W9-CAZ-483

ANGELS IN THE GLOOM

Also by Anne Perry and available from Headline

Tathea
Come Armageddon
The One Thing More
A Christmas Journey
A Christmas Visitor

World War I series
No Graves as Yet
Shoulder the Sky

The Inspector Pitt series
Bedford Square
Half Moon Street
The Whitechapel Conspiracy
Southampton Row
Seven Dials
Long Spoon Lane

The William Monk series
The Face of a Stranger
A Dangerous Mourning
Defend and Betray
A Sudden Fearful Death
Sins of the Wolf
Cain His Brother
Weighed in the Balance
The Silent Cry
Whited Sepulchres
The Twisted Root
Slaves and Obsession
A Funeral in Blue
Death of a Stranger
The Shifting Tide

ANGELS IN THE GLOOM

Anne Perry

headline

Copyright © 2005 Anne Perry

The right of Anne Perry to be identified as the Author of
the Work has been asserted by her in accordance with the
Copyright, Designs and Patents Act 1988.

First published in Great Britain in 2005 by
HEADLINE BOOK PUBLISHING

1

Apart from any use permitted under UK copyright law, this publication may
only be reproduced, stored, or transmitted, in any form, or by any means, with
prior permission in writing of the publishers or, in the case of reprographic
production, in accordance with the terms of licences issued by the Copyright
Licensing Agency.

All characters in this publication are fictitious
and any resemblance to real persons, living or dead,
is purely coincidental.

Cataloguing in Publication Data is available
from the British Library

ISBN 0 7553 0288 5 (hardback)
ISBN 0 7553 0979 0 (trade paperback)

Typeset in Galliard by Palimpsest Book Production Limited,
Polmont, Stirlingshire

Printed and bound in Great Britain by
Mackays of Chatham plc, Chatham, Kent

Headline's policy is to use papers that are natural, renewable and
recyclable products and made from wood grown in sustainable forests.
The logging and manufacturing processes are expected to conform
to the environmental regulations of the country of origin.

HEADLINE BOOK PUBLISHING
A division of Hodder Headline
338 Euston Road
London NW1 3BH

www.reviewbooks.co.uk
www.hodderheadline.com

To my father,
Henry Hulme,
Scientific Adviser to the Admiralty,
World War Two

... beyond that whisper
Going to look for angels in the gloom.

Siegfried Sassoon

Chapter One

Joseph lay on his face in the ice-filmed mud. Earlier in the night a score of men had gone over the top in a raid on the German trenches. They had taken a couple of prisoners, but been hit by a hail of gunfire on the way back. They had scrambled over the parapet wounded, bleeding, and without Doughy Ward and Tucky Nunn.

'Oi think Doughy's bought it,' Barshey Gee had said miserably, his face hollow-eyed in the brief glare of a star shell. 'But Tucky was still aloive.'

There was no choice. Under a barrage from their own guns, three of them went to look for him. The noise of the heavy mortars was deafening, but when they eased, Joseph could hear the quick, sharper rattle of machine guns. As the flare died, he lifted his head to look again across the craters, the torn wire and the few shattered tree stumps still left.

Something moved in the mud. He crawled forward again as quickly as he could. The thin ice cracked under his weight but he could hear nothing over the guns. He must get to Tucky without sliding into any of the huge, water-filled holes. Men had drowned in them before now. He shuddered, remembering. At least they had not been gassed this week, so there were no deadly, choking fumes in the hollows.

Another flare went up and Joseph lay still. Then, as it faded,

1

he moved forward again rapidly, feeling his way to avoid the remnants of spent shells, the rotting bodies of those never found, tangles of old wire and rusted weapons. As always he had emergency first-aid supplies with him, but he might need more than that. If he could carry Tucky back to the trench, real medics would be there by now.

It was dark again. He stood up and, crouching low, ran forward. It was only a few yards to where he had seen the movement. He slithered and almost fell over him.

'Tucky!'

'Hello, Chaplain.' Tucky's voice came out of the darkness, hoarse, ending in a cough.

'It's all right, I've got you,' Joseph answered, reaching forward and grasping the rough khaki and feeling the weight of Tucky's body. 'Where are you hurt?'

'What are you doing out here?' There was a kind of desperate humour in Tucky's voice, trying to mask his pain. Another flare went up and his snub-nosed face was visible for a few moments, and the bloody wound in his shoulder.

'Just passing,' Joseph replied, his own voice shaking a little. 'Where else are you hit?' If it were only the shoulder, Tucky would have made his way back. Joseph dreaded the answer.

'Moi leg, Oi think,' Tucky answered. 'Tell you the truth, Oi can't feel much. So damn cold. Don't seem they have summers here. 'Member summers at home, Chaplain? Girls all . . .' The rest of what he said was drowned in another roar of gunfire.

Joseph's heart sank. He had seen too many die, young men he had known most of their lives, even Tucky's elder brother Bibby, last year.

'I'll get you back,' he said to Tucky. 'Once you're warmer you'll probably feel it like hell. Come on.' He bent and half lifted Tucky on to his back, hearing his cry of pain as inadvertently he touched the wound. 'Sorry,' he apologized.

'It's all roight, Chaplain,' Tucky gasped, gagging as the pain dizzied him. 'It hurts, but not too much. Oi'll be better soon.'

Everyone said that, even when they were dying. It wasn't done to complain.

Bent double, staggering under Tucky's weight, and trying to keep low so as not to make a target, Joseph floundered back towards the line of the trenches. Twice he slipped and fell, apologizing automatically, aware that he was banging and jolting the injured man, but he could not help it.

He saw the parapet ahead of him, not more than a dozen yards away. He was sodden with mud and water up to the waist. His breath froze in the air and he was so cold he could hardly feel his legs.

'Nearly there,' he told Tucky, although his words were lost in another barrage of shells. One exploded close to him, on the left, hurling him forward flat on to the ground. He felt a sickening pain in his left side, and then nothing.

Joseph opened his eyes with a headache so nearly blinding, it all but obliterated his awareness that the whole of his left side hurt. There seemed to be other people around him. He could hear voices. It took him several moments to recognize that what he was staring up at was the ceiling of the field hospital. He must have been hit. What had happened to Tucky?

He tried to speak, but he was not sure if he actually made any sound or if the words were only in his head. No one came to him. He seemed to have no strength to move. The pain was appalling. It consumed his whole body, almost taking his breath away. What had happened to him? He had seen men injured, lots of them, their arms and legs blown off, bodies ripped open. He had held them, talked to them as they died, trying simply to be there so they were not alone. Sometimes that was all he could do.

He could not take up arms – he was a chaplain – but the night before war had been declared, he had promised himself he would be there with the men, endure with them whatever happened.

His sister Hannah was married, but Matthew and Judith had sat at their childhood home with him in Selborne St Giles watching the darkness gather over the fields, and spoken quietly of the future. Matthew would stay in the Secret Intelligence Service; Judith would go to the Front to do what she could, probably to drive ambulances; Joseph would be a chaplain. But he had sworn that never again would he allow himself to care about anything so much that he could be crippled by its loss, as he had been by Eleanor's death, and the baby's. Naturally Hannah would stay at home. Her husband, Archie, was at sea, and she had three children to care for.

There was someone leaning over him, a man with fair hair and a tired, serious face. He had blood on his hands and clothes. 'Captain Reavley?'

Joseph tried to answer but all he could manage was a croak.

'My name's Cavan,' the man went on. 'I'm the surgeon here. You've got a badly broken left arm. You caught a pretty big piece of shrapnel, by the look of it, and you've lost rather a lot of blood from the wound in your leg, but you should be all right. You'll keep the arm, but I'm afraid it is definitely a Blighty one.'

Joseph knew what that meant: an injury bad enough for him to be sent home.

'Tucky?' The words came at last, in a whisper. 'Tucky Nunn?'

'Bad, but I expect he'll make it,' Cavan answered. 'Probably going home with you. Now we've got to do something about this arm. It's going to hurt, but I'll do my best, and we'll repack that wound in your leg.'

Joseph knew dimly that the doctor had no time to say more. There were too many other men waiting, perhaps injured more seriously than him.

Cavan was right; it did hurt. For what seemed an age, Joseph swam in and out of consciousness. Everything was either the scarlet of pain or the infinitely better black of oblivion.

He was half aware of being lifted and carried, voices around him, and then a few very clear moments when he saw Judith. She was bending over him, her face pale and very grave, and he realized with surprise how frightened she was. He must look pretty bad. He tried to smile. He had no idea from the tears in her eyes if he succeeded or not. Then he drifted away again.

He woke up every so often. Sometimes he lay staring at the ceiling, wanting to scream from the pain that coursed through him till he thought he could not bear it, but one did not do that.

Other men, with worse injuries, did not. There were nurses around him, footsteps, voices, hands holding him up, giving him something to drink that made him gag. People spoke to him gently; there was a woman's voice, encouraging, but too busy for pity.

He felt helpless, but it was a kind of relief not to be responsible for anyone's pain except his own.

He was hot and shivering, the sweat trickling down his body, when they finally put him on the train. The rattle and jolt of it was dreadful, and he wanted to shout at the people who said how lucky he was to have 'a Blighty one' that he would rather they left him alone where he was. It must still be March and the weather was erratic. Would the winds make the Channel crossing rough? He was too ill to cope with seasickness as well! He could not even turn over.

In the event he remembered very little of it, or of the train journey afterwards. When he finally woke up to some kind of clarity he was lying in a clean bed in a hospital ward. The sun was coming in through the windows and making bright, warm splashes on the wooden floor, and there were bedclothes around him. Clean sheets? He could feel the smoothness against his chin and smell the cotton. He heard a broad Cambridgeshire voice in the distance and found himself smiling. He was in England, and it was spring.

He kept his eyes open in case, when he closed them, it all disappeared and he was back in the mud again. A slight woman, perhaps in her fifties, bent over him and helped him up to drink a cup of tea. It was hot, and made with clean water, not the stale dregs he was used to. She was dressed in a starched white uniform. She told him that her name was Gwen Neave. He looked at her hands around the cup as she held it to his lips. They were sunburned and very strong, as if she spent time outside.

During the next two or three days and nights she seemed to be there every time Joseph needed her, always understanding what it was that would ease him a little: the bed remade, pillows turned and plumped up, fresh water to drink, a cold cloth on his brow. She changed the dressings on the huge, raw wounds in his arm and leg without any expression on her face except a tightening

5

of her lips when she knew it must be hurting him. She talked about the weather outside, the lengthening days, the first daffodils flowering bright yellow. She told him once, very briefly, that she had two sons in the navy, but nothing more, no mention of where they were or how she feared for them amid all the losses at sea. He admired her for that.

It was she who was there at the worst times in the small hours of the morning when he was racked with pain, biting his lips so he did not cry out. He thought of other men's pain, men younger than him, who had barely tasted life and were already robbed of it, bodies broken, disfigured, and it was all too much. He had no strength left to fight, he only wanted to escape to a place where the pain stopped.

'It will get better,' Nurse Neave promised him, her voice little more than a whisper so as not to disturb the men in the other beds.

He did not answer. The words meant nothing. Pain, uselessness and the knowledge of death were the only realities.

'Do you want to give up?' she asked. He saw the smile in her eyes. 'We all do, sometimes,' she went on. 'Not many actually do, and you can't, you're the chaplain. You chose to pick up the cross, and now and again to help other people carry theirs. If somebody told you it wouldn't be heavy, they were lying.'

Nobody had told him that, though. Others had survived worse than this. He must just hang on.

Other fears crowded his mind, of helplessness, during the endless nights when he was awake while the rest of the world slept. He would be dependent, somebody else always having to look after him, too kind to say he was a burden, but growing to hate him for it, and having to remember to pity instead. Often he did not drift into sleep until dawn. Then the next night was almost as bad.

'What day is it?' he asked, one morning when finally it was light again.

'Twelfth of March,' a young nurse replied. 'Nineteen sixteen,' she added with a smile. 'Just in case you've forgotten. You've been here in Cambridge five days already.'

It was the morning after that when the same nurse told Joseph cheerfully that he had a visitor. She whisked away the remnants of his breakfast and tidied him up quite unnecessarily, and a moment later he saw Matthew walking down the ward between the other beds. He looked tired and pale. His thick, fair hair was not quite short enough for the army, and he was wearing a Harris tweed jacket over an ordinary cotton shirt. He stopped by the bed. 'You look awful,' he said with a smile. 'But better than last time.'

Joseph blinked. 'Last time? Last time I was home I was fine.'

'Last time I was here you weren't even conscious,' Matthew replied ruefully. 'I was very disappointed. I couldn't even shout at you for being a fool. It's the sort of thing Mother would have done.' His voice caught a little. 'Tell you she was so proud of you she'd burst, and then send you to bed with no dinner for frightening the life out of her.'

He was right. Were Alys Reavley still alive that is just what she would have done; then later send Mrs Appleton upstairs with pudding on a tray, as if she were sneaking it up and Alys did not know. In one sentence Matthew had summed up everything that home meant, and the impossible loss of their parents, murdered at the end of June two years ago, the same day the Archduke and Duchess were assassinated in Sarajevo. The loss washed over Joseph again in stinging grief, and for a moment his throat ached too fiercely to reply.

Matthew coughed. 'Actually for this she'd have had you down again, for hot pie and cream,' he said a little huskily. He fished in his jacket pocket and brought out something in his hand. It was a small case, of the sort in which good watches are presented. He opened it and held it up. It contained a silver cross on a purple and white ribbon.

'Military Cross,' he said, as if Joseph might not recognize it. 'Kitchener would have given it to you himself – it's good for morale, especially in hospitals. But he's pretty occupied at the moment, so he let me bring it.'

It was the highest award given to officers for consistent acts of courage over a period of time.

'I've got the citation,' Matthew went on. He was smiling now, his eyes bright with pride. He took an envelope out, opened it up and laid it on the table beside Joseph, then put the cross on top of it, still in its case. 'For all the men you rescued and carried back from no-man's-land.' He gave a tiny shrug. 'It mentions Eldon Prentice,' he added quietly. 'Actually there's a posthumous MC for Sam Wetherall too.' His voice dropped even lower. 'I'm sorry, Joe.'

Joseph wanted to answer, but the words would not come. He remembered Prentice's death as if it had been a month ago, not a year. He could still taste the anger – everyone's, not just his own. The night Charlie Gee was wounded he could have killed Prentice himself. And he had never stopped missing Sam. He had never told Matthew the truth about that.

'Thank you,' he said simply. There was no need for a lot of words; they understood each other without them.

Matthew dismissed it. 'I heard Tucky Nunn's not doing too badly. He'll be home for a while, but he'll get better. In the end he wasn't as bad as you.'

Joseph nodded. 'Doughy Ward got it,' he said quietly. 'I'll have to go and see his family, when I can. They'll just have the five girls now. The old man will find that hard. There'll be no one to take over the bakery.'

'Maybe Mary will,' Matthew suggested. 'She was always as good as her father at the baking, and more imaginative. Susie could keep the books.' He sighed. 'I know that's not what matters. How's everyone else? The people I know?'

Joseph smiled ruefully. 'Much the same, or trying to be. Whoopy Teversham is still a clown; got a face like India rubber.'

Matthew rolled his eyes. 'Last time I was here the Nunns and the Tevershams were still not speaking to each other.'

'Cully Teversham and Snowy Nunn are like brothers in the trenches,' Joseph said with a sudden ache in his throat, remembering them sitting together all night in the bitter cold, telling stories to keep up their courage, getting wilder with each one. Two men half a mile away had been frozen to death that night. They found their bodies when they brought the rations up the supply trenches the next morning.

Mathew said nothing.

'Thanks for the records,' Joseph changed the subject abruptly. 'Especially the Caruso one. Was it really a bestseller?'

'Of course it was,' Matthew said indignantly. 'That, and Al Jolson singing "Where Did Robinson Crusoe Go with Friday on Saturday Night?".'

They both laughed, and Joseph told him about other men from the village, but he spoke only of the pranks, the rivalries, the concert parties and letters from home. He said nothing about the terrible injuries – Plugger Arnold dying of gangrene, or handsome Arthur Butterfield with his wavy hair, drowned in a bomb crater in no-man's-land. He did not talk about the gas either, or how many men had been caught on the wire and hung there all night, riddled with shot, and no one could get to them.

He spoke of friendship, the kind of trust where everything is shared, good and bad, fear that strips you bare, and compassion that has no limit. He saw, as he had many times before, the guilt in Matthew's face, that he, a healthy young man, should be doing a job here at home when almost every other man he knew was either at the Front or at sea. Few people realized how important his job was. Without good intelligence, quickly gathered and correctly interpreted, tens of thousands more lives would be lost. There was no glory at the end; in fact seldom was there any recognition at all.

Joseph was simply grateful that his brother was safe. He did not lie awake at night, cold and sick with fear for him, or scan each new casualty list with his stomach churning. He knew that Matthew was responsible specifically for information concerning America, and the likelihood of the Americans joining the Allies, as opposed to their present neutrality. He could imagine his duties might involve the decoding and interpretation of letters, telegrams and other messages.

'How's Hannah?' he asked aloud.

Matthew smiled. 'Fine. I expect they'll let her in to see you this afternoon, or tomorrow. Not that there's been much to see, until now. You've been out of it most of the time.' The anxiety returned to his eyes.

'There are others a lot worse,' Joseph said truthfully. 'I've a cracking headache, but nothing that won't heal.'

Matthew's eyes flickered to Joseph's arm, which was heavily bandaged, and then the bedclothes carefully placed so as not to weigh on the wound in his leg. 'You'll be home a while,' he observed. His voice was thick. They both knew Joseph was fortunate not to have lost the arm. Perhaps had Cavan been less skilled, he would have.

'Any other news?' Joseph asked. He said it quite lightly, but there was still a change in his tone, and Matthew heard it immediately. He knew what the question really meant: was he any closer to finding the identity of the Peacemaker? That was the name they had given to the man behind the plot their father had discovered, and which had led to his murder, and that of their mother.

It was Joseph who had learned, to his enduring grief, who it was who had physically caused the fatal car crash. He and Matthew together had found the treaty, unsigned as yet by the King, on the day before Britain declared war. But the man with the passion and the intellect behind it still eluded them. Their compulsion to find him was partly born out of a hunger for revenge for the deaths of John and Alys Reavley. Others, too, whom they'd cared for, had died, used, crushed, then thrown away by the Peacemaker in pursuit of his cause. They also needed to stop him before he achieved the devastating ruin he planned.

Matthew pushed his hands into his pockets, lifting his shoulders in the slightest shrug. 'I haven't found anything helpful,' he answered. 'I followed everything we had, but in the end it led nowhere.' His lips tightened a fraction, and there was a moment's defeat in his eyes. 'I'm sorry. I don't know where else to look. I've been pretty busy trying to prevent the sabotage of munitions across the Atlantic. We're desperate for supplies. The Germans are advancing along the Somme. We've over a million men wounded or dead. We lose ships to the U-boats pretty well every week. If it goes on like this another year we'll start to know real hunger, not just shortages but actual starvation. God! If we could only get America in on our side, we'd have men, guns, food!' He stopped abruptly, the light going out of his face. 'But Wilson's still dithering around like an old maid being asked to . . .'

Joseph smiled.

Matthew shrugged. 'I suppose he has to,' he said resignedly. 'If he brings them in too fast he could lose his own election in the autumn, and what use would that be?'

'I know,' Joseph agreed. 'Maybe while I'm at home I'll have time to think about the Peacemaker a bit. There might be other people we haven't thought of.' He had his old master at St John's in mind, and he was startled how the idea hurt. The Peacemaker had to be someone they knew, which made it the ultimate betrayal. It was difficult to keep the hatred out of his voice. Perhaps Matthew would take it for pain.

'What else is happening in London?' he asked aloud. 'Any new shows worth seeing? What about the moving pictures? What about Chaplin? Has he done anything more?'

Matthew shrugged and gave a half-smile. 'There's some good Keystone stuff. *Fatty and Mabel Adrift*, with Roscoe Arbuckle and Mabel Normand, and a great dog called Luke. Or *He Did and He Didn't*, or *Love and Lobsters*, if you prefer. They all have alternative titles.' And he proceeded to outline some of the highlights.

Joseph was still laughing when Gwen Neave appeared, clean sheets folded over her arm and a roll of bandage in her other hand. She smiled at Matthew, but there was no denying her authority when she told him it was time for him to leave.

Matthew acknowledged it, saying goodbye to Joseph briefly, as if they saw each other every day. Then he walked out with a remnant of his old, very slight swagger.

'My brother,' Joseph said proudly. Suddenly he was filled with wellbeing, as if the pain had lessened, although actually it was just as bad.

Gwen Neave set the sheets down. 'He said he was up from London,' she remarked without meeting his eyes. 'We'll change those dressings first, before I put on the clean sheets.'

Joseph liked her and the distance in her voice hurt him. He cared what she thought of Matthew. He wanted to tell her how important Matthew's work was so she did not think he was one of those who evaded service, the sort of young man to whom girls on street corners gave white feathers, the mark of the coward. It was the ugliest insult possible to give.

She slid her arm round him and put an extra pillow behind his back so she could reach the raw, open wound where the broken ends of the bone had torn through the flesh.

'He works in London,' Joseph said, gasping as the pain shot through him in waves. He refused to look at the wound. He still needed to tell her about Matthew.

She was not interested. She dealt with the injured, the fighting men. She worked all day and often most of the night. No call on her care or her patience was too much, no clasp of the hand or silent listening too trivial.

'He can't tell us what he does,' he went on. 'It's secret. Not everybody can wear a uniform—' He stopped abruptly, afraid to say too much. The physical pain made him feel sick.

She gave him a quick smile, understanding what he was trying to do. 'He's obviously very fond of you,' she said. 'So is the other gentleman, by all appearances. He was upset you weren't well enough to see him.'

Joseph was startled. 'Other gentleman?'

Her eyes widened. 'Did they not tell you? I'm sorry. We had an emergency that evening. Rather bad. I dare say they forgot. They wouldn't do it on purpose. It . . . it was distressing.' Her face was bleak. He did not ask what had happened. It was too easy to guess.

'Who was he?' he asked instead. 'The man who came?'

'A Mr Shanley Corcoran,' she replied. 'We assured him you were doing well.'

He smiled, and a little of the tension eased out of him. Corcoran had been his father's closest friend and all of them had loved him as long as they could remember. Of course Corcoran would come, no matter how busy he was at the Scientific Establishment. Whatever he was working on would have to wait at least an hour or two when one of his own was ill.

Gwen Neave eased Joseph back as gently as she could. 'I see

your brother brought you your medal. That's very fine, Captain, very fine indeed. Your sister'll be proud of you too.'

A young man walked briskly along Marchmont Street in London, crossed behind a taxi-cab, and stepped up on to the kerb at the far side. He had come down from Cambridge for this meeting, which he had done at irregular intervals over the last year, and he was not looking forward to it.

Full of high ideals, quite certain of what end he was working towards and believing he knew what the personal cost would be, he had secured his place in the Scientific Establishment in Cambridgeshire. Now it was much more complicated. There were people and emotions involved that he could not have foreseen.

Not that he would say anything of this to the Peacemaker, because although he would understand it all perfectly with his mind, he would feel none of it with his heart. He had one belief, one passion, and everything in him was bent towards it. He would allow no person and no issue to stand in his way.

Still, this meeting would entail a certain degree of deception, at least by omission, and the young man was uncomfortable about that. There were changes to his own plans of which he could say nothing at all. It would be intensely dangerous, and he strode along the footpath in the sun without any pleasure at all.

In the afternoon Hannah was allowed to come to the hospital. Joseph opened his eyes to see her standing at the end of the bed. For a moment he registered only her face, with its soft lines, her eyes so like her mother's, and the thick, fair-brown hair. It was as if Alys were standing there. Then the pain in his body returned, and memory. Their mother was dead.

'Joseph?' Hannah sounded uncertain. She was afraid he was too ill to be disturbed, perhaps even still in danger. Her face lit with relief when she saw him smile and she moved towards him. 'How are you? Is there anything I can bring you?' She held a big bunch of daffodils from the garden, like cradled sunshine. He could smell them even above the hospital odours of carbolic, blood, washed linen and the warmth of bodies.

'They're beautiful,' he said, clearing his throat. 'Thank you.'

She put them on the small table near him. 'Do you want to sit up a little?' she asked, seeing him struggle to be more comfortable. In answer to her own question she helped him forward and plumped up the pillows, leaving him more upright. She was wearing a blouse and a blue linen skirt only halfway down her calf, as the fashion was now. He did not like it as much as the longer, fuller skirts of a few years ago, sweeping the ground, but he could see that it was more practical. War changed a lot of things. She looked pretty, and she smelled of something warm and delicate, but closer up, he could see the tiredness in her face and around her eyes.

'How are the children?' he asked.

'They're well.' Her simple words were said with assurance, probably the answer she gave everyone, but the truth in her eyes was far more complex.

'Tell me about them,' Joseph pressed. 'How is Tom doing at school? What is his ambition?' He was fourteen. He would need to decide soon.

A shadow crossed Hannah's face. She tried to make light of it. 'At the moment, like every other boy, he wants to join the war. He's always following soldiers around when there's anyone on leave in the village.' She gave a tiny laugh, barely a sound at all. 'He's afraid it will be over before he has a chance. Of course he has no real idea what it's like.'

Joseph wondered how much she knew. Her husband, Archie, was a commander in the Royal Navy. Such a life was probably beyond the imagination of anyone who lived on the land. Joseph had only the dimmest idea himself. But he knew the life of a soldier intimately.

'He's too young,' he said, knowing as he did so that there were boys even on the front lines who were not much older. He had seen the bodies of one or two. But there was no need for Hannah to know that.

'Do you think it will be over by next year?' she asked.

'Or the one after,' he answered, with no idea if that were true.

She relaxed. 'Yes, of course. I'm sorry. Is there anything I can

14

bring you? Are they feeding you properly? It's still quite easy to get most things, although they're saying that might change if the U-boats get any worse. There's nothing much in the garden yet, it's too early. And of course Albert's not with us any more, so it's gone a bit wild.'

Joseph heard a wealth of loss in her voice for the change to the world she had loved. At the Front they tended to think everything at home was caught in a motionless amber just as they remembered it. Sometimes it was only the thread of memory linking that order of life to the madness of war that gave the fighting any purpose. Perhaps they were as blind to life at home as the people at home were to the reality in the trenches? He had not really thought of that before.

He looked at her anxious face as she waited for his answer. 'Yes, the food's not bad at all,' he said cheerfully. 'Maybe they're giving us the best. But when I heal up a bit more, I'll be home anyway.'

She smiled suddenly, alight with pleasure. 'That'll be wonderful. It'll be quite a while before you can go back, I should think.' She was sorry for his wounds, but they kept him in England, safe and alive. She did not know where Archie was, or Judith. No matter how busy she was during the day, there was still too much time alone when fear crowded in, and helplessness. She could only imagine, and wait.

Seeing her loneliness far more than she realized, Joseph felt an intense tenderness for her. 'Thank you,' he said with a depth that surprised him.

It happened sooner than he expected. More wounded arrived. His bed was needed and he was past immediate danger. He was helped by Gwen Neave to dress at least in trousers, with a shirt and jacket over one shoulder and around his bandaged arm. He was taken to the door in a wheelchair and, feeling dizzy and very unsteady, helped into the ambulance to be driven home to Selborne St Giles. He was startled to find that he was exhausted by the time the doors were opened again. He was assisted out on to the gravel driveway where Hannah was waiting for him.

She held his arm as he negotiated the steps, leaning heavily on his crutch, the ambulance driver on his other side. He hardly had time to notice that the front garden was overgrown. The daffodils were bright; leaves were bursting open everywhere; the yellow forsythia was in bloom, uncut since last year; and there were clumps of primroses that should have been divided and spread.

The door opened and he saw Tom was kneeling on the floor in the hall, holding the dog by his collar as he wriggled and barked with excitement. Henry was a golden retriever, eternally enthusiastic, and his exuberance would have knocked Joseph off his feet.

Tom grinned a little uncertainly. 'Hello, Uncle Joseph. I daren't let him go, but he's pleased to see you. How are you?'

'Getting better very quickly, thank you,' Joseph replied. He did not feel that was true, but he wanted it to be. He was light-headed and so weak it frightened him. It was an effort to stand, even with help.

Tom looked relieved, but he still hung on to Henry, who was lunging forward in his eagerness to welcome Joseph.

The two younger children were at the top of the stairs, standing close together. Jenny was nine, fair, with brown eyes like her mother. Luke, six, was as dark as Archie. They stared at Joseph almost without blinking. He wasn't really Uncle Joseph any more, he was a soldier, a real one; and more than that, he was a hero. Both their mother and Mrs Appleton had said so.

Joseph climbed the stairs, hesitating on every step, assisted by the ambulance driver. He spoke to Luke and Jenny as he passed, but briefly. He was longing to get back to bed again and lie down, so the familiar hall and stairs would stop swaying and he would not make a spectacle of himself by collapsing in front of everyone. It would be so embarrassing trying to get up again, and needing to be lifted.

Hannah helped him to undress, anxious and fussing too much, asking him over and over if he were all right. He did not have the strength to keep reassuring her. She helped him into the bed, propped the crutch where he could reach it, then left. She returned a few minutes later with a cup of tea. He found his hand shook when he took it, and she had to hold it for him.

He thanked her and was glad when she left him alone. It was strange to be at home again in his own room with his books, pictures and other belongings that reminded him so sharply and intrusively of the past. There were photographs of himself and Harry Beecher hiking in Northumberland. The memory and the loss still hurt. There were also books and papers from his time teaching at St John's, even of his youth before his marriage when this house had been the centre of life for all of them.

His parents were no longer here, but when he lay awake in the night with the light on to read, he heard Hannah's footsteps on the landing. None the less for an instant it was his mother's face he expected around the door to check on him.

'Sorry,' he apologized before she could ask. 'My days and nights are a bit muddled.' It was pain that was keeping him awake, but there was nothing she could do to help it, so there was no purpose in telling her. She looked tired, and, with her hair loose, younger than she did in the daytime. She was far more like her mother than Judith was, not only in appearance but in nature. All he could ever remember her wanting was to marry and have children, care for them, and be as good a part of the village as Alys had been, trusted, admired and, above all, liked.

But everything was changing, moving much too quickly, as if a seventh wave had accumulated and drowned the shore.

'Are you all right?' she said anxiously. 'Would you like a cup of tea? Or cocoa? I've got milk. It might help you sleep.'

She wanted to be able to do something for him, but did not know what. He could see it as she half turned to go before he answered. 'Yes, please,' he said, as much for her as for himself. He would like cocoa, and it seemed they were neither of them able to rest.

She returned about ten minutes later with two cups on a tray, and sat in the chair beside the bed, sipping her own, having assured herself that he could manage his.

Joseph started speaking to fill the silence. 'How is Mr Arnold?'

Hannah's face pinched a little. 'He took Plugger's death pretty hard.' He was a widower, and she knew Joseph would not have forgotten that. 'He spends most of his time down at the forge doing odd jobs, cleaning up, taking people's horses back and forth. Mostly for the army, and to keep busy, I think.'

'And Mrs Gee?' Memory of Charlie Gee's death still twisted inside him. These were all people he would go to see when he was well enough. He knew how much it mattered to them to hear first-hand news. They wanted to ask questions, even if they were afraid of the answers. Mrs Gee's other son, Barshey, was still at the Front, and most of the other young men she knew as well. Everyone had friends or relations in the trenches; most had lost people they loved – dead, injured or simply missing. In some cases they would never know what had happened to them.

'She's all right,' Hannah answered him. 'Well, as all right as anyone can be. Charlie was such fun; he had so many dreams and ideas. She always has to make up her mind whether to go and look at the casualty lists or not. And she always does. Like the rest of us, I suppose. You go with your heart in your mouth, then when your family's names are not there you feel almost sick with relief.'

She bit her lip, her cocoa forgotten. Her eyes searched his to see if he understood the depth of the fear. 'And then you realize that other women next to you have lost someone, and you feel so guilty it's as if your skin has been ripped off. You see their faces whiten, eyes with all the light gone as if something inside them was dead too. You know it could be your turn next time. You try to think of something to say, all the while knowing there isn't anything at all. There's a gulf between you nothing can cross. You still have hope. They don't. And you end up not saying anything at all. You just go home, until the next list.'

He looked at the misery in her eyes.

'Mother would have known something to say,' she added.

He knew that was what she had been thinking all along. 'No, she wouldn't,' he answered. 'Nobody does. We've never been here before. Anyway, I don't think there is anything. What about your friends? Maggie Fuller? Or Polly Andrews? Or the girl with the curly hair you used to go riding with?'

She smiled. 'Tilda? Actually, she married a fellow in the Royal Flying Corps last year. Molly Gee and Lilian Ward have gone to work in the factories. Even the squire has only one servant left. Everybody seems to be doing something to do with the war: delivering the post, collecting clothes and blankets, putting together bags with mending supplies, needles and thread and so on, and of course knitting . . . miles of it. Mrs Appleton's back with us, thank goodness. Working on the land didn't suit her, but she achieves a formidable amount of knitting.' She sipped her cocoa. 'I don't know how many letters I've written as well, to men who have no families, things like that. And of course there's always cleaning and maintenance to be done. And lots of women drive now – delivering things.'

Joseph smiled, thinking of the vast organization of support, everyone striving to do what they could for the men they loved.

'I expect the squire will be round to see you,' she went on, changing the subject completely, except that he, by his very position, was part of the old way of the village. He belonged to the past that she trusted. 'He's bound to be a bit tedious, but it's his duty,' she added. 'You're a hero, and he'll want to pay his respects and hear all about your experiences.' She was watching him now, to see what he wanted, regardless of what he might feel compelled to say.

He debated it. He hated to talk about the men he knew. No words could draw for anyone else what their lives were like. And yet the people left at home who loved them had a need to know at least part of it. Their imaginations filled in the rest, which was still immeasurably better than revealing the whole ghastly truth.

'You don't have to see him,' Hannah cut across his thoughts, but her voice was gentle. 'Not yet, anyway.'

It was very tempting to say he was not well enough and put it off. But then on the other hand, when he was better, he would have no excuse to cut short the conversation. 'No,' he said aloud. 'I'll see him as soon as he feels like coming.'

She finished her cocoa and put down the cup. 'Are you certain? I can put it off very nicely.'

'I'm sure you can,' he agreed. 'I've seen you. Always a lady, but, like Mother, you could freeze anyone at twenty paces if they took liberties.'

She smiled, and lowered her eyes, for a moment too emotional to meet his.

'If he comes now,' Joseph went on, wishing he were able to lean over and touch her hand, 'then I can be very brief, and get away with it.'

She looked up with a flash of understanding. 'You don't like to talk about it, do you? Archie doesn't either.' There was loneliness in that, knowing she was being excluded. She stood up. 'Do you think you can go to sleep now? I'll stay if you like.'

That was just what she must have said to her children time and time again, after a bad dream. He felt so very much at home now, as if he were back in the past: the house, Hannah, the books and habits of the best from childhood – all these were familiar and comfortable with use. They were threads that held the core of life together. 'No, thanks,' Joseph said quietly. 'I'll be fine.'

Hannah went out, leaving the door ajar, in case he should want her. He felt like a child, and at least for a short while, just as safe. Surprisingly, he did fall asleep very shortly after.

Chapter Two

Hannah remained at home the following day until the squire had been in the morning. He seemed to be as relieved as Joseph was that he could just utter a few hearty platitudes and consider his duty done.

After he left, Hannah ascertained that Joseph was all right. Mrs Appleton was downstairs and would make him lunch. She herself needed to go into Cambridge and see the bank manager, and do one or two other necessary errands.

She caught the train in the village and was there in half an hour. The city did not look so different to her – the change had been gradual – but she still noticed the absence of young men. There were a few errand boys, junior clerks, delivery men, but most of all there were hardly any students. The streets used to be crowded with bicycles, and the cheerful conversations of the young with the world of knowledge before them. She could not bear to think of how many of them were already dead in France, and how many more would be.

Hannah went into the bank and asked to speak to the manager. She liked Mr Atherton. He was very capable and she always left reassured.

She waited just under ten minutes and a smart young woman in a plain, dark blue tailored skirt came out of a side door. The blouse was crisp, and the skirt was rather full and reached only to the middle of her calf. No doubt there was a matching jacket, long and equally fashionable. She had cut her hair short. She looked about Hannah's age.

'Good morning, Mrs MacAllister,' she said with a slight smile. 'My name is Mae Darnley. How can I help you?' She offered a cool, lean hand, without any rings.

Hannah accepted it only because it would have been rude not to, but it was an odd thing to do. 'I would like to speak to Mr Atherton, please.' She had already said as much to the original clerk.

'I am afraid Mr Atherton is no longer with us,' Miss Darnley replied. 'He works with the War Office in London. I am the manager now. How can I assist you?'

Hannah was lost for words. Surely things could not have changed so much? This woman could not be more than thirty-five at the most. What could she know?

Miss Darnley was waiting.

Hannah realized she was being discourteous and other people were beginning to look at her. 'Thank you,' she said awkwardly. 'Then . . . then I suppose I had better see you.'

It was a disconcerting experience. Hannah followed Miss Darnley into the office and even before she sat down she noticed how it had changed. The silver tantalus for whisky that usually sat on the side table had disappeared. In its place was a vase of narcissi. She smelled the perfume of them immediately. The photographs were different. Instead of Mr Atherton's wife and sons there was an elderly couple in a silver frame, and a young man in uniform, so far framed only in polished wood. And all the ashtrays had gone too. Apparently Miss Darnley did not approve of smoking in her office.

Hannah sat down while her mind raced through what she could ask this young woman, other than the advice she had come for, and would really trust only Mr Atherton with. Nothing came to her. You could hardly ask to see the manager in order to make a deposit or a withdrawal.

Miss Darnley was waiting expectantly.

There was really no civil alternative, and she did not have to accept the advice. Hannah cleared her throat. 'I have a small amount of money left after my parents' deaths,' she began. 'And continuing income from my husband's and my house in Portsmouth, which we are renting out because I now live in the family home here, while my brother, who owns it, is in the army.'

'I see. And you wish to invest it?'

'Yes. Mr Atherton suggested certain bonds, but I need more advice before I make up my mind. I don't wish to trouble my husband with the matter because he is home seldom, and only for a few days at a time.' Already she wished she had not told this smart young woman so much. Perhaps she should ask the family lawyer? He was always reliable.

'Will you require the money within a short time?' Miss Darnley asked. 'Two or three years, for example? Or is it a long-term investment, perhaps with your children in mind, or your husband's retirement?'

'Long term,' Hannah replied.

'How much are we speaking of?'

'Just over a thousand pounds.'

'Considerable,' Miss Darnley acknowledged. 'Houses are usually safer than bonds, which can be affected by a radical change in business, or the markets.' Her lips tightened. 'But in wartime houses can be bombed, and of course insurance does not cover war, or acts of God.' She looked at Hannah very steadily. 'Have you considered purchasing land, perhaps something that is presently agricultural, but on the outskirts of the city, where future development will take place? That is almost impossible to damage, except by flooding, and will increase in value as well as bringing you a small return now. There is also no upkeep required, as there is on rented houses.'

Hannah was astonished. Her mind raced through it for flaws, and found none. Could it really be so . . . so clear? Why had Mr Atherton not thought of it? 'Really?' she said.

'Give it a little consideration,' Miss Darnley suggested. 'You could ask your brother. I believe he is at home. How is he progressing?'

'Well, thank you.' That was a lie. Joseph was still in a great deal of pain. She saw it in the strain in his face, the hollows around his eyes and the slow way he moved, afraid of jolting fragile flesh, and the raw ends of bone as yet unknitted. Why did she exchange polite nothingness with this woman? Everybody admired those who did not complain, but the denials of truth cut them off from each other, making help impossible, to receive or to give. 'No, actually he's not,' she said suddenly. 'He was very badly hurt, and it's going to take ages, if he completely recovers at all.'

'I'm sorry,' Miss Darnley said with a sudden bleakness in her eyes.

Hannah wondered with a flash of perception if perhaps the man she had been going to marry had been killed, but it would be intrusive to ask. 'Thank you for your advice,' she said instead. 'It sounds excellent sense to me. I shall think about it, and make some enquiries as to what is available. I hope you will like it here at the bank.'

A quick enthusiastic smile lit Miss Darnley's face. 'Oh, yes! It's a marvellous opportunity. It's almost the only good thing about the war that women are at last getting the chance to do all kinds of jobs we were prevented from before. It's my belief that one day we really will get the vote. And then the next thing will be to become part of the government.'

Hannah had meant the remark only as a pleasantry. This was wildly further than she had thought of in her lifetime, let alone soon. She could feel all the familiar, beautiful world she loved slipping out of her grasp and changing into something harsh and strange where the natural roles of men and women were distorted, even broken.

'Yes, I suppose so,' she said confusedly. She thanked Miss Darnley again and took her leave. But outside in the street the sense of fear persisted. A horse and cart clattered past her, and an automobile went the other way. She had not realized until now quite what dignity and grace there had been in the certainties of life. It was not just the outer peace that everyone could see, but an inner quality as well, a gentleness that was utterly gone.

She almost bumped into the young man in flannel trousers and blazer coming the other way. She started to apologize, then realized it was Ben Morven, one of the scientists who worked for Shanley Corcoran in the Scientific Establishment. She had met him several times here in Cambridge or in the village. She liked his warmth, the way he laughed at some of the absurdities of life and yet treasured the old and simple things, just as she did.

'Are you all right?' he asked with a flicker of concern.

'Oh yes, perfectly,' she assured him. 'Just a little off balance to find my bank manager has been replaced by a young woman.' She smiled back at him ruefully, embarrassed to admit how much it frightened her.

'It's only temporary,' he replied with a little twist of his mouth. 'When the war's over and the men come home, she'll have to go back to whatever it was she did before. She'll have two or three years at most.'

'Do you think so?' Then as she laughed she was ashamed at her eagerness, and found herself blushing.

They were walking side by side in the sun up King's Parade. The traffic seemed to have eased. It was nice not to have to explain her feelings to him, even if it was a little embarrassing to be understood so well. She knew something about him already. He came from a small town on the coast of Lancashire, a scholarship boy from a very ordinary family. His mother had died when he was about Jenny's age and there was a yearning in him for the light and the sweetness of the past. When she had mentioned the death of her own mother she had seen the swift gentleness in his eyes. No words were necessary to tell him of the grief that still descended on her without warning, almost taking her breath away.

Should she apologize for being so quick to wish Miss Darnley back to wherever she had come from? She glanced sideways at his face, and knew it was totally unnecessary. It was very comfortable for a little while not to pretend.

That evening Shanley Corcoran came to see Joseph. Hannah was delighted for her own sake as well. Since her father's death her children had had no grandparents. Archie's parents lived in the far north, and poor health prevented them travelling. Corcoran told them marvellous stories and made the world seem like an exciting place, full of colour and mystery. No adventure was too wild or marvellous, at least to dream.

For Hannah he was inextricably tied to the memories of family life, childhood, times when pain was brief and permanent loss unimaginable.

Now she was delighted to see him. He came in with a wave of enthusiasm, leaving the door wide open on to the clear evening outside. He was of average height and build but he was remarkable for the vitality and intelligence in his face. His hair was white but still thick, and his eyes were unusually dark and seemed to burn with energy.

He spoke to them all, asking after each, but he was too eager to see Joseph to wait for more than the briefest of answers. Hannah took him upstairs after a few moments.

Joseph felt his spirits lifting simply because Corcoran was there. Suddenly the idea of rest seemed a waste of opportunity. He wished to be well again and do something. When Corcoran asked him how he was, he replied drily, 'It holds me up a bit.'

Corcoran laughed; it was a bright, infectious sound. He sat down on the chair beside the bed. 'Doesn't stop you talking, anyway,' he observed. 'It'll be good for Hannah to have you here, at least for a while. As soon as you're on your feet you'll have to come for dinner. Orla would love to see you. She'll drive over and fetch you. I'm so busy these days I practically have to be delirious with fever before they'll let me off.'

'I thought you were the head of the Establishment?' Joseph raised his eyebrows.

'Oh, I am! They are my own inner demons that drive me,' Corcoran admitted, then for an instant he was deeply serious. 'We've got marvellous work going on, Joseph. I can't tell you details, of course, but what we are creating could change everything. Win the war for us. And soon. So help me God, it'll have to be soon, the way it's going at sea. Our losses are appalling.' He spread his hands. 'But enough of that now. I imagine you know all you want to already. I've seen Matthew once or twice since you were last home, but how's Judith?' His eyes were bright and tender. 'Your father would be so proud of her, driving an ambulance on the Western Front! How times have changed, and people.'

Joseph smiled back. John Reavley would have been passionately proud of his young daughter, and he would probably even have said so, but only once. And he would have feared for her, as Joseph did, whilst assuring Alys that she was in no danger. Desperately as he missed his mother, he was glad she did not have to endure this.

They would both have been hurt, and perhaps confused by some of the things she had done. Joseph should have disapproved himself. He reminded himself that he did! And yet he had also understood. A year later he still felt the pain.

Corcoran was staring at him, his face puckered. 'Are you feeling worse, Joseph? Am I keeping you up? Please be honest . . .'

'No, of course not,' Joseph said quickly. 'I'm sorry, I was just thinking of some of the things Judith has seen, and experienced. She's a very different woman from the girl who used to tear around the lanes here in her Model T, scaring the sheep half silly.'

Corcoran laughed. 'Do you remember her at our Whitsun picnics?' he said with light in his face. 'I don't think she was more than five or six years old when we had our first. I've never seen a little girl run as she did.'

He and Orla had had no children. Joseph had caught the sadness in his face; but only for moments, and it never clouded his joy in his friend's family, nor stinted his generosity of praise and willingness to share the successes and the failures of their lives.

'And the time she decided to show us the cancan, and did a cartwheel that ended in the river.' Corcoran was laughing as he said it. 'Matthew had to pull her out, and what a sight she was! Soaked to the skin, poor girl, and looking like a piece of waterweed.'

'That was only seven years ago,' Joseph reminded him. 'It seems like another world now. I remember we had fresh salmon with lettuce and cucumber, and egg and cress sandwiches, and apple charlotte for pudding. It was too early for berries.' There was regret when he said that. He loved raspberries. He could never pass the bushes in the garden when they were in fruit without taking a few.

The mood changed suddenly. Both were returned to the present. They were lucky; safe and whole, and with people they loved. Joseph thought how warm he was, but it was as if the cold of the trenches were only beyond the door to the landing. So many of the men with whom he had shared it would be dead within the year. And without them the women in houses like this would never be the same.

'We'll win,' Corcoran said, leaning forward with sudden fierceness. 'We have the science, Joseph, I swear to you. We are working on an entirely new invention, something no one else has even thought of. And when we've solved the last few little problems with it, it will revolutionize the war at sea. U-boats will cease to be a threat. Germany won't strangle us. The shoe will be on the other foot; we shall destroy them.' His eyes were dark and brilliant with the knowledge of what could be, and the passion to bring it about. It was a kind of pride, but without arrogance. 'It's beautiful, Joseph. The concept is as simple and as elegant as mathematics; it's just the last few details of practicality we have to iron out. It will make history!'

He reached across and put his hand gently on Joseph's. 'But don't whisper of it to anyone, not even Hannah. I know she worries herself ill over Archie, like every woman in England who has brothers, husband or sons at sea, but she can't know yet. We are very nearly there.'

Joseph felt a surge of hope and found himself smiling widely. 'Of course I won't tell her,' he agreed. 'That should be your privilege, anyway.'

'Thank you,' Corcoran accepted with sudden emotion. 'To be able to tell her will be one of the greatest rewards of all. But I'm glad you will be home with her for a while. Take good care of yourself. Allow yourself to mend slowly. Build up your strength again. You've done such a lot already – you deserve a little time to see the spring.'

He left after another ten minutes, and even though Joseph was tired he felt as if there were a new warmth in the room, an easing of pain. Instead of going back to sleep, or trying to read, he contemplated how good it would be to be at home for the blossoming of the year. He would see the lambs and calves, the first leaves on the trees, the hedgerows filled with flowers, and all of it untrampled by marching feet, not ruined by gunfire, nothing broken, poisoned or burned.

He thought quite suddenly of Isobel Hughes, to whom he had been obliged, as chaplain, to write and inform her of her husband's death. She had written back thanking him for his kindness. A correspondence had developed – only a letter once a month or so. They had never met, and yet he was able to tell her his feelings of weariness, and guilt that he could do so little to help. She did not make futile suggestions, or say that it did not matter. Instead she told him about the farms and the village in Wales where she lived, little stories of gossip, the occasional joke. It brought him a remembrance again of the sanity of village life where quarrels over a piece of land or a churn of milk still mattered, where people danced and courted, made silly mistakes and gave generous forgiveness.

Should he write and tell her that he had been wounded and was at home for a while? Would she care or worry if she did not hear from him? Or would he be presuming on her kindness? He liked her very much. There was a gentleness and wry honesty in her letters he found himself thinking of more often than he would care to tell her.

He wondered what she looked like. He had no idea. It would be forward to ask, and it was only an idle curiosity. It did not matter; it was her friendship he valued.

In the end he asked Hannah for pen and paper and wrote a brief letter. After she had taken it, he wondered if he had been too terse, and rather silly to think Isobel would be concerned anyway.

He thought of the dugout where he had slept and where most of his belongings were, the books he loved best, and the portrait of Dante. That was where he wrote the almost daily letters he had to, to tell of a death, or a serious injury . . . presumably someone had done that for him, to tell Hannah? He had not thought of it until now. It would have been one of the easy ones to write, because he was still alive.

Who was doing it now he was not there? Would they have got another chaplain? But whoever he was he would not know the men, or their families! He would not know the rivalries, the debts of kindness, the weaknesses and the strengths. He himself should be there! But not yet. He still had time to watch the slow spring at least begin.

The next day he got up for a little while. If he didn't he would begin to lose the use of his muscles. The fever was gone; it was just a matter of his wounds healing and of gaining his strength again.

It also meant he was well enough to receive visitors outside the family. The squire was already dealt with; however the local vicar was not, and he arrived in the middle of the afternoon. Hannah showed him in to the sitting room where Joseph was resting quietly in an armchair, the dog at his feet, tail thumping on the floor now and then as Joseph spoke to him. Hannah shot them both a quick glance of apology.

Hallam Kerr was a man of medium height and build with straight hair parted in the middle. He was in his forties. His manner was full of enthusiasm, rather like a school sports master at the beginning of a match, but there were lines of anxiety in his face and something faintly dated in his dress.

'Ah! Captain Reavley! Congratulations!' He thrust out his hand; then, as if feeling that Joseph might attempt to get up, he snatched it back again. 'Please, please don't stand, my dear fellow. I simply came to see if there is anything I can do for you. And, of course, to say how immensely proud we all are. It's superb to have a holder of the Military Cross in the village – and for the Church as a whole! Shows that we men of God are fighters too, what?'

Joseph's heart sank. There was an eagerness in the man's eyes as if the war were all somehow magnificent. That was the moment Joseph realized how alien he felt here at home. What could he say to this man without betraying all that was true? 'Well . . . I suppose you could put it like that—' he began.

'Very modest,' Kerr cut across him. 'I'm proud to visit you, Captain.' He sat in the chair opposite Joseph's, leaning forward earnestly. 'I envy you. It must be superb to be part of such a fine, brave body of men, helping, encouraging, keeping the word of God alive among them.'

Joseph remembered the young men with lost limbs, lost sight, terrified, bleeding to death. Their conduct was heroic, certainly; it took the ultimate courage, going into the darkness alone. But there was nothing glorious about it. He was choked with the desire to weep just at the overwhelming return of memory. He looked at Kerr's idiotic face and wanted to run away. He had no desire to be cruel. The man could not help his blinding ignorance. He might in his own way be doing his best, but his every eager word was an insult to the reality of pain.

Joseph found he could say nothing.

'I wish I could have gone,' Kerr continued. 'Too old,' he said ruefully. 'And health not up to it. Damn shame.'

'There'll be plenty of people in hospital you can help,' Joseph pointed out, then instantly wished he had not. The last thing on earth crippled men wanted was platitudes about God or the nobility of sacrifice.

The light went out of Kerr's face. 'Yes, I realize that, of course,' he said awkwardly. 'But that's not the same as being with our boys in action, braving the gunfire and standing by them in their hour of peril.'

Joseph thought of real fear and its pathetic indignity, those who wept, or soiled themselves with terror. They desperately needed compassion and the willingness to forget as if it had never happened, the passionate, driving urgency to love, to reach out a hand in the bitterness of extremity, and never, ever let go. These easy words were a denial of honesty.

'We're bored most of the time,' he said flatly. 'And tired, and cold and fed up with the mud and the lice. The whole trench network is infested with rats, hundreds of thousands of them, as big as cats. They eat the dead.' He saw Kerr blanch and recoil, and it satisfied something of the anger inside him. 'We get used to them,' he said a fraction more gently. 'Believe me, you're needed here as well. And there will be plenty of widows to comfort who will require all your strength.'

31

'Well, yes, I suppose that is true,' Kerr admitted, but there was no expression in him any more. 'There is need for great faith, great faith indeed. And if there is anything I can do for you, please let Mrs MacAllister know.' He looked sideways, as if Hannah had been standing in the doorway.

'Thank you,' Joseph accepted, ashamed of himself now for having been so crushing. The man spoke from ignorance, not ill will. He wanted to help. It was not his fault he did not know how to. 'It was very good of you to come by,' he added. 'You must have a lot to do with so many men away. I don't suppose you even have a curate, do you?'

Kerr's expression lightened. 'No, no, I don't. Poor fellow felt obliged to go and do his duty. Went to the East End of London, actually, where they had no one. Had a game leg – no good for the army.' He rose to his feet. 'I don't want to tire you. I'm sure you need all the rest you can get, grow strong again and go back into the fray, what?'

'Yes, I expect so,' Joseph agreed. What else could he do?

After Kerr had gone Hannah came into the room. 'What did you say to him?' she demanded. 'The poor man looked even more lost than usual.'

'I'm sorry,' Joseph apologized. He drew in his breath to explain to her, then realized that he couldn't. She knew no more of the reality than Kerr did, and it would be unfair to try to force her to see it. She had her own burdens to bear, and they were suffi-cient. It was both cruel and pointless to want to make her see his pain as well, or live through the things that twisted and tore inside him. She had never asked him to look on her wounds of the heart or the mind. He was being unjust. He smiled at her warmly, meaning it. 'I'll be nicer to him next time, I promise.'

She shook her head very slightly. 'Don't push him into the water, Joe. He can't swim.'

He knew exactly what she meant. It was a touch of the old Hannah back again, from before the war, before the world changed, and youth had to grow wise and brave and die before its time. He hated the Peacemaker for the murders he had committed, and made other people commit, for the loss of John

and Alys Reavley, the betrayal of Sebastian. But he could understand the dream of avoiding war and the slaughter of hundreds
of thousands across the battlefields of Europe, the ruin of a gener-
ation, the grief of millions. It was the price that choked him –
the price in honour. Was betrayal ever right, even if it saved a
million lives? Ten million?

Perhaps every one of them was loved as much by somebody as
John and Alys Reavley had been by him.

He closed his eyes and drifted off into a half-sleep, aware of
his arm throbbing, and his leg, and longing for the time he could
turn on his side without pain.

Chapter Three

Calder Shearing looked up from his desk as Matthew Reavley came into his office. Shearing was of average height, strong chested, with heavy, black brows full of expression. It was an almost ascetic face with a powerfully curved nose and sensitive mouth.

'How is your brother?' he asked.

'Lucky to keep his arm,' Matthew replied. 'He'll be several weeks before he's fit to go back. Thank you, sir.'

'I suppose he will go back?' Shearing questioned him. He knew something of Joseph and had a deep respect for him rooted in his extraordinary actions a year ago.

'His conscience would crucify him if he didn't.' Matthew sat down as Shearing indicated the chair.

Shearing looked bleak. 'The sabotage is getting worse,' he said grimly, all pretence at courtesy abandoned. 'How much longer before we can act?' There was an edge of desperation in his voice. 'We're being bled to death!'

'I know—' Matthew began.

'Do you?' Shearing cut across him. 'The French are being massacred at Verdun. Last month the Seventy-second Division at Samogneux was reduced from twenty-six thousand men to ten thousand. The Russian Front is unspeakable. Stürmer, a creature of Rasputin's, has replaced Goremykin as Prime Minister.' His face tightened. 'Our people there estimate that a quarter of the entire working-age population is dead, captured or in the army. The harvest has failed and they are facing starvation. We are fighting in Italy, Turkey, the Balkans, Mesopotamia, Palestine, Egypt, and more than half Africa.'

Matthew did not interrupt. It seemed pointless to say that at least they had finally succeeded in extricating themselves from the disaster of Gallipoli, and without losing a single man. The actual evacuation had been a military masterpiece, though nothing could make up for the fiasco of the attempted invasion, which had cost the lives of over a quarter of a million men. On the worst days the reconnaissance aircraft had reported the sea red with blood.

Shearing was staring at him, his eyes shadowed with exhaustion and a deep, corroding knowledge. His emotion dominated the bleak room in which there was nothing of his home, his past, or the man he was outside these walls.

Matthew was compelled to offer all the brief information he could about his own specific task. 'The fact that they are putting smoke bombs in the holds of the ships, in among the munitions, so the captains have no choice but to flood the holds, can be deduced easily enough. It doesn't need any explanation,' he said. 'To trace the money to pay for the bombs, and the agents who plant them, all the way from Berlin to America needs several people. We can fabricate bank clerks, officials and so on, suggest bribery and betrayal, a degree of carelessness, but it all has to be verifiable.'

'I know that!' Shearing snapped. 'You've got men – do it!'

He was referring to Detta Hannassey, the Irish agent the Germans were using to test whether their vital naval code had been broken. It was Matthew's job to convince her, and them, that it had not, otherwise they would change the code and Britain would lose one of the very few advantages it had. All communication from Berlin to their men in the neutral United States hung in the balance. 'I am doing it. I can't just lay it out in front of her. I have to wait until she asks, or something happens to make it natural to talk about it. I've got a story about someone turned from their side to ours, but I need a cover to make it believable.'

Shearing kept his impatience under control with a visible effort. 'How long?'

'Three weeks,' Matthew estimated. 'Two if I'm lucky. If I rush it she'll know exactly what I'm doing.'

Shearing's face was pale.

'How is our status in Washington?' Matthew asked drily. He had little hope of change. Even rumour of a Japanese base in Baja California and all the violence and chaos in Mexico under Pancho Villa had made no real difference.

Anger and self-mockery lit Shearing's eyes. 'About equal with that of the Germans,' he said sourly. 'President Wilson is still aspiring to be the arbiter of peace in Europe. Teach the Old World how it's done.'

Matthew would have used an expletive had he not been in his superior's office. 'What will it take to make him change?'

'If I knew that I'd damn well do it!' Shearing told him. 'Work hard, Reavley. It can't be long before they take the next step up and start actually sinking the munitions ships. It only takes an incendiary bomb instead of smoke.'

Matthew was cold. 'Yes, sir, I know that.'

Shearing nodded slowly and had picked up the paper on his desk before Matthew reached the door.

The nightclub where Matthew had arranged to meet Detta was crowded with soldiers on leave. There was a hectic gaiety about them, as if it took all their energy of mind to absorb every sight and sound, to remember them in the days to come. Even the young women with them caught the mood – elegant, romantic, a little wild, as if they too knew that tonight was everything, and tomorrow might slip out of their hands.

There were only three musicians on the small platform: a pianist; a slender, wispy-haired man with a saxophone; and a girl of about twenty in a long, blue dress. She was singing a haunting lyric from one of the popular music-hall songs, but altered every now and then to be sadder, harsher, full of the reality of death. Her smoky voice added passion to the song, belying the innocence of her face. Her hair was short, and she wore a band around it, over her brow.

Matthew found a place at the bar and sat down.

He had nearly half an hour to wait, and he was surprised and annoyed with himself at how tense he became. He listened to the music. All the tunes were familiar, from the crazy Al Jolson 'Yaacka Hula Hickey Dula' to the heartbreaking 'Keep the Home Fires Burning'.

He sipped his drink, spinning it out, watching couples dancing. It was natural that he should be anxious to see Detta in order to further his work, convincing her that the code was unbroken, but his disappointment was personal. The emotion of the music, the fear in the eyes of the young men around him, made him overwhelmingly aware of loneliness, separation, clinging too hard to the present because the future was unbearable.

Then he heard a slight commotion in the doorway, a momentary silence, and Detta came down the steps. She was not tall, but she walked as if she were, with a unique kind of slow grace, as if she would never stumble or grow tired. She was wearing a black dress, cut low at the bosom, a red rose at her waist. The skirt was lined in satin so it rustled very slightly as she moved. It made the blemishless skin of her neck seem even whiter, and the cloud of her dark hair accentuated her eyes. One of her brows was a little different from the other, a blemish to perfect beauty that gave her a vulnerable, slightly humorous look.

As happened every time Matthew saw her, no matter how much he guarded against it, his pulse raced and his mouth went dry.

At first she did not appear to have seen him, and he really did not wish to stand up and draw her attention. Then she turned and smiled, walked elegantly past the young men who had crowded towards her, and came over to Matthew. She spoke to the bartender first, as if that were what she had really come for, then turned to Matthew.

'I haven't seen you for a while,' she remarked quite casually. Her voice was low, and the softness of the Irish gave it a unique music.

It was five days since they had last met, to be exact, but he did not tell her he had been counting. He must not let her know it mattered so much or she would be suspicious. Whatever he felt –

and it was far more than he wanted to – it must never affect his judgement. He could not afford to forget for an instant that they were on opposite sides. She was an Irish Nationalist, with sympathy for Germany, and perhaps any other enemy of England. Only here, in the lights, with the laughter and the music, did they pretend it did not matter.

He paid for her drink and another for himself, and they walked over to one of the few free tables.

'I went back to Cambridgeshire,' he explained. 'My brother was wounded rather badly and they sent him home.'

Her eyes widened. 'I'm sorry.' She said it instantly, without time to consider loyalties or causes. 'How is he?'

The girl in the blue dress was singing again, a sad, angry little song with downward falling notes.

'Better than many, I suppose,' Matthew answered. He could be reasonably dispassionate about other people – one had to be – but seeing Joseph grey-faced and obviously in appalling pain had shaken him more deeply than he had been prepared for. It brought back the memory of his father's broken body after the car crash, and his mother's. The police had called it an accident and nothing public had ever suggested otherwise.

To talk about numbers of losses was one thing; to see the blood and the pain in real people was quite different. He understood very well why soldiers ran away rather than take cold steel in their hands and plunge it into another human being. The fact that that other man was German was irrelevant. He was flesh and bone, capable of exactly the same emotions as themselves. Perhaps for some the nightmares would never entirely go. He did not want to be the kind of man for whom they would. He was intensely grateful that his job had never required him to meet his physical enemy face to face and exercise the violence of death. But he did not delude himself that he was somehow absolved from the results of any victory he might win.

Detta was looking at him curiously. He caught in her eyes an unguarded moment of compassion.

'He's a chaplain,' he said quickly, to explain that Joseph was not a soldier. Although since he was Protestant, not Catholic, perhaps in her eyes that would be even worse. He found himself smiling at the lunacy of it; it was that or rage, or tears. 'A shell ripped his leg open and smashed his arm pretty badly, but the doctor says he'll not lose it,' he added.

She winced. 'I suppose he's in a lot of pain,' she said gently.

'Yes.' He needed to go on; the next thing had to be said, but he hated it. 'The casualties are heavy at the moment. He was out over no-man's-land carrying back a pretty badly wounded soldier, someone from our own village – not that that makes any difference, I suppose. We're desperately short of ammunition. We're having to ration it, so many bullets per man. They're being shot at, and they can't shoot back. We're buying stuff from America, but it's being sabotaged at sea, and when it gets here it's no bloody use!' There was more anger in his voice than he had meant there to be, and his hand on the table next to his glass was clenched tight. He must think clearly. He was here to do a job, not to indulge his fury.

'Sabotaged?' She affected surprise, her dark eyes wide. 'The Americans would never do that, surely?'

'At sea,' he corrected her.

'At sea? How?' She did not disguise her interest.

That made it easier. Now they were playing the game again, threading the lies in with the truth, testing each other, tying the knots of emotion tighter and tighter.

'Smoke bombs,' he answered. 'Pack them in the hold, along with the shells, and set them to go off when the ship's at sea. It looks like fire. Then, of course, the captain has no choice but to flood the holds, and the shells are damaged. But not all of them, and there's no way to tell which. From the outside they all look perfectly sound. We're so desperate for munitions, we can't afford to turn them down.'

'How do you know they're smoke bombs?' she asked. 'Do you find them?'

'We know they're being put there,' he answered. 'We have men in several of the American east coast ports.' He was not sure whether to go on. Was that enough? Might she realize what he was doing if he added any more?

'Then why don't you stop it?' she said curiously, her faintly uneven brows giving her a quizzical look. 'You can't be squeamish! Or are you afraid of upsetting the Americans?'

He gave her a sidelong, incredulous look. 'Of course we aren't squeamish! What about? Taking out one or two saboteurs? Showing them up to the Americans? We can do it without causing a diplomatic incident. It's just too soon to act. We know who they are. If we take them out now, they'll only be replaced by others that we don't know. Far better to wait, and trace the whole organization, then we can get rid of all of them.'

'How can you do that?' She turned her hands up and smiled broadly. 'Sorry! Shouldn't have asked. I'm Irish – you'd hardly tell me.' There was laughter in her eyes. But then she did laugh. He had realized weeks ago that the hunt, the battle, was part of her life. The legends of Celtic conquest and mysticism, the heroes of the past with their love and their loss woven together inextricably, were part of her identity. If she won this struggle she would have to find a new one. She needed to seek the unattainable, to voyage beyond the known. Her crusades fed her dreams, and starved her heart.

If she were more realistic, if the fire in her burned under control, he might like her just as much, but the magic that enchanted him would be gone, and the vulnerability that made her so very human.

'If it were a secret I wouldn't tell you, even if you were English,' he replied, smiling at her as she winced at the insult. 'But it's only the obvious,' he went on. 'Just what you would do yourself, follow the money. If we get agents into the banking system at all the right points, we can prove to the Americans exactly what is happening. And the other thing, of course, is to put pressure at the right places, at exactly the right time, and turn one of their agents. Or should I say one of yours?'

She shook her head. 'Not ours! I'm strictly for freedom of my own land from British oppression, that's all.'

He did not challenge her on the truth of that. He might get into an argument where he would say too much and give away more of his purpose than he could afford, or too little, and make his reason for being with her obvious. Nor did he want to quarrel with her. He smiled. 'All right, not yours,' he conceded. 'German.'

The girl in blue was singing again, a light, sarcastic song to the tune of 'Pack Up Your Troubles in Your Old Kit Bag'.

Detta looked at her glass, twisting it slowly in her fingers. 'Do you think you can turn someone?' she asked with a lift of doubt. 'How would you know if you had, and they weren't just feeding you the information their masters wanted you to have? Even taking back bits and pieces about you?' She lifted her eyes quickly to meet his, bright and dark, full of a hidden laughter that was always on the edge of sadness.

He smiled back, a wall of humour against reality. 'I don't.'

She gave an elegant shrug. Her shoulders were beautiful. He had no idea whether she was conscious of it or not.

'There are ways,' he added, aware that he had not said enough. 'You measure one against another, advance information against what actually happens. But it's pretty hard to turn people. You have to have something very powerful to do it, and, unless they're stupid, they know the risks. Their own people will kill them if they're caught.'

She shivered and looked away across the room. 'Part of the price. I can't imagine betraying your own like that. I'd rather die.'

He said nothing. The Irish did not kill their traitors easily; more often they made examples of them by breaking their knees. Many a man never walked again. But this was not the time to tell her how much he knew about that.

'Probably spies for money rather than passion,' he said instead.

She did not answer. She was staring somewhere into the hollowness and hurts of her own mind.

'It's nasty to turn someone,' he went on quietly. 'But then if you see what's happening in the trenches that's pretty nasty too. We need ammunition we can rely on.' He thought of Joseph, and allowed the pain to show in his face. He knew she was watching him.

'I can't imagine you related to a priest,' she said softly. 'Actually I'm not sure I can imagine an English priest at all. You haven't the fire or the mysticism for it.'

'Is that what it takes?' He let the slight banter back into his voice.

'Isn't it?' she countered.

'I don't think there's a lot of room for mysticism when men are cold and frightened, squatting in the mud with the rats, or dying in crushing pain, armless, legless, their guts torn out. You need the reality of human pity and human love. It's about all there is left.'

Detta reached up and for a moment it was as if she were going to touch his face, then she changed her mind abruptly and the tenderness vanished from her eyes. 'So isn't that the time when you need a priest most of all?' she countered. 'To make sense of the senseless? Or don't Protestant priests do that?'

'I don't know. It sounds a bit like a retreat,' Matthew said with more candour than he had intended. 'Recite some comfortable piece of scripture and think you've solved the problem.'

'You've no magic in your heart,' she accused him, but she was looking at him with searching eyes now, gentle and surprised, as if she had seen something that had awoken a new emotion in her.

'Does magic help?' he asked with raised eyebrows.

Suddenly she was completely honest, all the laughter gone. 'I think when you're face to face with the devil, you'll find out. I've a horrible fear that maybe it doesn't after all. What then, Matthew? English courage, naked, without any pretty clothes and nice music?'

'Doesn't have to be English,' he replied. 'Any sort would do.'

She sat silent for a while, staring at the dancers on the floor. They were holding each other closely and moving as if the music carried them like a tide. There was sadness and anger in her face as she watched them.

'They know it, don't they?' she said after a while. 'You can see it in their eyes, hear it in the pitch of their voices, a bit high and with an edge. They could be dead in the Flanders mud this time next week.' She breathed in and out shakily. The passion welled up in her, a rage and sorrow that spilled over in tears on her cheek. 'It didn't have to happen, you know!' she said fiercely, her voice trembling out of control. 'You didn't have to fight the Germans. It could all have been avoided, but one misguided idealist, an Englishman with an arrogant, narrow patriotism, and

42

blind to any vision for the world, stumbled on to the papers that would have stopped it. And because he didn't understand that, he stole them and destroyed them.'

She blinked, but it did not stop the tears. 'I've no idea who he is, or what happened to him, but, Mother of God, if he can see what he's done, he must be in the madhouse with guilt and grief. All these men, so young, all gone, sacrificed on the altar of stupidity. Don't you despair of us sometimes?'

Matthew didn't hear her any more. The words ran through him like fire, scorching with a pain he could not have imagined. She was talking about John Reavley and the treaty he had found, and for which the Peacemaker had had him murdered. It was sitting in the gun room in St Giles where he and Joseph had replaced it after reading it.

Only one other man beyond the family knew of it, and he had paid with his life.

The document was a conspiracy to create an Anglo-German empire of peace, prosperity and domination, the cost of which was the betrayal of France and Belgium, and ultimately most of the world. It would be a dishonour that would cast a black pall over everything that England had ever been, or believed in. And how could Detta know that, unless she were part of it?

Detta was talking to him and the words were a meaningless jumble of sounds.

That she was involved with the Peacemaker was something Matthew had not even considered. Her Irish Nationalism he could understand. In her place he would have felt the same. He might have fought for Germany, if the reward were his own country's independence, even if half of them did not want it. But this had to mean that she was close enough to the Peacemaker to be trusted with at least the core of the plan, the dream of it. There would be no need to tell her the name or the fate of the man who had foiled it. His death was regarded by everyone else as an accident and no one in the family had challenged that. The Peacemaker himself never knew that they had found the treaty, or understood its nature. John Reavley had said simply that he had found a document that would dishonour England and change the world.

Detta was an idealist. It could be dangerous to tell her more of murder than she needed to know. The Peacemaker took no risks.

Until now Matthew had had little idea of his identity, hard as he had sought. It was not Ivor Chetwin; he and Joseph had proved that in Gallipoli. Nor was it Aiden Thyer; but then that had been only a passing thought because of his power in Cambridge as Master of St John's. Matthew's greatest fear had been that it was Calder Shearing himself, right at the heart of Britain's Secret Intelligence Service. Shearing was brilliant, charming and elusive, and Matthew knew almost nothing about him outside his work.

He had never even considered Patrick Hannassey. He had thought of him only as the cleverest and most dedicated fighter for the freedom of Catholic Ireland from British rule. Now he had to face the possibility – in fact the probability – that he was wrong.

Detta's father!

She was looking at him, her odd eyebrow raised in bitter irony. 'You didn't know about that paper, did you. You thought it was all inevitable.' It was a statement.

'Given the political tides,' he said very quietly, 'the alliances between Austria, Germany and Russia, and ours with France and Belgium, yes, I thought there was no way to avoid war.'

'You aren't asking me if I'm sure about it,' she pointed out.

'Would you say it if you weren't?' he asked, looking at her again now.

She turned away, avoiding his gaze. 'No. Is there a point where madness becomes so common we think it's sanity?'

'I don't know.' She was not going to say any more. He would not play the game of trying to make her. 'Would you like to dance?' he asked. He wanted to forget about talking for a while. He could not afford to say any more; he might far too easily betray himself. He simply wanted to hold her in his arms, feel the ease and grace of her movement, smell the perfume of her hair, and above all pretend for a few minutes that they were on the same side.

'Dance?' she asked, her voice rising. 'Perhaps you do understand magic after all! What's the difference between looking for a supernatural answer, and simply running away, Matthew?'

'Timing,' he answered. 'At the moment I'm just running away.'

'Yes,' she agreed, laughter touching her eyes again, but only with self-mockery. 'Yes, I'll dance. What better is there to do?'

The following morning Matthew arrived at his office in a mood of optimism. This was dashed the moment he encountered Hoskins standing in the corridor, his thin face twisted with anxiety.

For a moment Matthew thought of avoiding asking him what was wrong, and simply going on to his own door, but all bad news had to be faced sooner or later.

'Good morning, Hoskins. What is it?'

'Morning, Reavley. Just another ship gone,' Hoskins replied miserably. 'U-boats got it. It was carrying food and munitions. All hands lost.' Hoskins stood motionless apart from the slight tic in his left eyelid. 'That's the fourth this month.'

'I know,' Matthew said quietly. He could think of nothing else to say. There was no comfort to offer, and nothing to salvage.

'Shearing wants to see you,' Hoskins added. 'I'd go there first, if I were you.'

Matthew acknowledged the message, left his coat in his office and then glanced at his desk to see if there were any overnight messages of urgency. There was nothing that Shearing needed to know, just the usual reports from his men in the eastern United States. Progress was slow.

He crossed the corridor and, after a brief knock, went into Shearing's office.

Shearing looked up from his desk. There were hollows around his eyes, accentuating how dark they were. 'What's your progress with the Hannassey woman?' he asked.

There was a sour irony to the situation. Shearing knew of John and Alys Reavley's deaths and Matthew's belief that there was a conspiracy behind it, but because of John Reavley's warning, Matthew had not told even his own superior in the intelligence services.

'Well?' Shearing barked.

Matthew could not tell him that Detta had in one wild explosion of anger let slip her knowledge of the Peacemaker's conspiracy, but it pounded in his mind as if it could drive out all other thoughts, and he composed his expression with difficulty. One realization flooded out every other. Surely Hannassey had to be the Peacemaker? It was someone who trusted Detta with his life. It could not be Shearing.

He cleared his throat. He was still standing more or less to attention in front of the desk. 'I told her about the smoke bombs in the ships' holds, sir,' he replied. 'And that we have almost traced the money. We just need to turn one of their agents and we'll be able to close it down.'

'I see. And how do you propose to convince her that you have done that?' Shearing's expression was sceptical, his lips tightly compressed.

'With the information, and an appropriate dead body,' Matthew replied.

Shearing nodded very slowly, his eyes not leaving Matthew's face. 'Good. When?'

'Another week at the very least. I have to give it long enough to be believable.'

'I suppose you know we lost another ship last night? All hands.'

'Yes, sir.'

'When did you last hear anything from Shanley Corcoran?'

'Two days ago,' Matthew replied. For just over a year now he had been the link between the Secret Intelligence Service in London and the Scientific Establishment in Cambridge where they were developing an underwater guidance system that would mean that torpedoes and depth charges would no longer randomly hit their targets but would strike every time. It would revolutionize the war at sea. Whoever had such a device would be lethal. No skill or speed would enable an enemy to escape once they were found. The endless cat-and-mouse games that now meant a skilled and daring commander could outwit pursuit would avail nothing. Judgement of speed, direction, even depth, would be irrelevant. Every missile would strike.

And, of course, if the Germans were to have such a weapon

then the U-boats now reaping such a terrible harvest would become unstoppable. Britain would be brought to its knees in weeks. The supplies of food and munitions would dry up. There would be no navy to take reinforcements to France, or even to evacuate the wounded, and in the end not even to rescue what remained of the army, beaten because it had no guns, no food, no shells, no medicine, no new men.

Shearing was waiting for an answer.

Matthew smiled a little as he gave it. 'They are very close to completing it, sir. He said within a week.'

Shearing's eyes were wide. 'He's certain?'

'Yes, sir.'

Shearing eased back a little in his chair. There was a sheen of sweat on his brow. 'Thank God,' he breathed. 'Then if we don't have any more lunatic action like the Santa Ysabel massacre, and Pancho Villa doesn't lose his wits and storm over the Rio Grande, we just might make it. For God's sake be careful! Whatever you do, don't jeopardize the code!'

'No, sir.'

Shearing made a small, dismissive gesture, and returned his attention to the papers on his desk.

In Marchmont Street, in a discreet residential area near the heart of London, the man known as the Peacemaker stood in the upstairs sitting room facing his visitor. He hated war with a passion that consumed every other wish or hunger within him. He had seen the human misery of the Boer War in Africa at the turn of the century, the death and destruction, the concentration camps for civilians, even women and children. He had sworn then that whatever it cost he would do everything within his very considerable power to see that such a thing never happened again.

The passion of the man opposite was quite different. He was Irish, and the freedom of his country and its independence from Britain dominated every emotion he felt, and justified all acts that served its end. But they could use each other, and both knew it.

The subject under discussion was money, which the Irishman was going to use to continue his bribery of union officials in

Pittsburgh and in the east coast docks of America to sabotage the munitions destined for the Allies.

'No more than five thousand,' the Peacemaker said flatly.

'Six,' the other man answered. He was unimpressive to look at, the kind of man no one would notice in a crowd, average in height and build, nondescript of colouring and ordinary of feature. He was capable of a score of appearances depending upon his stance and expression, and the clothes he wore. That was part of his genius. He came and went as he chose, and no one remembered him. Another gift was his almost flawless memory.

The Peacemaker replied with a single word. 'Why?' He did not like the Irishman, nor did he trust him, and lately he had become too demanding. He also had a great deal of knowledge. Unless he proved himself more valuable than he had so far, he would have to be disposed of.

'You want to stop the American munitions reaching England safely?' the Irishman asked, almost without inflection. He had no accent; he had deliberately eradicated the soft music of his native burr. It was part of his anonymity, and he had learned never to let it slip.

In contrast to him, the Peacemaker was highly memorable, a man whose dynamic appearance and extraordinary character no one forgot.

'And keep your very considerable interest in Mexico?' the Irishman continued. 'It takes money.'

The Peacemaker had a strong suspicion that many of the guns in question, as well as the ammunition for them, were going to end up in Ireland, but just at the moment that was less important. 'I do,' he answered. 'It is in both our interests.'

'Then I need six thousand,' the Irishman told him. His face was expressionless, showing nothing at all that could be used against him. 'For the moment,' he added. 'We have to have men on all the ships, and they are taking a considerable risk planting smoke bombs in the holds. If they get caught they'll likely be shot. I can't rely on anyone doing that for love, or hate. We need at the least to guarantee that their families will be taken care of.'

The Peacemaker did not argue. He must handle this with exactly the right mixture of scepticism and generosity. Their goals were different – just how different he did not yet wish the other man to appreciate. He knew that the Irishman's aim was a free and independent Ireland, and a touch of revenge thrown in would add to the savour.

The Peacemaker's purpose was an Anglo-German empire that would lay peace not only on warring Europe, but upon the entire world, such as the British Empire had across Africa, India, Burma, the Far East, and the islands of the Atlantic and Pacific Oceans. This would be greater. It would end the strife that had torn the cradle of Western civilization apart for the last thousand years. Europe and Russia would belong to Germany, Africa was to be divided. The rest, including the United States of America, would be Britain's. They would have the best of the art and science and the richest culture in the world. There would be safety, prosperity and the values of free exchange, law, medicine and literacy for everyone. The price would be obedience. That was a fact in the nature of men and of nations. Those who did not obey willingly would have to be forced, for the sake of the vast majority whose lives would be enriched and who would be more than willing, indeed, eager, to grasp such moral and social wealth.

Naturally Ireland was included, and would have no more independence than it did now. It was by nature and geography part of the British Isles. But of course the Peacemaker would say nothing of this to the man opposite him.

'Very well,' he agreed reluctantly. 'Make sure every penny is used well.'

'I don't waste money,' the Irishman answered him. There was no emotion in his voice; only looking at the steady, pale steel-blue eyes did the Peacemaker see the chill in him. He knew better than ever to underestimate an enemy, or a friend.

The Peacemaker went over to his desk and withdrew the banker's draft. He had had it made for six thousand, because he knew that was what he would have to settle for. He had made his calculations in advance.

'Some of that is for Mexico,' he said as he handed it over. The

Irishman would never know if he had had two drafts together there, one for both missions.

The Irishman took the paper and put it in his inside pocket. 'What about the naval war?' he asked. 'I've heard whispers about this project in the Establishment in Cambridge. Are they on the brink of inventing something that will defeat the German Navy?'

The Peacemaker smiled, a cold, thin gesture. 'I will inform you of that if it should become necessary for you to know,' he answered. He was startled that the Irishman had even heard of it, uncomfortably so. He obviously had sources the Peacemaker was unaware of. Was that his purpose in asking, to let him know that? Looking at his smooth, blank face now with its prominent bones and relentless eyes, he judged that it was.

'So it is true,' the Irishman said.

'Or it is not true,' the Peacemaker replied. 'Or I do not know.'

The Irishman smiled mirthlessly. 'Or that is what you wish me to think.'

'Just so. Travel safely.'

When he was gone, the Peacemaker stood alone. The Irishman was a good tool – highly intelligent, resourceful, and in his dedication incorruptible. No money, personal power, luxury or office, no threat to his life or liberty would deter him from his course.

On the other hand he was ruthless, manipulative and devious. He was impossible to control, which the Peacemaker admired at the same time as he recognized its danger. The time was fast approaching when disposing of him would become a matter of urgency.

Half an hour later the post arrived with several letters and the usual bills. One envelope had a Swiss stamp on it, and he tore it open eagerly. There were several pages written in close script, in English, although the use of words was highly idiosyncratic, as of one who translated literally from another language before committing it to paper.

At a glance it seemed ordinary enough, the account of daily life of an elderly man in a small village at least a hundred miles from any battlefront. Fellow villagers were mentioned by Christian name only, most of them Italian or French. It was full of gossip, opinions, local quarrels over small matters of insult, jealousy, rivals in love.

Read with the Peacemaker's knowledge it was entirely different. The village in question was not some rural Swiss community but Imperial Russia; the local characters, the groups and players on that vast stage of tragedy and upheaval, war and mounting social unrest. New ideas were boiling to the surface and the possibilities were almost too huge to grasp. They could change the world.

But this was just one man's thoughts, sensitive and acutely observed as they were. The Peacemaker needed more information, a better ally, a man who could travel freely and make informed judgements, who had the width of experience and the idealism to see the humanity beneath the cause. The Irishman's intelligence was acute, but his dreams were narrow and self-serving. There was too much hatred in him.

The Peacemaker thought again with regret of Richard Mason. He had been wholehearted a year ago. He too had witnessed the abomination of the Boer War, and been sickened by it. And in this present conflict he had seen more than most men. His occupation as war correspondent had taken him from the trenches of the Western Front to the blood-soaked beaches of Gallipoli, the battlefields of Italy and the Balkans, and even the bitter slaughter of the Russian Front. He had written about them all with a passion and humanity unequalled by any other journalist, and unsurpassed courage.

He had been not only the ideal ally, but the Peacemaker had honestly liked him. Losing him last year had been a double blow. He could still remember his shock even more than his anger when Mason had stood here in this room, exhausted and beaten, and told him that he had changed his mind.

That had been the doing of Joseph Reavley, of all people! Reavley, whom he had totally discounted as a useless dreamer, a man who would wish well, and lack the nerve to act.

Damn Joseph Reavley and his stupid and desperately misguided emotionalism. He was exactly like his father, and he had cost the Peacemaker his best ally.

Nothing he could say afterwards had changed Mason's resolve.

51

But now, a year later, it was time to try again, even harder, to swallow his own pride and win him back. Argument did not work. He must use emotion, as Reavley had, and his very considerable charm. It might be inwardly humiliating, but for the sake of the greater peace it would be infinitely worth it. And such peace would not come without cost to them all. He should not expect to be immune, professionally or personally.

He moved away from the window. He would begin tonight.

Chapter Four

Hannah heard the front door bang, and Luke came running up the hall. She had told him a score of times not to run inside the house. She turned to tell him again just as she heard the vase topple off the hall table and crash to the floor. She knew from the sound of it that it had smashed, not into a couple of pieces, but dozens.

Then she heard Jenny's voice, strident and sharp.

Hannah stormed into the hall. 'Jenny! I've told you not to use that word! Go to your room!'

Jenny's face crumpled. 'That's not fair! It was Luke who broke the vase, it wasn't me!'

'Telltale tit! Telltale tit!' Luke sang, hopping up and down.

'And you go into the garden and pull the weeds in the vegetable patch until I tell you it's enough!' Hannah barked at him. 'Now!'

'But I—' he started.

'Now!' she repeated. 'If you want any supper?'

'It's not fair!' he complained. 'It was an accident! She called me—'

'If I have to tell you again, you'll have no supper,' Hannah warned him. She meant it. She was furious and frightened. Loss seemed to be crowding in on every side, like a darkness falling, and she knew no way out.

Both children went to obey, Jenny crying, Luke stifling his misery as a matter of pride.

Joseph came in through the side door, holding it open for Luke, who did not even glance upwards at him.

'Thank you!' Hannah called after him. 'Where are your manners?'

Luke ignored her and disappeared.

Just as miserable herself, she bent to pick up the pieces of the shattered vase. It had been her mother's, and was not just beautiful, but full of memories. There were too many fragments even to think of mending it. She felt bereft, as if a part of her history had been taken from her. In spite of all she could do, the tears welled in her eyes and spilled down her cheeks.

Joseph bent down beside her and, with his good hand, picked up the shards and put them on the table. He said nothing about her shouting at the children, nor did he go after either one of them to undo the pain she had caused.

'Say it!' she charged him accusingly as she stood up. 'You think I'm unfair, don't you?'

He looked at her, smiling, and it was a moment or two before she realized it was not kindness but amusement.

'You think it's funny!' she said furiously. She was ashamed of herself; Alys would have done so much better.

Joseph's smile did not lessen in the slightest. 'You're just like Mother,' he answered. 'I remember her flying off the handle at Matthew when he was late home from a football match, and some other boy had been hurt. She was afraid it had been him. Judith came in complaining about something else, and she shrieked at both of them and told them they'd get no tea. Mrs Appleton took them up plum pie and custard, but it was Mother who asked her to. I think it always was; it was just a fiction that it was Mrs Appleton's soft heart.'

'Are you inventing that to make me feel better?' Hannah demanded. But she needed it to be true. She wanted above all to be like her mother, to create safety, warmth, a sense of peace out of the uncertainty.

'No,' he assured her, then his smile vanished. 'They'll pick up your fear, Hannah, even if they don't know what about. They won't be frightened as long as they think you aren't, but if you crumble, so will they.'

She looked away from him. He was right, but she needed more time. 'Do you want to be the hero?' she asked.

'Hero?'

'Take up the pie and custard. It's Mrs Appleton's day off.'

'Yes . . . I'll do that.' He touched her gently on the arm. 'I'm sorry about the vase. I'll see if the antique shop in the village has something like it.'

'It doesn't matter. It wouldn't be the same.'

'It wouldn't to you. It might be for Luke,' he pointed out.

Tears threatened to choke her again, and she said nothing. She was still frightened, still hurt, but her anger was at herself.

Joseph went to bed early. He was tired after a very short time up, and the pain in his arm and leg was constant. He had said nothing, but Hannah saw the shadows in his face.

She sat alone mending sheets, turning their sides to middle. It was a job she hated because she was always acutely aware of the seam when she lay along it, and she imagined others were as well. She was playing Caruso singing '*O sole mio!*' on the gramophone. It had been a tremendous success a month ago. She knew that if Joseph could hear it upstairs he would like it, and she had left the door open on purpose. She was startled to hear the front doorbell ring. She put down her sewing and went to answer it, taking the needle off the record carefully as she passed. The sudden silence was breathless.

The woman on the step was in her late twenties, but grief and weariness had added years to her. Her hair was pretty, but she had tied it up and back without care and pulled the wave out of it. In the light from the hall, her skin seemed to have no colour. She was dressed in a plain dark blue blouse and skirt, and it was apparent at a glance that she had lost quite a bit of weight since Hannah had last seen her.

'Lucy! How are you?' Hannah said quickly. 'Do come in.' She stepped back to make the invitation almost a command.

Lucinda Compton hesitated, then agreed as if the battle against such determination were one she knew she would lose. 'I only came to ask if you could help to organize people for knitting more socks,' she said awkwardly. 'It doesn't matter how little time they can give – anything at all will help. Sometimes even children can do the straight bits, if an adult can turn the heel.'

'Of course,' Hannah agreed. 'Good idea. Would you like a cup of tea? I'm doing the mending and I hate it. I'd love an excuse to stop.' She smiled hopefully.

'Just for a moment or two,' Lucy accepted. 'I'd like to sit down, I admit.' She looked ready to drop.

'Kitchen all right?' Hannah led the way without waiting for an answer. Lucy looked so wretched, Hannah determined to get her hot pie as well. Her husband had been killed in France several months ago, but she looked as if the reality of it had struck her only now. There was an awkwardness in the way she moved, almost a clumsiness, as if she were only half aware of her limbs.

The oven was still warm. Hannah took the apple pie from the larder without asking if Lucy wanted any, and opened the damper for the heat to increase enough to crisp the pastry again. Then she filled the kettle and set it on the hob to boil.

'I heard about Plugger Arnold,' Lucy said softly. 'Gangrene. Is that true?'

'Yes. That's what they said.'

'Paul never told me about that sort of thing.' Lucy gave the ghost of a smile. 'Have you noticed how the newspapers have changed lately? They don't write about heroics so much. They don't use the sort of language that comes out of King Arthur any more. I like to read Richard Mason, even though it leaves me in tears sometimes. He makes people so real, they're never just figures.'

'I know what you mean,' Hannah agreed. 'You feel as if even the dead are not left without dignity. He must be a very fine man.' She indicated the chairs and they both sat down.

'Talking about fine men,' Lucy went on, 'Polly Andrews told me your brother Joseph was wounded. Is that true?'

'Yes, but he'll be all right. I haven't seen Polly for ages. You mean Tiddly Wop Andrews's sister? He's in Joseph's regiment.'

Lucy smiled. 'I used to be crazy about him when I was four-teen.'

'He was awfully good-looking,' Hannah agreed.

The kettle boiled and Hannah made the tea and served the warm, crisp apple pie. The custard was finished but she had a little cream. They ate in silence. Perhaps from pleasure, but more prob-ably from good manners, Lucy finished everything on her plate.

'Thank you,' she said with a smile. 'That's the best I've had in a long time. Are they your own apples?'

'Yes. This time of the year they've been stored all winter and they're not much good for anything but cooking,' Hannah replied. She wanted to be more help than supplying memories of the village and remarks about housekeeping, but she had no idea how to reach the pain that was so obvious in Lucy's face and the crum-pled bowing of her thin shoulders. What did one say or do to touch the loss of her husband? Perhaps that was the ultimate lone-liness; everyone was helpless in the reality of it and frightened because they knew it could happen to them too, tomorrow or the day after.

Alys would have known what to say that would offer some kind of healing, a moment's respite from the drowning pain. How did people survive it? They went to sleep with it, and woke up with it. It walked beside them close as their skin for the rest of their lives. What could Hannah offer that was not facile or intrusive, blundering in, making it all worse still? She remembered the name of Lucy's son. 'How is Sandy?' she asked.

Lucy's eyes filled with tears. 'He's well,' she answered. 'He's starting to enjoy reading and always has a book with him.'

Hannah seized the subject. He was about the same age as Luke, and it was easy to think of things to ask. 'Has he favourites? Tom used to love all sorts of imaginative things, but Luke's a realist.'

Lucy hesitated, and then answered slowly at first, trying to think of titles. Then, as they both recalled stumbled words, triumphant sentences and now finding boys curled up in bed reading in the middle of the night, the conversation became momentarily easy.

But all the time Hannah had the increasing feeling that there was something Lucy wanted to say, and yet dreaded it.

Outside the spring night was dark, the wind rustling very slightly in the leaves with a heaviness as if it might soon rain. Inside the heat from the oven was close on the skin, making the room seem oddly airless.

Finally the tension cracked within Hannah. She leaned forward across the table, reaching her hand towards Lucy's. 'What is it?' she asked: 'You can talk about Paul, if you want to. Or anything else. You can carry it alone if you want, but you don't have to.'

Lucy's eyes were swimming with tears. She wiped them fiercely, staring at Hannah through the blur, trying to make the decision.

Hannah did not know whether to speak or not. She waited while the silence settled. A few spatters of rain struck the window and she stood up to pull it closed.

'Someone from Paul's regiment came to see me about a week ago,' Lucy said suddenly. 'He was on leave. He . . . just came.'

Hannah heard the agony in her voice and turned round slowly. Lucy's face was twisted in pain. Her body was rigid, shuddering with the effort of trying to control herself and knowing she was failing.

Hannah felt her own stomach clench. What terrible thing had this man told her? Had he described the body of the man she loved blown apart, but perhaps still leaving him conscious to be hideously aware of it? Worse? Cowardice? A memory Lucy could scarcely bear to live with? Was that why she looked as if she longed for death herself?

Hannah went over to her, uncertain whether even to attempt to put her arms around the fragile, stiff body, or if it would seem like an unthinking intrusion. She stopped and simply took Lucy's hands instead, kneeling in front of her, awkwardly. The floor was hard.

'What did he say?' she asked.

'He told me about Paul,' Lucy answered, her eyes desperate. 'He told me how much he had liked him. What they did, what they talked about during the long days when they were bored stiff and had lots of time to be frightened, to think of what sort of night it would be, how many would be injured, or killed. He said Paul used to tell jokes, awful ones that went on and on, and sometimes he'd forget the end and have to make it up. Everyone knew he'd lost his place, and they all joined in, getting sillier and sillier.' She gulped. 'He said no one else ever made them laugh the way Paul did.'

Hannah felt the fear slip away from her. It was only pain that tore at her friend. Lucy was missing him all over again, the sharpness renewed. It wasn't any terrible revelation after all.

'It's good his men liked him,' she said. 'He was with friends.'

There was no comfort whatever in Lucy's eyes. 'This man – his name was Miles,' she went on. 'He told me about one concert party they had, all dressed up like women and singing songs. He wouldn't tell me the words because he said they were pretty racy, but Paul had a gift for rhymes, and he wrote a lot of them, even though he was an officer. He didn't take credit for it, but the men knew. All sorts of absurd rhymes, he said.' She tried to smile. 'Actually "ridiculous" and "meticulous" was one, and "crazy horse", "pays, of course" and "could be worse", only he pronounced it "worss". It was all incredibly silly, and it made them laugh.' She looked at Hannah wretchedly. 'I never heard him do that!'

Hannah was lost for words. She could see that Lucy was hurt almost more than she could bear, but not why. Everything this man had said about Paul was good.

'He told me Paul was incredibly brave,' Lucy went on. 'The men were filthy a lot of the time – mud and rats and things, and lice. Can't get rid of the lice. They shaved every day, but there was not enough water to wash any more than their faces.' Her voice was rising and getting faster. 'Miles told me you can smell the stench of the front line long before you get there. Paul never said that.'

Hannah waited.

'Miles said he'd never liked anyone more than he liked Paul.' Lucy did not even try to stop her tears now. 'His men trusted him, he said. He was hard. He had to be. But he was always fair. He agonized over mistakes, decisions he made which could have been wrong. Miles told me about once when he had to send almost twenty men over the top, and he knew they had hardly any chance of coming back, but he couldn't say that to them. It haunted him afterwards, that he had to tell them only part of the truth, so it amounted to a lie.'

She swallowed hard. 'They knew that, and they knew what he felt, and why he couldn't do anything else, but he still had nightmares about it. He'd wake up white-faced, shaking. I try to imagine it, him there alone in a dugout – I've seen pictures of them, tiny and all cramped up – thinking about looking men in the eyes and ordering them out to be killed while he stays behind. And they still loved him!'

'I expect they knew he had no choice,' Hannah spoke at last.

'That's the point, Hannah!' Lucy cried, her voice almost strangled with emotion. 'They knew him! They really knew him – they understood! I didn't! To me he wasn't that man at all. I never saw that kind of honour in him, that kind of laughter, or pain. I just knew him as he was at home, and that was so little. And now it's too late . . . I never will. I can't even tell Sandy what his father was really like.' She closed her eyes. 'It's all gone, slipped away, and I didn't grasp it when I could. I was too busy with my own life. I didn't look.'

'You couldn't have known what he was like in France,' Hannah said gently. 'None of us at home know what it's like for them.'

Lucy jerked her head up. 'But I didn't want to!' she hissed. 'Don't you understand? I knew it was terrible out there. I can read the casualty figures. I've seen the drawings and the photographs in the newspapers. I didn't want to hear the details! The sounds and smells, how cold it was or how wet, how filthy, how hungry they were.' She gasped in her breath. 'I didn't want to know what he felt like, what hurt him or what he was afraid of, what made him laugh or how he loved his friends, because I didn't know how to help him. I didn't want to know about the pain I couldn't touch, or the companionship I couldn't share. And now some man I never even met before comes to see me and tells me what Paul was really like. And I listen to him and try to remember every word, because that's all I'll ever have.'

She leaned forward and bowed her head in her arms across the table and sobbed, racked with a regret for which there was no healing.

With a fearful clarity Hannah knew exactly what she meant. If Archie never came home, how much would she know about what his life was really like? What would she understand of the joy or the pain he felt, how he weighed his decisions, what guilt kept him up all night? What did he laugh about when he was frightened, or trying to help other people through the long waiting for the moment of victory, or defeat? What did Archie's men think of him . . . really? Who was he, inside the carefully painted shell? Why did she not know? What would she tell her children of their father, if he was one of those who died?

She wanted to say something comforting to Lucy, but this was not the time for salvaging tiny pieces. She needed to face the emptiness and recognize it now; then perhaps it would not have to be done again. This time she was quite certain it was right to take Lucy in her arms and simply hold her until she had wept out her strength.

Afterwards she took her to the bathroom and left her to wash her face and straighten her clothes. She made no mention of what either of them had said, as if they had quietly agreed that it had not really happened.

'Thank you,' Lucy said, almost under her breath, as she stood by the front door to leave. 'The apple pie was lovely. You . . . I hope you don't mind my saying so, but you are very like your mother.' And with that ultimate compliment, she walked out into the darkness, leaving Hannah with a tumult of emotions.

She went back inside and found Tom in his pyjamas on the stairs. He looked worried. 'You all right, Mum?' he said anxiously.

She was about to dismiss it with 'of course', when she realized he would not believe her. It was not reassurance for himself he was seeking. He knew there was something wrong and he felt it was his responsibility to look after her.

'A friend came by and she was upset,' she said.

'Why?' he asked, coming down the last few steps. 'Has someone she loved been killed?'

'Yes. A little while ago now, but she just needed to talk about it a bit. Not everyone wants to listen.'

He smiled. 'I'm glad you did that for her.' He turned to go

back up again, then stopped. 'Uncle Joseph's still awake, Mum. I've seen his light go on and off a few times. I think maybe he can't sleep either.'

'Thank you. I'll take him a cup of cocoa, or something. Good night.'

'Good night, Mum.'

Hannah did not tell Joseph about Lucy Compton's visit other than simply that she had called, but she could not get rid of it from her mind.

She could just as easily have been the one to realize in a single, dreadful hour that she had turned her back on the chance to share the reality of all that love could be. Without the textures of pain and fear, the moments indelible in the mind, of blood, earth on your hands, a voice in the darkness, the ache of helplessness and pity, and guilt to haunt you afterwards, how much did you know anyone? You had impressions, ideas; you were not given the open heart.

It could still become her, if she did not confront Archie soon and face the things she did not want to know, and it seemed he did not want to tell her. But if she stayed shut out where it was safe, when she was ready to come in, it might be too late. She would be excluded for ever, as Lucy was.

She was frightened she would not have the courage to press him against his will. It would be so much easier to accept denial. She did not know what to ask, when to insist and when to keep silent. If she said something stupid, insensitive or without under-standing, she would never be able to take it back and pretend it hadn't happened. Perhaps it was already too late.

Why couldn't life have remained as it used to be? She had understood the problems then: love affairs that went wrong, child-birth and sometimes loss, quarrels, disloyalties, sickness, fractious children, long nights up watching the ill. Perhaps there had always been loneliness, but the long, quiet greyness of separation, not the searing scarlet of grief. But it had been all on a smaller scale, in homes and schools, churches and village greens; not on battle-fields and in warships. Such a life did not contain enough horror to drive people mad and divide men from women by gulfs they did not know how to cross. But there was no point in thinking further about it now.

Arranging the flowers in church the day before a service was one of the duties Hannah's mother had performed, and it would give her a sense of comfort to do it herself, as if at least some things had not changed. Before she left she checked on Joseph.

'Don't try to make tea yourself,' she told him, looking at his arm. 'Jenny's around and she can do it, if you stay in the kitchen with her. I won't be long.'

He smiled patiently, and she realized she was fussing. 'It's important,' she explained, hugging the daffodils she had picked, stems wrapped so they did not bleed on to her clothes.

'Of course it is,' he agreed. 'Daffodils always seem brave and beautiful, like a promise that things will get better. It doesn't matter what winter's like, spring will come, eventually.'

All kinds of thoughts crowded her mind about those who would not see it, but he knew that better than she, and it was maudlin to say so.

Was this a time to ask him about some of the things he had experienced, but never spoke of? When, if ever, would it be easier?

'Joseph . . .'

He looked up.

She plunged in. 'You never say much about Ypres, what it's like, how you feel, even the good things . . .'

His face tightened, almost imperceptibly, but she saw it. 'I'd like to understand,' she said quietly.

'One day,' he replied, looking away from her.

It was an evasion. She knew from his eyes and the line of his mouth that there would always be a reason why not. She turned quickly and went out of the door.

She walked along the village street in bright sunshine, but against a surprisingly cold wind. April was a deceitful month, full of brief glory, and promises it did not keep.

Inside the old Saxon church with its stained-glass windows and silent stones, the wooden pews were dark with age. Under each were hand-stitched hassocks to kneel on, donated by village women down the generations, some as long ago as the Napoleonic Wars. Hannah began to get out the vases and fill them with water from the outside tap and carry them back in one at a time.

Mrs Gee came into the vestry, red-eyed and shivering against the cold. She brought some blue irises, just a handful. Every time Hannah saw her she thought of Charlie Gee, who had died in Ypres last year. Mrs Gee did not know how horribly he had been maimed. Neither did Hannah, but she had seen the shadow of it in Joseph's face every time his name was mentioned. Anger and grief at this death still haunted him more than it did for others.

Hannah thanked Mrs Gee for the flowers and separated them to put a little of their rich colour in among the yellows. She needed to say something more than mere acknowledgement. 'I don't have anything blue,' she said with a smile.

'There'll be bluebells in the woods next month,' Mrs Gee reminded her. 'But they don't sit well in a vase. Oi s'pose woild flowers don't loike to be picked. Oi haven't been down to the woods in a while.' She did not say any more.

Hannah did not need to ask. The haze of blue over the ground, the sunlight and call of birds made the wood a place of over-powering emotion. She would not be able to go there in a time of grief herself. Odd how some kinds of beauty did not heal, but hollowed the pain even deeper.

'How's the chaplain?' Mrs Gee asked, concern in her voice.

'Much better, thank you.' That was more optimistic than the truth, but Mrs Gee needed every good word possible.

'Oi'm glad to hear it. Oi don't know what our boys would do without him. Tell him Oi was asking.'

'Yes, of course I will. Thank you.' Hannah felt a stab of fear again, as if she had deliberately excluded herself from the bond of knowledge other people shared.

Mrs Gee waited a moment longer, then turned and walked away between rows of seats, her footsteps heavy, her shoulders bowed a little.

Betty Townsend brought some yellow and red early wallflowers. It was a shame to put them in the cool church; in a warmer room in someone's home the perfume would have been far richer. Hannah thanked her for them, then noticed how pale she looked, as if she had not slept for many nights. She did not need to wonder what caused it. Everybody's problems were the same – bad news, or none at all when there should have been.

'How is your brother?' Betty asked, her voice a little husky.

Hannah held the wallflowers without beginning to arrange them. 'Getting better, thank you,' she answered. 'But it will be a while yet. He was lucky to keep his arm. Are you all right?'

Betty turned away quickly. 'Peter's been posted missing in action. We heard two days ago.' Her voice trembled. 'I don't know whether to keep up hope he's alive somewhere, or if that's just stupid, putting off the truth.'

Hannah wished with all her heart she knew of something to say that would help. She stood there holding the flowers in her hand as if they mattered. Her mother would have said the right thing! Why did loss hurt so unbearably? Standing here in this building where people had come in joy and grief for a thousand years, she should have had some sense of the promise of eternity, a resurrection when all this would not matter any more.

Betty gave a little shrug. 'Sorry. You don't know what to say, and whatever it was, it wouldn't make any difference. Thanks at least for not coming out with the usual platitudes.' She shrugged. 'The vicar came round, of course. He was trying to be kind, but I think he made it worse. Mother thanked him, but I just wanted to push him out of the house. He talked about glory and sacrifice as if Peter were somehow not real, a sort of idea rather than a person. I know he meant well, but all I wished to do was hit him. I wanted to shout, "Don't tell me about faith and virtue – this is real and it hurts. It hurts! It's Peter who taught me how to climb trees, and not to cry if I skinned my knee, and ate my rice pudding when I hated it, and told me silly jokes. It isn't just some hero! It's my brother – the only one I had!"'

Hannah jammed the flowers into the vase. Why was Hallam Kerr so useless? If religion wasn't any help now, what point was there in it? Was it really no more than a nice social habit, a reason for the village to meet and keep up the pretence that everything would be all right one day? Kerr was just as lost as the rest of them, perhaps even more so.

Was Joseph as empty and useless as that too? She did not think so, and not just because he was her brother. There was an inner strength to him; a place within him where his faith was real, and strong enough to bear up others. He was needed here at home. He should stay to help people like Betty, Mrs Gee, and God alone knew how many more before this was finished.

'All we can do is keep going, and help each other,' she said aloud. 'The vicar is just another cross to bear.'

Betty sniffed and gave a choking little laugh. 'He wouldn't like to be referred to like that,' she said, searching for a handkerchief to blow her nose.

'I know,' Hannah admitted. 'I'm sorry, I shouldn't have said it.'

By the time Betty went, Hannah was almost finished with the flowers she had, and thinking they needed a little greenery to fill them out. Then Lizzie Blaine came in with some catkin branches and budding willow. She was a dark-haired woman with a hot temper and bright blue eyes. Her husband was one of the scientists at the Establishment.

'Thank you.' Hannah accepted the additions with satisfaction: they gave bulk and variety to the yellow.

Lizzie smiled. 'I've always liked branches. They don't seem to know how to make an ugly shape.'

'You're right!' Hannah agreed with surprise. 'Even the knobbly bits look good.' She glanced at Lizzie again. There seemed to be a hidden excitement in her, as if she knew of something good that would happen, just beyond the sight of the rest of them. Would it be intrusive to ask what it was? 'You look well,' Hannah said pleasantly.

'I like Sundays,' Lizzie replied, then gave a little shrug. 'Theo doesn't usually work on Sunday, although he has once or twice lately. They're doing something critically important at the Establishment. He doesn't say anything, of course, but I know from the way he walks how alive he feels. It is as if his mind is racing on the brink of solving the final problems and finishing whatever it is. Please God, it will be something that will make a real difference to the war. Perhaps it will even be over soon. What do you think?' Her eyes were bright, her cheeks a little flushed. 'The men would come home. We could start to rebuild things again . . .' Her face tightened suddenly; perhaps she was remembering those who would not come back.

Hannah had no idea if Lizzie had other family far less safe than her scientist husband – perhaps brothers or friends. 'I can't think of anything better to pray for,' she said softly. 'And it would be right to pray for it, for everyone. We could all start again, making things instead of smashing them. And the Germans could too, of course.'

Lizzie nodded quickly, as if afraid to tempt fortune with words. Then she turned and walked away swiftly and almost soundlessly up the stone aisle and out of the door into the wind and sun.

Hannah finished the last of the vases and put them each in the right place for tomorrow, then went out as well. She almost bumped into Mrs Nunn coming up along the path through the graves.

'Hello, Mrs MacAllister,' the older woman said with a smile. 'Where's the chaplain?' She also spoke of Joseph by his occupation, because to her that was who he was. She had sons and nephews in the regiment at Ypres, and they wrote to her of Joseph often. 'Tell him Oi was asking after him, will you please?'

'Of course,' Hannah said quickly. 'He's recovering quite well, but it will be a few weeks before he can think about going back.'

A shadow crossed Mrs Nunn's face. 'But he will, won't he? Oi mean, he'll be all roight?' She was echoing Mrs Gee's words.

Hannah hesitated. She was overwhelmed by the power of her longing that he should stay. They needed Joseph's faith here to lean on if they were to survive. Kerr was useless. More loss, loneliness and pain lay ahead. Hannah thought of Betty Townsend and Mrs Nunn. They were only two of hundreds. 'I don't know,' she answered. 'He's thirty-seven, and he was pretty badly injured. They may not send him back.'

The colour and light vanished from Mrs Nunn's expression. 'Oh, Oi do hope that's not true. What will moi boys do without him?' She shook her head a little, her face crumpled. 'They don't tell us much, you know, but it's awful out there. Some o' them doi real hard. An' none of them come back loike they went. They need men loike your brother worse'n we need them. We're safe in our own beds, an' with food on the table in the morning, an' clean water to drink.' She looked very hard at Hannah, her faded eyes clear. 'Oi'd be out there for my boys, if Oi could, an' keep them safe here. What mother wouldn't? But at least Oi knowed Captain Reavley were there for them. He'd be with 'em in the worst, day or noight, winter or summer aloike.'

She smiled and her gaze was far away. 'He were hurt getting moi boy Tucky back out o' no-man's-land, you know? Saved his loife, the chaplain did.' She took a deep breath. 'God speed him back, Oi pray. Oi'm sorry, Mrs MacAllister, but the boys come first. They're foighting for England, and we got to do our part.' And sniffing fiercely she turned and picked her way back through the graves.

Hannah stood still on the path for a few moments longer. Then with her mind in increasing turmoil, she moved slowly towards the lich gate and out into the street.

She walked more rapidly. She had been sure, listening to Betty Townsend, that Joseph should stay here. He was needed to help their faith, grief, loneliness and fear of change.

Then listening to Mrs Nunn, seeing her tired, wounded face and the strength in her, the gratitude that Joseph was there with her boys, wanting him at home had become utterly selfish, the cry of a small, spoiled child.

But what about Joseph himself? Would his arm heal well enough for him to be able to go back? Perhaps it wouldn't. He might *have* to stay. That would be the best answer of all. He would be here, safe, able to help her, and the whole village, and honour be satisfied. Was that selfish? If it were her sons out there, she would want the best chaplain for them: the one who was strong enough to keep faith; brave enough to try to rescue the wounded, whatever the cost; the one who would not look away and leave them to die alone.

She opened the front door and went into the familiar hall. Mrs

Appleton was in the kitchen; the smell of baking drifted through the house. The dining-room door was open, the bunch of daffodils on the table reflected on its polished surface. She could smell the warm, heavy scent of them.

She found Joseph upstairs in his bed. His eyes were closed, but there was a book open upside down on his lap. It was one of those days when his arm was hurting more than usual; she could see the pain in the shadow on his face.

He must have heard her step, light as it was, because he opened his eyes.

'Hurts?' she asked with a half-smile.

'Not much,' he answered. 'Stop worrying. I'm perfectly all right – really.'

'It might not get strong enough for you to go back?' She lifted her voice at the end, as if it were a question. 'The vicar isn't much good. There'd be a lot for you to do here. Everything's changing, and we don't know what's right as easily as we used to.' She drew in her breath. 'The vicar hasn't the faintest idea what the men have been through, but you have.' Without meaning to, she was putting all the arguments at once. She could hear the urgency in her own voice, and knew she had said too much.

There was indecision in Joseph's face. He must feel the warmth around him, smell the clean cotton of the sheets, the flowers on the dresser, bright in the sunlight through the window. He must hear the sound of birdsong outside, and the wind in the branches, sweet off the fields.

'I'm sorry,' she said quietly. She was ashamed. His decision, whatever it was, would be hard enough. He was the one who would be cold, tired, hungry, perhaps injured in Flanders, not she. She was being unfair.

'I think Kerr will become better at it,' he said tiredly, 'with practice.'

'Yes, I expect he will,' she agreed, and went out again before she made another mistake, even if it were just to let him see her tears.

In the upper room in Marchmont Street the Peacemaker finished reading the letter on his desk and burned the pages one at a time.

It was a letter from his cousin in Berlin, one of the few men in the world he trusted absolutely. It was wiser to leave nothing to chance. German plans for the United States were crucial to success in the war. If America could be persuaded to join the Allies then the forces against Germany would be vastly increased. The American army was small as yet, but their resources were virtually inexhaustible. They had coal and steel enough to supply the world, and food, of course. In time it would tip the balance of the war fatally against Germany.

That was why America had to be kept occupied with the Mexican threat in its southern border, and possibly even with a Japanese base on the Pacific coast, just to the south in Baja California. Germany had brilliant men throughout the North American continent, agents who kept Berlin constantly in touch with every move of President Wilson and of Congress, and of public and private feeling in every state. With great skill and secrecy they moved money and guns into Mexico and judged the ambition and the violence in that turbulent country to an exactness.

The Santa Ysabel massacre was a piece of extraordinary good fortune, but with care it could be repeated on a scale large enough to keep America's attention focused entirely on its own affairs, but not so large as to precipitate a full-scale invasion of Mexico.

Detta Hannassey was becoming more and more useful. No doubt her principal aim was to free Ireland, but she was a far better tool in helping Germany to keep control of the sabotage in America than he had thought she would be. She was resourceful, clever without arrogance, and she had sufficient sense of humour never to betray herself by posturing or losing her temper. She was not as dangerous as her father, and therefore in many ways a better weapon to use.

He took the poker and crushed the ashes of Manfred's letter so there was nothing left.

The war at sea was the more urgent issue now. That could be won or lost on the invention being worked on in the Establishment in Cambridgeshire. He knew about its progress from the agent he had planted there over a year ago, a highly intelligent, eager man, as passionately against the war as he was himself. But he did not entirely trust him. Lately he had sensed a different mood in him, something more personal, a more particular emotion rather than the general horror against the destruction of war. It might be a weakness.

But it was thoughts of Russia, that other giant not yet fully awake, that crowded his mind now. Europe had never conquered it with armies. Napoleon had tried, and it had been for him the beginning of the end. Now, a century later, the war in Russia was a slow attrition eating away at the might of the German Empire, bleeding men and materials it would be far better to use towards the West, where victory could be complete and fruitful, the beginning of lasting peace and all that that meant.

What of the Tsar Nicholas II, and his Queen with her obsession with that unwashed lunatic Rasputin? And the only heir to the throne a haemophiliac boy who bled at the slightest bruise! The whole, vast sweeping country was riddled with centuries of oppression and corruption, injustices crying out for retribution, factions fighting one another, hunger and war slaughtering people by the thousands. The whole rotten structure was ready to collapse, and there were men who longed to bring it about, men of passion and dreams only awaiting the chance.

Whatever it took, however much latitude he had to give him, whatever flattery or yielding it required, he must get Richard Mason back. He had the passion, the courage and the intelligence, the supreme daring to pull together the pieces of the plan that was beginning to form in the Peacemaker's mind. As yet it was just a vague shape – huge areas were missing yet – but so supreme, so sublimely daring it would change the tide of history, carry it forward, not only to peace but to a justice undreamed of before.

He strode over to his desk, opened it, and sat down to write.

Chapter Five

Joseph picked up a fresh newspaper and read a long article by Richard Mason, the man regarded by many as the best of the war correspondents. He was writing from the Balkans. It was vivid, immediate and tragic in its evocation of courage and death. There was an anger in him at suffering that came through all the measured words.

Joseph remembered working beside him on the beach at Gallipoli. He thought of the cheerful Australian voices with their desperate jokes, their inventiveness, irreverence and good-humoured stoicism. He remembered the sinking ship afterwards, the cold, and facing Mason in the open boat as the wind rose, and the terrible decision he had made. For all the rage he had felt, oddly enough he had not personally disliked Mason, even then.

He knew that Hannah wanted him to stay at home after he was better, but he had refused to consider the possibility seriously until now. He thought about the men he knew who were still in the trenches – men from the village and from Cambridge itself. Some of them he had taught at St John's. In his dreams he was there also. He still woke with surprise to find himself in the quiet, familiar room of his childhood, birdsong against the background silence outside; no guns, no soldiers' voices.

Could he stay? There was certainly plenty for a man of the Church to do here: grief to comfort, confusion to try to ease, even anger and specific evil to fight against. He had been nearly two years at Ypres. No one would blame him if he said it was enough. He was thirty-seven, far older than the vast majority of the men. Even most of the officers below the rank of colonel were in their twenties, some even less.

He would never have to face the noise again, incessant, battering the mind until thought and sense were almost impossible. He need never see another rat, another mutilated body, or watch another young man die, and try to find meaning or hope in the closest one could see of hell.

Of course, that would not stop it being there! The suffering and the loss would be just the same, it would simply be that he did not have to share the physical reality. He could stay at home and only hear about it, imagine it, remember, and of course see the results in the faces of the women. And after it was over, he could help to rebuild again, whether they won or lost.

Was that what he wanted? With every nightmare, with every aching bone or stab of pain, yes! Yes, he longed to find a reason never ever to go back. He longed to stay here where he was safe and clean, where he could sleep at night, where he could see the slow, sweet spring blossom over the earth, watch the patient horses pull the plough, walk with his dog and see the birds circle in the sky at sunset and fly low to roost in the elms.

Could he do that with an easy heart, knowing his men in Flanders expected him back? No one wanted to return after leave. The only ones who imagined it in heroic colours were those like Hallam Kerr, who had never been there. Even most of them were a little wiser, a little more sober now.

The morning post had brought Joseph a letter from Isobel Hughes. He was surprised how much it had pleased him to see her handwriting on the envelope. He had torn it open eagerly.

She was concerned for his injuries in case they were more serious than he had said. They were. He had underplayed their enormity. But then he would have felt childish telling her the pain had been so consuming he had, at the beginning, even wished he could die to escape it. That sounded so cowardly now he was intensely grateful he had not said anything.

As always she told him of village life in Wales, the changing seasons, a little gossip about those she knew and cared for, making light of the hardships without denying them. Only this time there was something darker, a story she introduced quite casually, but her choice of words was different and even her handwriting had an urgency about it.

A young man here on leave from the Front has deserted. They say he has run away, but those are simple words. I don't think they tell anything like all the truth. I saw his face when he was in the village shop. He spoke to me quite pleasantly, but his eyes looked beyond me to some hell I could not see, though perhaps I had a glimpse of it for an instant.

I know there are a million men out there who are staying and facing everything there is, no matter what, and that many of them will not come back. Every reason in my mind tells me that if I knew where he was hiding in the hills, then I should tell the authorities so they can hunt him out. I imagine he will be court-martialled and then shot. I can see how that is necessary, or maybe thousands would desert, leaving only the bravest to face the enemy alone.

His father is so ashamed he won't go to chapel any more. His mother weeps, but for her son, I think, not for herself or for shame. Perhaps it is something in us because we are women, we admire the strong and the brave, but we protect the weak. Is that pity, or simply that we do not think far enough ahead to see the damage it does?

I have troubled myself about this quite a lot. I ask you because I hunger for the answer and I know no one wiser or more able to weigh the matter from the view of both the army and the kinder and greater judgement of God as well. Or at least as much of God as it is given us to know.

Joseph had thought about the letter, rereading it to make sure his first impression was right. She did not dare write it openly, but he was convinced she knew where the deserter was, and wanted his opinion as to whether she should betray him or not.

Then he realized with a jolt that by the very use of the word 'betray' he had allowed his sympathies to be as engaged as hers were. He knew the blind stare on young men's faces when they had seen too much for the mind to bear, when their ears never ceased to hear the roar of the guns, even in the silence of the fields or the chatter of a village street.

And yet if she knew and sheltered him, even by her failure to report it, she would be held accountable for aiding a deserter. At the very best she could be shunned by her own people; at worst she could be charged with a crime. His instinct was to protect her, urge her to take no risks.

But there were other risks – to the conscience, to the grief and the shame afterwards, to the belief in one's own compassion or morality. All her life she would remember whatever she did about it, and the life or death of this young man, and his family. One wanted to save everyone – and it was impossible.

He folded up the letter and put it away. He must answer it today. It would not wait. But he was not ready yet. If he was right and she wanted his judgement, then he too would never escape the consequence of it. He drifted off to sleep pondering the dilemma, the newspaper on the floor beside him.

Joseph was jerked awake by the sound of shouting in the hallway: excited voices, high-pitched, over and over again, 'Daddy! Daddy! Daddy!' and Henry barking.

He stood up stiffly, papers sliding to the floor, just as Archie came in through the door, Jenny on one side of him, Luke on the other, and Tom and Hannah behind him. Archie was smiling. He was still in uniform and there was something enormously impressive about the navy jacket with the gold braid. Tom's eyes were blazing with pride, Hannah's face shining, her eyes brimming with tears, and Jenny looked up at her father as if he were close to a god.

But the momentary joy did not hide the tiredness in Archie's face, and Joseph recognized it with aching familiarity. He had seen that battle-weariness countless times before, the slowness to refocus the eyes, the way the shoulders were tight as if movement were not quite co-ordinated. Archie's skin was wind-chapped and there was a razor-cut on his left cheek. His dark hair had a touch of early grey at the temples.

'Joseph!' He held out his hand. 'How are you?' His glance took in the heavily bandaged arm and the awkwardness of stance as he stood up. Archie understood injury.

'Good to see you, Archie,' Joseph replied, gripping his hand firmly. He met his eyes only for a moment, giving away nothing.

Tom carried his father's case upstairs. Luke stood around, longing to ask questions and not sure how to begin. Archie sat down and Jenny slipped on to his lap and leaned against him. Hannah went to get hot tea and cakes.

'How long do you have?' Joseph asked, hoping it was at least a week.

Archie shrugged very slightly. 'Three or four days,' he replied. 'We've lost a few men. Had one or two nasty scraps. Gun turret caught fire.' He did not add that there were no survivors. Joseph knew enough about such things not to need explanation and Archie did not want the children to hear. There was so much that was better unsaid, nor would he ask Joseph about whatever shellfire or explosion had caused his injuries. One did not relive it – there was no point, no explanation, nothing eased.

Tom came back into the room silently.

'I hear the Duke of Westminster's unit has reached Bir Hakkim and rescued the crews of the *Tara* and the *Moorina*,' Joseph observed, struggling to think of something hopeful.

Archie smiled. 'That's good. All I heard in London was the political news, and word about Verdun. We're taking bets as to whether Lloyd Geroge will be Prime Minister by autumn.' He stood up restlessly, sliding Jenny on to her feet, and began walking around the room, looking at the familiar ornaments, pictures, the way the afternoon light fell slanting through the windows on to the worn patches in the carpet.

Joseph knew what he was doing. He had done it also, making sure in the deeper parts of his mind that he was really home, that it all remained the same, whatever happened to the world away from here. Later, alone, Archie would probably touch those things, steeping his senses in their feel and their smell, to carry with him when he had to leave.

'Last bets I heard were on conscription by the middle of the year,' Joseph said quietly.

Archie was by the mantelpiece. He turned, glancing at the children, seeing their faces as they watched his every move and gesture. 'Which way is your money?' he asked.

'For it,' Joseph replied. 'About sixpence.' He made himself smile. He knew the news was bad and he was reading in Archie's eyes the things he would not say in front of anyone else. There was a tacit understanding that one never spoke of defeat, or even its possibility, in front of women or children.

'Sounds about right,' Archie agreed.

'I'm going to join up,' Tom announced. 'Navy, of course. Sorry, Uncle Joseph, I don't mean to be insulting. Of course the army's good too, but we're naval, aren't we, Dad?'

Archie's face tightened, but he knew better than to argue, especially in front of anyone else. 'Yes. But we're officers, not ratings, so you'll study properly first.'

'But, Dad—' Tom started.

Archie gave him a quick smile. 'And you'll obey the captain! You'll not discuss it over tea!'

Luke turned to see if Tom would obey.

'Yes, sir,' Tom said reluctantly.

It was a strange, unnatural evening. Everyone was overwrought emotionally, uncertain what to say. One moment they were silent, the next everyone speaking together.

'Dad, what's the worst battle you've ever seen?' Tom asked, his face tense, eyes unwavering.

'Was it terrible?' Luke added immediately.

Hannah drew in her breath, then changed her mind and said nothing. Her eyes also were on Archie, waiting.

Even before he spoke, Joseph knew Archie was going to evade anything like the truth, just as he would have done himself. So far he had used his injuries to deflect any such discussion.

Jenny sat next to her father, squashed up in the armchair. He had his arm around her with a gentleness that was intensely concentrated, as if in the softness of her hair and the angular grace of her young body, he touched the infinite value of life itself.

'We're patrolling most of the time,' he answered lightly. 'We meet the odd U-boat, but the main German fleet has stayed in port so far, you know.' He smiled. 'I think they're scared of us.'

Luke believed him. 'Are they?' he said with pleasure. 'Good, eh?'

Tom was more doubtful. 'But they sink a lot of our ships, Dad. We'd be winning if they didn't. There are a couple of boys at school whose fathers went down.'

Hannah looked quickly at Joseph, then at Archie. She needed truth, but she was afraid of it, afraid of the nightmares. She would be the one left at home to find the answers, the comfort, to make going on possible, schoolwork seem worth it, anything at all make sense.

'Not a lot of ships,' Archie replied, considering as he spoke. 'It just seems like a lot because we hear about it, and it hurts. But most of the Grand Fleet is still here. We can't persuade the Germans to come out of harbour and face us.'

'But the U-boats do,' Tom persisted.

'Oh, yes. They're pretty nasty, but we've got a few tricks of our own, and getting more all the time. And don't ask me what they are, because it's secret stuff, and I don't know all of it myself. Now tell me about school, I'm much more interested in that.'

Tom gave up and dutifully answered the questions, but the enthusiasm was gone from his eyes. Half an hour later Luke and Jenny went to bed and Joseph walked alone down towards the orchard.

He did not hear Tom's footsteps on the grass and was startled when he spoke.

'Sorry, Uncle Joseph,' Tom apologized, his voice laden with misery.

Joseph turned and saw him. His young, smooth face was solemn, his eyes shadowed in the dappled light through the trees.

'Why doesn't Dad talk to me about anything real?' he asked quietly. 'Is it because we are going to lose the war?'

Joseph had been half waiting for the question, but now that it had come it was more difficult to answer than he had expected.

'I don't know,' he said simply. 'I don't think so, but of course it's possible. We won't give up, ever, but we might be beaten.'

Tom looked startled. Joseph realized he should not have been so candid. Tom was only fourteen. Now he would have nightmares Hannah would not be able to comfort, and it was Joseph's fault. How could he undo it?

'I don't think we'll be beaten,' Tom said clearly. 'We won't let it happen. But Dad was just trying to protect us, wasn't he? A lot of people are being killed. I heard in school today that Billy Arnold's elder brother was killed. They heard yesterday. He was twenty. That's only six years older than I am. Did you know him, Uncle Joseph? Perhaps I shouldn't have told you like that? I'm sorry.'

Joseph smiled. 'People aren't going to stop being killed just because I'm here on sick leave. And I knew him, but not very well. I don't think we'll be beaten either, actually. I just don't want to tell you lies.'

Tom was silent for a while. They stood side by side, watching the light fade beyond the elms.

'Why won't Dad tell me that?' Tom said at last, his voice thick with hurt. 'Does he think I can't take it?'

'We all try to protect people we love,' Joseph answered. He watched as in the distance a shire horse walked gently over the slope of the rise, the light catching on its harness. It moved slowly, head low with weariness at the end of the day. 'We don't think about it, we just do it,' he added. 'It's natural.'

'You don't! Don't you love me?' Tom asked.

Deliberately Joseph did not look at him. He knew there would be tears on his face, and it was better they were private.

'Yes, I do, very much,' he answered. 'But not in quite the same way. I've seen boys not much older than you in the trenches, and I know you can take a lot. However bad it is, not knowing is sometimes worse. At least that's what I think. But your father may think differently.'

'I suppose so. It seems as if Jenny's the only one he's really pleased to see!' That last sounded raw with hurt. 'Is that because she's a girl?'

'Probably. And too young to go and drive ambulances, like your Aunt Judith.' The horse disappeared under the may blossom in the lane, and a flock of birds whirled up in the sky, startled.

'Is that pretty dangerous?' Tom asked.

'Not most of the time, but it's very hard work, and you see a lot of badly injured people.'

'I wouldn't like that.'

'No, but it's better to help them than stand around doing nothing much.'

'What do you do, Uncle Joseph? You can't pray all the time – people don't want that, do they? Anyway, it doesn't work, does it?'

Joseph turned to look at him. There was pain and disillusion in Tom's face, oddly naked in the warmth of the evening light. 'What would you like God to do?' he asked.

Tom drew in his breath. 'Make it stop, of course.'

'How?'

Tom blinked. 'Well . . . I don't know. Can't God do anything He wants to?'

'He could force us, I suppose. But if you are made to do something, is it any good?' Joseph asked. 'Is it worth anything, if you had no choice?'

'Well . . . well, we've got no choice about fighting! We have to, or get beaten – and killed.'

'I know. The only decision for us is whether we do it well or badly, whether we're brave and, even at the worst times, remember what we believe, and the kind of people we want to be.'

Tom bit his lip. 'Is that what you pray for?'

Joseph looked out over the fields again. There was no longer anybody there, just an emptiness of dark ploughed earth and fading sky.

'Mostly. But I don't spend a lot of time praying. Mostly I fetch and carry, dig the broken trenches along with everyone else, try to help the wounded, write letters, that sort of thing.'

'Is that what you got the Military Cross for?' There was sharp pride in Tom's voice now.

80

'That sort of thing.' The sunset breeze smelled of the earth and in the distance the elms were little more than shadows against the sky.

'I'm going into the navy as soon as I can,' Tom said as if challenging Joseph to argue.

'Yes. I expected you would,' Joseph agreed.

Tom let out a sigh of satisfaction and they stood together in silence, but now it was comfortable.

In the sitting room Hannah was glad to be alone with Archie. There was only one lamp on and the gathering darkness outside cast long shadows, leaving the glow like an island of warmth, picking out the familiar shapes of chairs, books, pictures on the wall.

Time was infinitely precious. She might never have a better chance than this to ask him about the things she needed to know.

She thought of Paul Compton, the friends who knew him, and the wife who did not. Where could she begin? She couldn't just ask baldly: what hurt, and what makes you laugh? What are your friends like? Are you frightened, and how do you face the horror? What do you tell yourself to make it bearable? What do you miss most about home, the little things? Why do you not talk to Tom, who is aching to be close to you? He loves and admires you so much. He needs to know – almost as much as I do!

'I wish you could tell us something about your ship,' she started. 'Tom is longing to know.'

'He already knows all about destroyers,' Archie answered, looking a little beyond her. 'He can tell you length, tonnage, size and number of guns, range, complement of men.'

'I don't mean that!' Hannah tried to keep the loneliness out of her voice, and the anger that he seemed to be wilfully misunderstanding her. 'That doesn't tell him what it feels like! Anybody can read the facts out of a book. He wants to know it from you. I do! What is your day like? What do you care about? What does it taste like? What's funny? What's horrible?'

He smiled, his face wrinkling in the old laughter lines she remembered. 'It tastes pretty much the same as at boarding school,' he replied wryly, passing it off as a joke, still keeping her from the pain. 'Bit staler, and it smells like salt, engine oil, old rooms with windows that have never been opened.'

She swallowed. She was touching reality at last, even if obliquely. 'And in battle?'

His face changed so subtly she could not have named the difference – something in the tautness of the skin across the planes of his cheek, the line of his lips. 'It smells of smoke, cordite, burned rubber and the sweat of fear,' he answered. 'I'm on leave, Hannah. I don't want to spend it talking about war. I want to be at home. Tell me what you're doing. Tell me about the children.'

The door to his inner self was closed and locked. She knew from the set of his face and the way his eyes avoided hers that he would not allow her into that part of him where fear or pain were real, or any of his passionate and vulnerable self. They were alone together in the familiar room with the light fading outside, the last birds circling in the sky, everything exactly as it had always been. They could talk of their children, and nothing could be dearer or of more meaning, yet it would be only the often-used words, so predictable as to add nothing. The gulf between them was infinite. She could have said the same things to a stranger.

When Joseph came back in from the garden Tom went to bed, and a short while afterwards Hannah followed, weary but wide awake, ridiculously close to tears. But she must not weep, or when would she stop, and how could she explain it to anyone?

Joseph sat across the room from Archie and saw his tired, closed-in face. Archie was in command of a destroyer in the most desperate and crushing war England had known. There were no great victories like Nelson's a century ago, just the slow erosion of sudden attack, and loss. It was his job never to show fear or doubt, regardless of what he felt, or the greater weight of what he knew. He protected his men from the demons of the mind as well as the violence of the seas. Hannah would not understand that any more than she could understand the blood-soaked trenches of Flanders. Why should she? Her own responsibilities were enough.

*   *   *

82

The next day was quiet. Archie took Henry for a walk in the early evening. Joseph could understand if the sheer silence of the countryside offered him a kind of healing that nothing else could, and perhaps he needed a time of solitude away from the questions and the unceasing hunger for his company. The dog's was a happy and undemanding friendship.

Joseph knew that he could no longer put off writing to Isobel. He went into his father's study to do it. He had never taken it as his own, and was grateful that Archie had not even placed anything of his there either.

He opened the door and went in. It was clean – there was no dust on the polished surfaces – but it had a forsaken feel that was surely more than just his knowledge that John Reavley would never come back to it again. The Bonnington seascape still hung where it always had, its grey-green water almost luminous, its lines small and delicate.

Joseph stood for only a moment before sitting down at the desk, then pulling out paper and opening the inkwell. He could not even know if his advice was right or not, but he must have the courage to give it. Indecision was a choice as well. Better to be in error than to take the coward's way of silence.

Dear Isobel,
    Thank you for your letter. I was delighted to hear from you. I am recovering rather more slowly than I wish, and so I expect to be here for several more weeks.

He would not yet tell her that he was considering not returning at all; somehow it was not a thought he wished her to know of. Of course, if he followed it through then he would have to tell her, but that lay in the future. He had considered describing the slow, sweet fragrance of the spring, longing to share it with her, but it seemed a luxury out of place with the urgency of her question.

I am sorry to learn of the young soldier you write about. I have seen that look on men's faces. We call it 'the thousand-yard stare'. It happens to men who have seen more terrible things than the mind can bear. Some of them are very young. I wish I knew of a way to reach the agony and ease it, touch with healing what is broken inside, but I have not found it. All I know for certain is that I cannot bring myself to blame anyone that is so terribly wounded, and through no fault of their own. I would be no man's judge in what I can barely understand, even though I have heard the incessant, beating noise myself, and seen the mud and the death. Who knows what hell another man walks through?

But others may think very differently. Their own losses, or their anger, fear and ignorance may make them wish for a violent resolution that they feel represents justice. In any decision you make, please never forget this, and take the greatest care.

Then he went on to speak of his own village, the garden, the orchard and the fields. He hoped he had made his advice plain enough that she would understand. He dared not be clearer. There was always the possibility the letter would be censored, and greater clarity would in itself prevent her from doing anything but turning in the young soldier.

He could not even tell her that he had an indecision in his mind. He sat alone in the study and stared at the small, exquisite painting of the sea, and prayed, please God, his advice was good.

The following morning Joseph was barely dressed when Hannah knocked hard and peremptorily on his bedroom door, calling his name.

'Come in,' he said, alarm too swift for irritation. 'What is it?'

She stood in the doorway, her face pale. 'The vicar is here to see you,' she said breathlessly. 'He looks absolutely terrible, and he says it can't wait. He won't even sit down. I'm sorry, but you'd better come. He looks beside himself, but he won't tell me anything at all. Joseph, do you think the Germans have landed?'

'No, of course not,' he answered suddenly, moving towards the door. 'The vicar wouldn't be the only one to know. Where's Archie?'

She swallowed. 'He's still asleep. Should I waken him?'

'No! No. I'll go and see what Kerr wants.' He was annoyed at the disturbance. 'It might be nothing much. He panics rather easily. But just in case it's someone in the village lost a son, or brother and can't cope, you'd better keep the children busy. We don't need them frightened.'

'If it is, you'd better tell me who . . . in case I can help.' Her face was even whiter, her voice husky.

'I will.' He moved to go past her on to the landing.

'Here.' She reached out to retie his sling where it was roughly done. 'It needs to be taut or it won't support your arm.'

He stood obediently while she redid it, then went down to the sitting room. He realized how good it had been not to have to face death, maiming, grief, not to be the one who had to be first there and try to deal with the pain of it and make sense to the people left.

Hallam Kerr was standing in the middle of the room, his body rigid, his hair wet and sticking up in spikes. His face was so pale as to be almost grey. Joseph was used to the signs of shock, but it still caught him by surprise.

Kerr took a swaying step towards him. 'Thank God you're here!' he gasped. 'Something terrible has happened! Ghastly!' His breath caught in his throat, his chest heaving. 'I simply don't know where to begin . . .'

'You had better sit down and tell me,' Joseph said firmly. He closed the door. 'What has happened?'

Kerr stood rigidly, flapping his hands as if trying to grasp something that eluded him. 'There's been a murder, right here in the village!' His voice was high-pitched and unnatural. 'Theo Blaine from the Establishment! Found dead in his own garden. He was a scientist! One of their best, I believe. Who would do such a thing? What's happening to us?'

Joseph was appalled. He had thought nothing violent could shock him any more, but this did. A scientist! One of Shanley Corcoran's men. Fear chilled him to the pit of his stomach. Did the Germans know about the invention? Was this their way of stopping Britain from winning, even from surviving? No. He was being hysterical. There could be any number of reasons.

He sat down slowly. Kerr could remain standing if he wanted to. 'How did it happen?' he asked. 'Who is responsible?'

Kerr flopped into the chair opposite him, clasping and unclasping his hands. 'No one knows,' he said wretchedly. 'The police have been sent for, of course. I mean someone from Cambridge. There'll have to be an investigation. It's going to turn the whole village upside down. There'll be scandal. As if we hadn't enough to . . .' He covered his face with his hands. 'What can I say to his wife? I can hardly go in with condolences as if she had lost him in France. This is hideous . . . personal hatred so terrible . . .' He looked up, his skin blotched from the pressure of his fingers. 'What do I say?' he pleaded. 'How do I explain this, and tell her there is some kind of God who is in control and can make sense out of it all? What can I do to comfort her?'

'You won't know until you see her,' Joseph answered. 'There's no formula.'

'I can't do it! I don't know the words . . .' the vicar gestured helplessly. 'If he'd died in the army, or the navy, I could say he made a great sacrifice and God would . . . I don't know . . . watch over him, take him home . . .' he floundered to a stop.

Joseph wanted to argue the futility of saying such things however anyone had died, but Kerr was not listening to him. He was not ready or able to be of any help to Mrs Blaine. He had not come for advice. He wanted Joseph to do the job for him, and for Mrs Blaine's sake, as well as for Kerr's, he must.

'You'll have to drive me,' he answered, and saw the flood of relief in Kerr's face, and then apprehension. 'I haven't got a car, and I couldn't drive it with one hand if I had,' Joseph pointed out.

'Oh! Yes, yes, of course.' Kerr stood up. 'Thank you. Thank you. Will you . . . er . . . come now?'

'I must tell my family, then I'll come.' Joseph stood also, finding himself oddly stiff and a little dizzy. 'I shall be back in a moment.' He left Kerr in the sitting room and went through to look for Hannah.

She was in the kitchen. She turned to face him as soon as she heard his footsteps, even before he was through the door. She had a dish mop in one hand, dripping unnoticed on to the floor. 'What is it?' she asked. 'What's happened?'

'One of the scientists at the Establishment has been murdered,' he answered gently. There was no point in trying to protect her. The whole village would know in an hour or two. 'Kerr wants me to go with him to see the widow.'

'You don't have to.' She put the mop down and took a step towards him. 'You're still sick.'

'Yes, I do have to, for Mrs Blaine's sake.'

She drew in her breath to argue, then let it out again, the struggle over before it began. 'Can I help?'

'Maybe later.' He turned to leave.

'Joseph?'

'Yes?'

'Is that going to stop Shanley from completing the invention?' She was frightened and it was naked in her face.

He knew that fear, tight gripping in the stomach, shivering cold. It was of something far bigger than one life or death, however terrible. It could be the loss they all dreaded, the beginning of the final defeat.

'I don't know.' He tried to sound calm, braver than he felt. 'This man might not even have been working on it.'

'Shanley's going to be so distressed – either way. Don't forget him, will you?' she warned.

'No, of course not.' He hesitated a moment more, touched her briefly with his good hand, then went out into the hall.

He sat silently beside Kerr as they drove along the main street of St Giles. It was the first time Joseph had seen it since his last leave in October. In the ambulance from Cambridge he had been lying down, and in too much pain to think of peering out. Now he looked at the familiar buildings whose shape he could have drawn in his dreams with the name of every shop, and who owned them, the post office, the school, the village pond, and of course the lich gate to the church and the graveyard beyond. John and Alys Reavley were there . . .

Once again Joseph was dealing with murder, the shock and the grief of it, and the anger that would certainly follow. And he thought of Mrs Prentice. He had loathed her son. He could have imagined killing him himself, especially the night of Charlie Gee's injury. That still sickened him. He understood Sam. God! – how he understood Sam! And missed him still.

At least he did not know the poor woman he was going to see now, and whoever had killed her husband would also be someone he did not know. This time he would be a bystander, and perhaps he could be of some help. He might eventually even help Kerr! He needed it as much as anyone.

Kerr drew up abruptly alongside a hedge white with early black-thorn blossom. 'The house is just the other side of that,' he said, nodding towards it. 'I'll wait here. I don't want to seem to be watching. It would make the poor woman feel even worse.'

Coward, Joseph thought, but he said nothing. He opened the car door with his good hand and stepped out. The air was cool and sweet, and the earth slightly damp as he walked to the gate and then up the path. He loathed doing this, and was prepared to be told pretty briskly to go away.

He knocked on the door, and waited long enough to believe it would not be answered. He stepped back and was about to turn away, both disappointed and relieved, when it pulled open slowly and he saw a slender, dark-haired woman with a face bleached by shock.

'Mrs Blaine?' He did not wait for her answer. It could be no one else. 'I am Mrs MacAllister's brother, Joseph Reavley. I'm a chaplain in the army, home on sick leave.' His bandaged arm in the sling was obvious. 'If I can be of any help or comfort to you, please call on me.'

She stared, then looked past him as if to make certain he was alone.

He waited without moving.

'I don't know what anyone can do,' she said helplessly. 'It's . . .' She made a small gesture of complete loss.

He smiled very slightly. 'Well, I'm not a lot of practical use at the moment,' he admitted. 'I couldn't even make you a decent cup of tea. But if the paper is held down for me, I can write letters, or get in touch with solicitors or banks, or anyone else you need to notify. Sometimes doing that sort of thing is terribly hard because you have to keep on repeating the same things, and it doesn't get any easier. It's like hammering home the reality of it.'

Her blue eyes widened very slightly. 'Yes . . . it . . . it will be. I hadn't thought . . .' She gave a little shake of her head. 'I suppose you do this all the time.'

'No. I just write letters to tell people that someone they loved is missing or lost,' he answered. 'Sometimes it's just that they are wounded and can't write themselves.'

'You sound as if you know . . .'

'I lost my own wife.' He did not want to add anything more. It was over three years ago now, and the whole world had changed in that time, but it still hurt.

'I'll make the tea.' She pulled the door wider. 'Please come in. I suppose I need advice, and I'd rather not do this alone.'

He followed her through to the kitchen. It was an ordinary house, tidy but obviously lived in. There were coats hanging in the hall, a basket of clean laundry on the bottom of the stairs ready to be carried up. An open book lay on the hall table and letters waiting to be posted. There were two umbrellas in the stand next to outdoor shoes, and a pair of binoculars.

The kitchen was immaculate. She must have found the body before starting to make breakfast. What had she done since then? Perhaps nothing, just moved from one place to another aimlessly, suddenly without purpose, too stunned to care about anything.

Now she had something to do, tea to make for a visitor. Her hands were shaking slightly, but she managed, and Joseph allowed her to do it without interfering. She offered him biscuits and he accepted. All the time he talked, just trivia, letting the conversation wander wherever she wished it to, half-sentences, irrelevances.

'We came here because of Theo's work at the Establishment,' she said as she sat down at the wooden kitchen table opposite him. 'He's brilliant. Mr Corcoran isn't going to know how to replace him. Of course he won't be able to; Theo was unique.

He seemed to be able to get ideas out of the air, to think sideways.' She looked at Joseph questioningly to see if he understood what she meant. It seemed to matter to her that he believed her. Small pieces of sense seem to, absurdly, at such times. He knew that.

He nodded. In a while he would ask her about letters, people to tell, anything that needed cancelling. The practical things could be very hard to do alone. Even sorting through a dead person's clothes was desperately painful. The very familiarity of it was overwhelming, the smell, the remembered touch of someone you loved. With only one useful arm he would be little physical help, but he would at least be there.

They were discussing such things, when to do it, which charity to give them to, when they were interrupted by another knock at the front door. Lizzie Blaine answered it and returned to the kitchen, followed by a very ordinary-looking man of barely average height. He was wearing a suit of indeterminate brownish-grey and brown leather shoes scuffed at the toes. His hair was sprinkled with grey and definitely receding. When he spoke one could see that his teeth were crooked, and two were missing.

''Morning, Captain Reavley,' he said with slight surprise. 'Home on sick leave, are you? Hope it's not too bad. That your driver outside, reading his Bible?'

A tide of memory washed over Joseph. It was as if for a moment he were back in Cambridge before the war, and it was Sebastian who was dead, not some brilliant young scientist full of promise whom he had never met, never taught or cared about, or whose work he had loved and believed in so fiercely. All the ugliness of suspicions came back to him, the angers, the jealousies uncovered, the hate where he thought there had been friendship, the shabby deeds that life could have left covered, and death had exposed.

'Good morning, Inspector Perth,' he replied, his voice suddenly scratchy. 'It's the vicar. Yes, I suppose you could say he is my driver. How are you?' He had found Perth intrusive then, worrying at injuries and hidden pain like an animal with an old bone. He had returned to the vulnerabilities again and again, but in the end he had not been without compassion. Now he looked tired and anxious. Probably the police were short-handed; all the fit young men had gone to France. 'I expect you are here to see Mrs Blaine,' he concluded. 'Am I in the way?'

'Please stay!' Lizzie Blaine said quickly. 'I . . . I'd like you to, if you don't mind?' She looked frightened and on the edge of losing the fragile control she had managed to cling to so far.

Joseph did not move. He met Perth's eyes.

'If you don't interrupt, Captain,' Perth warned. He nodded his head fractionally. There was a respect in his eyes as if Joseph were in uniform. He was a man from the trenches, the front line of battle, and in a country at war that meant he was a hero. He could ask for and receive almost anything. It was an artificial role, and he disliked it. The heroes were the men who went willingly to the Front, to live and all too often to die on the line, the ones who went over the top into no-man's-land and faced the bullets, the shells and the gas. A lot of the time they did it with a joke, and so often when they were injured appallingly, if asked if it hurt, would say, 'Yes, sir, but not too much.' By the next day they might be dead. Many of them were not yet twenty.

He forced his attention back to the present and the white-faced woman of perhaps twenty-five or so, looking at Perth and trying to find the words to tell him what had happened.

'When did you last see your husband, Mrs Blaine?' Perth said calmly, waiting until she sat down in one of the kitchen chairs, then doing the same.

'We quarrelled last night,' she admitted, her face flushed with shame. 'About half-past nine. He went out into the garden. I went up to bed about half an hour after that. I . . . I didn't see him again.'

'What did you quarrel about?' Perth asked, no expression in his voice or his tired, ordinary face.

'Nothing, really,' she said miserably. It was a lie – Joseph knew it as he watched her – but not a guilty one. Perhaps it was defensive – to hide the foolishness of a man already dead. 'It was stupid, just tiredness and short temper,' she went on. 'He'd been working very hard at the Establishment. He didn't often get home before eight or even nine in the evening.'

91

Perth's expression was unreadable. Had he seen the lie as well?

Joseph did not believe Lizzie Blaine this time either. There was a change in the way she sat, not a movement but a lack of it, as if she were rigid inside, guarding herself. The quarrel had been specific, and she did not want to admit it. Did she know who had killed her husband?

Perth looked at her curiously. 'Were you angry that he worked late so often, Mrs Blaine?'

She hesitated. 'No, of course not.' She met his eyes. 'It's for the war. It's something we all have to do. It would be worse if he were in the army, or the navy, wouldn't it?' Suddenly her eyes filled with tears. 'At least it might have been,' she corrected herself.

Perth glanced at Joseph, then he nodded again. 'I'm afraid, Mrs Blaine, that terrible as it is out there, we've got our own troubles at home too. Crime doesn't stop just 'cos of the war. Wish it did. You went to bed, you say? Did you hear Mr Blaine come back inside?'

'No.' She swallowed.

'That didn't worry you?' There was scepticism in his face.

She looked at him defiantly now. 'No. He used to stay up sometimes, thinking. He was a scientist, Inspector, not an office clerk. He was always thinking.'

Perth's face tightened. Not many people worked office hours these days, certainly not police, but he did not say so aloud. 'And you didn't wake up in the night and wonder where he was?'

'No,' she answered. She was sitting stiff-backed on the wooden chair, her shoulders rigid, her knuckles white on the table top. 'I slept right through. I'd worked pretty hard during the day too, and I was exhausted.'

Perth's eyes flickered around the tidy kitchen. Had he noticed that there was nothing belonging to children downstairs, and no mention of them? 'Working?' he asked.

'With the VADs,' she answered. 'We had a garden party where everybody brought a blanket. We got nearly three hundred, but it took a long time afterwards to fold and pack them.'

'I see. So you would have been late home also?'

'Half-past six. I wanted to cook dinner for him.'

Perth's voice dropped a little and became gentler. 'And this morning, Mrs Blaine?'

Her lips quivered and she swallowed as if there were an obstruction in her throat. 'When I woke up and saw he still wasn't there I knew something was wrong. We . . . we have a shed at the bottom of the garden, where the walk is, at the end under the trees.' She shivered although it was warm in the room from the black lead stove still alight from the night before. 'I thought he might have been so angry that he had slept down there,' she went on. 'I know that's ridiculous – it's far too cold for that – but I went down anyway, after I knew he wasn't in the house. I . . .' she dragged her hand over her face, pushing her dark hair back, 'I found him lying on the earth just by the path, and the . . .' She stopped. Every trace of colour left her face. Joseph could only imagine the horror in her mind. He realized he did not know how Blaine had died.

'I see. And what time was that?' Perth asked.

'What?' She looked lost, as if the meaning of what he said had evaded her.

'What time was that?' he repeated. He was uncomfortable, aware of the clinical coldness of the question.

'I've no idea.' She blinked. 'It was light so it must have been after six o'clock. I don't know. It seems like ages ago, but maybe it wasn't. I came back up to the house. We have a telephone for Theo's work. I called the police.'

'Yes. The constable said so.' He went on asking her questions, quiet and persistent, about her husband's habits, his friends, anyone who disliked him, anything else she could think of.

Joseph listened as a picture emerged of a quiet, somewhat impatient young man with a dry sense of humour, a love of the late chamber music of Beethoven, and a rather impractical desire to have a dog, preferably a large one.

In spite of every effort not to, Joseph felt a wave of grief for him. Considering the number of men who were dying in war, it was foolish, irrelevant, and made him less able to think clearly and be of help, but he had no power over it. He looked at Lizzie Blaine, and perhaps she saw something of his emotion in his face, because for an instant there was gratitude naked in hers.

'Thank you, Mrs Blaine,' Perth said at last. 'I'll go down and look at this shed now.' It was odd to hear him being so delicately oblique. It was ridiculous, but Joseph liked him better for it.

Perth stood up. 'You stay here, ma'am. Captain Reavley can take me down.'

'He doesn't know . . .' she started, then realized it did not matter. They could hardly get lost in the small, slightly overgrown back garden.

They went out of the back door and walked down the lawn bordered on either side by walls with espaliered trees and low shrubs in front, some of them chosen for flowers, others for leaves. Beyond the garden was a wood stretching perhaps half a mile to the right, and rather less to the left. There was a gate in the fence behind the potting shed, so apparently there was a path on the other side. A uniformed constable stood by the wall, his face pale. He recognized Perth with a slight stiffening to attention.

The body of Theo Blaine had been moved an hour or so before, and the place where he had been was marked out very carefully with little sticks in the wet earth, and tape tied to them. Perth regarded the scene with tight lips, shaking his head.

'Garden fork right through the neck,' he said, his voice quiet and sad. 'Savage. Never seen anything like it, to be honest.' He glanced sideways and away again. 'That's it over there, propped up against the wall.'

Joseph looked at it. It was a perfectly ordinary piece of garden equipment such as he had himself – grey steel with a wooden shaft and green handle at the top, now heavily smeared with mud. Three of the prongs were stained with blood. There was something obscenely brutal about such a domestic tool used to tear a man's flesh and veins apart until the red, arterial blood gushed out on to the ground.

'How . . .' his mouth was dry, 'how could you swing that to . . . ?'

Perth went over and picked it up, his mouth twisted in distaste. 'No fingerprints as we could use on it,' he said. 'Not with all this mud. S'pose that's why they did it.' He picked it up with one hand at the top, the other where the shaft met the metal tongues of the tines to hold them on. He swung it round as if to hit Joseph on the side of the head. 'Damn!' he swore. 'Sorry,' he apologized instantly. Repositioning his grip, he then stabbed it into the ground. 'When his man fell down he must have pierced him something like that.' He replaced the fork where it had been and wiped most of the mud off his hand with his handkerchief, then examined it ruefully.

'Hurt yourself?' Joseph asked.

Perth grunted. 'Just a scratch. Must be a screw high on it with a rough edge. But useful, that. If I cut myself, then he might have too. Or she, I suppose. More likely a man, though. Man's sort of thing to do.' He looked at the gate. 'What's the other side of there, Constable?'

'Lane, sir,' the constable replied. 'Goes along past the houses, all the way to the river, then up to the main road. Down to the road to Madingley the other way.'

'So whoever it was probably came along it one way or the other?'

'Yes, sir, 'less they came through the garden, or from one o' them other houses.'

'Did you look along the path? Ask anyone?'

'Yes, sir. Nobody saw anyone, but then if it were after dark, they likely wouldn't. But there was tracks here an' there in the earth, like a bicycle'd bin down very recent. Somebody of a fair weight, to judge by the depth o' the marks.'

'Good work.'

'Thank you, sir.' The constable straightened his shoulders.

'No one seen a bicycle, by any chance?'

'Not yet, sir, but we're still looking. There moight have bin someone out walking late, courtin' couple, or someone with a dog. Never know.'

'Good. Don't stop.' Perth turned back to Joseph, his voice lowered, his eyes anxious. 'I understand this Mr Blaine was one of the top scientists at the Establishment. This isn't good, Captain Reavley.'

'You think it had to do with his work?' Joseph asked. Corcoran would miss Blaine appallingly if he was really one of his best men.

Would it actually affect the invention he had spoken of, and the time in which it could be completed?

Perth chewed his lip. 'Don't know about that, sir. Could be German spies, an' no doubt that's what some folks'll think. But seems a bit odd to me. Why the garden fork, eh? Looks more like a crime of opportunity, don't you think?'

'You mean a German spy would be better organized?' Joseph asked. The morning air smelled of damp leaf mould and it was muddy underfoot, but there was nothing left to mark what had happened except the dark patch of blood already soaking into the earth. Joseph looked at it, and thought he must arrange for some-body to come and perhaps lay a stonework path over it. It shouldn't be left like this. There were plenty of men in the village who would do that, as a kindness, a mark of decency. Albie Nunn, Tucky's father, or Bert Arnold. They were good with their hands. 'Perhaps he *was* better organized,' he said aloud. 'But he saw the fork, and used it precisely so we would think it was impulse, a passion of some sort.'

Perth looked sideways at him. 'You're getting clever at this, Captain Reavley. If that arm of yours don't get really right, mebbe we could use you in the police force?'

Joseph had no idea if Perth was being sarcastic or not, and he could think of no sensible reply. He was painfully conscious that a young man had died here, suddenly and violently, and that someone, for whatever reason, had committed a crime that would surely mark them for ever too.

They walked slowly back up to the house. Perth spoke briefly to Lizzie Blaine, then took his leave. Joseph stayed another half-hour to help her with some of the most immediate arrangements, simple things like informing the bank, her solicitor, putting her own notice of bereavement in the newspapers, separate from the Establishment's. Then he too left, but promising to return, and giving her his telephone number if she needed him for anything.

Hallam Kerr had waited patiently in the lane, reading his Bible, as Perth had observed. He looked up, startled and unhappy, when Joseph reappeared, but he asked no questions, as if the entire visit fell within the realm of confidentiality, and in truth, Joseph had no wish to confide in him. They drove back in silence.

Hannah was waiting in the hall. She must have been listening for the car.

'Are you all right?' she said urgently as Joseph came in. 'You look terrible. I'll get you a cup of tea and something to eat. How about a boiled egg and some toast? Unless you're too tired?'

He smiled in spite of the grief inside him. 'I'm fine,' he assured her. 'I did what I could to help Mrs Blaine. There's not a great deal, other than assist with a few practical things, and be there to sit beside her while she goes through the ordeal of telling people. I'm afraid it's going to be very ugly. Because of his work, it is possible Theo Blaine was killed by a German spy.'

Hannah frowned. 'Isn't that better than by somebody in the village, which would mean one of us, and that would be awful?'

'My dear,' he said gently, 'he died in his own garden. Whoever killed him has to be one of us. It is only their reason for doing it that is in question.'

'We don't have any . . .' She stopped. Her voice dropped to a harsh whisper. 'I suppose we wouldn't know, would we? I can't believe anyone here would betray us. But then I can't believe anyone here would murder him for any other reason either.'

'Three years ago I would have believed you,' Joseph replied. 'But I am afraid we are not so naïve any more.'

She avoided meeting his eyes. 'Archie's going on the night train to Portsmouth. Nancy Arnold will drive him to Cambridge.'

'Nancy Arnold?' he said in surprise.

'She runs the taxi service now. I can't make up my mind whether to go with him or not.'

'I wouldn't,' he said immediately. 'Railway station goodbyes are always pretty rotten. Let him think of you here at home.'

'Did he say that?'

'No.' Archie had not spoken to Joseph of anything so intimate. They had discussed the news, and more seriously the possibility that England could lose the war, and what that would mean, how their lives would change. They might both be killed, in fact Archie almost certainly would be. For Joseph it would depend more upon whether he was in Flanders at the time, or was home, but well enough to carry on the fight in whatever resistance was left. The same would surely be true for Matthew. To imagine him surrendering was impossible. But what would happen to the women and children?

There was no answer, and they left it only as a dark shadow it was better to share than face alone.

'No, he didn't say so,' Joseph expanded. 'It's just how I would feel.'

'But you're not ready to go back!' Hannah said urgently. 'And we need you here. Kerr went to pieces today. What good is he when someone loses a son or a husband in France, or just as bad, has come home armless, or legless, or blind? Who else will help them get over it? Who even knows what to say to them, except you?'

It was true. And either the war would be over soon, if Shanley Corcoran was right and the project could still be completed. Or it would drag on in senseless slaughter until every home in the land had lost someone and women everywhere worked in quiet, numb grief, trying to find meaning where they had only loss.

Who would be there for Hannah if Archie died? Who would help her not only with her own loneliness but for Tom and Luke and Jenny? How many women all over Europe were going to have to manage alone, all the rest of their lives?

But Hannah was his sister, they weren't. Any one person could do only so much.

'No need to think of it now,' he said aloud. 'It'll be ages before I'm well enough, anyway. Yes, I'll have a boiled egg, in fact two.'

She clung on to him for a moment, fiercely, kissing his cheek, then let go and went straight-backed into the kitchen, her skirt twitching a little as she walked. She had always had that little sway, a part of her character that surprised. One might have expected it of Judith, but not of Hannah.

Kerr turned up again the next morning. Hannah seemed pleased to see him and regarded Joseph's exasperation with patience.

'He needs you,' she said simply. 'The poor man is totally out of his depth. I'm going to the shops to get more wool, and then to the VAD centre for supplies to sew ditty bags. I'll be back at lunchtime.'

Kerr was in the sitting room as before, standing in the middle of the floor and looking just as white-faced as he had the previous day.

Joseph's heart sank. 'What is it now?' he said, somewhat less than graciously. He was afraid Kerr was going to ask him to conduct the funeral, and he should not do it. It should be the incumbent of St Giles.

'I have a moral dilemma,' Kerr replied. 'I have never been in this position before!'

'Life is full of positions we have never been in before,' Joseph pointed out a little tartly. Kerr's failure was tempting him more than he wished. He could feel the yielding to impatience in himself.

Kerr's hands were clenching and unclenching again. He would not be put off. 'This policeman seems to think it was someone in the village who killed poor Blaine,' he said abruptly. 'He's like a ferret with his teeth in your leg – he won't let go until he has someone in prison.'

Joseph smiled bleakly. 'I think your acquaintance with ferrets must be better than mine.'

Kerr brushed it aside. 'A figure of speech. He is going to hound us all until he knows everything about everybody. It will do untold harm.'

'Murders do,' Joseph assured him bitterly, every vestige of humour gone. He remembered acutely what it had done to St John's and the students there, and what it had done in the trenches, even though no one was sorry to see Prentice dead, and they were drenched with death every day. They were nearly all of them under twenty-five, and they had hopes and dreams and passions like anyone else, and their life expectancy could be counted in weeks. 'I'm sorry,' he moderated his tone a little. 'It's a wretched thing, but there is no dilemma because there's nothing we can do about it.'

'But I know people's secrets!' Kerr protested, his voice rising.

'It is part of my calling. You know that! What am I supposed to tell this awful man?'

'It's perfectly simple,' Joseph replied. 'You tell him nothing.'

'And if what I know allows a murderer to go free? Or worse than that, an innocent man to be hanged?' Kerr's face twisted in misery. 'It isn't as simple as you are saying. This crime may be linked with the war. Perhaps poor Blaine was killed because of his work at the Establishment, and whoever is guilty is a German spy. Have you thought of that? Doesn't that alter my duty? I may not be in the army, but I am as loyal to my country as you are.'

Joseph saw the wretchedness in the man's face, the confusion and the longing to be accepted.

'I'm sorry,' he apologized. 'Of course you are. And it is a dilemma. If you observe anything for yourself that has bearing on the crime, or could have, then you should tell Inspector Perth. But if it is only something that you have been told by someone else, then you do not know if it is true or not. You can't judge. Let Perth find it out for himself, or not.'

Disbelief filled Kerr's face. 'You make it sound so simple.' It was almost an accusation, as if Joseph were still attempting to evade the issue.

Joseph looked away. 'Judgement is anything but simple.' He thought of Prentice, and Corliss, and Charlie Gee, and General Cullingford, and above all of Sam. Judgement was impossible. You stumbled from hour to hour, trying to understand, trying to get it right, hardly ever sure whether you had or not. It all mattered far too much: love and hate, loyalties torn in too many directions, uncertainty, guilt, decisions that had to be made too quickly and without a chance to think and weigh.

Could there really be a spy, or enemy sympathizer here in St Giles, this quiet village in the heart of everything that was English to the root and bone? Or was it simply the ordinary rage and jealousy, the greed or rejection that is as common in England as everywhere else where people live and strive for what they want?

'Just do your best,' Joseph said to Kerr. 'Perth will probably find out eventually anyway. Don't betray anybody's trust in you.'

'Thank you,' Kerr said with a rush of overriding gratitude, his face suddenly pink. 'I knew you would advise me.' He hesitated a moment as if to repeat himself, then straightened his shoulders and went to the door.

Joseph suddenly felt exhausted and his arm ached appallingly. It seemed as if a hideous pattern was starting all over again.

Chapter Six

Matthew was in his office as usual on the morning Blaine's body was found. He was reading a letter and he finally put it down with a sense of relief. He was always pleased to hear from Judith because he worried about her, not only because of the very obvious danger of her being injured, or even killed, but that the threats of ordinary illness were made far worse by the long hours she worked, and the wet and filthy conditions.

In her letter she accepted that every avenue of enquiry had been followed to its end, and they – she and her siblings – knew no more about the Peacemaker than they had before. He could still be almost anyone, except Ivor Chetwin or Dermot Sandwell. Aidan Thyer, Master of St John's, was still possible. Most painful to Matthew, and perhaps most frightening, was the chance the man was Calder Shearing himself. That thought touched Matthew now and then like the cold fingers of nightmare. His father had hated Secret Intelligence and all its works; in his very brief experience they had proved devious, manipulative and dishonest in spirit. Was Shearing's involvement what he had meant when he had warned Matthew to trust no one because the corruption reached right to the very top?

Matthew had had no difficulty in deciding not to tell Judith anything of his thoughts on Patrick Hannassey yet. There was still too much to test. Where had he been at the time of John and

Alys Reavley's deaths? And was it imaginable that John Reavley had known him? Could he possibly have had private access to the King and the Kaiser? Had he access to Eldon Prentice, and power to influence the press? He could tell Judith if the answers to all these confirmed that Hannassey could be guilty.

He still had these questions in his mind when Desborough put his head around the door and told him that Shearing wanted him immediately. 'Something bad,' he added with a frown. 'By the look on his face, pretty bloody. Thought I'd warn you.'

'Thanks,' Matthew said drily, rising to his feet.

He put Judith's letter in his pocket and went along the corridor to Shearing's office. His mind raced over the most probable disasters in the Atlantic, or worse still, in America itself. Either one of their own agents had been caught, or there had been another major incident on the Mexican-American border.

He knocked and heard the order to come in. Shearing was standing by the window, unusually for him. Matthew almost always found him at this desk.

'Yes, sir?' he said, closing the door behind him.

'There's been a murder in St Giles,' Shearing said bluntly. 'Theo Blaine. He was Corcoran's best man – in fact he was brilliant, key to the whole project.'

Matthew was stunned. It was the last thing he had been expecting. 'Yes, sir,' he said. 'Do we show our interest by investigating it, or leave it to the Cambridge police?'

Shearing looked exhausted. He had the dazed, rather stiff air of someone newly bereaved, but Matthew knew it was not the young scientist personally whose loss bruised him so deeply, but the wound it dealt to the project that was possibly crucial to Britain's survival in the war. He could not keep away the thought that perhaps this was another brilliant act of the Peacemaker's. A blow like this, with such surgical precision, was just the sort of thing he would do. It was like his own parents' deaths – swift, murderous, but hideously economic.

'Reavley!' Shearing's voice broke Matthew's moment of inattention.

'Yes, sir,' he said again. 'I can go to St Giles without drawing any particular notice, if you want me to. I can stay at home, visit my brother. He's still far from recovered. But if it was a German agent who killed him, that won't fool our enemies.'

'We've no idea yet who it was,' Shearing replied. 'He was only found this morning.'

'Where? By whom?' Matthew asked. It was still hard to grasp as reality. Blaine was someone he had never met, but his death could affect the entire country, millions of lives, perhaps the course of history. It was too vast to have meaning yet.

'By his wife,' Shearing answered. He moved to stand with his back to the window, the late morning light shadowed from his face for a moment. 'By the potting shed at the bottom of the garden. He was probably there all night.'

'She didn't miss him?' Matthew was startled. Perhaps this was nothing to do with Germany, but was simply a domestic tragedy.

Shearing must have read the thought in his expression. The ghost of a smile touched his eyes and vanished instantly. 'Don't cling on to that, Reavley. It means nothing.' He walked slowly over to his desk, but without sitting down in the leather-padded, round-backed chair, as if it would in some way imprison him. 'His throat was torn out with the prongs of a garden fork.'

Matthew winced.

Shearing saw it. 'It could still have been a woman's crime,' he pointed out. 'That doesn't mean it had nothing to do with Germany. It could be any of a dozen things, and whatever it was, it is still the loss of the best scientific brain in the country. That matters more than any one man's life.'

There was nothing to argue. 'What do you want me to do, sir?'

'Get your brother the priest to resurrect the man!' Shearing snapped, his eyes blazing for a moment. Then, with fear and will suppressing the panic, he levelled his voice. 'We need to know whether it was personal or enemy-inspired,' he answered. 'We've done everything we can to keep the project secret, but it's almost impossible. If there is a German spy or sympathizer in St Giles we must find them and destroy them, preferably without exposing them publicly. It's devastating for morale to know we are so vulnerable. And of course we need to guard ourselves better in the future.'

Matthew did not interrupt.

'In the hope that it was personal, possibly domestic,' Shearing went on, 'we must avoid drawing more attention to the murder than necessary. We mustn't go swarming down there with men all over the place, questions and orders. It's a murder. Leave the local police to do what we have to hope they are trained for.' His lips tightened. 'What I need you to do, Reavley, is find out from Corcoran the absolute truth, however bitter – can we complete the project without Blaine?'

Matthew had been thinking about the murder, finding out whether it was a private tragedy or an act of war. He should have been prepared for this. In the end it was the only thing that was crucial; the rest was simply one more loss in a nation already counting its dead by the hundreds of thousands. There was not a village, a hamlet however small, a street in any town that did not have someone wounded, dead or simply missing.

But it would be extremely hard to go and face Shanley Corcoran and ask him if this was defeat. He dreaded it.

'Yes, sir,' he said quietly.

'We can allow other people hope,' Shearing said. 'I need the truth, Reavley, whatever it is.'

'Yes, sir. I know that.'

Matthew assigned his immediate duties to his colleagues and cleared his desk, then early the next morning he drove to Selborne St Giles. There was no point in going the same day. The police would need time to assemble the preliminary facts and, more important than that, Corcoran would have to assess the situation at the Establishment. He would have to see what Blaine had left in the way of notes or instructions to others, who else he had trusted, or who might understand his calculations. It was not a judgement that could be made in haste.

It was one of those brisk spring days when the sky was blue, the wind sharp, and clouds gathered in a matter of minutes, giving sudden squalls of rain that left everything dripping.

There was a haze of green over the fields and the first leaves were beginning to open in the hedges. Every so often a burst of white blossom showed.

Matthew was one of the few people who had access to as much petrol as he needed, but he was acutely aware of the shortages and he did not abuse the privilege. However, he would need to travel not only to St Giles but also to the Establishment, to Shanley Corcoran's house in Madingley, and probably back and forth to Cambridge. This time he had a reason to drive, and he enjoyed the surge of power in the engine of his Sunbeam Talbot, and the sense of freedom it gave him to race along the open road.

He tried to plan in his mind what he would say, then decided it was useless. Grief could not be met with prepared speeches; in fact it could not be met at all, only treated with the dignity of being honest.

He went to the Establishment first. It was less than half an hour beyond St Giles through the winding, familiar lanes, verges deep in grass. He was not in uniform, since the whole visit was ostensibly a private one, but he carried identification, and was obliged to produce it before being allowed in to see Corcoran.

There was an air of gloom about the large, utilitarian building. Doors were closed and locked until opened by discreet guards. Their faces were tense, shoulders stiff, and if they recognized Matthew from previous visits they gave no sign of it.

After what seemed like endless corridors, indistinguishable from one another, he found Corcoran in his office, sitting at his desk with a mass of papers in front of him. Even at a glance Matthew could see that many of them were covered with formulae and calculations; less than half were merely written on. He would not have understood them, but even so, Corcoran automatically covered them with a couple of large sheets of paper before standing up to greet him.

'Matthew! It's good to see you.' He clasped Matthew's hands in both of his. He looked shocked, his face crumpled, every line heavier and more deeply scored than previously, as if dragged downwards. There was no colour in his skin except for shadows, but his eyes were vivid as always, and his hands were warm and strong. 'Of course you've come about this dreadful situation. Poor Blaine was brilliant. One of our best.' He let go of Matthew's hands.

'I know. Can you complete the project without him?' Matthew asked.

Corcoran winced and gave a half-smile. 'You're blunt! I suppose you have to be. It will be difficult, but yes, of course we will. We have to. I know every bit as well as you do that victory could depend on it, and very probably will.' His mouth tightened. 'I can do it, Matthew. I'll work on it myself, day and night. I have good men left. Ben Morven is first class – well, good second,' he amended. 'And Francis Iliffe, and Dacy Lucas. Every man will throw all he has into it, believe me.'

'I know you will, but will it be enough without Blaine?' Matthew hated having to persist. 'I need the truth, Shanley, not optimism, and not just hope or faith. How hard will it be? What difference will it make to the time, being without Blaine? Your best estimate?'

Corcoran considered for several moments, his eyes dark and bright.

'For whom am I guessing, Matthew? Calder Shearing?'

'Yes. And I would think for Admiral Hall too.' Admiral 'Blinker' Hall was head of Naval Intelligence.

Corcoran grimaced again as if stabbed with pain. 'Of course it will make the work very much harder,' he admitted soberly. 'If I have to be specific, the project may take us two or even four weeks longer.' His voice trembled with the fierceness of his emotion. 'But I swear I will do it!' He gestured towards the desk. 'I've dropped everything else and I am personally going over all Blaine's notes to project what he was planning and follow it. I know what lives will be lost by even that much delay.'

Matthew believed him, but he was also concerned. Corcoran was well over sixty and he looked shattered by weariness and now shock. He had lost considerable weight in the last year and was working himself to exhaustion without this added burden. This kind of intense mental drive over such extraordinary hours would be enough to break the health of a young man, let alone one his

107

age. Matthew understood sacrifice, and it was selfish and absurd to make different rules for those you cared about, whatever the reason. And yet it was almost beyond his ability not to.

'Don't work yourself into the grave,' he said, almost lightly, but there was a catch in his voice. Corcoran was more than a great man whom he admired intensely, he was a deeply loved friend, a link with the past and all that was precious in it. Memory stretched back into a childhood so sweet it held a pain for all that had slipped away with John Reavley's death, the war, the need to fight at such hideous price for what they had once taken so lightly for granted. 'We couldn't do without you,' he added.

'Oh, come on!' Corcoran smiled suddenly. 'It's only work! Work is a challenge!' He held up his hand in a fist. 'It's what man was born for – work and love. That's who we are, isn't it? A life that doesn't challenge you to give all you have is only half a life, unworthy of the possibilities of man. Your father would say that, and you know it.'

Matthew looked away, feeling suddenly stripped, and too vulnerable to meet Corcoran's eyes. If he lost him too it would hurt more than he was prepared to face. He must think of something practical to divert the torrent of feeling that threatened to sweep away his balance.

'Shearing said to tell you that if there is anything you need, he'll get it for you,' he said abruptly. 'That might not be quite *carte blanche*, but it's close.'

'It'll do,' Corcoran assured him. 'I'll write a list. Give me half an hour. I'll get someone to take you around the place, show you the two or three things that you can be allowed to see – like the canteen and the lavatory! Not that I think for a moment you would understand the rest anyway. But it's a protection for you as much as for us. Come with me, I'll find someone.' He went to the door. 'Lucas! Come, meet Matthew Reavley from the Special Intelligence Service. Show him what you can for half an hour, then bring him back here. Be nice to him. He's not only my friend, he's the man who'll bring us all the tools and funds we want!'

'Well, all there is,' Matthew amended.

* * *

Richard Mason left the nightmare of Verdun behind him, thinking, as he rattled over the torn-up roads towards Ypres, of what he could write in his report on the slaughter in the French Army. Twelve days of incessant rain had made the landscape a sea of mud broken only by skeleton-like limbs of shattered trees and the occasional length of barbed wire.

The French had taken Dead Man's Hill back from the Germans, a few thousand square yards of hell. The ground, like that of Ypres, was strewn with the blood and bones of both sides. Mason could not see them as essentially different. The rotting corpse of a German soldier did not smell the same as that of an English one, or French. But it was only to do with what they ate, nothing at all with what they believed or cared about, how much they loved, their dreams or their pain.

The whole thing was an obscene parody of what life should be, like something one of the early Flemish or Dutch artists, such as Hieronymus Bosch, would have created as a vision of damnation.

The car hit a shell hole in the road and careered to one side, the driver righting it only with difficulty. Ypres was still ten miles away. Mason had not told the man why he wanted to come here. There would be nothing different to see. It was a struggle to make his reports in any way separate from one another, or one lot of dead men unique and identifiable, except to those who had known and loved them.

He was going because here he might see Judith Reavley again, even if it were only for an hour or two. He had seen her twice since their first meeting at the Savoy in London nearly a year ago, when she had been so furious with him. Both times had been just behind the lines in Flanders.

Once she had been at the side of the road by her ambulance, changing the wheel when one of the tyres had obviously burst. He had been in a staff car going the other way, and had stopped and offered to help. He had half expected to be told with asperity that she could manage perfectly well. No doubt she could, and had had to often enough. She had surprised him by accepting assistance without a murmur, and giving him a smile at the end which he still remembered with a warmth that was unexplainable.

'I thought you might be offended,' he had said with a sense of relief.

They had stood together side by side on the road, he tidy, dry-footed, actually quite smart, she with her boots caked in mud, the bottom of her skirt sodden wet and blood on her sleeves. Her hair had been pinned up hastily and untidily, but her face was designed for fire, tenderness, and to be hurt, and there was a kind of beauty in her nothing could hide.

'Then you don't know me, Mr Mason,' she had replied. 'I am not interested in proving to you that I can change a wheel. I care only about getting these men to a hospital as quickly as possible, and two of us will do that more quickly than I can alone. Thank you.' And with another smile, cooler this time, she had climbed up into the driver's seat. She directed him to crank the engine for her and pass her the handle, which he had done obediently.

The second time had been less accidental. He had wanted to talk to injured men in one of the field dressing stations and had deliberately chosen one where he knew she would be. He had watched her working quickly, grim-faced, cleaning the inside of her ambulance from a particularly bloody trip. He could smell the vinegar and carbolic in the water she had used. Her hands were raw with it.

He had brought her a cup of tea, pretty disgusting stuff made in a dixie can and tasting of petrol and grease, but at least fairly hot. She had thanked him and drunk it without comment. It was one of the most telling observations about her life that she was so used to it she did not seem to notice. He still found such a brew revolting.

They had talked a little, even laughed at a couple of current jokes. The occasion stood out in his memory because they had not quarrelled about anything. For a while he had deluded himself it was agreement; later he had thought it was more likely she simply cared too much about her men, and too little about him, to expend energy on argument.

That was partly why he had wanted so urgently to go back to Ypres this time. He needed to know how she would see him now, if they could talk again and touch minds, ideas, if he could know a little more about her that was real.

Ahead of him the mist was thickening as darkness approached. He could hear the guns in the distance and the smell of the trenches was in his nose and throat. As long as he lived he would never forget or become immune to the nausea of the taste of death in the air.

He should report to the commanding officer as a matter of courtesy. He would be busy. Bombardment usually increased at this time of the day and would go on all night. There would be raiding parties, possibly a serious assault, even a whole battalion going over the top. Casualties could be heavy.

He thought of Judith and in his mind's eye she was smiling. Perhaps that was what he wanted to think, to remember. She was a moment's grace in a world drowned in ugliness. 'Drowned' was too appropriate a word. It was raining again, not hard, just a steady grey pall over everything, blurring the road, smearing headlights, shining back off the pools of muddy water everywhere around them. With the coming of darkness the air was getting colder.

Star shells went up, briefly lighting the sky. The guns were louder now. They were not more than a mile from the trenches. There was a slight wind carrying the smell of the latrines.

It took Mason another hour to reach the brigade headquarters and report his presence. He was received with courtesy but no one had time to do more than be civil. He had bread, and hot tea tasting of oil and tinned Maconochie stew. No one told him where he could or could not go; his reputation was his passport to anything he wished.

It was a hard night. The Germans mounted a raid and were fought off with heavy casualties. No prisoners were taken, but there were half a dozen dead, and at least three times that many wounded.

When dawn came grey and bitterly cold, the east wind slicing through the flesh as if it could strike the bone, Mason was helping wounded men from stretchers to field dressing stations and then to ambulances. He saw Wilson Sloan, the young American volunteer he had met six months ago with Judith. He looked older; his face was thinner and there was something different about his eyes. There was no time to talk, except for a moment, about the practicalities of moving men, lifting without causing further hurt, not getting the ambulance stuck in the mud, which was everywhere. Sloan worked singly, uncomplainingly, and now with considerable skill.

It was broad daylight when Mason saw the outline of the ambulance, dark in the fine rain, a shadow against the grey trunks of trees. One of the doors was blown off the back and it sat at an angle. He ran forward, a surge of panic inside him, floundering in the mud. The driver in the front seemed to be unconscious, slumped over the wheel. It was not until he was level with the cab, his feet slithering, that he even realized it was a woman.

'Judith!' he shouted, his heart pounding. It was ridiculous; the driver could be anyone.

He leaned in. Yes, it looked like Judith. She sat motionless, head bowed over the wheel, resting on her arms. He was sick with the thought that she was dead, although there was no wound visible, but it was hard to see when her clothes were dark-stained with rain. She must be wet to the skin, and frozen. Perhaps she had died of exposure.

He gulped air, gagging, and put out his hand to touch her arm. The muscles tensed to resist him, and the vitality poured back into him, with overwhelming relief.

'Go away,' she said expressionlessly. 'There's nothing to do.'

'Judith?' She sounded so different, now he was uncertain it was her after all. With her profile hidden she did not look the same. He could not see the planes of her cheek or the line of her nose.

She ignored him. Did she not recognize his voice either?

'Judith!' He felt the panic back again, high in his throat. What if she were injured, seriously? He did not know enough first aid to save her, not when it mattered so savagely! Not when it was her! 'Judith!' The cry was high-pitched, strangled.

She raised her head very slowly and looked at him. Her wide

blue-grey eyes held only slight expression, a mild uninterested surprise. She did not bother to speak to him.

'Judith . . .' he gulped. 'Are you hurt?'

'Not particularly,' she answered. 'There's nobody here. They took them. There's nothing more to do.'

'You must be freezing!' he exclaimed. 'Does the engine work?'

'No.' She offered no explanation. The anger was burned out of her, and the hunger, and the hope. For an instant he felt robbed: the light he had come to find was not here. Then he saw her pale face, empty-eyed, and the sad, wounded line of her mouth and all he could think of was how to heal her, not for himself, but for her, even if he never saw her again.

'Judith,' he said softly, 'you must get out and we'll go and find something to eat, something warm. The ambulance is no good. Someone else will come and take it away. Come on . . .' He held out his hand.

She did not bother to argue; she simply remained there, motionless.

The guns were firing only sporadically now. In between there was something almost like silence.

Mason hated being abrupt, but he had seen shell shock before, that terrible, thousand-yard stare of those who carry the horror within themselves, for whom the gunfire is in the brain.

'Judith! Do as you're told! Give me your hand – now! You are in the way and you have to get out.'

She obeyed. It was probably out of habit. She moved slowly, stiff with cold, but he was dizzy with relief to see that she did not seem to be hurt more than a few bruises, a stiff leg, and one blood-stained bandage on her lower arm.

'Come on,' he insisted. 'Walk.'

She hesitated, looking over her shoulder at the ambulance.

'It's all right,' he told her. 'Someone will come for it.'

'I shouldn't leave it,' she said with a frown.

His heart surged upward. It was a sign of emotion, of concern for something.

'Yes, you can.' He took her arm. 'You've got to report in.'

She looked at him with a brief flare of humour. It died instantly.

113

'What for? Because you say so, Mason? What in God's name do you know about it? If we aren't dead today, we will be tomorrow, or the day after.'

'It's bad,' he agreed. 'So is Verdun. But we're not finished. And even if we are, we're not going down moaning.'

She was walking slowly, squelching in the mud. 'Perhaps you were right about war and peace, and it's all pointless,' she said.

What could he say to make her argue, make her fight? At the Savoy he had wanted her to agree with him, force her to think clearly instead of fostering the mindless heroics she had seemed to believe in then. Now her passive surrender was the last thing on earth he wanted. How could he get back the fire she had had then, the grace and courage of dissension, the passion to live and believe, even if it was futile and completely Quixotic?

He pulled her forward to hurry her up and she increased speed without complaining, even though her feet must have hurt in her wet, stiff boots. He could have wept to see the change in her. Only now did he realize that what he admired in her was far more than beauty, it was the inner light of a uniquely precious belief, one person's heart and vision, that he would miss irrevocably should it be destroyed by the terrible experience of war. That she was wrong, that the war was pointless, that she was Joseph Reavley's sister, did not matter; only that she was alive, and she hurt.

How could he light a spark of the old anger?

'I never said it was pointless!' he denied it. 'I said it was . . .' He could not remember what he had said. Anyway, it did not matter. All that mattered was catching some passion in her, any passion at all – anger, hope, love, hate. He would have said anything to free her from the grip of despair. 'I said we shouldn't start a world war over one boundary dispute.'

She looked at him with a slight puckering of her brow. 'No you didn't. And it wasn't one boundary dispute. Wars never are.'

He felt a flame of exultation. She was going to argue! 'Yes it was! The Kaiser crossed through Belgium. If he'd gone straight across the French frontier we would probably have stayed at home!'

114

'No we wouldn't!' She turned away sharply. 'If it hadn't been Belgium it would have been somewhere else. I don't know much history, but even I know enough for that. It's bloody, it's consuming half Europe and beginning to stain the rest of the world. Perhaps it's even senseless now. But it wasn't ever just a squabble about boundaries, and you can't be stupid enough to think it was.'

Was he losing her again? He looked at the weary slope of her shoulders. She was trudging along, too exhausted in body to do more than barely pick up her feet. But it was her heart he needed to reach, her will. She needed to believe there would be something left to win, no matter how hard it was or how long it took. He was not sure that he believed it himself.

What could he argue now? What did he need from her – gentleness, anger, laughter, even just disagreement?

'Perhaps I'm too close to it,' he said, although it was a pointless observation.

'Where've you been?' she asked.

It was broad daylight now and the rain had eased off. There would soon be other traffic, even though this was not a main road, and too badly cratered for convoy use.

'Verdun,' he answered.

She turned to look at him. 'Was it bad?'

'Yes.'

'Poor devils.'

He needed to think of something else to say, but for a moment memory of Verdun drove out everything else. He did not realize that she was still looking at him.

'Don't tell people they're losing,' she said firmly. 'It might be true for the moment, but it would be a betrayal. They need our faith.'

He stared at her, incredulously.

She gave a tiny, twisted smile. 'You have to have faith, even to die well,' she explained.

It was there! The old fire, just a tiny light, but the grace and the courage he loved. He seized hold of her, ignoring her bandaged arm, and hugged her, half lifting her off her feet and swinging her round. She was wet and cold, and her skin smelled of antiseptic and engine oil, but the warmth inside him was enough to make all of it sweet to him.

He put her down on the rutted road again and went forward, increasing his speed, willing to drag her if necessary. They had to reach an outpost, one of the field dressing stations, a command dugout, anything where she could get warm and dry and eat something.

Two hours later she was asleep and Mason had eaten the usual front-line breakfast of stale bread, beef stew and strong tea, when a corporal brought up the mail, and ten minutes after that the major in command of the station handed Mason a sealed letter.

'Thank you.' Mason took it, and the moment the man had moved away, he tore it open and read it.

The handwriting was clear and strong, the wording casual, as any man might use to a friend. The message within was anything but ordinary. It was from the man he knew as the Peacemaker and, masked by pleasantries, was the information that he had heard about the social unrest in Russia – the vast possibilities of relieving the Eastern Front and stopping the slaughter there. Which would in turn alter the balance on the Western Front, and perhaps bring an early end to the war.

It was all couched in terms of village politics, but Mason knew enough of what it meant for his interest to be held as if in a vice. When he had read the letter he put it in his pocket and sat crouched on an ammunition box, his feet on duckboards awash with rain-water, the weak spring sun thawing some of the chill out of his flesh. He could hear the sounds of men moving about. Someone was singing a bawdy song. There was a burst of laughter, and then others joined in. There was a kind of desperate courage in it he admired with a passion so intense he found his hands were shaking on the tin mug he was holding, slopping the tea over. Anything that would save them was worth trying. Tiredness, defeat, bereavement, fear, none of them was an excuse for not trying. Pride was not even the beginning of an excuse. He would go back and listen to the Peacemaker, see if there was anything worth attempting.

Then men like these around him could go home, and a woman like Judith could drive ordinary cars crazily along country roads instead of carrying the bleeding and dead through this carnage.

He was on his way back to London anyway. He had only come through Ypres in the hope of seeing Judith. He was startled and a little afraid how much that had mattered to him. He was not at all certain it was what he wanted, not now, not when nothing could be held on to, treasured, promised for life.

But there should be life, for all these tens of thousands of men around him, its possibilities and hopes and chances for good or ill.

He drank the rest of the tea and climbed to his feet. He could not afford to stay here any longer. He must leave before the night's bombardment began, and cadge a lift towards the train.

Mason arrived in London on a troop train, and climbed out stiff and cold on to the platform at Waterloo station. He heard the doors open and men call out, the clatter of boots, the whistle and hiss of steam as the engine belched. The platform was crowded, people pushing and jostling together, all straining eagerly to catch sight of a particular face, and growing more and more desperate if they didn't. There were nurses in long, grey uniforms, always busy, too much to do, too little time; porters with luggage, men too old to fight, or not fit enough; and endless men in khaki with white bandages, some spotted with blood.

Outside the station the line of people waiting for taxis was long, and most of them were wounded. Mason was stiff and cold, but he was unhurt. He walked to the nearest stop and waited for an omnibus. It could even be quicker in the end.

He stared around. London looked tired and drabber than he remembered it. The women wore smart, elegant jackets, skirts to the mid-calf with often a longer one beneath, but there was no colour, no reds or pinks, nothing extravagant, no lace parasols as there used to be before the war, no hats with big flowers on them.

There was both horse-drawn traffic and automobiles on the street, all the familiar advertisements, the noise and the movement, but everything looked dirty in the sun.

Since the last time he had been to Marchmont Street he had not only reported from the Western Front, and Gallipoli again, but also on the desperate Italian resistance to Austria, and the fighting in the Balkans. His emotions were raw with the bitter sameness of the loss. And now Judith's face, blank with misery, haunted his mind and drove him to want to see her laugh again, walk with a lift in her step and that old arrogance and certainty of her passions that had caught his eye, and his temper, before.

The horns and the traffic brought him back to the present and the street again. The bus came and he boarded it, glad to find a seat.

What was unique to Judith that she stayed in his mind? A quality of the dreams in her face, the power to care, and to be hurt? She had the same blind courage and loyalty that her brother Joseph had. It infuriated Mason, but commanded his admiration. He did not even know if Joseph were still alive. Considering how much time he spent in or near the front line, quite possibly he wasn't. Mason was startled by how much pain that thought gave him, first for himself, then savagely, like a blow, for Judith. He had not even asked her!

He alighted while he was still half a mile from Marchmont Street. It was easier and certainly faster to walk the rest of the way than wait for another bus.

He thought of the first time he had come here, before the war. He had been full of hope and the belief that they really could make a difference, that the horror of the Boer War need never happen again. Their ideals had been vast – a new age of peace and progress for mankind. Of course there was a price; nothing came without one, least of all change. But it had seemed then to be infinitely worth doing. How long ago that was now.

He reached the door he was looking for and rang the bell. It was answered by a manservant and he was shown upstairs. Mason felt self-conscious, here again after a full year in which so much had happened. The whole world was drawn in and seemed bent on slaughter, except the Americans. Only they remained the same, huge and aloof, blanketed in peace and prosperity while Europe drowned in its own blood.

Now he stood in the Peacemaker's house again. Nothing had changed in the hallway or the landing. The walls were the same soft red. There were still the same pictures hanging there: masterpieces of scenery – mountains and lakes, country by-roads, fields with great trees and quiet cows beneath them. There was even the same Chinese porcelain ginger jar on the stand at the top of the stairs.

The Peacemaker himself looked no different either, except perhaps around the eyes. He was tireder, more guarded. Something of the fire was spent, but when Mason looked more closely he knew the determination was the same.

The Peacemaker held out his hand. 'Good to see you, Mason. How are you? Tired, I imagine. Tea, or whisky? I have a good Glenmorangie if you'd like it.'

'Not if you want me to stay awake, thank you,' Mason declined. 'But tea would be excellent.'

'Earl Grey?'

'Thank you.'

The Peacemaker gave instructions, adding the request for sandwiches as well, then returned, closing the door and inviting Mason to sit down. 'I imagine Verdun was worse than you wrote in your dispatch?' he said quietly.

'Everything is worse than I write,' Mason answered. He knew roughly why the Peacemaker had sent for him. Russia, of course, but to do what? Mason believed in the same cause, with a passion even deeper and more consuming than before, but he was not prepared to bring it to pass in the same way. Watching the slaughter at Verdun until he could hear the guns in his dreams and taste blood, he knew there was still no such thing as peace 'at any price'. Some prices in their very nature made peace impossible, except in a way that could not last; its destruction was built into it. He had said as much last year.

Was it conceivable that the Peacemaker had finally realized this himself?

Mason looked at the man opposite him with a kind of desperate hope. He had the intelligence, the power and the vision to stop the war! Personal feelings, likes and dislikes, even individual pride, were nothing compared with that gain, if it were possible.

'You can't tell people what it's really like,' he finished quietly. 'The only pain of it we know is in the broken bodies that return, and the faces of the women who have lost their men.'

The Peacemaker sat motionless, his mouth drawn into a tight grip of pain. 'We came close to stopping it, Mason,' he said softly, his voice thick with emotion. 'We missed by hours! God knows what absurd chance made Reavley find that treaty, or what Quixotic idiocy made him take it.' He drew in a deep breath and let it out in a sigh. 'But we have to deal with what we have now. That much of the past is irrelevant. It's blood under the bridge,' he said with a bitter smile. 'The situation is approaching a crisis. That is why I asked you to come.'

The Peacemaker was intensely serious. He leaned forward a little, as his face caught the light, the fine lines in it etching his skin with a mask of weariness, and his voice was raw with emotion. 'We are bogged down in France and Flanders, losing a thousand men a day! Gallipoli was a disaster. Italy may survive, but it hangs in the balance. The news from German East Africa is not good. Van Deventer is leading twelve hundred men to Kondoa Irangi, but the going is hard and they are being decimated by disease. In Mesopotamia our forces have still not lifted the siege of Kut-al-Amara and saved our men inside. The Tigris Corps' casualties number about ten thousand men! That's a quarter of General Aylmer's total force, which means it's a loss altogether of twenty-three thousand.'

Mason had not known the figures. They were far worse than he had assumed, but what puzzled him was what the Peacemaker wanted of him. Had he misunderstood the letter, and it was not Russia at all?

'But the change that matters most is that in the German High Command,' the Peacemaker went on, lowering his voice still further, his face tense. 'With every week that passes they too are losing more men, and their attitude hardens. They have held Naroch to Russian losses estimated at well over a hundred thousand men. There will be a counteroffensive, probably next month. So far the Germans have resisted withdrawing men from Verdun to redirect them to the Eastern Front, but that may not last.'

120

'Exactly what is it you want?' Mason asked.

The Peacemaker smiled, softening his features startlingly, as if he had seen across a crowded room someone he liked enormously. 'An understanding on both sides that there will be no victors in this war, except those who did not participate,' he answered. 'Mason, it must be stopped somehow, before there is such bitterness on both sides that there can be no realistic peace after it. Too much bloodshed, and the fury for vengeance may become so overwhelming that no settlement is possible, except when one side or the other has been utterly destroyed. I think the way it is going at the moment, that may be Britain. And God knows, that would be a tragedy unsurpassed even in the futile and terrible history of the world.'

Mason felt cold, as if he were overtaken with illness.

'I don't want it for Germany either,' the Peacemaker continued earnestly. 'They are a great people, with a culture which has enriched mankind. Who can read their poets, their philosophers or benefit from their science without gratitude? Who can listen to Beethoven and not be enlarged in spirit? His genius bestrides the world and transcends the petty language of words.'

Mason agreed with everything he said, but he was still waiting for the spark that was new, the reason the Peacemaker had sent for him.

The manservant brought the tea tray with delicate sandwiches and left it on the table.

'The death toll is already hideous,' the Peacemaker resumed, pouring for both of them as the door closed. 'It is mounting every day, and it is the best who die, the bravest and the most honourable, and very often the strongest, those who would have been the leaders of the future. In a little while Europe will be impossible to rebuild because the best will be gone, the workforce will be decimated. All the time and skill of those who are left will be used up in caring for the human wreckage and pain of those who survive.'

His lips pursed into a dry smile terrible with sadness. 'The social changes are already irrevocable. Women are doing the jobs men used to. Many of them will not marry because the men who would have been their husbands are dead. Generations will pass before the loss is caught up. And we will all be degraded by the savagery, the starvation and the betrayals that follow war.'

His eyes searched Mason's face.

'We have a duty to save them, and ourselves, from that, and we haven't much longer in which to do it,' he said, emotion cracking his voice. 'The old governments, the men who wanted peace, are being replaced by warmongers who make their name and fame out of ruin. Are you still willing to help? Do you still have the strength and the courage to care?'

'Of course I care!' Mason retorted, angry that the Peacemaker felt any need to ask the question, even rhetorically. 'What is it you plan? What has it to do with Russia, beyond dreams?'

The Peacemaker's expression did not alter, but something in him relaxed so his elegantly cut suit eased into different lines on his body.

'Simply?' he asked. 'Have you any concept of how many troops, how many tanks and guns could be released if Russia came out of the war?'

'I'm sure I could calculate it,' Mason replied. 'But I can't see any likelihood of that happening. It was the Tsar's treaties within Europe that took them in, in the first place. None of that has changed.'

'It could do,' the Peacemaker answered, the excitement sharp in his voice now. 'What do you know about Russia – not the army, but the society, the government, the mass of the people?'

Mason thought for a few moments. 'Hunger, social injustice, crop failure,' he replied. 'I suppose it could be summed up as chaos, and shocking numbers of dead, not only in battle but right across the land, due to poverty and climate, and lack of resources except in the hands of the few. They won't beat Germany!' He frowned. 'But Germany won't beat them either. Nobody ever has. It's not just the stoicism of the people and their unbelievable sacrifice.' He shivered as he remembered the carnage he had seen. 'It's the land itself. We Western Europeans can't begin to comprehend how vast Russia is. It's . . . endless! It swallowed Napoleon. It will swallow the Kaiser if he's stupid enough to try to invade it.'

'And God knows how many people,' the Peacemaker said, a

hush of awe in his voice, as if he were already in the presence of the dead. 'And what of the Russian government?'

'The Tsar? Out of touch with everything,' Mason replied. 'No concept of reality at all. His only son is haemophiliac and not likely to live long. The Tsarina is terrified for him, poor woman, and seems entirely dominated by the lunatic Rasputin. The whole edifice is corrupt from floor to ceiling.'

'Exactly,' the Peacemaker agreed. 'Ready to fall. It will need only a little assistance . . .'

Mason stiffened. 'Assistance?'

The Peacemaker's face was tense, his eyes burning. 'If it does not happen soon it will be very violent, worse than the revolution in France in 1789, when the gutters of Paris ran with blood. Russia needs change, and it needs it soon, before it is catastrophic and tears the country apart. The Russian people have no stake in the war! They should make peace with Germany, pull out, gain a new government and a new order of social justice.'

Mason could not help smiling, although with a kind of wry despair. 'And how can we bring that about?'

It was a rhetorical question, but the Peacemaker gave him an answer. 'By helping their own reformers – revolutionaries, if you like. Every great change begins with a dream, a man with a vision of something better, who inspires others.'

A memory seared across Mason's mind of a cramped office in London in 1903, a wild energy in the air, passionate ideals of a new social order, justice, the rule of the people at last. There had been men with fire in their eyes and in their brains. The Mensheviks and Bolsheviks had split from each other, the latter unwilling to wait on the former's moderation.

The Peacemaker saw it in his face. He was smiling.

Mason had been a journalist then, sharing his office in Clerkenwell with the editor of *Iskra*, Vladimir Ilyich Lenin.

'Now is the time,' the Peacemaker said, his voice little more than a whisper, as if he could be overheard even here. 'We must assure that it happens while Russia is still self-contained, and the violence, when it erupts – and it will – does not spill over into the rest of Europe, and eventually the world.'

Mason struggled to accommodate the enormity of what he was hearing.

The Peacemaker held his gaze. 'Once Germany conquers Russia, even part of it, it will be too late. Then it will be Germany's problem, and we can't afford that. Rebuilding Europe after this war will take every ounce of our strength, all our courage, skill and resource. Our people will be exhausted, God knows how many dead or crippled. Mason – we've got to put a stop to it! Before it's too late . . .'

'How?'

'We have two possibilities,' the Peacemaker answered very softly. 'There are two men who could light the fires of revolution in Russia. I know Lenin, so do you . . .'

Of course Mason knew Lenin. The passion in the man was unforgettable, once one had really looked at him. At first he might seem insignificant, another quiet worker with his head bowed in books, but meet his eyes and all thought of the ordinary fled.

'I know what he thinks,' the Peacemaker went on. 'He doesn't want war any more than the Russian people do. But he's in Zurich now, and unwilling to leave. His fire is all in his mind, not yet in his belly.'

Mason waited. The clock on the mantelpiece ticked like a minuscule heartbeat.

'You know Trotsky as well,' the Peacemaker said, his eyes on Mason's face. 'I need to know what he wants – revolution, of course – but war or peace with Europe. That is the only question we have to answer to.'

'And if it's war?' Mason found his voice was shaking. He knew Leon Trotsky as well. Even as the name came to his mind he could see the square face and piled-up mass of curling, dark hair, the vitality of the man. He was small, and yet the passion of him filled a room. Instinctively Mason had liked him more than the dry, inward-looking Lenin.

'You know the answer to that,' the Peacemaker answered. 'The revolution will happen in Russia, Mason. It is as inevitable as the phases of the moon. We must have peace. Five million men are dead in Europe already. What is one more?'

Mason gulped air, his heart racing. He had seen countless dead men. He had waded through corpses. It should not matter, and yet it did. The thought repulsed him.

'Have you only the stomach for dreams, not reality?' the Peacemaker challenged.

'No.' Was it the truth? He knew Trotsky. He had talked with the man, eaten with him, even liked him. Trotsky had actually told him about his exile in Siberia and Mason knew he had escaped and come to England. 'No,' he repeated. The man he remembered would be for peace. But was he still the same?

'Find him,' the Peacemaker repeated. 'We can change what is to come, Mason. We can end this storm of slaughter! My God, someone has to!'

Mason was hardly aware of his hands and feet, as if he were detached from his body. He held history in his hands, life and death, choice. He thought of the men in Verdun, of Judith by the side of the road in Ypres, and all those like them across the battlefields of Europe. 'Yes, of course,' he said firmly. Suddenly there was no doubt. He would have killed an enemy soldier with regret, but without hesitation. If Leon Trotsky was in favour of war, then he must be prevented from returning to Russia, and Lenin go in his place.

The Peacemaker was talking about arrangements. Mason barely heard his voice. His mind was stunned by the enormity of what he had agreed to do, but there was no escaping it. Please God, Trotsky would be for peace.

When Mason was gone the Peacemaker poured himself a glass of Glenmorangie and was surprised to find his hand trembling. It was excitement, release of tension because finally he had succeeded in getting Mason back. To use him to contact Leon Trotsky was a stroke of genius. It would be the beginning of accomplishing a great goal.

He sipped the whisky and walked back to his chair, sitting down and crossing his legs. He relaxed at last. He had control again.

He had told Mason nothing of affairs at the Scientific Establishment in Cambridgeshire – not of the murder of Theo

Blaine, nor of the man the Peacemaker had so carefully placed in the heart of the work there. Mason did not need to know.

He also had not told him anything about his concerns over the safety of the German naval code. There was nothing specific that he could name, no incident, nothing said that made him think the British had broken it; it was just a sense of discomfort, a certain satisfaction in the manner of 'Blinker' Hall, a man for whom the Peacemaker had the most profound respect. Hall should have been more worried, more anxious than he was.

The Peacemaker had a plan to test it already well in progress. It involved Matthew Reavley, and his attraction to Detta Hannassey. She was a beautiful woman – in fact more than beautiful. She had grace and intelligence, a kind of fire inside her that few people possessed. She was unpredictable, daring, sometimes tender, a mixture of madness and sanity that was almost unique. Not surprising Reavley was fascinated by her. That could be used very well indeed. At the very best, the Peacemaker would find out if British Naval Intelligence had broken the code. If they had he would have to make sure Admiral Hall knew it was Reavley who had betrayed the fact, and that would give the Peacemaker a sharp, sweet pleasure. One day he would have to destroy Joseph Reavley too, but that could wait. Never place pleasure before business.

It was a pity Patrick Hannassey was becoming a nuisance. He might have to be got rid of quite soon.

The Peacemaker really was very pleased indeed that Mason had accepted the task to go to Paris. He quite genuinely liked him.

He took another sip of the whisky.

Chapter Seven

It was a fine day, and Joseph decided to walk to the village and visit a few other people he knew, particularly Tucky Nunn, who was home now, and Charlie Gee's mother, and Plugger Arnold's father. He took the stick, and Hannah watched him go down the path and out of the gates. He turned around once with a wry smile, knowing she was watching him, and then disappeared along the sunlit road, Henry trotting happily at his heels.

Hannah went back to her work, forcing the thoughts out of her mind as to how far he was recovered, whether he would ever really be completely strong again. She scrubbed the floor fiercely and moved everything around in the larder for no adequate reason. There was mending and ironing to do, and she wrote a long letter to Judith.

Joseph returned shortly after two, having eaten in the village. He looked tired, definitely limping quite badly, but extraordinarily pleased with himself.

'Look!' he said as soon as he was through the door. He produced out of a large paper bag a beautiful, softly curved pewter goblet with an ornate handle. The lines were simple, the sheen on it like dark grey satin.

'Oh, Joseph! It's gorgeous!' Hannah said enthusiastically. 'It will look really good on the shelf in your room. You need a few things to replace those you took with you to Flanders. This'll be perfect. How old is it?' She knew without asking that it was not a reproduction; Joseph would never accept such a thing. No doubt he had found it at the junk shop at the end of the High Street, where John Reavley had spent so many hours.

'It's not for me,' he answered happily. 'It's Shanley's birthday in a couple of weeks. I thought it would be perfect for him. Don't you think it would?'

She was momentarily confused.

He saw it in her face. 'You don't think so?' He was disappointed. 'He loves things like this. It's seventeenth century. It's real!'

'Of course it's real,' she said quietly. She saw the gentleness in his eyes, and with a lurch of sorrow so violent it caught her breath, she knew what had happened. She did not wish to tell him, but she had to. 'But Shanley's birthday isn't until next February, Joe. It's Father's birthday at the beginning of May.'

He stared at her.

She gulped. 'You . . . you just got them mixed up. It'll keep . . . if . . . if you want it to.'

Joseph stared at the goblet, frowning. 'I suppose I did,' he said. 'Stupid.' He stood up and went limping out into the hall and she heard his uneven step up the stairs.

She had dwelled on her own loneliness without Archie; she had hardly even thought about Joseph, so busy trying to deal with everybody else's fears and griefs he had no time for his own. He must miss his father appallingly. There had been a friendship between them nothing else could replace, but at times perhaps Shanley Corcoran came close. His warmth, his optimism and humour, his wealth of memories were more precious than probably she had any idea. It would be a good thing to give him the goblet, not to mark any occasion, just as a gift. She would say that to Joseph, later on.

In the afternoon she took a bundle of knitted squares to the village hall and was passed by Penny Lucas cycling along the road, and waved to her. She knew her slightly and had liked her warmth and enthusiasm, but she had not seen her in several weeks. Penny had no children, so perhaps she was involved in war work that had kept her out of St Giles.

Penny pulled in to the kerb ahead and dismounted with dexterity and a certain grace. She waited until Hannah caught up with her.

'How are you?' Hannah asked.

Penny gave a little gesture of resignation. She was a handsome woman with chestnut hair, blue-green eyes and a lightly freckled skin that always looked blemishless. Now some of the colour was gone from her cheeks, in spite of the exertion of bicycling.

'Well enough, I suppose,' she answered with a little shrug. 'How about you?'

Hannah smiled. 'A day at a time,' she replied.

Penny pushed the bicycle and they walked slowly side by side.

'I haven't seen you for ages,' Hannah went on. 'Are you doing something interesting?'

'Not really.' Penny gave a rueful smile. 'Just organizing the laundry room at the hospital in Cambridge. It's important, I suppose, but once you've got a system going it's hardly ground-breaking science.'

Her use of words jarred on Hannah, reminding her forcibly of Theo Blaine and his terrible death.

Penny must have seen it in her face. 'Sorry,' she apologized. 'I suppose it's at the top of everybody's mind. He was an extra-ordinary man, you know.' She brushed her skirt aside from being caught in the wheels of the bicycle. 'No, of course you wouldn't. He hardly had any time to know anyone. Corcoran works them all the hours they're awake, practically. It must be necessary, for the war, I suppose, but it's hard to take sometimes.' Her face tightened. 'He forgets that those men are young, and maybe not as obsessed with science and making history as he is.' She looked sideways at Hannah. 'Sorry again. He's a friend of yours, isn't he?'

'He was my father's closest friend, actually,' Hannah corrected her, wondering how Penny Lucas knew so much. She could remember meeting her husband, Dacy, only a couple of times. He was a quick-tempered man with a ready smile, who collected chessmen from various cultures, and liked to talk about them.

'But your friend too,' Penny added, watching her.

'Certainly, and he's my brother Joseph's godfather.'

'He's the one in the army? He was wounded, wasn't he? How is he?'

The baker's cart passed them, pulled by an old black horse, looking shiny in the sun, harness bright.

'Recovering, but it takes time,' Hannah replied.

'You'll miss him when he goes back.' Penny turned away, as if to guard some emotion she knew her eyes betrayed. It sounded from her voice like pain, a sudden loneliness too strong to govern.

Hannah wondered how well Penny had known Theo Blaine. Or was it someone else she was thinking of that hurt so deeply. Had she lost brothers or cousins in the war? 'Do you have family in France?' she asked aloud.

'No.' The word was oddly flat. 'We're all girls. My father's so ashamed of it. No sons to send to the Front.' She gave a little shiver, a gesture oddly vulnerable. 'He doesn't even think much of a son-in-law who works in a scientific place. It could be a factory, for all he perceives, except that it isn't really work – pushing a pen around. Actually Dacy works far longer hours than anyone else I know. Except Theo; he was really brilliant, probably one of the best brains alive today.' She took a breath and almost gagged on it. 'At least . . . yesterday. Isn't that awful!'

'Yes, it is,' Hannah agreed, taken aback by the depth of emotion in the other woman's voice. It seemed odd to stand together on the footpath in the sun, knowing each other so slightly and speaking of the deepest passions of life and loss as if they were friends. But that had probably happened to women all over the country. Just as the trenches made brothers of men, so the ripping apart of the old certainties, the aching loneliness of change and bereavement, made sisters of women who might never have known each other in peacetime. 'You think you can't bear it, except that there isn't any way out,' she added.

Penny straightened her shoulders and started to walk again. Plugger Arnold's father passed them, leading a shire horse, and Hannah smiled at him.

'That loathsome policeman keeps coming around asking questions,' Penny said angrily. 'Poking and prying into our lives. I

don't suppose he's going through my laundry basket, but I feel
as if I can't even take a bath without the chance that he'll knock
on the door to see how much hot water I'm using.'

'It must be a very difficult job.' Hannah matched her step to
Penny's. 'Where could he even start? If there really is a German
spy in St Giles, it could be pretty well anyone, couldn't it?'

'I suppose so,' Penny agreed. 'It's a horrible thought!
Although I can think of dozens it wouldn't be. He wouldn't
even bother with the old village families, especially those with
sons or brothers at the Front. When you think of it, that doesn't
leave many.'

'He'll have to look in the other villages near enough to drive
to, anyway,' Hannah reasoned.

'You wouldn't get a car down that back lane,' Penny pointed
out. 'You'd scratch it to pieces and leave tyre tracks all over the
place. Our busy inspector would have seen them. Maybe that's
why he's questioning everyone close enough to walk . . . or, I
suppose, bicycle.' She gave a rueful little smile. 'It's incredibly
grubby!' Then suddenly she was angry again. 'I hate it! It's not
his fault, but I hate him too, with his devious remarks and probing
little eyes, as if he's all the time imagining . . . I don't know what.
Think what it would be like married to such a man who spends
his days pawing through the sins and tragedies of other people's
lives?' She waved her hand, dismissing it. 'I'm sorry. You haven't
even met him. How could you know?'

Thoughts raced through Hannah's mind, memories of things
she had said and done that she would prefer no one knew – not
necessarily bad things, just foolish. But she had thought of other
things too, about Ben Morven, the way he laughed, the easy way
he walked, the look of his throat in a clean cotton shirt. He had
good hands, brown and slender.

Was that why Penny Lucas felt so very strongly about Perth
that it frightened her? Did she know the narrowness of the back
way to Theo Blaine's house because she had been there?

'Do you know Mrs Blaine?' Hannah said aloud.

Penny was caught by surprise. Her face had a closed look. 'Well
. . . a bit, of course. Theo worked with my husband.'

What an odd way of putting it! She did not speak of Theo as Lizzie Blaine's husband, as if she wanted to avoid the thought.

'Why?' Penny demanded, her blue-green eyes narrowed.

'I was thinking how dreadful she must feel,' Hannah lied. 'It's an awful way to lose someone. I hope she has good friends – I mean other than just people like the vicar, or . . . or that sort of thing.'

Penny looked at the road ahead. 'We all lose people, especially these days. I don't really know if she has friends or not. She's rather a cold, self-contained sort of person. We each deal with things as we can.'

'Of course. And I expect the policeman will bother her most of all.'

Penny stopped abruptly, swinging around, her eyes wide and angry. 'What do you mean by that?'

'I don't know.' Hannah assumed an expression of innocence close to apology. 'I suppose because she must have known him best, and the home, the garden, everything.'

Penny looked beaten. The courage and spirit inside her were suddenly deflated.

'I'm so sorry,' Hannah said quickly, pity overtaking sense. 'I can't imagine what it's like to lose someone you know and have been friends with in such a way.' She had grown so used to the lie that her parents' deaths had been an accident that she almost believed it herself. And regardless of that, she knew, from the time Joseph had told her, that it must never be spoken of. 'If . . . if you want to talk to anyone who understands a bit, my brother would listen,' she offered to Penny. 'A couple of years ago one of his very best friends was murdered. That's how he knows Inspector Perth. It was pretty awful.'

'Really?' It was surprise in Penny's face, but not much more than polite interest. 'Perhaps. Just now I need to get home. I have a mountain of things to do, and I'm due back at the hospital in the morning. Thanks for . . .' She did not know how to finish the sentence, and she mounted her bicycle and with a quick smile, pedalled away with considerable speed, leaving the words unsaid.

Hannah stood on the kerbside and watched Penny Lucas go,

her blouse billowing in the wind and the sun bright on her hair, until she disappeared round the curve in the road. She seemed to feel the loss of Theo Blaine very deeply indeed, and yet she obviously did not like his wife, or know her very well.

Was it possible she had had a love affair with Blaine, and her husband had discovered it? Was that what Perth was sensing, searching to prove, and that was why Penny felt so threatened and intruded upon?

If she had met Theo Blaine secretly, where would it be? And when? Certainly not where he had been killed, but what about the woods beyond? Hardly in the winter, but in the spring or summer? Only in the evening. Too much chance of children playing in daylight.

But outside of romantic novels, did people really make love in the woods? It would be uncomfortable, almost certainly damp and a bit muddy, and with a hideous chance of being stumbled on by someone out walking their dog, or an enthusiastic botanist or collector of butterflies. What a ghastly embarrassment! She felt her own face colour, and in spite of herself, visualized it and began to giggle.

So much for illicit passion in the woods!

It would not do to find anywhere in the small villages either. Someone would be bound to find out sooner or later. You could hardly sneeze without it being noticed. You would be inviting disaster, crude jokes, even a little grubby, small-time blackmail.

She walked slowly, thinking. Really you would have to go somewhere big enough for you to remain anonymous, and that meant Cambridge. Penny was there anyway, at her duties in the hospital. What about Theo Blaine? He would have a car to drive to and from the Establishment. He could very easily go to Cambridge. The Establishment would think he had gone home, Lizzie Blaine would think he was working late.

Perhaps Dacy Lucas had even borrowed Penny's bicycle to go along the back lane through the trees to confront Blaine, and they had quarrelled. Blaine had refused to give up his affair, and Lucas had attacked him in fury? Or perhaps Lucas had threatened to tell Lizzie Blaine, and Blaine had attacked him, and Lucas had defended himself rather too well? Then seeing what he had done, he had been horrified and run away. Who would believe he had not meant it?

Hannah was walking more slowly, unaware of passers-by.

Probably Inspector Perth knew all this. But what if he did not? He might still be convinced that the murderer was a German spy. That thought was so horrible she felt suddenly as if her own home had been violated, someone dirty and violent had broken in and soiled everything. It would take months, years before it could be made clean again.

Perhaps she should tell Perth at least where to look! She had grown up with the code of honour that you did not tell tales on people, and if you were caught in something you owned up to it. Above all, you never ever let someone else take the punishment for what you had done. That was the ultimate cowardice.

But this was different. How much would everyone suffer if Perth stayed in the village and continued going through everybody's lives, poking and prying, awakening suspicions, resurrecting old feuds? There was more than enough grief already, and no doubt more to come. The first whispers of suspicion had started.

Without realizing it, she had changed direction and was walking more briskly again, toward the railway station.

Inspector Perth was not in when Hannah arrived at the police station in Cambridge, and she had to wait over half an hour before he came. He looked hot and tired, as if his feet hurt, which quite possibly they did. His shoes were worn down at the sides and he limped a little.

'Yes, Mrs MacAllister, what can I do for you?' He waited until she was seated, then lowered himself into the chair opposite her, taking his weight off his legs with visible relief.

Briefly and quite succinctly she told him what she had heard, and what she suspected.

'Really?' He was guarded, but certainly not without interest. 'She was on a bicycle, you say?'

'Yes. Most people ride bicycles in Cambridgeshire, especially now. It's the best way to get around.'

'I know that, ma'am. I'm local born and bred,' he said patiently. 'A lady's bicycle that'd be?'

'Yes, of course!'

'You didn't happen to notice her hands, did you?'

'Not particularly. Why?'

'She didn't have a little cut or scratch, or a plaster, maybe? About here.' He indicated a small sticking plaster on his own hand, across the palm near the base of his forefinger.

'I don't think so. I don't remember. Why? You . . .' Her imagination raced. 'How did you do that?'

'You don't want to know that, ma'am.' He winced slightly.

'You picked up . . . the . . . fork!' She realized with a shiver why he was reluctant to tell her.

'Yes, ma'am. It's just a little sort of nick. A screw sitting a bit too high. But it drew blood, all right. Tore the skin.'

She had not really looked at Penny Lucas's hands. It was a repulsive idea to allow into her mind that she could have had such a bestial rage that she would have killed Theo.

'If she picked it up, couldn't you tell?' she asked.

'No, ma'am. Whoever used it smeared it with so much mud there was nothing to see. No fingerprints at all, nor any blood. Could be they had gloves.'

'Why would she kill him?' she asked. 'If she loved him . . .'

'In love, Mrs MacAllister,' Perth corrected sadly. 'It's a very different kind of a thing, sometimes. It's about wanting, sort of owning, not about caring what happens to the other person. I've known people kill someone they reckoned was unfaithful to them. Or maybe just rejected them, let them down hard.'

'I don't . . .' she began, then stopped.

'Course you don't,' Perth agreed. 'Nobody does. Wouldn't need detectives in the police if it were clear. Thank you for coming in.'

She left, feeling queasy in her stomach. She was wrong for coming, and yet if she had not come, that would have been wrong too. There was no good path.

She walked back towards the station to catch the next train home and was almost there when she nearly bumped into Ben

Morven crossing the road and apparently going the same way. His face lit up with pleasure immediately.

'We'll make the next one easily,' he said. Then he frowned, looking at her more closely. 'You all right?'

'Does it show that much?' She was rueful.

He blushed. 'Sorry. That was a bit clumsy. But you look as if something nasty has happened.'

She saw the anxiety in his eyes and found herself laughing. 'I've been talking to that miserable policeman,' she told him. 'I really can't bear the thought that either there is a German spy in St Giles who killed poor Mr Blaine to stop his work, or that there was some sort of personal hatred so awful that it ended in murder.'

'I'm afraid I don't see any other conclusion,' Ben said unhappily as they continued towards the station, crossing the road through the traffic and up on to the kerb again. 'From what I hear it could hardly have been an accident,' he went on.

'No.' Hannah refused to picture it in her mind.

He took her arm, not roughly, but his strength was enough to draw her to a stop. 'Don't think about it, Hannah. Leave it to Perth. It's his job and he probably knows how to do it. Either you'll waste your time and learn nothing, or you'll discover a whole lot of things about people you would far rather not know. We all need a little space . . .' he hesitated, letting go of her. 'A little room to cover our mistakes and let them go. It's a lot easier to do better next time, if last time isn't printed in your neighbours' eyes.'

They were in the way of the crowd, but she did not care. She looked at him gravely. 'You knew him. Did you like him?'

'Yes,' Ben said without prevarication. 'Actually he was a good chap, nicely eccentric. A bit selfish at times, but I think that was because he was so absorbed in his work he didn't realize that most people didn't even know what he was doing, let alone care. I did like him.'

'Was he really brilliant? I mean – someone who would go down in history, like Newton, or . . . whoever?'

He smiled slightly. 'I'm not sure, but I think so.'

'Might he hurt somebody without meaning to, just because he

wasn't . . . paying attention to them?' She did not know how to phrase it without being obvious.

He understood immediately. 'You mean like Lizzie?'

'Or anyone else,' she added.

'I don't know.' He frowned. 'Lizzie wasn't in that evening. I telephoned to speak to Theo. I called two or three times, but there was no answer. I suppose I'm going to have to tell that damn policeman, if he asks. I'd rather not. I like her too.'

'Does that make a difference?' Hannah asked candidly.

He lifted his shoulders a little. 'No, I suppose not. And as long as he doesn't have the answer, he'll go on looking, turning the village inside out and opening old wounds of all sorts. Somebody did it. We have to know who. Poor Theo. What a terrible way to die.' He took her arm again. 'Come on, or we might miss the train.'

They hurried along the pavement and went in through the entrance to find the platform crowded with people. A troop train had just pulled in, carrying wounded from the Front, and everywhere they turned there were white-faced women hopeful of seeing the ones they loved, eyes wide and dark with fear as to how bad it would be. Some had heard only a little news and were almost numb with the exhaustion of waiting.

The engine still belched steam, doors clanged to, voices were shouting, echoing in the vast roofs above. Someone called out for help, orders were barked. Nurses in grey uniforms were trying to organize stretchers, find ambulance drivers. Porters were doing their best to get the most severely wounded away first.

Hannah could see motionless figures lying on stretchers; some were bandaged. One she saw very clearly had thick swathes of cloth, already bloodied, where his right leg should have been. She thought of Joseph, and how easily that could have happened to him.

'I've got to help,' Ben said urgently, cutting through the clamour in her mind. 'I'll get the next train. I can carry some of these. You go on.'

'Maybe I can help too,' she answered without thinking. What use was she?

'Come on then,' he agreed. 'You might be able to steady someone, lend a hand.'

They worked without consciousness of time. Their train to St Giles came and went. Ben helped carry stretchers and load them into the waiting ambulances; Hannah lent her strength and balance to walking wounded, grey-faced, exhausted with sleeplessness and pain.

It was over an hour before they were all gone, and the medical orderlies had thanked them. Hannah was rumpled and marked with dust and occasional smears of blood. Her shoes were scuffed where she had been accidentally trodden on.

Ben was far more creased and his shirt was torn and soiled. He pushed his hair back and smiled at her. There was no need for words between them – it was a kind of silent victory.

'You have blood on your face,' she noticed. 'Have you a hand-kerchief?'

'Have I? Oh.' He shook his head. 'It's just off my hand. I caught it on a rough piece on one of the stretchers.' He looked at it. It was on his left hand, just below the base of his index finger, exactly where Inspector Perth had caught himself on Blaine's garden fork. Only Ben's was fresh, and still bleeding, a small tear, caused by gripping something sharp.

Hannah felt ice sudden inside her.

'Don't tell me blood makes you faint!' he said incredulously. 'You've just been helping people with real wounds!'

She controlled herself with an effort, trying to smooth the horror out of her eyes. 'No, of course not! Nobody with children is. I was just thinking . . . I don't know what. I suppose remembering Joseph coming back. He was such a mess. I dread him having to go again. It could be worse next time.'

'Don't think of next time.' He tried to smile at her, anxiety in his face, and gentleness. 'Maybe there won't be one. The war's got to finish one day. It could be soon. Come on, or we'll miss this train too.' He moved swiftly towards the platform where the engine was coming in, gushing steam in clouds and the doors were beginning to swing open ready for people to alight.

*　　*　　*

138

The following afternoon Perth came again to see Joseph. They went out into the garden, followed by Henry, and through the gate at the bottom into the orchard, partly to avoid any chance of being overheard by one of the children when they came home from school.

Perth looked tired and harassed. Joseph remembered that expression from St John's two years ago, and all the misery of suspicion then. Except that in St John's he had known that whoever had committed the crime had to be either one of his own students, or a lecturer who was at least a colleague, more probably a friend. This time there was no such certainty. He was ashamed of how precious that relief was.

'Not much progress,' Perth said lugubriously. 'Haven't found anyone with a cut on their hand, and I've looked. But it does seem, from information given, that it's possible Mr Blaine was having an affair with the wife of one of his colleagues.' He gave Joseph a startlingly penetrating glance, then turned away again to watch a thrush land on the grass near one of the apple trees. 'Need some rain to bring the worms up,' he added.

'And the bicycle?' Joseph asked.

Perth shook his head. 'Can't find anyone willing to say they saw it. Least not at a time of any use to us. We know when he must have got home, because of when he left the Establishment, and that's certain.' He chewed his lip. 'Not that Mrs Blaine says any different. He ate his dinner. They had a quarrel about something and nothing, she says, and he went outside and she stayed in and had a long bath. Nobody to prove that right or wrong. But then there likely wouldn't be. Was after dark, so not many people out, and no one anywhere to see a lone cyclist along the lane, which no doubt the cyclist was counting on.'

'If it was after dark, a cyclist would have a light,' Joseph pointed out. 'Only a fool would cycle along a wooded track in the dark. Asking to trip over a tree root, or even a pothole. That lane has plenty of them. And lots of people might take a dog out for a last walk.'

Perth looked at Henry, happily rooting around in the long grass. 'Don't have a dog myself,' he said regretfully. 'But you're right. I'll have to go and ask all the dog owners again: did one fellow see a woman on a bicycle, half a mile away from the Blaines' house? Bit odd, though, don't you think? Could you see a woman doing a thing like that, Captain Reavley?'

'No,' Joseph said honestly. In spite of all the death he had seen, the thought of a woman knocking a man down and then, when he was on the ground, deliberately tearing his neck with the tines of a garden fork, was sickening.

Perth looked at him unhappily. 'Thing is, Captain, if he was killed by a German spy in the village, who would that be? And why Blaine rather than any of the other scientists up at the Establishment?'

'Opportunity?' Joseph suggested. 'Maybe whoever it is was watching everyone, and Blaine was the first one who gave him a really good chance.'

Henry put up a couple of birds and went charging after them, barking.

Perth watched him dolefully. 'Doesn't work out that way,' he argued. 'Been asking around a bit, looking into who was where, and that sort of thing. Plenty of chances to kill Mr Iliffe, if anyone wanted to. Wanders around by himself quite a lot, it seems. Goes down to his local pub of an evening, and across back through the lanes to his house after dark. Single man. No reason why he shouldn't. Relax his thoughts after a long day working on figures, and the like. Says he never thought of any danger. Same with young Morven. Could have caught him, if anyone'd been trying. Lives alone. Got a cottage out on the Haslingfield Road. Small place. Easy broke into, if you'd a mind. Could look like a burglary.'

'Then I don't know,' Joseph admitted. 'Looks as if they wanted Blaine. Mr Corcoran told me he was the best mind in the place, brilliant and original.'

Henry came trotting back, wagging his tail, and Joseph bent slightly to acknowledge him.

'Nice dog, that,' Perth observed. 'Always wanted one of them. So we come to the question of who knew that Mr Blaine was so important? And another thing – why now?' He looked at Joseph with a challenge. 'Why not a month ago, or next week? Chance again? I don't like chance, Captain Reavley. I've found that it doesn't play much of a role in these things. Mostly when people do something like murder, there's a pretty big reason for it. I want to know what that reason was, and who knew about it.'

'If Blaine really was crucial to the work they're doing,' Joseph said thoughtfully, 'then I imagine everyone at the Establishment would know it, and probably those immediately connected with him, such as Mrs Blaine, and perhaps the wives of the other scientists there.'

'That says who,' Perth agreed. 'And people talk. A woman would be proud of her husband. Perhaps a little rivalry, a little boasting? If there's a spy in the village, then he'll be listening to every bit of gossip there is. That's his job. Still leaves the question, why now? What happened that day, or the day before?'

'Something to do with the work at the Establishment,' Joseph replied. 'I suppose you've spoken to Mr Corcoran?'

'Oh, yes. He says they were getting very close to a breakthrough on some secret project they have. Couldn't tell me what, of course.'

'That's significant if the murderer was a spy, and the motive not some personal enmity,' Joseph said.

'Exactly. And if Mr Blaine really was having an affair with someone, then it would likely have been nothing to do with the work.'

'Any reason to suppose he was?'

'Looks like it, Captain. Which is a pity. And seems as if Mrs Blaine might not have been in the house, as she says she was. Could have been she was just in the bathroom like she said, and didn't hear the telephone. Hard to say, isn't it?' He looked around at the apple trees. 'You'll have a good crop, if the wind doesn't get them. Lose a few myself. Set all right, then the wind knocks them off before they're ripe. Not that I've as many trees as you have, of course.'

'They're mostly cookers,' Joseph told him. 'Do you really think Blaine was having an affair? Not just a possibility you have to consider?'

'Consider,' Perth agreed sadly. 'Consider carefully. Very fond of an apple pie. Nothing to beat it, with a good drop of cream on. Have to be new to the village, this spy. Can't see any of the old families turning a hand to such a thing. Most of them got boys up the Front anyway. Been looking into who's come here in the last couple or three years. Since about 1913, say. Not many. For example, what do you know about the vicar, Captain? You being a churchman, and all, how do you reckon him?'

Joseph was startled. It had never crossed his mind to think of Hallam Kerr as other than the kind of man who falls into the Church as an occupation because he really isn't adequate to make a respectable living at any other profession. It would offer him the kind of security and social standing to which his family might well be accustomed, and allowed him to expect from life. The fact that he was totally unsuited for it may only have become apparent after he was ordained.

'Not naturally gifted,' Perth observed wryly.

Joseph caught a flash of humour in his eyes. 'No,' he agreed. 'Not at all.'

'And no wife to help him either,' Perth added. 'Is that usual, Captain?'

'Not for a parish, no. But then wartime isn't usual. The previous vicar went to Birmingham, I believe. Needed in a bigger area. More to do than here. And now his curate's gone to London.' Was it even conceivable that Kerr was not the ass he appeared, but something far more sinister? It was a peculiarly chilling thought because it was so unexpected.

'No, it isn't,' Perth agreed. 'It's mighty different. You've been a priest, Captain. In a way you still are. What's your opinion, sir? Is he good?'

Joseph was embarrassed now. Kerr irritated him, but part of that very irritation was because he was sorry for the man. Pity was an acutely uncomfortable feeling.

Perth was waiting, watching his face.

'He's inadequate,' Joseph replied. 'But what can you say or do for those you visit who are faced with unbearable suffering that you can do nothing to help? Who can explain God to someone who has just lost everything they care about in a way which seems totally senseless? You can't hold Kerr accountable because he can't either.'

Perth shook his head very slowly.

'Isn't it a matter of degree, Captain Reavley? You can't help it all, just some of it. Have the courage at least to look at it square, and not tell people lies, or speak to them in quotes.'

That was more perceptive than Joseph had expected and it took him aback. 'Yes,' he agreed quickly. 'And Kerr has a lot to learn yet, but that doesn't mean to say he won't.'

'No, sir, I dare say not. All the same, I think I'd like to find out a bit more about him. Where he's from, and where he trained for the ministry, things like that. Did he know Mr Blaine, do you know?'

'I have no idea.'

'Maybe you could find out, sir, without putting the wind up him, like? I'd be greatly obliged.'

In the event, Joseph was prevented from deciding when to go to see Kerr, or how to explain his visit. That evening Kerr arrived at the front door and Hannah had no acceptable alternative but to show him in to the sitting room where Joseph had been reading.

'Don't stand up!' Kerr said quickly, holding out his hand as if to keep Joseph in his seat by force. He looked harassed and frightened. There were shadows around his eyes and a tightness in his mouth. In the morning he had probably parted his hair in the middle and plastered it down with water, but now it was dry and poked up in spikes.

'Sit down, Reverend,' Joseph invited, trying to sound at least reasonably welcoming. The man was obviously in some distress. 'How are you?'

Hannah drew in her breath to offer him tea, but he was already oblivious of her. She shrugged very slightly and withdrew, closing the door behind her. Joseph knew, with a sinking heart, that she would not interrupt them.

'This is terrible,' Kerr replied, sitting down wearily in the chair opposite Joseph. 'In a way it's worse than war. It's the ultimate enemy, isn't it? Fear, suspicion, everyone thinking the worst. We aren't united any more. Or were we ever? Was it only a comfortable delusion?'

143

Joseph could not find the energy to argue with him, but Perth's words came back with a darkness that seemed more intense now. Was it really possible Kerr was a German agent or sympathizer?

'What's happened?' he asked. In the end that was the question that mattered.

Kerr leaned forward in the chair. 'One of my parishioners – I can't name them, of course – told me that on the night poor Blaine was murdered, this person overheard Dacy Lucas and his wife quarrelling violently! It was very angry, shouting voices, both his and hers, and then he stormed out of the house and drove away.'

'People do quarrel occasionally,' Joseph replied. 'It doesn't mean a great deal.'

Kerr did not look in the least soothed or reassured – in fact, if anything he seemed more agitated. 'It was not a slight or usual thing,' he said urgently. 'I am not married myself, but I know that women can feel neglected at times. They don't understand the moral and ethical demands of certain callings, and during wartime scientific invention and discovery must be at the fore-front of our endeavours. Perhaps it would be easier to understand if a man were in the army, but all that is irrelevant.' He jerked his hand sideways to dismiss it. 'In this quarrel – and it was a quarrel, Captain Reavley, not just a little complaint – jealousy of the worst, most terrible kind was spoken quite unmistakably.'

For a moment Joseph wondered what was the worst kind of jealousy to Kerr, as if there were any kind that was acceptable. But remembering what Perth had said, he understood the euphemism.

'I see,' he said quietly, not sure whether he wanted Blaine's murder to be ordinary sexual rage instead of a German sympathizer in the village. Perhaps he did. They had seen and understood that since the dawn of mankind. There was betrayal in it, but of one man, not an entire community.

'That is not all,' Kerr went on miserably. 'Theo Blaine, the dead man, quarrelled with his wife the same night, also very savagely. He left the house to go down to his shed in the garden, which is where he was killed. Mrs Blaine swore that she did not leave the house, but neither did she see nor hear anything at all to make her suspect something wrong. At least that is what she says.' He stared at Joseph expectantly.

'Oh.' Joseph sat still, wondering how Kerr knew all this. It was an old story with many possibilities, all of them sad and very predictable.

'Can that be true?' Kerr demanded, leaning forward a little, and staring at Joseph. 'Do you suppose she really saw and heard nothing?'

'I should think so.' Joseph tried to remember the Blaine house from his visit there. The shed was some distance even from the back door, let alone the front where the sitting room was, and the main bedroom faced the front as well. 'If he did not cry out, there wouldn't be much to hear. Let Inspector Perth sort it out.'

'But that's it!' Kerr said desperately. 'He doesn't know!'

'Know?' Perth had to be aware of the proportions of the house and garden.

Kerr was exasperated. 'He doesn't know about the quarrels! I was told in the utmost confidence, by a parishioner, don't you see?'

Joseph was familiar with parishioners' utmost confidences. 'They will have to use their judgement whether to report it to the police or not,' he said to Kerr. 'You did not hear those quarrels yourself, so you have no knowledge of them—'

'But I do!' Kerr protested. 'The person who told me is absolutely honest. I have known them for years, and there is not the slightest malice in them. They were distressed, I may say terrified, that the poison that there is an enemy sympathizer among us will spread, when in fact it may be no more than a domestic tragedy, with no one else involved at all.'

'Is there really so much fear that we have a sympathizer here?' Joseph asked, uncertain quite what answer he wanted. Was one betrayal better or worse than the tragedy of murder by one of their own?

'Yes!' Kerr's eyes opened wider. 'Of course there is. It is a terrible thing to believe that one of us is actually an enemy. Surely you, of all people, must understand that? Our men are giving their lives out there in France, in terrible conditions, to save England.' He flung his arm out sharply. 'And here is this person willing, even eager, to sell us to Germany by murder and treason. It's . . . it's so evil it defies imagination.' His cheeks were stained with pink, his eyes bright.

'And what about our spies in Germany?' Joseph asked, thinking of Perth's suspicions. Then, seeing the look on Kerr's face, he wished instantly that he had not. The man was confused, and because he did not understand, he perceived himself to be attacked, and was angry.

'I don't know what you mean!' he protested. 'Are you suggesting there is no difference between us, Captain Reavley? If that were so, why on earth would our young men be fighting and dying out there? What you are saying is manifestly ridiculous.'

'In theory there's all the difference in the world,' Joseph said wearily. If Kerr were really a German agent as Perth had considered, then his acting skill amounted to genius. 'When it comes to fact,' he went on, 'the difference isn't much more than that they are fighting against us, whereas we are fighting against them.'

'I don't know what you mean!' Kerr repeated.

'I'm not sure that I do either,' Joseph conceded, although it was not the truth, it was just pointless to argue. 'Are you so sure that God is an Englishman? Might He not see little difference between one nationality and another, only between a man who does the best he can, and one who doesn't?'

Kerr blinked. It was quite clear in his face that he was being presented with a vast idea that had never occurred to him before. Suddenly the simple had become savagely and impossibly complicated.

Joseph was sorry he had given the man more than he could accommodate, but he could not bring himself to say so. One thing he was convinced of: Perth was utterly wrong – Kerr was every bit as big an ass as he seemed.

'It's probably a domestic tragedy, just as you're supposing,' he said quietly. Conscience demanded that he be kinder to the man. 'But leave it to Perth to find out. He's really very good. I've seen him work before. He'll uncover the truth, but carefully, piece by piece, without error. All you can do is tell him what you know, not what other people have told you. They may be malicious, or simply mistaken, and you would unwittingly compound the injustice. If the time should ever come when you know for certain that the wrong person may be convicted, then reconsider. But we are far from that now. You can't carry the world. Don't try. You'll break your back, and that won't help anyone. Then you'll be no use for when you are needed by the next person who requires your comfort or help.'

Kerr gulped, but his shoulders were relaxed, his hands still. 'Yes,' he said, then again more firmly. 'Yes, of course. You are very wise. Very fair. I'm sorry I didn't see that at first.'

Now Joseph was ashamed for his abruptness. He made himself smile. 'I should have explained myself a little more clearly.'

Kerr stared at him. 'It's all . . . it's so alien! Everything's changing.'

Joseph thought that it was not so much that the world was changing as that they were being forced to see it more realistically. He did not say so. 'Yes,' he agreed, feeling like a hypocrite. 'I think it's hard, one way or another, for everyone.'

Kerr was obviously still disturbed about something. 'This man Perth,' he said anxiously, 'he's digging up all sorts of things about people that have nothing to do with poor Blaine's death. Indiscretions, old quarrels which were beginning to heal!' He waved his hand uselessly. 'It's like tearing the bandages off everyone's wounds. I've tried, but I can't do anything to stop him. I feel so . . . helpless! People expect me to look after them, and I can't!'

Joseph felt a sudden, completely humble sympathy for him. 'People expect too much of us altogether,' he said ruefully. 'A bit like doctors. We can't cure everything, only ease the pain a bit, and give advice which they don't have to take. And they'll quite possibly blame us if it goes wrong, when we never said it wouldn't, they just chose to believe it. Perhaps that was the only way they could cope.'

'I'm . . . I'm so grateful to talk to you,' Kerr said impulsively, his face pink. 'This whole thing is quite dreadful. The other young men at the Establishment can't prove where they were when Blaine was killed either. Everyone is under suspicion. And of course they knew him. It could simply have been a personal dislike, I suppose, a rivalry or quarrel over work. Do you think?'

'It would be an easier answer for the village, if not for the war effort,' Joseph conceded. 'I understand what you mean.'

'Good. Good. You've been very kind.' Kerr rose to his feet, satisfied. He stood straight, as if with some new sort of strength. 'I'm very grateful to you, Captain. You see it all so clearly.'

Joseph did not deny it. That was a truth Kerr did not need. Joseph had made sufficient difficulties for him for one visit.

After Kerr had gone he walked outside in the garden. The spring evening was mild and close. The air was still full of gold from the lowering sun. There was no breeze to whisper in the branches of the elms, but the starlings whirled up in huge flocks, wheeling against the blue of the sky and the shredded mares' tails of cloud glowing to the west.

He stood alone amid the burning colour of the tulips, crimson and purple and hot scarlets. Kerr had been satisfied when he had finally gone, perhaps because he no longer felt alone in his responsibility. That was what Joseph had promised himself when he had first committed his life to being a chaplain in the war. He would try to do what he could for everyone, regardless of their need. He could not cure, he could not even share physical or emotional pain, but he could be there. At least he would not run away.

But had he turned away inside himself? By trying to be all things to others, had he ended being nothing to himself? He had said what he thought Kerr needed to hear. He was thinking of Kerr's weakness, his very apparent confusion. He was doing the same for Hannah, thinking of her fear of change, of losing the familiar that was so sweet.

In all that he said and did, where was his own passion, his integrity, that part of mind or spirit that was so rooted in belief that it would anchor him no matter what storms blew? What would he live or die for? What would hold him upright if he faced the ultimate storm and there was no one else to consider, no single voice that cried 'Help me!' and gave him something to do, a direction to consume his thoughts so he had no time and no need to examine himself?

If he faced the silence, where was his inner strength? What colour was the chameleon itself? No colour at all? Nothing, except as reflected by others? That would be a kind of moral suicide, the final emptiness. Is that what he was doing to himself?

He prayed with all his heart. 'Father, do I stay here and pick up the task Kerr can't and won't do? These are my people too! Or do I go back to the trenches, the mud and the stench of death, and be with my men there? What do You want me to do? Help me!'

The starlings wheeled back and settled in the elms. The light was deepening, the colours in the sky growing hotter. The silence was total.

Chapter Eight

Hannah walked away slowly from the women gathered in the street around the casualty notices. There had been one man killed from Cherry Hinton, another missing from Haslingfield, no one from St Giles. Relief welled up inside all the people standing together. They could look each other in the eye for a while longer. There were hesitant smiles, the freedom to think of ordinary things: mending and sewing, shopping, work, the upcoming Easter weekend. But voices were quiet, hushed with the weight of knowing that just beyond that sloping hill, the copse of trees, the spire of the next village church, was the loss that next time might be here.

Hannah walked homeward slowly in the still, damp morning. The sun broke through in misty shafts, making everything silver and green, shining through the raindrops on twigs and grass heads. Some of the early blossom had blown off and lay in white petals on the path.

She was a couple of hundred yards from the corner when she met Ben Morven coming out of the ironmonger's. He was wearing a corduroy jacket over a crisp, white shirt and grey slacks. His face lit up with pleasure seeing her. It was really out of all proportion, but his smile suddenly lifted her spirits also, and she found her step lighter and a warmth inside. She remembered how he had worked at the railway station in Cambridge, the intensity of his concentration, trying not to jolt the injured, to be quick and gentle, and how he had ignored his own bruises.

He fell into step beside her, matching his stride to hers.

'The news is not very good,' she said, biting her lip. 'Apparently someone has been arrested bringing a vast amount of guns into Ireland. As if we hadn't enough trouble there already.'

He shook his head. 'I heard. It's insane. The last thing anyone needs is more turmoil in Ireland! They can't win – we can't afford to let them! It'll just mean more bloodshed.' He glanced around at the peaceful, almost deserted street, the tension gone, the people dispersed. A little brown dog scampered along the footpath. Two young girls stood absorbed in conversation. An old man sat in the seat near the duck pond, chewing on the stem of his pipe. The wind gusted, but it was warm to the skin.

'There's so much bad news at the moment,' Ben added. 'I sometimes wonder if we are all insane. Or perhaps I'll wake up and discover it's still 1914, and all this never happened. It's me that's wrong, not the rest of the world.'

'I'd like that,' she said quietly. 'I would give anything I can think of to go back to the way it used to be. It was so . . .'

'Sane,' he said with a smile, his eyes bright and soft.

'Yes, it was, wasn't it! Do you think it will ever be like that again, when the war is over?' She wanted him to say it would, even if he could not know or dared not believe.

'Yes, of course it will.' He did not hesitate and his voice was full of warmth. 'We'll make it. It may take a little time, and there'll be so many people to look after. But we haven't changed inside. We still believe the same things, love the same things. We'll heal, like getting over an illness. The fever breaks, then we begin to get our strength back.' He gave her a quick, bright glance. 'Maybe it will give us an immunity?'

She smiled; it was such a commonplace idea it made sense. 'Like getting the measles, or chicken pox?'

'Yes,' he agreed. 'Exactly. We'll have had a dose so strong we'll never do it again. If you get burned badly enough, you don't ever go near the fire in the future.'

'I like that!' she said quickly. 'Then perhaps in a hideous way it would even be worth it. We would crown our folly with something so awful that future generations would learn from it. Then our price would have bought something worth having. Thank you . . .'

He looked at her with a softness in his eyes so undisguised she was suddenly embarrassed. For the first time it was impossible for her to mistake his thoughts.

The moment broke with a shriek of outrage twenty yards up the street and Hannah was so startled she froze, the blood hot in her face.

Ben jerked round and stared.

Mrs Oundle, a very large lady in a green dress, was standing outside the butcher's shop, clutching a torn piece of paper, and the brown dog was racing across the road with a brace of lamb chops in his mouth.

The old man on the bench beside the village pond stood up and reached out to stop the dog, who veered sideways, splashing through the water and soaking the man. Mrs Oundle was still shrieking.

The butcher came out to see what the trouble was and she rounded on him furiously. Two little boys hopped up and down in glee, then when Mrs Oundle saw them, turned and fled, boots clattering on the pavement.

Hannah tried to stifle her laughter and totally failed.

The dog dropped the chops in the water and started to bark.

Ben doubled over, tears of delight running down his cheeks.

Mrs Oundle and the butcher both got angrier and angrier, but it was no use at all, Hannah was incapable of stopping laughing either. All the fear and misery exploded inside her in a glorious release of hilarity, and the sheer joy of sharing it with someone else who saw the divine absurdity of it in exactly the same way as she did. There was no point in even trying to apologize to Mrs Oundle. For a start, she was not sorry, and everyone could see that. On the contrary, she was supremely grateful for the sane absurdity of it.

She took Ben's arm and they turned away, still laughing.

The brown dog was ducky-diving in the pond to find his chops and Mrs Oundle and the butcher were sizing each other up to decide who was to blame, when Ben left Hannah at her gate where Joseph was pulling weeds, one-handed, in the garden.

He spoke briefly to Ben, then followed Hannah inside to the kitchen.

'Tea?' she asked, still smiling. 'Thank you for doing the weeding.' She filled the kettle under the tap.

'It's my garden,' Joseph replied.

She froze. It was an extraordinary remark. She turned around slowly to face him. He was standing in the middle of the kitchen floor; his sleeve was rolled up, his good arm slightly scratched, and stained with mud and the green sap of grasses.

'Why did you say that?' she asked. 'I know perfectly well that this is your house. When the war is over, and you come back here, I shall return to Portsmouth, or wherever Archie . . . if he is still alive . . . is posted. Or are you saying that you are going to stay here, and you want it back now?'

He blushed. 'No, of course I'm not. I meant it's fair that I do something of the work to keep it up, while I'm here. And even if I do stay, it's still your home for as long as you want it to be.'

'But you might stay?' she asked eagerly, ignoring the fact that something had obviously angered him.

'I don't know.' His expression was deeply unhappy.

'You don't have to decide today,' she tried to comfort him. 'It will be another three or four weeks before your arm is completely better.'

'I know.' None of the misery left his face.

'Why are you so angry?' she asked. 'Is it the Irish news? Do you really think there'll be war there too?'

'No, it's not the Irish news,' he replied. 'Hannah, that young man is falling in love with you, and don't pretend you don't know it. That would be unworthy of you.'

She felt the blood scald up her face. Yesterday she could have denied it, but today it was impossible. She felt intruded upon. Joseph had no right to enter that part of her life. It was not only embarrassment that burned in her but anger.

'I didn't deny it!' she snapped at him. 'How dare you accuse me like that, of something I haven't done? I said nothing to you about it because it is none of your business.'

He did not flinch, as if he had expected her to react exactly as she had. It added insult to the turmoil of feelings inside her.

'Is that as honest as you can be, Hannah?' he asked. 'You are afraid something will happen to Archie, so you are allowing yourself to care for someone safe, and letting him care for you. I understand fear, and loss, but that doesn't make it right.'

Her temper snapped. All the loneliness, the tension and fear, the sense of exclusion tumbled out of the tight repression in which she had kept it.

'No you don't!' she said savagely. 'You don't understand the waiting, the being shut out. You don't understand having to pretend it doesn't hurt all the time so you protect your children. You don't understand being a family for a few days, and then being on your own, then having a family again, and then wondering if it's for the last time. When it goes one way or the other, you can begin to recover from it, but this never lets you get used to anything!' She drew in a shivering breath, still glaring at him. 'I hate all the changes! I don't want women bank managers, women police, women taxi drivers, and I don't want to be able to vote for Members of Parliament. I want to do what women have always done: be a wife to my husband and a mother to my children! I hate uncertainty, anger, fighting, destroying everything we used to value.'

'I know.' His face was bleak and very pale. 'I don't like it much myself. I think a lot of people who make the best of it do so because they have no choice. You can be dragged into the future, kicking like a child, or you can walk in upright and with some dignity. That's almost all the choice you've got.'

'You sound pompous, Joseph. This is just about Ben Morven being a little in love with me,' she responded. She knew Joseph despised pomposity. She ached for the warmth and the brightness of being cared for, that softness in Ben Morven's eyes when he looked at her. It gave her hope that even if Archie were killed, there was still someone who could love her. She had put words to it at last – if Archie were killed. It was like a miniature death just to think it.

Joseph leaned back a little against the kitchen table, easing the weight from his damaged leg. 'Is that how you would explain it to Tom?' he asked.

'That is horribly unfair! Tom is fourteen!' she protested. 'He has no idea—' She stopped. Joseph was standing there with his eyes wide, his dark eyebrows raised a little. She felt her face burn.

'Really?' he asked with surprise.

She turned round and marched out of the kitchen, slamming the door behind her.

Jenny was standing in the hall, her face solemn. 'Are you cross with Uncle Joseph?' she asked seriously. 'Because he has to go back to the war again and leave us?'

Hannah was taken aback. 'No. No, of course not . . .'

'We'll look after you, Mummy. I'll help more. I won't make a mess in my room. And I'll make my bed.'

Hannah wanted to weep, and hug Jenny so hard she might even hurt her. The passion inside her was too much, but she must control herself, or she could frighten Jenny. She was a child. She would not be afraid so long as Hannah herself was not. It all depended upon her. That was the trouble, it was always the trouble, and Joseph did not understand.

'You help a lot already,' she said, making herself smile. 'I was just upset because of something that happened in the village. Uncle Joseph was telling me I did the wrong thing, and I was cross with him because I don't like to be told I'm wrong, especially when I am. And Uncle Joseph isn't going back to the war for a long time yet, maybe not at all. He isn't well enough.'

'Is he going to get well? Margaret's daddy isn't going to get well. She says he was gassed, and he'll always be sick.'

Hannah touched Jenny's hair, pushing it out of her eyes automatically. It was too soft to stay in grips.

'That's terrible. But it isn't what happened to Uncle Joseph. He will get well, just not for a while yet. Perhaps you could help a bit by going and making him a cup of tea. Let him put the kettle on, and you get out the pot for him. I need to go out quickly, just for a little while.'

'Are you coming back?'

'Yes, of course I am! Tell Uncle Joseph I've gone to put it right.'

'What right?'

'He'll know.'

It was an extraordinarily difficult thing to do because she knew she had been guilty of deceit, both of Ben and of herself. Several times she hesitated, actually stopping on the footpath, wondering if she was ridiculous to seek him out at the tearoom where she knew he would be having an early lunch, perhaps not even alone. Was she making more out of a glance than he had ever meant? Would she end up embarrassing herself even more? It would be far easier simply to let it go until the next time they happened to meet.

That would probably be at church tomorrow, and that was the last place to have the sort of conversation she needed to. How could she be brief, honest, and retain some dignity for both of them? She should leave it until the opportunity arose by itself. Which could be a week from now!

She reached the tearoom and stopped outside. The sun was winking on mullioned windows and there was a black and white cat basking on the sill inside. She could go in and buy something for Joseph, and still change her mind. A chocolate cake to have with dinner?

She pushed the door open. It was noisy, cheerful. Half a dozen couples were there already, eating sandwiches and talking. She saw Ben at a table with another man, a few years older, perhaps in his middle thirties. That was the perfect excuse to avoid the whole issue. She could not possibly say such a thing to him in front of his friend.

She walked to the counter and smiled at Mrs Bateman. She had known her for as long as she could remember.

'Afternoon, Miss Hannah,' she said cheerfully. 'Chocolate cake, is it, for Mr Joseph?' Without waiting for a reply she disappeared to go to the kitchen, leaving Hannah alone at the counter.

The next moment Ben was behind her. 'Are you all right?' he said gently. 'You look . . .' He could not find a tactful word.

'Flustered,' she supplied for him, meeting his eyes, then wishing she had not. The warmth was still there, all the possibilities she was willing and afraid to see. Now was the moment. 'I am,' she answered. 'I realized that I behaved rather badly an hour ago when poor Mrs Oundle lost her chops.'

He grinned broadly. 'So did I! I haven't seen anything so funny in months, and I needed to laugh. Do you think we should apologize to her? Or would that only make it worse? There are some things you need to pretend didn't happen, or at least that you didn't see.'

'Since we doubled up and howled with laughter, I don't think that's going to work,' she answered, smiling in spite of herself. 'But actually that wasn't what I meant.'

He looked puzzled.

She hurried on before he could say something that would make it impossible for her. How on earth could she do this without sounding awkward, humourless, and incredibly arrogant? The only thing was to be honest. She looked at him steadily, seeing the laughter and the intelligence and the capacity for pain in his face. 'I've been behaving as if I were not married, and I am,' she said quietly. 'I'm very married, and I love my husband. I just miss him a great deal when he's away, and I've forgotten how to behave properly. I owe you an apology for that, and I am sorry.'

The colour bleached from his skin, leaving the freckles standing out. 'I see.' His voice was husky. 'Yes, of course you are . . . married, I mean.'

She knew she had hurt him, and despised herself for it. How incredibly, contemptibly selfish. Whatever Joseph felt for her, it was mild compared with the disgust she felt for herself.

Mrs Bateman returned with the large chocolate cake. 'There y'are, Miss Hannah. You tell Mr Joseph it's the best Oi've got, an' it's on the house.'

'I can't do that!' she protested. 'I'll—'

'You'll take it,' Mrs Bateman said with a satisfied smile. 'If Mr Joseph won't accept it from me, then let 'im bring it back an' say so to me face. He'll not do it, Oi'll wager. Whole village thinks the world of 'im, Miss Hannah. You tell him that. Now, Mr Morven, what can Oi get for you, sir?'

*　　*　　*

Joseph accepted the cake. He knew Mrs Bateman had an excellent kitchen, and it was her pleasure to give away the best now and then. It was her way of marking her respect for certain favourites. It would hurt her for him to have refused.

It was a warm, comfortable evening. Hannah said nothing, but he knew from the direct gaze she gave him, and the very slight, rueful smile, that she had faced her problem, and dealt with it.

But later, alone in his room, he lay awake, conscious of how abrupt he had been with her, and how sure of himself when he had not even considered what might lie ahead for her. What if Archie were one of the thousands who would not come back from the sea?

She had accused him of being pompous. Was she simply lashing out with the charge she knew would hurt him most? Or was she right? Was he a hollow man, criticizing where he had not walked? How much life and love was there inside him? Was he judging a passion he had forgotten how to feel, a warmth and a hunger he had lost?

He had been so busy trying to answer other people's needs that he had stifled his own. And without that ache of life, the vulnerability to hurt, what understanding did he have of any of it? Or of anybody who had the courage to be all they could, to be hollowed out by joy and pain into a vessel big enough to hold all of life?

'Coward' was a terrible word, the ugliest known to a soldier – and perhaps, if they were honest, anyone at all. He was used to the reality of courage in the trenches, what it cost a man to face misery daily, to see his friends blown apart and so much torn flesh they were barely recognizable as having once been men. And he had seen them do it with quiet dignity.

What courage had he? The courage to face other people's wounds, but not to risk sustaining them himself?

No, that was unfair. He was hurt by their pain. He realized with shock just how much he dreaded going back to Flanders. For over a week now he had avoided even thinking about it. His mind had been filled with the need for him here, among his own people, in the village where he was born and the incumbent priest was useless.

He fell asleep still troubled, not liking himself much.

On Saturday Joseph was invited to dinner with Shanley and Orla Corcoran. Hannah had been invited also, but more as a courtesy than with the belief that she would come. She had a previous commitment to take the children to a party in the village.

'I have no way to get to you,' Joseph protested.

'Lizzie Blaine will come for you,' Corcoran replied. 'She has a friend to visit a mile or so away from us, and will be happy to do it.'

So Joseph accepted. He wrapped the pewter goblet carefully, making it as tidy and elegant as he could, and took it with him. He was excited at the thought of Corcoran's pleasure when he saw it.

Lizzie arrived at exactly the time she had said, and he got into the car. It was a utilitarian Model T Ford that reminded him sharply of the one Judith had driven with such reckless pleasure before the war. He mentioned it to her as they set off.

'Your sister?' she said with interest. 'Is she the one who drives an ambulance in Flanders now?'

'Yes.'

'I've thought of that. I should try to do something really useful. Take my mind off myself for a while.' She said it with a small, rueful gesture. 'What sort of qualifications would I need?'

'Are you sure it's what you want?' he asked, looking sideways at her face, as she stared through the windscreen, intent on the road ahead. She was not a pretty woman but there was a kind of individuality and intelligence in her that he liked. Her nose was a little crooked and too long for beauty. Her eyes were very clear blue, in spite of her dark hair, and there was humour and vulnerability in her mouth. She looked less numb than she had when he first met her, the day of her husband's death, but she must still be suffering a bitter bereavement. It was simply that the pain had settled deeper and she had managed some fragile mask to hide the surface.

Was she also feeling passionately betrayed? Was that why she wanted now to go to France and lose herself in the war? That was not a good reason to go. Injured men needed someone who wanted to live, whose mind was free to give wholly to the job of getting them back to hospitals, and help.

They turned off the village street on to the road towards Madingley. The fields were hazed with green and an old man, shoulders bent, led weary horses along the lane to the Nunns' farm.

'You should think about it a little longer,' Joseph advised. 'Wait at least until you have had a chance to heal a little from your loss. You are still shocked now.'

'You think it will get better?' Lizzie said wryly, glancing at him for an instant, then back at the road. 'Are all the ambulance drivers in France calm and comfortable inside? None of those girls have lost husbands, brothers or fiancés?' She swerved round a pothole in the road. 'Haven't you lost people you cared about? Did they send you home?'

Of course it was preposterous. You cared about the men you were with. No one who had not been there could understand the friendships in the trenches, the sharing of everything: food, body warmth, dreams, letters from home, jokes, terror, secrets you would have told no one else, perhaps even life's blood. The bond was unique, fierce and lifelong. There were ways in which no one else would ever be so close, memories that locked you together beyond words.

He thought of Sam Wetherall, and for a moment a pain of loss engulfed him like a fire burning out everything else. It was as if it had been only yesterday that they had sat in the dugout together and talked about Prentice, and shared the last of Sam's chocolate biscuits. Joseph could still smell the Flanders earth – slick, wet clay – and the latrines, and the odour of death that got into everything.

'No, they don't send us home,' he answered her. 'And sometimes when we've lost someone particularly close, or made mistakes, got too tired to think, someone else pays for it. But we don't deliberately start out too bruised to care.'

She smiled faintly. 'You're very blunt.'

'I'm sorry.'

'Don't be. I prefer it that way. That policeman doesn't seem to have any idea yet who killed Theo, you know.'

'He will, but it could take time.'

A weasel ran across the road, sleek and bright. Lizzie braked a little, then accelerated again. 'You knew him before, didn't you?' That was more of a statement than a question.

He was surprised. 'Yes. A friend of mine was murdered, just before the war.'

'I'm sorry. That must have been horrible.'

'Yes, it was. But Perth's a good man.'

She was driving with unconscious skill, as if she loved the feel of the control and the power. It sat easily with her; there was no rushing, no arrogance. Her hands were relaxed on the wheel. She would be a good ambulance driver, if she were not too angry and too hurt to give herself to it.

'I knew he was having an affair with Penny Lucas,' she said quietly. 'I'm not sure how. I'm not even sure if it was partly my fault.'

Joseph's mind wheeled around thoughts of Hannah, and Judith, and then other people he had known. Love, envy, loneliness, the need to know beyond question that you mattered to someone – relationships were complicated, full of hungers so intense they overrode all wisdom and understanding of morality and loss.

He should have been gentler with Hannah. What had crippled his imagination so badly that he had allowed himself to be so much angrier with her than he would with anyone else? 'How could it be your fault?' he asked aloud.

Lizzie kept her eyes on the road. 'I don't know. Sometimes I wish life could be as it used to, but part of me is excited by the changes, the new things opening up. I've always just waited on Theo.' Her face was motionless in the evening sunlight. 'He was truly brilliant, you know, perhaps one of the best scientists we've ever had. It's not just me who's lost him, it's Britain, maybe the whole world. But in a way now I can be me.' A wobbly smile touched her lips. 'I've got to. I'm scared stiff, but there could be good things about it too. I can't wait at home to look after him any more.' She blinked back sudden tears. 'What I mean is, perhaps I wasn't doing it so well anyway.'

He believed her. The emotion was so palpable inside the small car as it drove between the hedges bursting with leaf that it was impossible to doubt. She was filled with regret, and her determination was a balance between fear and hope, and a mask for the pain too deep to face.

Had she loved Theo enough to be passionately jealous? Joseph did not want to consider even the possibility. But he had been wrong before. Other people he had cared about, loved, and known far better than he knew her, had had the courage, the violence and the moment's unreasoning fire inside them to be blinded to the values of eternity and see only the need of the moment – and kill.

There was death and bereavement all around them. Casualty lists were posted every day. How easy was it to think of France, only twenty miles across the Channel, and keep sanity untainted here?

'Wait until Perth has solved it and you've had a little time to get your strength and make a firm decision,' he said to her. 'Maybe you'll make a pretty good ambulance driver.'

Lizzie smiled and took a deep breath, reaching for a handkerchief in her pocket. She was too busy trying to master herself to repeat her thanks.

They were almost at the Corcorans' house and they did not speak again until arranging what time she should return to take him home.

The visit was just what Joseph needed: the warmth of welcome, the familiar rooms with their memories of the past, old pictures, old books, chairs that were long worn into the shape that held his body. The french doors were open to birdsong in the garden, even though the air was growing cooler. There was a comfort about it all that put mistakes in perspective.

Corcoran was delighted with the goblet. He held it up to let the light play on its satin surface, and touched it with his fingertips, smiling. The beauty of the artefact itself captivated him, but far more than that was the fact that Joseph had chosen it and given it to him. He set it in the middle of the dinner table and his eyes kept going towards it.

Over dinner they talked of things other than war and tragedy: timeless ideas and the beauty of poetry, music, paintings that outlasted the storms of history.

Afterwards Orla excused herself, and Joseph and Corcoran sat alone in the twilight. At last they turned to the matters of the present.

'You must have known Theo Blaine quite well,' Joseph said almost casually. 'Did you like him?'

Corcoran looked surprised. 'Yes, actually I did. He had a very pure enthusiasm it was impossible not to like.'

'Was he really one of the best scientists in England?'

A very slight shadow passed over Corcoran's face, hardly more than a change in his eyes. 'Yes, I have no doubt he was, or at least he could have been. He had some distance yet to mature and realize his full potential. Certainly he was remarkable. But don't worry, Joseph, we will finish our project even without him. He was not indispensable.'

'Do you think it was a German spy or sympathizer who killed him?'

Corcoran chewed his lip. 'I've been thinking about it, not from choice, but it is hardly a thing one can keep forever out of one's thoughts. The more I consider, the less I am certain.' He was looking very steadily at Joseph. 'At first I assumed, because of the work we were doing, that it had to be. Now I am beginning to remember that as well as being a superb mind he was also a young man, with a young man's appetites and occasionally an impractical way of looking at things, and particularly at people.'

Joseph smiled in spite of himself. 'Is that a euphemistic way of saying that he ignored other people's feelings? Like, possibly, his wife's? Or those of Dacy Lucas?'

Corcoran's eyes widened. 'You know about that?'

'I've heard. Was he self-centred?'

A flash of bleak humour crossed Corcoran's face. 'I suppose so. A lot of young men are, in that area of their lives. And I think Mrs Lucas is a headstrong woman, perhaps a trifle bored with being the wife of a man devoted to his work, in which she has no part, and very little understanding.' He shook his head. 'She has a hot temper, and I think considerable appetite, at least for admiration.' His face puckered. 'I'm truly sorry about it, Joseph. Sometimes we ask a great deal of people, and forget that other than a marvellous talent or a superb intellect, they may have the same human weaknesses and needs as the rest of us.'

'Shanley, are you speaking of Theo Blaine, or of Mrs Lucas? Or Dacy Lucas?'

'Or Lizzie Blaine,' Corcoran added wryly. 'I really have no idea. And to be honest, I prefer not to. I don't want to look at the people I know and like, and think such things of them.' His mouth twisted a little. 'Perth told me that a woman was seen on a bicycle about half a mile from Blaine's house, and bicycle tyre marks were in the damp earth of the path along the back. I wouldn't like to think that the perpetrator was Mrs Lucas. That would be a terrible thing. Although I suppose I have to admit that it is possible.'

'Why would she kill Blaine? She had nothing to be jealous of. If she wished to end the affair then she could have done it,' Joseph reasoned.

'Perhaps she didn't wish to,' Corcoran responded, looking at Joseph with a patient smile. 'Maybe he did.'

Joseph realized the obviousness of that now, but the thought was ugly. 'And kill him?' he protested. 'That seems . . .'

'A very violent passion,' Corcoran observed. 'Of course it does. Insane, to you or me. Very probably it was a German spy. I rather hope so. It would be infinitely preferable to it being someone I know, and probably like. Perhaps I am naïve, but I should like to keep my illusions . . . at least some of them.'

'Did you know about his affair before?' Joseph asked.

Corcoran spread his hands in half-apology. 'I chose not to look, but I suppose I was aware.' Guilt creased his face. 'Do you think I should have intervened somehow?'

Joseph drew in breath to say that he should, then changed his mind. 'I don't know. It probably would have looked more like interfering than the warning of friendship. I doubt it would have stopped him.'

'I could hardly threaten to dismiss him,' Corcoran said ruefully. 'His genius put him above such law, and he knew it.'

'And whoever killed him?' Joseph asked, then almost instantly wished he had bitten the words into silence. Would Corcoran protect a man, even from payment for murder, if his brain were needed to finish a project that might be crucial to the war?

He remembered Prentice, Mason and what had happened at Gallipoli. Was he so different?

'Don't ask me, Joseph,' Corcoran replied very quietly. 'I don't know. Do the ordinary laws of society apply to men like Newton, Galileo, Copernicus, or geniuses of the spirit like da Vinci or Beethoven? Would I have saved Rembrandt or Vermeer from the gallows, if they had warranted it? Or Shakespeare or Dante, or Homer? Yes – probably. Wouldn't you?'

Joseph had no answer to offer. Did you weigh one gift against another, count the price in other people's lives – innocent people – make judgements? He refused to think whether such a thing had been necessary, or would yet be. Shanley Corcoran had no more idea than he had who had killed Theo Blaine.

He smiled, and they indulged in a pleasant argument as to who was the greater, Beethoven or Mozart. It was one they had had before, more times than they could count, and it was a sort of game. Corcoran always favoured the lyrical clarity of Mozart, Joseph the turbulent passion of Beethoven.

When Lizzie Blaine returned it seemed as if she had come early, but actually it was already half-past ten, and of course Corcoran had to be up in the morning and at his office in the Establishment, regardless of the day. Only then did Joseph realize how tired he must be. He moved slowly and as he walked with Joseph to the door, there was a dry, papery look to the skin around his eyes.

'I'm sorry,' Joseph said, ashamed of the time he had taken up. He should have said at the outset that he would leave earlier, and asked Lizzie Blaine to come before ten.

'My dear boy,' Corcoran shook his head. 'It has been delightful to see you. No matter what work there is to do, even I am allowed a little self-indulgence now and then. A few hours of doing what you wish restores the spirits and gives you strength to resume. I am the better for seeing you, I assure you.'

Joseph thanked Orla as well, and went outside into the darkness smiling.

He could not help Lizzie crank the engine, but she seemed just as capable as Judith of doing it herself, and within moments they were retracing their way back towards St Giles.

'He looks terribly tired,' Lizzie said after a while. The night-time road did not seem to disconcert her at all. The overhanging hedgerows, tilting camber and heavily overgrown verges made her hesitate no more than the bright bars of moonlight on the smooth tarmac of the stretches between.

'Yes, he was,' Joseph agreed, recalling now the strain in Corcoran's face in repose, the tension in his hands, usually so relaxed. 'It must be hard for him to carry the extra load. Your husband's loss is very great.'

'Does he think it was Germans?' she asked quickly.

He did not know how to answer. What should he say to hurt her the least, and yet still be honest? 'Do you think the Germans would pick on him particularly, more than Iliffe, Lucas or Morven, or Corcoran himself?'

She smiled, a tight, bleak little gesture of the lips. 'Theo was the most original thinker. He would come up with something that seemed crazy at first, completely unrelated, then after a moment or two you could see that it was just sideways, not the way you'd been thinking. He could turn things inside out and show you a new sense to them.'

Joseph was surprised. 'He talked about his work to you?' He tried not to sound incredulous.

Again the flash of humour. 'No, but I knew him pretty well.' Then the light vanished. 'Or at least part of him,' she corrected herself. 'Before the war we used to talk about things, ideas. You should have seen him play charades. It sounds ridiculous now. He used to invent the wildest clues, but once you caught on to what they were, they made perfect sense. He loved the Gilbert and Sullivan patter songs. And Edward Lear's nonsense verses. He could recite Lewis Carroll's *The Hunting of the Snark* from beginning to end. Carroll was a mathematician too, or I suppose I should say Charles Dodgson was. Theo loved mathematics. He got excited about it, the way I would about really beautiful poetry.' She stopped abruptly.

Joseph was aware with pain how very much she had loved him. Perhaps she was realizing it too, in spite of all the effort to pretend otherwise. She was staring ahead of her, blinking hard, leaning forward a little as if the moonlight on the road dazzled her.

Of course she would never replace Theo, no matter what she said. He left an abyss that would remain unfilled. Would he leave such an emptiness for Corcoran too, professionally? That was the fear that gnawed inside Joseph's mind. Was it nothing to do with anybody's love affair, loyalty or betrayal, but a simple matter of an enemy somewhere in their midst? Was there someone, unsuspected, clever enough to have killed the one man capable of inventing a machine that would change the war? What was one woman's widowhood compared with that? A small, terrible fraction of a whole that stretched on unimaginably.

He must think about it more. He knew the village and its people in a way Perth never would. He would not only hear the whispers but he would understand them. Passive goodwill was not enough.

They arrived back in St Giles, and as they drew up, Joseph recognized Hallam Kerr's Ford parked outside the house. The lights were on in the hall and sitting room in spite of the hour.

Joseph glanced at Lizzie. She was looking at him, understanding the sudden leap of anxiety in his eyes.

'Thank you,' he said with more sincerity than his haste suggested. He did not even know what he was afraid of, but Kerr would not be here, or Hannah still up, unless there were something deeply wrong. He leaned over and opened the door with his good hand.

'Good night,' she answered as his feet crunched on the gravel.

Hannah and Kerr were in the sitting room and both whirled round where they stood, their faces white, eyes hollow and wide, as if they did not know how to blink.

'What is it?' Joseph demanded, his heart pounding, breath choking him. 'What's happened?' He was terrified it was Archie.

Hannah came to him quickly, and something in the very fact that she moved, dispelled a little of his fear. 'What's happened?' he demanded again, his voice rising.

'Joseph, a ship went down today. Gwen Neave's sons were on it – both of them. She's lost everyone she has!'

Joseph remembered her patience, the strong hands, slim and brown, the way she had always been there in his blur of pain, every time he needed her. He was sick, hollow inside with misery for her. He could not imagine losing children, adult ones that you knew as people. His child had died when he was born, with his mother.

But this was not a time for his loss; it was Gwen Neave who mattered. He touched Hannah, holding her arm with his good hand, and looked beyond her to Kerr. 'Have you been to see her?' he asked.

'I can't! For God's sake, what can I say to her?' Kerr's voice strangled in his throat. 'Tell her there's a God who's in charge of this . . . this . . .' he swung his arm around in a gesture of despair . . . 'parody of life?' He was out of control, teetering on the edge of hysteria. There was a desperation in his eyes as if he were seeking an escape he could not find.

Joseph turned to Hannah. 'I know it's late, but would you get a cup of tea, please?' He did not want the tea so much as an excuse for asking her to leave. He closed the door behind her when she did, then turned to Kerr.

'I can't!' Kerr said again, his voice rising thin and sharp. 'What use am I to her? Do you want me to go into her home, in her time of terrible grief, and repeat a lot of platitudes to her as if I had no idea what she's really suffering?' Now he was angry, lashing out at Joseph. 'What do you suggest I say, Captain? That they'll all meet up again in the Resurrection? Have faith, God loves you, perhaps? Does He?' he accused. 'Look me in the face, Captain Reavley, and tell me you believe in God!'

He waved his hands again. 'If you can do that, then tell me what He's like, where He is, and why the hell He allows this to happen. We're all facing inconceivable loss. The world's gone mad! It's the destruction of everything. It's an insult to the reality of other people's pain to mouth meaningless words at them. They don't want or need reasons, they need hope, and I haven't any to give them.'

Joseph thought of the warmth and vitality of Shanley Corcoran, of his will to pick up the pieces of Theo Blaine's job and work day and night to try to put it together, and complete it as he would have if Blaine had lived. He would keep on through exhaustion, defeat, grief, even fear of failure, and perhaps uglier than that, fear of the same man who had killed Blaine coming after him too. He never considered the possibility of stopping or giving up.

And here was Kerr, snivelling because he had to see Gwen Neave and try to think of something to say to her that offered meaning or hope in her pain.

'Then stop thinking about what you know or believe,' Joseph replied tersely, hearing the anger in his voice like a slap to the face. 'Think about what you can say to help Gwen Neave. She's a widow who has just learned that she's also lost both her sons. She's your job, not your fear or doubts. And she needs you now, tonight, not when you think you're ready to go.'

Kerr's face was grey, his eyes lifeless. 'I can't go,' he said flatly. 'I've nothing to say. If I try telling her to have faith, lean on God, she'll know I'm lying.' There was open rage in him now. 'I don't think there is a God, not one I can worship. He may have created the universe – I have no idea and I really don't care. If He exists, He has no love for us, or else it's all spun out of control, and He is as incapable of doing anything about it as we are. Perhaps He's just as lost and frightened as the rest of us, don't you think, Captain?'

He stared at Joseph as if seeing him clearly for the first time, his eyes wide and hectic. 'You told me what it's like in the trenches, really like – not some propaganda we read in the newspapers and recruiting posters about heroes fighting and dying to save us. That's what I used to think, but you showed me it's a lie. The truth is that it's hunger and cold, filthy food, rats, and at the end of it a slow, hideous death. Perhaps there won't even be enough of you left to bury.' He gasped in his breath. 'Or worse than that, half of you alive, armless and legless, hearing the screaming going on even when you're asleep, feeling the mud suck you down, and the rats' feet run over your face.'

He was swaying a little, his skin white. 'You see, I've been listening to some of the other wounded men in the hospital, as you told me to. Do you still think there's a God in control of all this, then?' He started to laugh, a jerky, obscene sound on the edge of weeping. 'Or did the Devil win after all?'

Joseph looked at the anguish in his eyes, the fury and despair, the knowledge that he was falling into an abyss that had no bottom, and he was helpless to stop it.

'I've no idea,' Joseph replied bluntly. 'But I know whose side I'm on. And it's about time you made up your mind. War isn't a new invention, nor is death, or doubt, or any of it.' His own voice was high now. 'Did you imagine all the men in the past, the ones we read about and admire so much, didn't have bodies that bled and broke just like ours? Did you suppose they had some certainty that stopped them doubting, or kept them from being terrified and thinking they were abandoned?'

'I . . . I . . .' Kerr shook his head, the idea was totally new to him.

'For God's sake!' Joseph's voice was growing louder without his being aware of it. 'They were just as lost as we are! The difference is that they didn't give up! And it's the only difference!'

Kerr kept on shaking his head and staggered backwards, collapsing into the big chair by the fireplace, hands flapping. 'I . . . can't! I could recite all the things I'm supposed to say, but they're just words. They mean nothing. I mean nothing, and she'll know that. I'm a failure, but I refuse to be a hypocrite.'

'Who cares what you are?' Joseph shouted at him. 'She's the one who matters tonight, not you! Just be there!'

But Kerr bent over, his face in his hands, nothing in him moving.

'Then drive me there,' Joseph ordered him. 'If that's what you want, I'll go.'

'I can't face her.' Kerr was speaking through his clenched hands, knuckles white. 'God didn't create us, we created Him, out of our own terror of being alone. I can't say that to her.'

'I just asked you to drive the damn car!' Joseph snarled.

The door opened behind him and Hannah came in. She had not bothered with the tea. 'I'll look after him,' she said quietly. 'You'll have to go and see Mrs Neave, Joseph. She needs you every bit as much as you needed her when you were frightened and in pain.'

'How do I get there?' he said helplessly. His arm ached like a broken tooth and his leg was pounding. He was so tired he was dizzy with it.

'I went after Lizzie Blaine. She's waiting for you,' Hannah answered.

There was no excuse left, and he did not really want one. He would not sleep anyway. Perhaps being with Gwen Neave would be only marginally harder than staying here and trying to pull Hallam Kerr out of the morass he had sunk into. Doubt was not a sin; intelligence demanded it now and again. He had just picked a damned selfish time to let it overtake him.

Lizzie Blaine was sitting in the car waiting for Joseph, the engine running. He got in and thanked her. He was already half ashamed of himself for being so harsh with Kerr. He had seen shell shock in men in the trenches, and pitied it. Perhaps Kerr was suffering a kind of religious shell shock, spirituality stunned by too much challenge to a faith that had been slender at the best of times.

Lizzie did not speak. Perhaps she was too bitterly acquainted with grief to feel any need to make conversation. It was an odd, wordless companionship they shared driving through the lanes. The moon was now hidden by cloud, and the headlamps swept hedges and tree trunks as they careered round corners. Cottages were dark and beasts silent in the fields. Once an owl swooped low and large, gone again almost before its short body and huge wingspan identified it.

They pulled up outside Gwen Neave's house, along the road towards Cambridge. The blinds were drawn here too, but there was light around the edges.

'I'll come in and make tea, or something, if you like?' Lizzie offered. 'Tidy up, whatever's needed. I can stay the night with her, if she wants me to. You can't do that.'

He smiled at her. Whatever madness had made Theo Blaine begin an affair with another woman? Who knew why anyone fell in love? Who knew why one person would betray another, or a belief, a nation?

'Thank you,' Joseph accepted. 'She might feel better if you do. We'll . . . we'll see.'

It was time to move. There was no point whatever in putting it off. This was always a kind of hell. He undid the door with his good hand and eased himself out before Lizzie could come around and open it for him. He walked up to the front door and knocked.

It was several moments before it was opened, then Gwen Neave stood there like a ghost, a woman from whom life had departed. There was no recognition in her eyes.

'Joseph Reavley,' he said quietly. 'Broken arm and shell injury in my leg. You looked after me in the hospital in Cambridge when I first came back from Ypres, about four weeks ago. You were there every time I woke up, always knowing what I needed. I wish I could do as much for you, but if you would like me to stay, to talk a little, or not, I'm here.'

'Oh . . . yes.' Her voice was hoarse, the words hard to form. 'I remember you. A chaplain . . . weren't you?' She stepped back a little.

'I still am,' he answered, following her in. 'Mrs Blaine drove me. Can she do anything to help . . . practical, perhaps? I'm afraid I'm still rather useless.'

She backed further in towards the sitting room, but with a blank look in her face as if she had not understood what he had said. Lizzie followed, but went towards where the kitchen must be.

'Chaplain . . .' Gwen Neave repeated the words. 'I'm not sure that I want . . .' There was fear in her face, as if she thought he would start telling her something unbearable.

'It's irrelevant,' he said with a slight shrug. 'Just to help you place me. You must have so many patients.'

'Military Cross.' She stared at him. 'For bringing injured men back from no-man's-land. I remember you.' She sat down, not so much in any kind of ease but simply because she was losing both her balance and her strength to remain standing.

What on earth could he say? This proud woman, who had helped so many men in their extremity of physical distress, perhaps even death, did not want platitudes about suffering or resurrection. She must have heard it all. She might not even be a Christian, for all he

172

knew. It would be a presumption of extraordinary insensitivity to start speaking as if she were. No words had helped him in the first shock of Eleanor's death. There was only a vast, aching hole inside him where there had been light and love just a few hours before. What had he wanted to hear, to say? Nothing comforting, nothing prepared and necessarily impersonal. Other deaths did not matter to him; only Eleanor's was real, eating into his heart. He wanted to talk about her, as if it kept her close and real a little longer.

'Tell me about your sons,' he asked her. 'My brother-in-law is at sea, on a destroyer. For all the hardship and the danger, there's a part of him that wouldn't do anything else. The sea has a kind of magic for him.'

She blinked. 'Eric was like that. He had a toy boat he sailed in the village pond, when he was little. He had very fair hair, straight as stair rods. It flopped up and down on his head when he jumped with excitement. His father used to rig his boat for him and put it in the water, and when the wind caught it, it went right to the other side. Terrified the ducks.'

There was a moment's agonized silence, then she went on, memories crowding her mind, falling over each other as she found words for them. Lizzie brought tea in and went away again. Gwen ignored it, still exploring the terrible wounds of her love. Joseph drank.

Then at last she could cry. She bent over, great wrenching sobs of raw, tearing loss for her children who were gone. He said nothing, but very gently kneeled on the floor, awkwardly because of his injured leg, and held her with his good arm.

When finally she was exhausted and pulled away, he was too cramped to be able to move.

'I'm sorry,' she apologized. 'Here. I'll help you up. No! Don't do that, you'll make it worse!' Expertly, used to helping injured men, she eased him to sit, turn sideways and clamber to his feet.

'Thank you,' he said again. 'A good thing one of us is competent. Would you like Mrs Blaine to stay with you? She will if you wish, if you'd rather not be alone.'

'Oh God! Didn't the poor woman just lose her husband?' She was aghast.

'Yes. But she'll stay, if you like.'

'Do you know who did it yet?'

'No. They're still looking.'

'I saw him . . . I think.' She frowned. 'I'd been to see Mrs Palfrey. She lost her brother a month ago. Posted missing. I saw the man just on the edge of the woods, in the dark. He had a pale coat on. He was terribly upset, sick with it. I thought it was a woman at first, then he relieved himself, so I knew it was a man.'

He was stunned. 'With a bicycle? A woman's bicycle, coming from the track past the Blaines' house?'

'Yes,' she agreed. 'It was very late. It must have been . . . after . . .' she stopped. 'Does Mrs Blaine want to stay?' she whispered. 'I'd rather be alone, but if she—'

'No, I don't think so,' he answered. 'She just offered. If you want to talk again, or I can do anything for you, let Mrs MacAllister know, and I'll be here.'

'Thank you,' she said automatically, then concentrated for a moment, looking at him as if she really saw him. 'Thank you, Captain Reavley.'

He could not sleep. At two o'clock he was still wide awake, seeing Gwen Neave's shattered face in his mind, her consuming grief, not furious, not questioning or railing against fate, simply a kind of inner death.

He got up and went to the window, pulling the curtains back. Now the night was radiant with moonlight. It flooded the sky, catching every flake of the mackerel clouds with silver. Just below the sill the first white roses were out, single flowers, pale as the moon, like apple blossom.

He stood gazing at the scene. The beauty was almost too intense to bear. Then he heard the piercing sweetness of a nightingale, once, twice, then the silence washed back again like a deep ocean, drowned in light.

He ached with a measureless hunger to hold the moment for ever, make it part of him so he could never lose it.

He was needed here. It was a lifetime's work to touch this grief and heal even a fraction of it. He must stay.

Chapter Nine

Patrick Hannassey might be the Peacemaker; in fact the probability stabbed like a knife into Matthew's thoughts no matter which avenue he followed. He told himself it was ridiculous. He had always known that Hannassey was an enemy of England, willing to resort to violence. But it was different to think that he could be the man behind the murder of his parents. It was personal in a way that could never be put aside. It was close as his skin, a memory that would never entirely heal. He found that Detta's words filled his mind even when he wanted desperately to escape them.

He and Joseph had done everything they could to learn the Peacemaker's identity. They had considered all they knew that must define him: first, his access to both the King and the Kaiser in a manner sufficiently confidential to present the treaty and its astounding contents for their consideration; secondly, John Reavley had to have known him well enough to have stumbled accidentally on the treaty and taken it. There were times when in order to commit other acts he knew the Peacemaker had been involved in personally, he had to have been in London. And lastly there was little doubt that he had also had a powerful influence on Eldon Prentice, and upon Richard Mason. Therefore he had strong connections with the press; not the national newspapers who obeyed the government's restriction notices, but the smaller, less responsible provincials.

How did these criteria apply to Patrick Hannassey? Matthew had to put it to the test, whatever the answer.

The appalling violence of the Easter risings in Dublin and the British suppression of them gave him the opportunity he needed. On Easter Monday the gunboat *Helga* opened fire on Dublin, setting light to Liberty Hall and several other buildings, and killing civilians. British troops landed at Kingstown and marched to Dublin, entering the city, in spite of de Valera's men ambushing them.

The next day General Sir John Maxwell's troops, sent by the Prime Minister, Mr Asquith, and mostly untrained, began shooting Irishmen on sight, and the General Post Office went up in flames. It became obvious that even worse was to come. Questions about leading Irish Nationalists did not need to be explained.

Matthew was dining with a friend with whom he had been at school. They had played in the same cricket elevens and shared a brief enthusiasm for collecting stamps. Now Barrington had a position in the Foreign Office. It was a quiet restaurant and they sat in the corner discreetly, with a bottle of claret and a rather good game pie. He asked the questions that pounded in his mind, hoping for the answers, and dreading them.

'Hannassey?' Barrington said thoughtfully. 'Do you think he's behind this uprising? Behind Connolly and Pearse?'

'Can't say,' Matthew replied, meaning to imply that he was.

Barrington smiled. 'So what is it you want to know?'

Matthew began with the least controversial issue. 'His history. For example, before the war what sort of influence did he have? Where did he travel?'

'Travel?' Barrington was surprised. 'Europe. He had some sort of diplomatic position regarding Anglo-Irish interests.'

'Including Germany?'

'Naturally. Hadn't you better tell me what this is about, Reavley?'

'I don't know what it's about yet,' Matthew evaded. 'Still in the stage of seeing if it's anything at all. Diplomatic service in Germany?'

'If you're asking me if he's a German sympathizer, yes of course he is. Sympathizes with anyone who's against us.'

'I took that for granted, given other circumstances. Would he know anyone connected with the Kaiser?'

Barrington frowned, twiddling his coffee spoon in his fingers.

'Yes. He's a very personable man, highly intelligent and if he wants to be, very cultured. Certainly the Kaiser. King too, come to that.'

'And Members of our Parliament?' Matthew persisted.

'He might have known pretty well anyone of influence.' Barrington shook his head a little. 'Who do you have in mind, Reavley? You are being very evasive. Are you sure this isn't something we should know?'

'It's to do with something my father said before he died.' That was obliquely true, more or less.

'I heard about that. Road accident, wasn't it? I'm very sorry.'

'Yes. Rather got swallowed in the news at the time.'

'Oh?'

'Same day as the assassination in Sarajevo.'

'Oh. That's too bad. Do you think he knew something about Hannassey that still matters?'

'I'm chasing a possibility. Do you keep tabs on Hannassey?'

'Sometimes. Lose him pretty regularly. He's a master of looking so damn ordinary he disappears. What dates are you interested in?'

'Late May, early June last year.'

'London, mostly. Can't tell you where exactly.'

'Thank you. Last question, has he any influence with the press?'

'None that I know. I should doubt it very much.'

'Not even local press, small papers in the north?'

'No idea. Why?'

'I'll tell you, if it comes to anything.' He drank the last of his coffee. 'Do you fancy a brandy?'

In his office again Matthew received a wireless message from America and decoded it. He read it with acceptance and perhaps a kind of satisfaction, grim as it was. A stevedore in the New York docks had been murdered.

He wrote his reply. It was not necessary to say much. His man already had his instructions. The corpse was to be made to appear a spy, trained by Germany and then 'turned' to betray their plans to Britain. His murder was payment for that act, an object lesson to would-be traitors.

Now also was the time to show the evidence on paper of a fictional agent in the German-American banking system, who had revealed the details of all the transactions paying the man in the docks who had placed the bombs in the ships' holds.

Matthew reread his letter once more, making certain of every detail, then encrypted it and gave it to the operator to send.

He reported to Shearing in the late afternoon as if no thoughts teemed in his mind except those of the allied shipping crossing the Atlantic with smoke bombs hidden among the tightly packed munitions. He forced away all thought that he was on the verge of exposing the Peacemaker at last, and the deeply painful knowledge that it was Detta's father. The thought of how she would be hurt was something he could not face. He concentrated instead on the vast entanglement of loyalties, political office and judgement that made up the Anglo-American relationship.

'Well?' Shearing asked. He looked tired. His usually immaculate suit was a little creased and his tie was not quite straight. Once again Matthew wondered where he lived, and why he had never mentioned even a parent or a brother. Why was there nothing in his office that betrayed any love or memory, any ties to place or culture? He seemed a man without roots. That very anonymity was vaguely frightening. It made him less than human. Every other man had a photograph, an ornament, pictures, some ties to who he was. At least the fear had gone that he could be the Peacemaker.

'We have a suitable body for the double agent,' he said briefly. 'I'm going to tell Detta Hannassey about it this evening.'

Shearing nodded. 'Don't rush it, Reavley. She'll know if she's being fed. Don't do it all at once.'

'I won't.'

Shearing smiled with a bleak humour. 'But be quick. Time is short.'

'Yes, sir.' Matthew stood to attention for a moment, then turned and left. As so often before, he wished profoundly that he could trust Shearing. Perhaps now he could, but the old caution was too deep to cast aside. John Reavley's last words to him had been that the conspiracy reached right to the top. Who also was tainted? And if he did trust, who else would die?

There were moments when he missed his father with exactly the same desperate, incredulous pain as on the very first day. There was an emptiness inside him that no one else could fill. They would have sat together, probably on a bench in Regent's Park, watching the ducks, and talked about whatever the problem was. They might have walked around an art gallery, seeing what was for sale, looking for bargains, old watercolours that needed cleaning and restoring, the foxing taken off, and refreshed to show their beauty.

Matthew would have wanted to tell him of his strange relationship with Detta Hannassey, and how they knew that each was playing a game with the other, with a mixture of lies and truths. In the big matters – the ideals and the battles – they were against each other, even to the extent of using deceit and counterdeceit. In the little things – the jokes and the teasing, the tenderness, even the fleeting pleasures of flowers or music, a moment of sunlight on the water, the flight of a bird – they were passionately honest. But he could not have confided in his father. John Reavley would have seen it as one more example of the duplicity and betrayal innate in the nature of the work, and despised it. Would he ever have understood how many lives it saved? Matthew wished he could have told him! It would have undone an ache inside him if he could.

This was all in his mind when he met Detta at the theatre that evening. He never collected her from her home, as he would have with another woman. She did not permit him to know where she lived. He thought it more than possible she did not always sleep in the same bed each night. He preferred not to know. Jealousy would be ridiculous, but he knew its taste well enough to avoid even the suspicion.

He had intended to be there well before she was, which ought not to be difficult. She was often late, arriving casually at the last moment when he was on the point of giving up, her smile as bright as usual. But this evening she was there already. He saw her standing in the foyer as soon as he was through the doors. She was dressed in dark blue. She tended to choose cold colours, but she never looked cold. They heightened her drama, as if she did not belong in the everyday world but was merely visiting it from a more mystical place. Her gown was very simple and she wore a dark cloak over it as the evening would be cooler after the performance.

She did not come towards him; she stood quite still, smiling, until he should reach her. He wondered if she was always as intensely sure of herself as she seemed. Perhaps her doubts were more of others, of life itself. In spite of her humour there was a sadness in her he could never touch, as if she knew something too subtle and complicated to frame in words.

'Hello, Matthew,' she said warmly. She never abbreviated his name. 'This was a fine choice. I'm in the mood for farce.' She looked up at him, her eyes so dark. He could see the laughter in them, and the pain as well. He had already determined not to mention the uprising in Dublin, unless she insisted on it, although too often his resolutions as far as Detta were concerned went astray.

'Hello,' he replied. 'It's supposed to be a good show – been on for a couple of weeks and they're getting used to their parts and working with each other.'

She glanced around at the other people coming in. As so often these days, they all seemed very young, no more than in their mid-twenties, but there was a gauntness to their faces that was deeper than hunger or tiredness. It was something in the skin, a certain look to the eyes. They were men on leave from the trenches, for a few days pretending nothing existed but these lights and laughter, the jokes, the music, the girls on their arms. They wanted to have fun, to taste youth and irresponsibility again, gulping at it like a diver coming up for air.

'Poor devils,' Detta said quietly. 'They know, don't they!' She did not add any more, the soft lilt in her voice told of a long familiarity with the dark side of love. 'They're as Anglo-Saxon as you are.' Then her mouth twisted in wry laughter. 'But they know, all the same. I suppose if you make it plain enough, often enough, then even an Englishman will see it eventually.'

'As opposed to an Irishman, who'll see it immediately, whether it's there or not?' he asked. If he were too gentle with her she would detect pity, and hate him for it.

'Something like that!' she shrugged.

They did not speak while they found their seats.

'*Mr Manhatten*,' she said the play's title when they were comfortable. 'Your mind still on America?'

It was the opening he wanted, but actually he had chosen the show because it was a light musical comedy, with emphasis on the comedy. The star, Raymond Hitchcock, had a reputation for engaging the audience in a way that drew them in whether they intended it or not. A friend had said that Iris Hoey was excellent in the burlesque, and the music was very good.

'Hard for it not to be,' he answered Detta's question. 'Our men are still getting dud ammunition.'

She did not look at him. 'But you're doing something about that, aren't you? That is, when you're not here with me, forgetting your responsibilities and having fun!' It was more a comment than a question, and there was a play of humour around her mouth.

Matthew knew the complexities of her thought. This was a jibe at him that he was too sober, that he had not the wild, Irish imagination. His feet were earthbound, and his mind as well. And she was leaving the opening wide for him to pursue the subject, which was what they were both here for. Was she also testing to see if he cared about her and was willing to say so? She knew he did; he was not a good enough actor to pretend. Perhaps her sudden vulnerabilities were all a pretence on her part? He should not let that thought hurt so much.

'I forget all my responsibilities when I'm with you,' he answered, allowing both honesty and laughter into his voice. He saw the pleasure in her, too real to be hidden immediately. 'Until I look at the faces of the soldiers on leave,' he added. 'Then I remember

I'm part of it all, whether I want to be or not.' He had to remember there was a war on, to prevent his feelings for her from sweeping him away. The price of forgetting could be their lives.

She swung around to face him, eyes wide as if he had slapped her. But there was admiration as well as the sudden loss of happiness. 'Of course you are,' she said quietly. 'You've come to work, even if it has its pleasures. If I weren't Irish, you wouldn't be here.'

'If you weren't Irish, you wouldn't be here either,' he pointed out, but he kept the banter in his voice, and the smile.

'And do you imagine I know who is sabotaging your bullets and shells?' she asked, turning away so he could see only her profile.

'Possibly,' he replied. 'But it hardly matters. I'm quite sure you wouldn't tell me. But I think it's far more likely you simply know that it's being done, and probably how. But I don't need you to tell me that because I already know.'

'Then why are you here?' She still did not look at him. Her voice was light and very soft. He had to lean closer to her to be sure of catching every word. He could smell the perfume of her hair and see the shadow of her lashes on her cheek.

The orchestra started to tune up in the pit. People were still busy settling in their seats, waving to friends they recognized, calling out greetings. Girls were laughing and flirting. There was a hectic pleasure in the air. No comedian could fail to amuse them, nor on the other hand could they totally block out the shadow of knowledge of world events just beyond the edge of the lights.

'I'm here deceiving everybody,' Matthew replied in a whisper. 'I tell myself I'm here to gain confirmation from you, but that's not true, because I don't need it. We turned the spy in New York. We got all the information from him that we wanted, even the name of their man in the German bank, and the account numbers. But he paid for it with his life.'

She was silent for several minutes.

He waited. What she really wanted was to know if they had broken the code, but what would she pretend to want? Suddenly he longed for her to be like the people around them, here just for fun, to flirt with each other, perhaps even to love and lose, but without deceit. He longed for it so fiercely it was a hollow, physical ache inside him.

She turned and met his eyes. In a glance she understood, and allowed the mirror of it to show in her own face. Then deliberately, like smashing a glass into a hundred shards of light, she broke it. 'Did your people kill him?' she asked.

He was cold in the heat of the theatre. 'No. I imagine his own people did,' he replied.

'Then they knew he had betrayed them,' she pointed out. 'They'll change their routine. Your intelligence will be no good to you.'

He smiled bleakly. 'We'll act before then, if we haven't already.'

'What good will that do?' She shrugged very slightly, a gesture of futility. 'Are you going to turn another, and let him be killed too?'

Why had she said that? To smash the momentary imagination of peace, before either of them could grasp it and be sure it was good?

'Once will be enough,' he answered, trying to keep emotion out of his voice. 'The Germans won't risk angering the Americans by doing it again. They'll have to think of something else, and no doubt they will. But Wilson has this grand idea of stepping in to be the arbiter of peace in Europe. It seems to matter intensely to him. His place in history. Neither we nor Germany can afford to destroy that illusion, especially with presidential elections in November. Far more of this is about internal American politics than you might think.'

'There are a lot of Germans in America,' Detta said, looking at the stage where the tempo of the music had quickened.

'And Irish,' Matthew added. 'But plenty of British too, and even a few French, and Italians. Don't forget the Italians. God knows how many of them have been slaughtered on the Austrian border.'

She did not answer. Her face was bleak with misery, as if she had suddenly remembered a vast, ancient grief.

The music swept over them. All around them, young people

were living in the moment, refusing to think of yesterday or tomorrow. Some sat close, arms around each other.

Detta said no more until the interval and they went to the foyer and bar. Matthew bought her a drink and some chocolates. A few yards away a group of young men in uniform were repeating one of the jokes and laughing too loudly, too long. The undertones of despair in their voices caught his ear like a cry.

He glanced at Detta. There was a naked pity in her eyes so powerful he put his hand on her arm without thinking what he was doing.

She turned to him in surprise, and the pity vanished, although hiding it cost her an effort. Then she read in his face that it had stirred a softness in him, no sense of victory over her because she had yielded a moment. How Matthew longed for her then, hungered to be able to break through the barrier of lies and games so that for a moment they could cling to each other in the passions of the mind and heart that hold people together. They had the understanding of the same beauty, the same gentleness, pity for hurt and loss, the infinite treasuring of life's sweetness, and above all the need not to be alone in it.

But he was alone. Their separate loyalties held them both too hard. To yield anything would be betrayal, and if they gave up that much of themselves, what had they left to give to anyone, let alone to each other?

Did the loneliness cut her as deeply to the bone as it did him? Or was that unreadable part of her, the Celtic dream with its plaintive music, its myths that stretched back through history, enough to feed her hunger?

He looked at the vitality in her face, the delicate curve of her neck, her shoulders a little too thin for perfection, and felt as if the impenetrable glass between them could never be broken.

Then she turned and he blanked his expression just in time to stop her reading his hurt. At least he thought it was in time.

'Don't you feel for them, Matthew?' she asked, a pucker between her brows, just a tiny, fleeting confusion. 'They have this moment, and they know that could be all. They've been snatched from hell for a few hours, and tomorrow or the day after, they

184

go back. Perhaps they'll never come home again. Can't you see it on their faces, hear it on the edge of their laughter? It's in the air, like the smell of a storm coming.'

He looked at her. She was beautiful, so alone, chasing a dream. What would happen if she ever caught it? Would she stop and hold it close, taste its sweetness and be happy? Or would she then create another dream to pursue, her heart as elusive, as unsettled as it was now? He feared the answer to that. Not that it mattered! The pursuit itself would always stand between them.

She reached out her hand and touched his cheek. She was smiling, but the pain behind her eyes was real. 'I don't understand you English,' she said huskily. 'I'm sure there's somebody fierce and wonderful behind that throwaway calm. I just can't crack the shell. I want the curtain to go up on the play for a while, so I can laugh, or the pain inside me is going to burst.' And she turned and walked away across the foyer, as elegant as a reed in the wind.

He followed her, knowing irrefutably that they were already on the brink of that point where they would have to betray each other, or themselves. If she won the battle of wits, hundreds, perhaps thousands more young soldiers like these around them might pay with their lives. He did not want to think what his victory would cost. The Irish were not kind to those who failed them.

Richard Mason found the streets of Paris surprisingly empty. It was late April, just after Easter, when he turned into the narrow rue Oudry where he knew Trotsky lived, and yet there seemed nothing of spring in the air. The sun was warmer and there was a slight breeze and it blew old newspapers and pamphlets along the pavement. There was no one sitting in the cafés and too many of the women he had seen were wearing black, even young ones who at any other time would have had a smile and a word for him.

He had noticed on the way here how many of the street clocks had stopped, and the statue of the Lion de Belfort had dirty straw sticking out of its mouth. All anyone could think of was the news from Verdun.

It was early evening. Mason hoped Trotsky would be at home. He worked on a Russian emigré newspaper, scratching a living, and, as always, pursuing his dreams for a revolution of social justice, a world where workers overthrew oppression and there was food and warmth for all.

Mason's hands were sweating, and he found it hard to catch his breath. In the days since he had left London the Peacemaker's words had beaten in his brain: 'Kill him! If he will continue the war, kill him!'

Of course he could not do that tonight! All he had to do now was meet Trotsky again, and start to make some judgement of the man. But he would not have changed, would he? People like Trotsky never changed! There was a fire in him nothing would quench. He had been sentenced to exile to Siberia, escaped from Russia to Sèvres and then Paris. He had been poor to the point of starvation, and a stranger in a foreign land. Still he wrote with the same passion as of old, greater if anything. The Peacemaker might not know Trotsky, but Mason did.

He knocked on the door. Then he wanted to run, but his feet were like lead and his knees weak. Whatever Trotsky said, Mason could not murder him, and that was what the Peacemaker wanted.

A woman in black passed him, her face mask-like in grief. How many loved ones had she lost? Mason had seen the corpses piled in Verdun too deep to count, too many to bury. They would be there until the rats ate them and the earth itself subsided in the rain and mud and covered them over. His stomach clenched. Yes, of course, he could kill one Russian exile, if it brought peace even a day nearer.

The door swung open and another woman in black looked at him without interest.

He asked in French if Monsieur Trotsky was at home.

She said that he was, and showed him up to the apartment where Trotsky lived with his wife and two sons.

Trotsky himself opened the door. He was a small man, stocky, with a wealth of black curling hair so thick it added inches to his height. Intelligence lit his square face with its full lips and powerful chin, so utterly different from the sparer, more ascetic Lenin. He stared at the tall man on his doorstep in bewilderment, then as Mason spoke, memory and pleasure lit his eyes.

'Mason!' he said incredulously. 'Come in! Come in!' He stepped back, making way for Mason to follow him inside the small room. 'It's been an age! How are you?' He waved at a chair, and indicated a bottle of Pernod. 'Drink?'

Trotsky introduced his wife, who gave a quick smile and excused herself, saying she was just going to put their young sons to bed. Mason greeted her with circumspection, uncomfortably aware of Trotsky's other family in St Petersburg.

Mason told him of his travels as a war correspondent, allowing him to assume they were what had brought him to Paris. However, he was obliged to be economical with the truth, having to leave out anything to do with the Peacemaker, his recent visit to Ypres, and Judith Reavley. He was acutely conscious of the small room, and its contrasts. All over the table there were papers covered with scribbled political argument. And yet scattered around the room were the physical details of family life: children's toys, handmade and well used; a piece of mending with the needle still in it, thread hanging; a small bowl with half a dozen leaves and flowers; a plate with a chip on one side; a book with a paper marking the place.

Trotsky was talking about Jean Jaurès, the great French socialist who had been murdered just before the outbreak of war.

'He might have stopped all this!' Trotsky said savagely, watching Mason's face. 'I went to the Café Croissant, where he was killed, you know. I thought I might still feel something of him there. I did not agree with him politically, of course, but I admired him. How he could speak! Like a great waterfall, elemental! And yet he could be gentleness itself, endlessly patient in explaining.'

Mason watched him as he went on about Jaurès, and then Julius Martov, the leader of the Mensheviks in Paris, a man of towering intellect but irresolute will. He spoke of a dozen others, his own enthusiasm flooding through it all.

But did he want peace? If he returned to Russia to overthrow the Tsar and the whole rotten edifice of oppression surrounding the old government, would he then take Russia out of the war?

Or remain with the Allies, for whatever reason, and pursue it to the end through more seas of blood?

It was ludicrous! Mason was sitting here in this man's home, talking of a world revolution of social order and justice, and thinking about whether he would have to murder him or not!

But men who had never met each other were crushed in the mud only a few score miles away, killing by the thousands. Surely the only sanity left was to stop it, any way at all?

The conversation had come round to Trotsky's plans of returning to Russia.

'When you go back to Russia, when you get rid of the Tsar, what then?' Mason asked him. 'What will you do? What about the war?'

'We can't help the rest of Europe,' Trotsky said with resignation. 'We'll make peace, of course, as soon as we have a voice at all!'

Mason felt relief well up inside him almost as if he were drunk. But then, he wondered if he were being hasty in accepting this answer. Was he leaping to conclusions, so it might hasten the end of the war, or so he himself did not have to exercise the ultimate barbarity, and kill this man sitting across the table talking to him about reform, justice, hope, revolution!

'You don't feel that if you withdrew from the war, the rest of Europe might not support the Revolution?' he asked.

'What's the matter with you?' Trotsky demanded. 'We can't keep fighting, with the losses we're sustaining. And we've got so much to do to put our country to rights. The last thing we need is war, more death, our people killed. It is the ordinary men, the soldiers, the workers, who will bring about the new order. This is an unjust war – proletarian against proletarian. It must come to an end as soon as possible.' He frowned, puzzled by Mason's apparent stupidity.

It was true. Of course it was true. How could Mason fail to believe it? Nothing else made sense. He leaned across the table. 'When?' he asked with more urgency in his voice than he had intended. 'You cannot afford to wait until Germany has beaten you, or you will merely exchange the Tsar for the Kaiser. And if

America comes into the war that will not help you. Then the Allies will win, and that means the Tsar again. You will be back where you started, but with God knows how many of your people dead.'

'I know,' Trotsky said with pain marked deep in his face. 'It must be soon. But we are persecuted on every side, even here in Paris. Martov is brilliant, but cannot make up his mind on anything. Lenin is in Zurich, and afraid to move. Believe me, I am doing everything I can. If I had not friends here I would be in danger of being driven out of France myself. But never give up hope, my friend, we will overcome in the end, and it is not far – another year, perhaps less.'

'Less,' Mason said quietly. 'It needs to be less.' There was a kind of peace inside him now, a freedom from a terrible weight.

It was not until he had at last taken leave of Trotsky and was walking along the quiet street in the dark that he even considered how many people might be slaughtered, starved or dispossessed in the 'peace' that Trotsky dreamed of.

The evening light was fading in a high, pale blue arc across the sky, like washed silk, and the colour was lost beneath the trees where Joseph and Corcoran had been walking on the edge of the fields.

'It's so mild I forget it isn't summer yet,' Corcoran said with a smile.

Joseph stared across the wind-rippled grass towards Madingley, and the west. It had been a brief interlude of escape from the present, the dilemmas of grief and decision, even awareness of the terrible losses in Verdun and the uprising in Ireland. That had now been quelled with a savagery that had forfeited all the goodwill the Dubliners had originally felt towards the British troops.

Then he turned to Shanley and saw in the yellow sunset light the haggard planes of his face, the sunken skin around his eyes, the lines etched deep in the flesh from nose to mouth. He looked an old man, beaten and worn out. It touched Joseph with unexpected fear. The confidence of a few moments before vanished. It had been an illusion created by courage and force of will, the need to believe the impossible because it was all that lay between them and defeat.

The instant passed. Joseph replaced his own mask of ease, as if he had not noticed anything. Since his decision to remain in St Giles his mind was genuinely easier. There was nothing in the future to dread except the burdens of the village, the familiar pains of confusion and bereavement.

Corcoran smiled, a sad, weary look. Joseph had blanked the understanding from his face too late. 'You know this man, Perth, don't you.' It was an observation not a question.

'A little,' Joseph conceded. 'He might have changed in a couple of years. Is he making things difficult for you?'

Corcoran did not answer immediately. He seemed to be weighing his words. A ploughman leading two shire horses passed along the lane at the bottom of the field, harness clinking gently. He must have been harrowing up on the slope beyond the woods.

They had not spoken of the murder. Now the subject lay between them like a third presence.

'Gwen Neave saw him,' Joseph said. 'A man in a light coat, on a woman's bicycle, coming out of the path through the trees shortly after Blaine must have been killed. That would be why the tracks were deeper than if the cyclist had been a woman – the greater weight.'

Corcoran was stiff, as if the idea froze him in horror.

Joseph felt a moment's guilt for having mentioned it. 'I'm sorry,' he said quietly.

Corcoran did not move and when he spoke his voice was hoarse. 'Not your fault, my dear fellow. Did you say Mrs Neave saw a man coming out of the woods? Was it light enough to tell?'

Joseph was aware of his own clumsiness. 'No, she said not. But he was in a state of considerable distress. He was sick, and then he relieved himself. That was the point at which she realized that the person was without question a man. Until then she had assumed it was a woman, perhaps because of the woman's bicycle.'

Corcoran's face was almost blank. It seemed the idea was too ugly for him to grasp.

'Shanley?' Joseph moved closer to him, suddenly anxious.

Corcoran turned slowly. 'What a dreadful time we live in, Joseph,' he said softly. 'I knew about Blaine's affair and, God forgive me, but I hoped it was only that old evil of jealousy which had spurred this awful action. To tell you the truth, I thought Blaine had seen sense, and ended it. Mrs Lucas is a woman of intense and rather selfish appetite. I assumed she had lost all control of herself and in a fit of jealousy had struck at poor Blaine.' He closed his eyes as if he could block out the idea. 'It is peculiarly disgusting, and perhaps I wronged her in allowing the thought into my mind.' He looked guilty and profoundly regretful. 'I suppose it is what I wanted to think. It seemed . . . more ordinary. Not a new threat, if you see what I mean?'

'Yes, of course I do.'

'But you say it was a man?' He still looked as if he were hoping Joseph might be in some doubt.

'Yes. And I suppose when you consider the way in which Blaine was killed, it would be remarkable if a woman could have achieved it. The strength necessary . . .' he trailed off. The thought was repulsive.

Corcoran's mouth tightened in distaste, pulling his lips crooked. 'Women can be strong, Joseph. If she was driven by rage, and she took him by surprise. A garden fork, you said?'

'Yes.'

'She could have struck him with it first.' He swung an imaginary weapon in his hands. 'And then . . .' he could not finish. He closed his eyes and shuddered at what his inner vision showed him.

'I should think that is what happened,' Joseph agreed. 'Actually Perth picked up the fork and did the same thing. It nicked his skin.' He held up his hand and showed Corcoran where.

Corcoran imitated his gesture, looking at his own unblemished skin. He had good hands, strong and well-formed. Joseph remembered how they always seemed to be warm.

'Dacy Lucas?' he asked aloud.

Corcoran shook his head. 'I thought so, Joseph, but I was deceiving myself. I fear very deeply that the murder has nothing to do with Blaine's unfortunate lapse from morality. I have to

191

think he was killed because someone believed he was on the verge of making a breakthrough in scientific discovery which would blaze the way for a totally different era of naval warfare, and would unquestionably win the war at sea for Britain.'

Joseph felt a coldness as if the fields in the long light of evening had suddenly been mantled in snow. The world he loved was slipping out of his grasp, and no strength of passion or grief could hold on to it.

'We'll have to finish it without him!' Corcoran said abruptly. 'Work harder.' He turned till his face shone like bronze in the light. 'I'm almost there. Believe me, Joseph, it will be a turning point in history. Future generations will look back on this summer in Cambridgeshire as the beginning of a new age. I only have . . .' he lifted his shoulders slightly and smiled, 'a little way to go. A few more steps. If only they give me time!' Then he shivered and fear touched his eyes before he turned away again.

'Shanley!' Joseph reached towards him.

'No, no!' Corcoran denied his anxiety softly. 'I just hate having this wretched, pedestrian little man poking into everything, asking questions, awakening ugly thoughts. I suppose he is simply doing his duty, as he sees it. And of course he is not aware of the wider issues and he cannot be told.' He pulled his mouth into a thin line. 'I loathe the suspicion everywhere, like a disease in the air. Nothing is as it used to be. One cannot afford to trust anybody, and it would not be a kindness to do so. A slip, a word or an omission, anything at all, and a person falls under suspicion. To know nothing is the only safety.'

Joseph saw a whole landscape of fear he had not even imagined before. No wonder Corcoran was exhausted. There must be things he could share with no one. The pressure to succeed was almost unbearable, knowing what lay in the balance, even the difference between victory and defeat. And closer and more urgent than that was the knowledge that one of his own men must probably be guilty.

But there was another thought in Joseph's mind even worse again, filling him with fear like a hand crushing his chest. 'You can finish the work? You are sure?' he asked, hating his own doubt.

'Yes!' Corcoran looked startled, as if the question angered him. 'It will take longer, that's all.'

'Do the others in the Establishment know that? Surely they will deduce it from the fact that you are still working on the prototype?'

'Yes . . .' Then Corcoran saw what it was that had struck Joseph like a physical blow. A softness filled his face and his eyes were bright. 'I shall take great care, I assure you.'

'Will you?' Joseph demanded. 'How? What will you do to protect yourself? Look over your shoulder all the time? I know you better than that. Have you even the faintest idea who the murderer is?'

Corcoran raised his eyebrows. 'Faintest?' He sighed. 'If I rely on the honesty and the ability of Inspector Perth, then I know at least that it was not Dacy Lucas.'

'Do you? How?' Joseph challenged.

'Because Perth checked on where he was, and he could not have been anywhere near Blaine's house.'

'Are you sure? Absolutely certain?'

Corcoran half turned away. 'No. I don't know for myself. Actually I was at the Cutlers' Arms just outside Madingley, talking to your brother-in-law about possible sea trials for the prototype.' His voice was heavy with irony. 'That's how sure I was then that we were on the brink of completing it. It seems now like another world.'

The shadows were so long that the trees in the distance seemed to stretch across half the field. The black scatter of starlings drifted up against the gold of the sky, turned and were swept sideways, curving around and settling again.

The unhappiness in Corcoran's face was clear. Joseph knew him far too well to misread it. And there was fear as well, but subtle as a half-forgotten scent. Did he suspect who it was, and the grief in him was for a man he had worked beside and trusted, with whom he had shared food and dreams? Did he now understand a truth so bitter the hurt of it was more than he could confront?

Or was he waiting for the final proof before he put away the last denial and faced its reality? Or worse – an idea so ugly it wrenched the stomach – was he protecting him because he was necessary for the completion of the project?

Joseph did not even know what the prototype was, or what it was designed to do. He could deduce its importance from Corcoran's manner, from Matthew's involvement, and above all from the fact that Corcoran himself believed one of his own men could be driven to commit murder to prevent its creation. That had to mean that the Germans had placed a man in the Establishment, secretly waiting his time, perhaps as long ago as the beginning of the war, an Englishman prepared to betray his own people.

Would Corcoran condone murder to preserve the invention? If it saved as many lives as he implied, if it even turned the tide of the war at sea, then yes, of course he might! War was about death and destruction, smashing and killing, ruining everything possible. It was about your own and your country's survival, and the cost of that could be high. It could be violence, betrayal, acts unthinkable in peace.

'Shanley . . .' Joseph turned towards him again, 'for God's sake be careful. If you know who it is, protect yourself! If he killed Blaine to sabotage the project, he'll certainly kill you to protect himself! He's ruthless, and you have no idea who he is.' The thought of Corcoran murdered was unbearable. He was laughter and bright memories, reason, courage and hunger for life. He was the bond with all that was good in the past, now slipping away like the light fading on the horizon as the wind rose rustling in the elms. Joseph needed to cling to him, save him, protect him, comfort him as if in some way he could even reach his father through him.

Corcoran smiled, and for a moment there was an intense joy in his eyes. 'Thank you, Joseph,' he said with a huskiness in his voice. 'But I'll be safe. You don't need to worry.'

'Do you know who it is, Shanley?' Joseph demanded an answer.

'Do you think I would defend him if I did?' Corcoran countered.

'Wouldn't you? If he were crucial to the project?'

'And he would give it to the Germans?' Corcoran said with mockery in his disbelief.

Joseph would not be diverted: 'If you thought you could use him until exactly the right moment, then betray him before he betrayed you? Is that not what this kind of battle is about?'

Corcoran smiled. 'My dear Joseph, I can't answer that. I don't know, because I haven't faced the situation yet.' His eyes were dark and gentle as he looked back in the fast-fading light. 'But don't fear for me. I'm very careful. Believe me, I care about the project more than anything else in my life. It is brilliant! More than I dare tell you. It would save not only a million lives, but Europe itself. That has to outweigh individual justice or even individual lives, hard as that is.'

There was no argument to make. Joseph stood silent, but the fear for Corcoran sank deep into him.

It was not enough for Joseph simply to pity or to fear. All the love in the world was worth nothing if he did not act. He had unravelled murder before now, even when he had not wanted to know who had done it. Now, when it mattered desperately, he must try again, harder.

He forced himself to smile, but there were tears in his throat.

Chapter Ten

'This!' Detta said with complete conviction, her eyes alight, her lips smiling. 'It's perfect!'

Matthew looked at it. It was a man's wristwatch of a highly individual design, with a thin green circle around the face, which was only visible when the light caught it. 'It's excellent,' he agreed, more bitterly aware of the irony than she was. It was a gift for her father, to her an Irish Nationalist fighting for his country against the British oppressor. There was nothing in her face, in its passion, laughter or wild imagination that let him believe she also knew that her father was the man who had ordered the murder of his parents. For Matthew it was not just a war of nations but an acutely personal violation that would last as long as he lived.

'Yes, it's excellent,' he agreed, struggling to mask his feelings. He refused to imagine Hannassey wearing it.

'Thank you for being so patient,' she said warmly. 'It's always difficult to know what to choose for a man. Women are easy.' Her expression was pinched with momentary pain.

Detta had never mentioned her mother. Matthew had not wondered before what had happened to her, or if she were still alive. Perhaps she too had died tragically, even violently, and Detta had a burden like his to bear. Why had he not considered that? Why had he not considered a lot of things, now that it was almost over, and one of them was going to pay the price of losing? He forced that thought from his mind.

'It was a pleasure,' he said aloud.

She gave a little laugh. 'Liar!' she retorted, but there was no anger in her. She paid for the watch, and he could see that it was more than she had intended, but the extra sacrifice gave her happiness. It was ridiculous that it should hurt him so much. He could give nothing to his father now. And here was the Peacemaker's daughter, eyes soft with joy because she could give him something that cost her dearly. He walked outside while she finished the transaction, so she would not see his face before he could control himself and take up his role again.

A moment later she joined him in the street and they crossed over and went into the park. The late afternoon sun was warm and there was an illusion of timelessness about the day that both of them seemed willing to indulge in.

From where they were they could see at least twenty other couples, some walking arm in arm, many standing idly under the trees, some sitting on the grass. They passed one man wobbling on crutches, his left leg missing below the knee. The girl with him was white-faced and she kept looking away, as if afraid she would embarrass him by seeing his awkwardness. Perhaps she was revolted and knew he would see it in her eyes. Matthew caught it in her face, and for an instant hated her for it.

Detta touched his arm. 'Some people can't help it,' she whispered.

'We have to help it!' he returned savagely when they were out of earshot. 'Won't she expect him to love her when she's older, when she's put on weight and her bosom sags, or her skin has blemishes? Or does she think she's always going to be so pretty?'

'She isn't thinking, Matthew,' Detta answered drily. 'She's just feeling. She loved him as he was. You grow old slowly; this is all in a few days. And maybe he pushed her away? Have you thought of that? When we're hurt in body and dignity, sometimes we take it out on those closest to us, and they don't know what to do or how to help. She's maybe hurting too.'

He looked at her with surprise and a flood of perception he

197

knew he should have had before. 'You've seen that.' It was not a question.

She gave a little shrug, swinging her skirt with the elegance of her stride. 'Irishmen are no different,' she answered.

He was about to ask who it had been, but she was walking ahead and had her back to him, the sun gleaming on her hair, catching rich, red lights in its darkness. She was slender, and there was the grace of a wild creature in her, moving when and where she would. The elusiveness of her was part of what he loved. She made other women seem tame, too easily caught and held.

She could not be held at all, except in rare, fierce moments when she seemed to give everything of herself, her thoughts, her beliefs, even the sudden tenderness of her dreams.

Far in the distance a band was playing, something patriotic and sentimental. Before the war the German bands had played here. Funny that he should equate that music with peace now! What a blessed, lost innocence that was.

Three young men walked by together, in the uniform of the same regiment. They were laughing, teasing each other. They moved with a kind of unity, as if there were an invisible thread that governed them all.

A nursemaid pushed a perambulator. She seemed like a relic from another age when that was the sort of job women looked for, men performed their peacetime labours, and there were no throngs labouring in munitions factories.

A man stood in the middle of the grass, looking from side to side as though utterly lost. His face was bleak. Matthew had not seen these symptoms before, but Joseph had described it to him. The man had been so battered and deafened by the guns, seen such horror, that his mind had refused to accept any more. He had no idea where he was; the only reality was inside him, and that was unbearable.

This one looked about thirty years of age. Then, as Matthew and Detta drew closer to him, Matthew realized with a twisting pity that he was probably more like nineteen or twenty. His eyes were old, but the skin of his cheek and neck said that he had barely reached maturity.

'Are you lost?' Detta said to the young man. She spoke softly, with a sweet, urgent gentleness.

He did not answer.

She asked again.

He looked at her, then the present returned to his mind. 'I suppose so. I'm sorry. You look different. You've grown your hair. I thought you said you'd cut it off. Machines, or something. Caught in it – tore it right off. Someone's scalp, you said.' There was no emotion in his face or his voice. He had seen so many people torn apart one more made no impact at all.

Detta was startled.

An older woman came across the grass, running as fast as she could with her skirts flapping around her legs.

'I'm so sorry,' she apologized. 'I just stopped for a moment. Saw someone I knew.' She looked at the youth. 'Come on, Peter, this way. We'll get a cup of tea at the Corner House, then it's time to go home for supper.'

He went with her uncomplainingly. It probably made little difference to him where he was.

Detta watched them leave, her face tight with misery. 'Why do we do this, Matthew?' she said bitterly. 'Why do we care what happens to Belgium? Why do we let our young men be crucified for it?'

'I thought you liked fighting!' he retorted before he thought to guard his tongue. 'Especially for a piece of land.'

She swung around to face him, her eyes blazing. 'That's different!' she said between her teeth. 'We're fighting for—' Then she stopped, a tide of colour rushing up her cheeks.

Matthew smiled. He did not say anything; it was no longer necessary.

They walked a hundred yards or so in silence. A group of young women were laughing, absorbed in their own conversation. A man in striped trousers and a bowler hat strode briskly in the other direction, stiff and rhythmic, as if he were marching to his own, inner beat.

'Is that really how you see us?' she said at last. 'Pretty much the same as the Germans invading Belgium!'

'I think you see it from your own point of view, as we all do,' he replied. 'You make rather a holy crusade of it, passionate and self-righteous, as if you were the only ones who loved your land, which is a bit of a bore.' It was the most honest answer he had ever given her. But today was different. It would be the last time he would see her. Even now he had no excuse to be here; it was emotion that brought him, his need to see her once more before it was over. The arrests would be made today and the sabotage ended. Perhaps she knew it also. Their ability to use each other was drawing to a close. The pretence was so thin it was almost broken.

She stopped a step ahead of him, forcing him to stop as well.

'Have you thought that all this time?' she asked. 'Is that what has bred your calm, English tolerance?' There was curiosity and sadness in her eyes. Oddly, the anger had gone. 'Your idea of being fair!'

'I suppose so,' he agreed. 'You think that's cold, don't you?'

She looked away and started walking again. 'I used to.'

He refused to ask if she had changed, still less why.

'I don't mind fairness,' she added.

He remained silent. He did not really want to say the sarcastic words that rose to his lips. They would be easy to say but they were not what he meant. He had always wondered if there was anything in him that she really liked, rather than those things that amused her or made the task of trying to extract information from him enjoyable to her. He did not want the answer.

It would be dusk in an hour. The air was still warm and the park was full of people, more soldiers on leave, more girls returning from work, two middle-aged ladies, a handful of children. Whoever had been making the music seemed to have packed up and gone home.

'In fact I admire it,' Detta added, still keeping her face half turned away. '"Play up and play the game",' she went on. 'That's what we love, and hate, in you. You're impossible to understand.'

He laughed outright, a guffaw of sound with an underlying edge to it. This was the end of their time together, and he wanted to cling on to it, impossibly, with a hunger that raged through

200

him, hurting, twisting old certainties in burning temptation. He loved her laughter, her grace, her vitality and her imperfections.

They were at the end of the grass and crossed the path, then followed it to the gates. The shadows of the trees were long and the light had a muted tone. The traffic was a mixture of engines and the rattle of horses' hoofs.

'Are you hungry?' he asked. They had said all they had to; they had shared time and laughter and pain. She had wanted to know if the code was safe. He had deceived her that it was unbroken, and therefore British Intelligence could continue to use the information it gave them.

He looked at her. Her face was gold in the sun, a lock of hair straggling over her brow, and there was dust on her shoes. Could there possibly be any way not to let her go without betraying all those who trusted him, and the young men who went without question to the slaughter, believing in those who sent them?

'I'm thirsty,' she answered. He knew with a tightening of the throat that she did not want to end it any more than he did. They were spinning it out, like a thread of gossamer, bright and fragile.

The traffic stopped and they crossed the road and walked in the close heat of the footpath, bumping into others, weaving their way. They crossed another street and came to a café. They went inside and had tea and hard-boiled egg sandwiches with cress, which was sharp and a little mustardy. They talked about books, and ended up arguing over the virtues of Irish playwrights as opposed to English. She said all the best English ones were Irish anyway.

He asked how she would know, since she only read the Irish ones. She won the argument, then they moved to poets. She lost that argument, but she did it graciously, because the magic of the words enraptured her.

It was almost dark when they went out into the street again. The traffic had lessened a little, and the lamps were lit, but there were still people out walking. The breeze that ruffled the leaves at the edge of the park was warm on the skin.

There was nothing else to cling on to, no more to say. Detta started to walk and Matthew lengthened his stride to keep up with her. Each was waiting for the other deliberately to make the break.

Then suddenly she stopped. 'Lights!' she said hoarsely. 'Look!'

He followed her gaze and saw searchlights probing the sky, first a couple, then more, long fingers poking into the vastness of the night.

She drew in her breath in a gasp, her body rigid. There was a silver tube, soundless, floating so high up it looked small, like a fat insect drifting on the wind. He knew it was a dirigible; the Germans called them Zeppelins. There was a whole ship below the balloon itself, which in peacetime carried passengers. Now it carried a crew, and bombs.

Detta swung around to face him, her eyes huge, her body stiff. She put her hands on his arms and gripped him till he could feel the strength of her fingers through the cloth of his coat. She was breathing hard. She knew it could drop bombs anywhere. There was no point in running, and nowhere to run to anyway.

They stood together, staring up as the lights picked out the gleaming thing, then lost it, and found it again.

Then the first bomb came. They did not see it fall, only heard the crash and the explosion as it landed somewhere to the south, near the river. Flame burst upward, then rubble and dust. Not far away a woman screamed. Someone else was sobbing.

Matthew put his arms around Detta and held her. It seemed a totally natural thing to do, and she leaned against him, still clinging to his coat.

Another bomb came down, closer and far louder. They felt the jar of it as the ground trembled. He held her more tightly. To run away made no sense because the balloon could change direction any moment, drift or hover as it willed, or as the wind took it, before it finally turned and powered its engines to take it home again.

'How many does it have?' Detta asked.

'I don't know,' he replied. He wondered if she had ever been bombed before. There was something in her fear that made him think the violence of the explosion woke memory in her. He wished it had not been Englishmen who had done it, whatever it was.

He looked up and saw the next bomb quite clearly. He could make out the dark, cigar-shaped shadow, black against the lighter sky. He watched it fall with a growing sickness inside, his stomach clenched as it came closer until finally it landed in the next street, shattering the night with a sound that bruised the eardrums, and the blast knocked him sideways and tore them apart. He staggered against the wall of the shop behind him, and Detta fell to her knees on the pavement. The air was full of dust and they could hear rubble landing on the roofs and in the street. People were screaming.

Then the flame shot up and the red glare of it lit the clouds of dust and smoke, and the stench of burning caught in the throat.

Matthew went to Detta, but she was already climbing to her feet. She was dirty, her beautiful dress torn. 'I'm all right,' she said clearly. 'Are you?'

'Yes. Yes, I'm fine. Stay here. I'll go and see if I can help.' He looked at her, his eyes stinging. He could feel the heat already. 'Stay here,' he repeated.

'I'm coming with you.' She did not even consider obeying him. 'We've got to do what we can.'

'No . . . Detta . . .'

She started forward, moving swiftly towards the corner and the only clear way around to where the shattered building had collapsed into the street.

He went after her, afraid for her and yet with a lift of pride that her only thought was to help. For the moment English and Irish were the same, all capable of courage and pity.

The scene was horrible. Broken walls gaped, and scattered about were household goods, furniture, bedding, a mattress on fire on the footpath, clothes tattered like rags. The body of an old man, his legs missing, lay in blood on his own footpath.

A woman was standing paralysed, her dress on fire.

'Oh, Mother of God!' Detta gasped, then swung to Matthew. 'Coat!' she demanded. 'Quick!'

He tore it off and she snatched it from him, lurching forward to throw it around the woman and then knock her to the ground, rolling her over and over.

Someone was shouting, words indistinguishable.

The fire was taking hold of the buildings. Timbers were exploding and showers of sparks arcing through the air. Another blast shook the street and splintered glass crashed on to the pavements.

Matthew saw a body trapped under a fallen beam.

'Help me!' he yelled as loudly as his lungs would bear. 'Help me lift this!' He charged forward, still shouting, and put all his weight to moving the massive length of wood. 'Stay still!' he ordered. 'We'll get you out. Just don't move.'

More rubble was falling and the heat was getting worse. Someone was there beside him and he felt the timbers begin to give. Then Detta was heaving at the fallen man, trying to reassure him.

An ambulance crew appeared and took the man away, and Matthew and Detta moved to the next person, an old woman lying in the rubble, broken-legged and helpless.

'Don't!' Detta said sharply as Matthew bent to lift her. 'We'll have to tie those legs or the jagged ends could cut an artery.'

Matthew understood immediately, and wondered how he could have been so stupid. But what could they use?

Detta was balanced on one leg. 'Here.' She gave him a flashing smile, and two stockings. He grinned back at her, then bent to work. Another man came to help, hands trembling, sobbing under his breath. The noise around them was sporadic – shouts, sirens, more rubble falling, and above it all, what sounded like the crackle of gunfire. The air was full of dust and smoke, but it was beginning to settle.

Fire engines pulled up, horses tethered, eyes rolling, and another ambulance. The heat subsided as the water hit the flames with a roar of steam. Matthew returned from helping to carry the last injured person to find Detta filthy, her dress torn at the shoulders and her ankles bare beneath the hem of her skirt. There was a kind of triumph in the angle of her head and, weary and bruised as she was, she stood with grace. She smiled at him.

He gave her a half-salute. It was not meant in mockery, it was the acknowledgement from one fighter to another. For once they were on the same side, and there was a sweetness to it he wanted to remember through the long loneliness ahead.

She looked into his eyes, and saluted back.

The fire was nearly out inside the house. Somewhere beyond sight another wall collapsed, but with a thud not an explosion.

'If we get out to the main road we might find a cab,' Matthew said, looking down at her feet. He had never thought of feet being beautiful before, but hers were: neat and strong, high-arched. 'Where are your shoes?'

She grimaced. 'Under that wall,' she replied, gesturing towards a heap of shattered brick a dozen yards away. 'But I still have my bag.' Miraculously she was holding the handbag into which she'd carefully put the watch in its box.

'I'll carry you as far as the pavement,' he answered, picking her up before she could argue. It felt good to hold her; she was lighter than he had expected. The grace of her movement hid a certain boniness. He knew he was smiling in the dark. He liked it that she should be less than perfect. For all her fire and courage, it made her human.

He reached the end of the street and reluctantly put her down, slowly, so she was standing close to him and he could still feel the warmth of her. Then he saw the plane. It was a tiny thing, double-winged, like a truncated dragonfly. It crossed the beam of light and disappeared. Then there was another one, climbing upward, veering right and left again. Gunfire tore into the silver ship, not the sturdy lower part carrying the bombs and the crew, but the huge, bright balloon.

There was a moment's silence. He and Detta stared upwards as the searchlights crisscrossed the darkness, catching the planes like angry insects. Tracer bullets arced through the night. And then it happened – an explosion of flame in the air as the gas caught fire and billowed up, lighting the sky.

'Oh, merciful God!' Detta said in horror. 'What a terrible way to die!' She huddled closer to Matthew, clinging to his arm. Without his coat he could feel the warmth of her fingers.

Matthew wasn't thinking of the men in the Zeppelin, but of

the fireball sinking more and more rapidly, new explosions ripping it apart as the bombs left in it went off. He was realizing as it loomed above him that it would come to rest on the streets below it in an inferno of destruction.

'Who?' he said hoarsely. 'Them, or us?'

She turned to look at him. Then she understood and her face went sheet-white. She started to say something and stopped. They stood close together, arms around each other, as the funeral pyre in the sky sank closer to the rooftops. It stretched out, an eternity – and no time at all – too little to escape. The glare increased. It was seconds away. They could feel the heat from where they were. What irony. Perhaps the parting he dreaded would never happen after all.

Everyone was transfixed, staring upwards, shielding their eyes. A man in a long black coat crossed himself. An old woman was shaking her fist. A small dog barked furiously, racing round and round in circles, terrified and not knowing what to do.

A piece of burning debris landed fifty yards away.

People were passing them in the street, cars and wagons, everyone trying to get out of the way, but there was no time. What was left of the balloon and its gondola crashed on a row of houses and shops, and another wave of fire billowed up.

Matthew started forward. He had no idea what on earth he could do, but it was instinctive to try. It was Detta who held him back.

'No,' she shouted, her voice harsh. 'There's nothing. No one will get out of that. Come. They need trained people now. We've done what we can. We'll only be in the way.'

It was true, but it seemed a kind of defeat. He was exhausted. His whole body ached, and he realized only now that he was also cut and burned. But hurting more deeply than that was the knowledge that they had said all there was, all the lies about England and Ireland, the half-truths about America, the evasions about Germany. Tonight they had seen a moment from the reality of war in the broken houses and shattered lives, the grief and the blood, and tried together to help, a little. They had seen the best in each other, but there was nothing to add to it. This was a clean place to break.

They both thought they had been true to their causes, and each had deceived the other. Time would show who was right, and who was wrong would pay. It hurt almost beyond bearing that if he could, Matthew had to make it her.

They walked slowly. The first available cab that passed would mean the time to say goodbye. Detta would not want him to know where she went home to. For minutes he did not look at the stream of traffic passing. The glare of fire made everything red. There were sirens behind them and the sound of other explosions: probably roofs caving in, slate, timbers and glass bursting in the heat, gas mains exploding.

Was it going to go on like this, war from the air? No one safe anywhere?

He looked at the street and saw a cab moving slowly. It was time to put an end to the waiting. It would end anyway, one minute or another. He could not hang on to her. It was up to him to do it. He put up his arm and the cab drew in to the kerb.

'Where to, guv?' the driver asked. 'You 'urt, sir? Yer didn't get caught in that bombing, did yer? 'Orspital?'

'No, we're not hurt. Just tried to help a bit,' he replied. 'Please take the lady wherever she wants to go.' He handed the driver half a crown, and opened the door for Detta.

She stood for a moment, the gleam from the fires red on the sides of her face, her dark eyes wide. There was no laughter in her at all, none of the old daring and imagination, only sadness. She looked very young.

'You're wrong, Matthew,' she said quietly, a catch in her voice. 'I don't always like fighting. Sometimes it's a rotten way to do things. Don't change – that's a battle I wouldn't like to win.' She reached up and kissed him quickly on the mouth, then got into the cab and closed the door.

The taxi pulled away from the kerb, and he watched it until he could no longer distinguish it from the others in the darkness. Then he started to walk. He walked all the way back to his flat. It took him an hour and a half, but it seemed like all night.

*　　*　　*

207

Joseph was getting considerably stronger. It still hurt him to walk, but far less now, and he wore only a light sling on his arm. The bone was knitting well, and as long as he did not jar it he could ignore the occasional twinge.

He had been to see Gwen Neave. He was returning now across the fields, his footsteps soundless on the grass. He had meant to find out how she was, to offer any help, however slight, in the practical duties she would have to perform, although he thought she was probably extremely capable. And so it had proved. It was company she needed, and someone with whom she could speak in confidence about mounting tension in the village. Suspicion was cutting like acid into old friendships, leaving scars it might take years to heal. The Nunns and the Teversams were whispering about each other. Someone had seen Mrs Bateman with a foreign letter. One of Doughy Ward's sisters had been accused of loose talk, or worse. There were fights at school. Children had broken old Billy Hoxton's windows. It was all stupid and ugly, and growing worse.

Joseph had also felt compelled to pursue the investigation into Blaine's death because it threatened Shanley Corcoran, and that was something he could not leave, however cruel or inappropriate it might seem to others. He had asked Gwen about the person she had seen on a bicycle coming out of the path through the trees. He had questioned her persistently, but she could add nothing helpful.

Now he walked across the field and turned over in his mind all he knew. It was little enough. Theo Blaine had been on the edge of solving the last problem with the prototype of the invention, perhaps only a day or two from completing it. He had been having an affair with Penny Lucas, and no one was likely to tell the truth as to how serious that had been, or whether it was over, or in what circumstances.

Blaine had quarrelled with his wife and gone down towards the potting shed on the evening of his death. She had said she had remained in the house, but there was nothing to corroborate that, or disprove it.

Dacy Lucas was accounted for, according to Perth. No one else was, unless you considered Shanley himself, and Archie, at the Cutlers' Arms.

Someone had cycled along the path in the woods: the tyre marks were there. According to the depth of the tracks in the earth, Perth had estimated that someone to be of heavier build than most women, or else a lighter person carrying something. Gwen Neave had seen a man, she was adamant about that.

The fork had a raised screw that had scratched Perth's hand when he swung it experimentally. Whoever had killed Blaine with it had either protected their hands, or would have a similar scratch. Except that it would probably be healed by now. But it might still have been noticed by someone.

Or else they had worn gloves, and smeared the fork with mud to disguise that fact too. There were no fingerprints. Was it a crime of passion and opportunity? Or a carefully planned killing, and the fork simply a chance taken at the last minute?

Joseph had talked to Kerr as well, probing, insisting, asking everything he knew and had observed for himself. That had amounted to nothing of use. Perhaps he was stupid to have imagined it would have. It had all ended in Kerr begging Joseph to deliver the sermon on Sunday. The village was frightened. People who had known each other all their lives were filled with suspicion and imagined ugly acts without reason, and then lashed out when they did not understand. Kerr had no idea what to say to them.

Joseph had stood in the pulpit and looked at the familiar faces turned towards him. He could see the squire, Mrs Nunn, Tucky still swathed in bandages, Mrs Gee, Plugger Arnold's father, Hannah and the children, all the families he knew. They were waiting for him, full of confidence that he could give them some comfort, guidance, meaning to what was happening.

For a moment he had felt panic seize him. No wonder Hallam Kerr was overwhelmed. Did any of the old stories in the old words answer the confusion of today? Would anyone hear the truth wrapped up in the phrases they were so used to?

He thought not. The Bible was all to do with other people, two thousand years ago and somewhere else. They would nod and say Joseph was a good man, and go out exactly the same as they had come in, still angry, frightened and lost.

What use was religion if it was about somebody else? It was about you, or it was about no one. He had abandoned the story of Christ walking the road to Emmaus, unrecognized by the apostles, although it was one of his favourites. He told them instead of the reality of war in Ypres, where their own families were dying. He reminded them of the corpse-filled craters of no-man's-land, and the agony endured in terrible wounds. He did not make it anything like as harsh as the reality, only enough to tear them out of their own present.

'These are our sons and brothers!' he had told them. 'They're doing this because they love us, they believe in home, the dignity and peace, the laughter and the tolerance we stand for, the things of labour and decency, fields that are ploughed and sown year in, year out, streets where men walk without fear, where children play and women carry home their shopping. If we don't keep it a good home, if we soil it with bigotry and intolerance, if we learn how to hate and destroy, if we forget who we are, what are they dying to save? What is there left for those who survive to come home to?'

Now he stood in the grass, in the sweet-smelling air, and was afraid he had said too much. No one had spoken to him afterwards, and Kerr had looked grey-faced enough to be buried in his own churchyard. Only Mrs Nunn had smiled at him, tears in her eyes, and nodded before she went on her way home.

The elms were heavy out over the fields, clouds towering high and bright into the blue of the sky, and there was hardly a sound in the wide peace of it except for the wind and the larks.

Joseph reached the edge of the field and the orchard gate. He unlatched it and went in. There was someone coming towards him, floundering awkwardly. For an instant it took him back to men floundering like that in the mud, the crash and thud of shells around them. But there was no sound amid the apple trees foaming with blossom, except Inspector Perth up to his knees in the uncut grass.

'We should get a scythe to it,' Joseph apologized. 'Nobody's had time.'

Perth dismissed it with a wave. He was a town man, and he did not expect to find things here comfortable. He looked grim, lips drawn tight and brow wrinkled. 'I've bad news, Captain Reavley,' he said, perhaps unnecessarily. 'Can we stay out here, sir? This mustn't go any further. In fact, I would probably be in trouble if anyone knew I'd told you, but could be as I'll need your help before we're through.'

'What is it?' Joseph felt a flutter of fear making him a little sick.

'The Scientific Establishment's been broken into again and . . .'

Shanley Corcoran! He had been murdered, as Joseph had dreaded. He should have done something when he had the chance. Shanley knew who killed Blaine, and he had let himself be . . .

'I'm sorry, Captain Reavley,' Perth continued, cutting through his thoughts. 'Mr Corcoran's very upset, and knowing you're a friend of his for a long time, I . . .'

Joseph felt his heart beating in his throat. 'He's upset? Then he's all right?'

'Well, I wouldn't go so far as to say "all right",' Perth qualified, biting his lip. 'He looks like a man at the end of his strength, to me.'

'You said the Establishment was broken into. What happened? Was anyone hurt? Do you know who did it?' Joseph could hear his own voice out of control, and he could not stop it. Corcoran was safe! That was all that mattered. He was dizzy with relief.

'No, we don't know,' Perth replied. 'That's the thing, sir. Whoever it was smashed the piece of equipment the scientists were working on. Prototype, they called it. Broke it to bits. Mr Corcoran says they'll have to start again from the beginning.'

'But he wasn't hurt?' Joseph insisted.

'No, sir. He was in a different part of the building. Nowhere near it, thank heaven. But he looks proper wore out, like he was coming down with the flu, or something.' He shook his head, his plain, pleasant face twisted in concern. 'He's a very brave man, Captain Reavley, but I don't know how long he can go on like this. It looks as if there's no question we've got a spy in the village, or hereabouts, and that's a bitter thing.' His mouth was pinched as he said it and there was a downward tone in his voice, as if he had struggled a long time to avoid facing that conclusion.

Joseph looked at Perth with a sudden clarity, seeing not just a methodical policeman who was tackling a difficult case, but a man of deep loyalties to his country, perhaps who had sons or brothers in the services, no longer able to deny to himself that his own small area of land, his own people, had bred a traitor. It could be someone he knew, perhaps even liked.

The blossom was drifting off the pear tree, the white petals lost in the high grasses, and a thrush was singing in the hedge.

'War changes us,' he said to Perth.

Perth swung his head around, his eyes miserable and challenging. 'Does it, sir?'

'Strips us down to the best, and the worst in us.' Joseph smiled at him very slightly, just a warmth in his eyes. 'I think so. I've found heroes where I didn't expect, as well as villains.'

'Yes, I suppose,' Perth conceded. 'I'd like to put men in the Establishment to keep Mr Corcoran safe, but I haven't got anyone to spare. I wouldn't know who to tell him to watch, and the intelligence people wouldn't let me anyway. There's nothing to do but find the bastard and see that he's hanged! And they will hang him – for what he did to poor Mr Blaine, apart from anything else. I'd like to know what ideas you have, Captain. I know you've been thinking on it a great deal.'

Joseph nodded. It was a miserable thought, but an inevitable one. He wished with a savage depth that he had more to tell Perth, something of meaning. 'I'll go and talk to Francis Iliffe, and see what I can find out,' he said. But he resolved first to go and try to comfort Shanley Corcoran.

In the house on Marchmont Street the Peacemaker received a visitor. It was the same young man who had called before to bring him word from Cambridgeshire. He stood in the upstairs room, his young face tired. He was trying to hide at least some of his unease, but it was more out of courtesy than any hope to deceive.

'Do the police know who killed Blaine yet?' the Peacemaker asked.

'No,' the young man replied. 'To begin with they considered the probability that it was a domestic matter. Blaine was having an affair with Lucas's wife. But Lucas couldn't have killed him, he can prove quite easily that he was somewhere else.'

'You're certain?'

'Yes. I checked it myself.'

'What about Blaine's wife?' the Peacemaker asked.

'Possible. But they aren't considering her seriously, I think . . .'

'Couldn't be a woman's crime?' the Peacemaker said with derision. 'Rubbish. A strong, healthy young woman, driven by jealousy, could easily have done it. From what you say, it was a crime of opportunity and passion anyway. The weapon was already there – no one brought it! That's hardly planned.'

'I know that.' A flicker of impatience crossed the young man's features. 'But someone broke into the Establishment the day before yesterday, late in the evening, and smashed the prototype—'

'And you come to tell me now?' the Peacemaker demanded, his hands clenching, fury rising inside him like bile.

The young man's eyebrows rose, his eyes wide. 'And if I'd come racing up to London the morning after, don't you think Inspector Perth might have started looking at me a great deal more closely than either of us want?' There was no respect or fear in his voice. That was a change the Peacemaker noted with interest.

'Smashed it? Didn't take it?' he asked.

'Exactly.'

'Why? Any ideas?'

'I've been giving it a lot of thought,' the young man answered. 'The actual guidance system is not too large or too heavy for one man to carry, and that's all you would need. The rest of it is pretty standard, that's the beauty of it. It could be used on anything: torpedo, depth charge, even regular shell, if you wanted.'

'I know that!' the Peacemaker snapped. 'Is that the best you can do?'

A flash of temper lit the young man's eyes, but he controlled it. 'The Establishment would be extraordinarily difficult to break into. They have doubled the guards, but no one was attacked.'

'Bribery?'

'It's possible, but they'd have had to bribe at least three men in order to reach where the prototype was.'

'Money would be no object,' the Peacemaker pointed out.

'No, but the more people you bribe the more chance of one of them changing his mind or betraying you. And you've not only got to get in, you've got to get out again. And what about afterwards? Do you want to leave three men who have that knowledge?'

The Peacemaker waited.

'I think no one came in or went out,' the young man said. 'It was broken precisely because it was someone inside all the time.'

The Peacemaker relaxed. It made perfect sense. 'And I assume if it were you, you would tell me?' he said with an edge to his voice, half humour, half threat.

'I wouldn't smash it before it were finished,' the young man replied levelly. 'If you don't believe my loyalty, at least believe my intellectual curiosity.'

'I hadn't thought to question your loyalty,' the Peacemaker said very carefully. 'Should I?' There was something in the young man's manner, a change in the timbre of his voice since the last time he had been here. Or perhaps, on reflection, it dated further back than that.

'I still believe exactly as I did when we first met,' the young man said intently, his concentration sudden and very real. 'More so, if anything.'

The Peacemaker knew that that was the literal truth, but was there some double edge to the meaning of the words? 'Then it seems we have a third player in the game,' he said very slowly.

The young man paled. 'I think perhaps we have. And before you ask me, I have no idea who.'

'Are they still going to try and complete it?'

'Yes. Corcoran is determined, whatever the cost. He's working all day and half the night as it is. I don't know when he eats or sleeps. He looks twenty years older than he did two months ago.'

'Were you close to success?' It was a question he hardly dared ask. If Corcoran did succeed, then Britain would gain a whole new lease of life at sea. It could prolong the war another year, even two. It could stretch on into 1918 and beyond, and God alone knew how many more lives would be lost.

The young man did not answer the question. His face was bleak, his eyes unhappy.

'If he does succeed, you must take it for Germany,' the Peacemaker said with a sudden flare of passion. 'Tell me when he's anywhere near it, whatever it costs you! I'll see the prototype is taken, if I have to burn the place to the ground.'

The young man nodded. 'Yes, sir. I'll watch. I'm working on it myself. Unless Corcoran gets a sudden breakthrough, I'll be able to see it in advance.' His voice was oddly flat; there was no excitement in it, none of the hunger there used to be. Was he tired, harassed by the police presence, the questions intruding on his work, the suspicion? Or was he really afraid there was a third player, and his own life was at risk?

Or was he going soft, learning to become too much part of one small village in Cambridgeshire, and its people? He must be watched. The work, the goal was too important to indulge any individual.

Two days later the Peacemaker had a very different visitor. This was not a young English scientist with a pleasant freckled face and brown hair that waved off his brow. It was a Irishman closer to fifty, of average height, lean-bodied, his hair neither dark nor fair. If one did not study the expression in his face, he was unremarkable. Only his eyes reflected his intelligence, and then only if he chose that they should.

He stood in front of the Peacemaker, carefully balanced as if to run or to strike, but it was only habit. He had been here many times, and his weapons in this battle were of the intellect.

'Have they the code?' the Peacemaker asked him bluntly.

'No,' Hannassey replied. 'They've worked out how the saboteurs get their funding and who they are by turning a German agent in the docks, and using a double agent in the banking system.'

'Are you sure?' the Peacemaker asked with a lift of interest.

'Yes. The double agent was murdered,' Hannassey replied. 'We found the body. The main thing is that our plans in Mexico can go ahead. The code is safe. We can run rings around the Americans, keep them busy on the Rio Grande for another year at least. Bleed them dry. After that it won't matter whether or not they enter the war.'

'And you trust Bernadette – not just her loyalty, but her judgement?' the Peacemaker persisted. There was an arrogance in Hannassey that he did not like.

Hannassey smiled, a cold expression of mirth without pleasure. 'Sure I'd trust her loyalty to the end of the earth and beyond,' he replied. 'She has the courage to take on God Himself.' There was a shadow in his face, but he did not explain it. Bernadette was his daughter. If he saw a flaw in her he would admit it to no one else, least of all this man.

The Peacemaker offered no comment. He had assessed Bernadette for himself. He trusted no one else's judgement.

Hannassey was motionless. His intense, controlled stillness was one of the few things that marked him out physically. 'Who are the leaders of British Naval Intelligence?' he asked with the slightest smile. 'One superannuated admiral who blinks like an owl, a chief with a wooden leg, and a couple of dozen assorted academics from this college and that.' He was not being dismissive, it was simply fact. The British were amateurs.

The Peacemaker relaxed. He knew the men of British Intelligence. 'Tell Bernadette we are grateful,' he said generously. 'It's a fine piece of work.'

'She didn't do it for you,' Hannassey told him. 'Or for Germany. She works for Ireland as a united country, free of British rule, and with its rightful place in Europe. We've a proud heritage, older and better than yours, and far older than Germany's.' His lip curled very slightly. 'Neither do I work for you. We've a bargain, and I expect you to keep your side of it, starting with more money to support our men, and the right word in the ear of the right man about how the Easter uprising is dealt with. We'll need a great deal more support next time, not only financial but political.' His eyes were unflinching and there was an ugliness in his face, as if threat were very close to the surface.

The Peacemaker saw it, and understood exactly what it was. 'Give us a list of your requirements,' he said calmly. 'I'll consider them.' He made a mental decision to get rid of Hannassey as soon as the opportunity offered itself. He had already exceeded his usefulness. If things worked out as he intended in Cambridgeshire, that opportunity would come very soon.

He looked up at Hannassey and smiled.

Chapter Eleven

Joseph needed far more to take to Perth than vague ideas about Blaine's death and the terrible fear for Shanley Corcoran corroding inside him. It was now inescapable that there was a German sympathizer within the Establishment. No one had broken in to smash the prototype; Perth had proved that beyond doubt. Whatever Theo Blaine's romantic affairs had been, it was now ridiculous to suppose they were the cause of his death, or that Lizzie was involved.

It was for that reason that Joseph felt it was acceptable to ask her to drive him to meet with Francis Iliffe in the evening after his conversation with Perth in the orchard.

It was dusk as they left the village street in St Giles and turned on to the road towards Haslingfield. She was concentrating on the twists, verges now almost hidden by the tall grass and bursting leaf of the hedgerows. Here and there, early may blossom was white. And there was always the possibility of coming on a farm implement in the roadway, or horses, sometimes even a herd of cows.

'Do you know Francis?' Lizzie asked, slowing down for a bend.

'No.' That was the part that Joseph was going to find most difficult. He was intruding into the home of a man he had not even met, with the intention of asking him impertinent questions, and even implying that he might be guilty of murder. He smiled ruefully, aware of his own absurdity. 'I was hoping you would introduce me. I apologize if I am placing you in an embarrassing position.' However he did not offer her the chance of retreating.

She glanced sideways at him for a second. 'You're really worried about Mr Corcoran, aren't you?' she said quietly. There was sympathy in her voice, a sudden gentleness.

'Yes,' he admitted. 'Whoever it is has already killed once, and smashed the machine.'

She winced.

'I'm sorry.' He was callous to have mentioned it to her so clumsily. He realized that he was requiring her to take him to see the man who might have murdered her husband, with as little thought for her feelings as if she had been a taxi driver. He blushed with shame for himself. 'Mrs Blaine, I really am sorry! I've behaved with terrible insensitivity. I was so afraid for Shanley I forgot your feelings altogether. I—'

'It's all right,' she cut across him. 'I know what you're thinking. Truly. You can't bring Theo back, and you're trying to save a man who can finish his work and create something to win the war, and – far more important to you – a man whom you love as a friend and something like a father. I understand.'

He was embarrassed for her gentleness, and his own stupidity. 'You are very forgiving,' he said sincerely.

She gave a little laugh, sad and self-deprecatory. 'Not usually. It's something I need to learn. I didn't forgive Theo much, and now it's too late. I expected him to be clever in everything, not just some things, and people aren't like that. Just because he could invent new and extraordinary machines didn't mean he was wise as well, where people are concerned. I think mathematicians are young, the men that are geniuses. Understanding of people tends to come with age.'

'Is Iliffe brilliant as well?' he asked.

She looked at him quickly again, then back at the road. 'You mean is he a fool over women? Probably, but I don't know.'

'Do you know Ben Morven too?' He thought of Hannah, but he would not ask Lizzie if she knew about the situation.

'Yes. He's a bit naïve also, an idealist,' she replied. 'But a nice one. Not as abrasive as Francis Iliffe.'

'What sort of idealist?'

'Social justice, that sort of thing,' she answered. 'He thinks education is the answer for everyone. He's rather sweet, but very provincial.'

They were out on the Haslingfield road and drove in silence for a while. The western sky in front of them flamed with colour, and faded as they headed towards Iliffe's home. Joseph tried to prepare what he would say. It was late to call on anyone, and discourteous to do so without notice in advance, but urgency precluded such niceties.

Iliffe opened the door himself. He was in his early thirties, lean and dark-haired. At the moment he was wearing rather baggy trousers, a white shirt and an old cricketing sweater against the evening chill. The lighted hallway behind him had the cleanliness of a house kept by a domestic servant, and the untidiness of one lived in by a young, single man who was interested in ideas and to whom physical surroundings were of little importance.

'Yes?' Iliffe looked at Joseph curiously, not immediately seeing Lizzie beyond the circle of the light.

Prepared explanations deserted Joseph and he was left with nothing but bare honesty, and his fear for Corcoran made anything else ridiculous.

'Good evening, Mr Iliffe,' he said candidly. 'My name is Joseph Reavley. Shanley Corcoran is a friend of mine – he has been for years. I'm deeply afraid for his safety, and that of anyone else working at the Establishment.'

A flicker of humour lit Iliffe's thin, intelligent face. 'Thanks for your concern. Did you come here to tell me that?' There was an understandable edge to his voice. 'A letter would have sufficed.'

Joseph felt himself blushing. 'Of course not. I'm on sick leave from Ypres, where I'm a chaplain.' He saw Iliffe's expression change and knew he had redeemed at least something of the situation. 'I know Inspector Perth from another case, before the war. I intend to help him, whether he likes it or not.'

Iliffe smiled and stepped back. 'Come in.' Then he saw Lizzie and his eyes softened. 'If you're a friend of Lizzie's, you can't be as bad as you seem,' he added, leading them to a sitting room where books and papers were scattered on every surface. He tidied them from the sofa, putting them in a pile on the desk, and offered his visitors seats.

'It's not secret stuff,' he said disparagingly, seeing Joseph's surprise. 'I'm designing a sailing boat, one of those to put on ponds. I want to be able to steer it from the shore.'

Joseph found himself smiling.

'So what do you want from me?' Iliffe asked with interest. 'If I had any proof who it was I'd have done something about it myself.'

Joseph knew what he wanted to ask; what he did not know was how to measure the truth of the answers he received. 'How brilliant was Theo Blaine?' he asked. He wished Lizzie were not there, but the advantage was that she was at least some measure for accuracy.

'The best,' Iliffe said frankly. His eyes went to Lizzie with a smile, then back to Joseph again.

'Can you finish without him?' Joseph continued.

Iliffe shrugged. 'Touch and go. Not if some swine smashes the prototype again. It's worth a try, but I'm not sure.'

'With Corcoran working on it personally?'

Iliffe looked unhappy.

Joseph waited. There was a keen edge of intelligence in Iliffe's face. He understood the reasoning, and guessed the personal gain and loss.

'If Morven works on it, perhaps,' he answered. 'Corcoran alone, no.' He offered no apology and no prevarication.

'What can you tell me about Morven?' Joseph asked.

'Intellectually? He's outstanding. Almost in Blaine's category.'

'And in other ways?'

Iliffe looked at Lizzie, but she allowed him to answer without adding anything herself.

'Grew up in working-class Lancashire,' Iliffe said. 'Grammar school, Manchester University. Opened up a new world to him. Don't know if you can understand that, Mr Reavley. Sorry, I don't know your rank . . .'

'Captain, but it's irrelevant. Yes, I can understand it. I lectured in biblical languages in Cambridge before the war. I had many students with a similar background. Some were even brilliant, in their own field.' He ignored the pain inside him as he said that.

Iliffe saw it. 'Gone to the trenches?' he asked.

'Many of them, yes. It's not exactly a war-exempt skill.'

'Then you know the impact of ideas on a boy from a narrow, working-class town suddenly in a ferment of social, political and philosophical ideas, realizing he's got a dazzling mind and the whole world is out there, and his for the conquering. Morven's an idealist. At least he was a year ago. I think some of the dreams have been hampered a bit by reality since then. One grows up. Are you thinking he's a German sympathizer?'

'Are you?' Joseph countered.

Lizzie looked from one to the other of them, but she did not interrupt.

'No, frankly,' Iliffe replied. 'But a socialist possibly. Even an internationalist of sorts. I can't see him killing Blaine.' He glanced at Lizzie. 'Sorry,' he apologized gently. He turned back to Joseph. 'But then I can't see anyone doing that, and obviously someone did. Does your pastoral experience teach you how to recognize violence like that behind the everyday faces, Reverend?'

'No,' Joseph said simply. 'We all have the darkness – some act on it, most of us don't. I can't tell who will, or who already has.'

'Pity,' Iliffe said drily. 'I was hoping you had all the answers. I'm damn sure I don't.'

Outside on the way home again Lizzie said very little. Joseph apologized once more for having asked her to drive him on such a journey.

'Don't.' She shook her head. 'In an obscure sort of way it makes me feel better to think I'm doing something. It isn't right to carry on with my life as if Theo were going to come back one day. I was his wife. I loved him . . . I ought to be trying to find out who killed him, and prevent them from killing his work as well.'

Joseph looked at her face, concentrated on the dark road and the bright path of the headlights. He could only see her profile, lips smiling, and tears on her cheek.

He did not say anything and they drove home in an oddly companionable silence.

The next day was Sunday. Archie had come home late the previous evening for a short leave, but he made the effort to get up and they all went to church together, dressed in their best clothes. Archie and Joseph both wore uniform and Hannah walked between them, her head high with pride. They spoke to everyone they knew, assuring them they were well, asking in return but never mentioning other members of families. One could not be certain from day to day who was critically injured, posted missing in action, or even newly dead. There was kindness in it, sensitivity to pain and fear, and the knowledge that if the blow did not come today, then it could tomorrow, or the day after. There was so much that could not be said, or the dam would break.

Joseph saw Ben Morven in a pew to their left, and caught his eyes on Hannah, watching her with a bright gentleness that betrayed more than he could have known. Once he saw Hannah look back at him, and then away again quickly, blushing.

The submerged tension in the air was crackling. Everyone practised their Sunday-best behaviour, along with the suits and dresses and hats, but the anger and suspicion were there, the tight lips, the whispers and the silences.

Joseph wondered, could Ben possibly have killed Theo Blaine? Perhaps in a fistfight; he was young and strong and passionate in his loves and his dreams. But not in the dark, ripping his throat out with a garden fork! Could he?

That was absurdly naïve. Idealism had crucified men, burned them at the stake, broken them on the wheel. Of course he could. It was hypocrisy that made the hand fail, cowardice, apathy, all the half-hearted emotions. Ben Morven was not half-hearted, right or wrong.

Kerr's sermon was better than previously and Joseph caught his anxious glance two or three times. However much he would prefer to avoid it, he must speak to him. He told Hannah he would follow them home, and waited behind after everyone else had left.

Kerr was standing at the church door, moving uncomfortably from one foot to the other. His hair was slicked back with its exact centre parting, a slight sheen of sweat on his forehead in the warmth of the sun.

'The suspicion is tearing us apart,' he said before Joseph had time to speak. 'All sorts of stupid whispers are going around the village. Old feuds we all thought were settled years ago are being opened up again. Anybody gets a letter from a stranger, an overseas stamp on it, and the stories begin. That wretched inspector talks to everyone and either someone says he suspects that person, or they're telling stories about someone else, trying to plant suspicion. And the awful thing is, sometimes that's true. People are using this to settle old scores, take advantage, even to threaten.'

'It's bad,' Joseph agreed sombrely. 'I came just to say that you gave a good sermon, but . . .'

Pleasure lit Kerr's face, and Joseph suddenly realized, with surprise and a degree of guilt, that Kerr admired him intensely. He cared what Joseph thought. His impatience or indifference would wound with real pain, perhaps lasting.

'. . . But perhaps we should think a little about this,' he added. 'It's a very serious problem.'

Now Kerr was surprised. He had not expected help, and that too made Joseph aware of a streak of unkindness in himself. He had had the time, simply not the inclination. If he were going to stay here then he should face the villagers' needs, not simply use them as an excuse not to go back to the trenches.

'I've been thinking about it,' Kerr was saying. 'I can't decide whether it would be better to speak about it generally, without making anyone feel singled out, or to go to each one I know is guilty, and tackle it unequivocally.' He was talking too quickly. 'Sometimes an oblique approach is better. It allows people to deny it and at the same time do something about it.' He looked at Joseph hopefully.

They smiled at the Teversham family as they huddled together along the path.

'It's a good point,' Joseph conceded. 'You touched on it today. I didn't realize at the time quite how bad it had become.'

Kerr nodded. He began to look less tense and he stood still at last as if he were easy in front of his own church. 'Of course the difficulty is that if you speak of something in a sermon, so often the people you mean it for are quite sure it is directed at everyone but them,' he said.

Joseph put his hands in his pockets. It was a curiously valuable sense of freedom to be rid of the sling at last, even though he tended to carry his arm bent a little. 'Then you will have to speak to people as you become aware of their behaviour,' he said decisively.

Kerr gulped.

Joseph smiled at him, but it was an expression of sympathy, devoid of judgement. 'Rotten,' he agreed. 'But there are ways of doing it. Have you considered asking their help?'

'Help?' Kerr said incredulously, sure he had misheard. 'From the ones creating the most damage?'

'Exactly. Tell them how much pain and fear it's causing, but attribute it to someone else. Think how they can then agree with you and save their pride, and at the same time crush what's happening.'

'I see! Yes. Yes, I think . . .' he gulped again, 'that might work,' he smiled, 'rather well.'

'It's somewhere to start,' Joseph said encouragingly. 'And you are quite right, it must be addressed, and there isn't really anyone else who has the moral authority.'

Kerr squared his shoulders. 'Thank you, Captain Reavley. You really are a very great help. There is something valuable for me to do here. I see that.' He held out his hand. 'Please believe me, I shall do my best.'

It was a kind of farewell, as if Joseph would be leaving soon. A sharp guilt stabbed him that he was not. He had not actually sent the letter yet, but it was on the desk in the study, ready to go. He just had not got around to posting it. He had not told Hannah he would stay, but he had allowed her to believe it, to hope, and now in the silent graveyard it seemed a coward's thing to do, a desertion. He could not make himself tell Kerr that he had decided not to return. There were all sorts of phrases in his mind, ready to say, and none of them sounded good. And above all Tom would no longer see him as a hero, but just one more man who had escaped when he could, who no longer faced forward.

If he changed his mind now he would be letting Hannah down, but whatever he did he would be letting someone down. It was not that Tom's opinion of him mattered more than hers, and he would have to make her understand that it was his own opinion. This quiet village with its ancient church, its graveyard where his parents were buried, its vast trees and sunlit fields, its domestic lives, its quarrels, was infinitely precious. The only way to help it was not to cling, but to be willing to let go, to give, not to take.

Kerr was looking at him, waiting for the acknowledgement he needed.

'I have no doubt of that,' Joseph said sincerely. 'And it will be enough. But don't be afraid of failure. No one wins all the time. If you win most of it you will have done a great thing.' He took Kerr's hand and gripped it hard before turning away and walking down the path to the lich-gate and on to the road.

Archie was reading the newspaper in the sitting room when Joseph burst in.

'Can you drive me to the Establishment, now, to see Ben Morven?'

'This afternoon?' Archie said in disbelief.

'Sorry,' Joseph apologized. 'It can't wait.'

'You think it's Morven?' Archie still looked doubtful.

'I don't know. I can't afford to take the risk that it isn't.'

'And he'll kill Corcoran as soon as he's sure the prototype is complete?' Archie's whole attention was engaged now.

Joseph was confused. He had wrestled with the thoughts, turning them over and over in his mind. He would far rather have come to a different conclusion. He had liked Ben, but the theory fitted too well: the brilliant boy growing up where he could see and taste plenty of anger and social injustice, attending a university where suddenly the whole world expanded before him with its infinite opportunities and thought had a power close to God!

Joseph had seen it in so many young men, the passion of idealism overwhelming patience and caution. Words of warning infuriated where pain was seen on a vast scale, and a solution beckoned.

A man like the Peacemaker would find recruits there so easily. Joseph had experienced it before at St John's. It was happening again, it was bound to, as long as there were young men with dreams, and powerful men willing to use them.

Last time the price had been John Reavley's life; this time it could be Shanley Corcoran's. The difference was that now Joseph could see it, and stop it.

'Probably,' he answered Archie's question. 'He has no need to keep him alive once it's finished.'

Archie was still hesitant.

'He killed Theo Blaine!' Joseph said with bitter regreat. 'He tore his throat out with a garden fork. Why wouldn't he kill Shanley?'

'He would,' Archie conceded. 'We'd better go. Are you going to tell Hannah why?'

'No . . . at least . . .' Joseph was uncertain. 'I'll tell her it's to do with Blaine's death, then at least she'll know why you have to go. I can't ask Mrs Blaine to drive me again.'

'I'll borrow Albie Nunn's car. It's not exactly elegant, but it goes. I'll see you in half an hour. I suppose Shanley will be at home?'

'If he isn't we'll wait,' Joseph replied simply.

They spoke of other things as they drove – memories, family affairs, nothing of the war. Joseph had wondered whether to say anything of Hannah's desire to know more of Archie's life at sea, and decided it was up to her whether or not she asked further. Any intrusion might be clumsy, and, apart from that, if what she learned was more than she afterwards wanted to bear, then it must be of her own choosing.

Orla Corcoran was surprised to see Joseph on the step. Archie had decided to remain in the car, possibly to walk a little once Joseph had gone inside.

'He's not home yet,' she said, showing Joseph into the drawing room. The curtains were still open to let in the afternoon light.

Orla looked elegant and faintly exotic with her smooth, dark hair and her eyes so black it was impossible to read their expression.

Joseph could not afford to worry about keeping Archie waiting outside. 'Then may I wait?' he asked. 'It's important.'

She stood motionless, lean and graceful, the sun on her shoulders. 'Is it about Blaine's death?' she said quietly. It was a natural guess. What else would bring him here at this hour, uninvited and with such insistence?

'Yes. I'm sorry.' Did she know too? Was she just as afraid for Shanley as he was? Joseph realized with shock that in spite of all the years of superficial familiarity he did not know her anything like as well as he knew her husband. She never spoke of herself, always of him. Joseph knew nothing of her dreams, beliefs, or what she might have wanted, apart from to be Mrs Corcoran. How deeply did it hurt her that she had no children? He had never seen her spend time alone with any of his own family, nor did she now call on Hannah. It was always Shanley who took the lead.

Was she simply shy? Or uninterested? Or guarding a hurt too deep to expose, even to friends? The mask of shadow created by the sunlight behind her showed nothing in her face. Joseph made the decision. 'I'm afraid for him,' he said suddenly.

'Of course,' she agreed. 'We're all afraid. What happened to Theo Blaine was terrible.'

'Who did it?' he asked.

Her fine eyebrows rose. 'Do you think I know?'

'I think Shanley does.'

She turned away. 'Would you like a glass of sherry while you are waiting?'

So she was not going to answer. Perhaps that was an answer in itself? He accepted the sherry in a small, crystal glass, and they talked of other things. Corcoran arrived fifteen minutes later, pale-faced and clearly exhausted. He could not hide that it cost him an effort to be courteous, even to Joseph, close as they were.

'I didn't recognize the car,' he said without expression. 'You're well enough to drive. I'm glad.'

'Archie borrowed one,' Joseph explained. 'I expect he's gone for a walk.'

Corcoran turned away. 'I see.'

'I'm sorry,' Joseph apologized immediately. 'If it could have waited I wouldn't have come.'

Corcoran sighed. He accepted a glass of sherry from Orla, but did not touch it. He probably had not eaten, perhaps all day. Joseph was consumed with guilt, but his fear for his friend overtook it all.

Orla slipped out without bothering to excuse herself.

Corcoran turned to face Joseph. 'What is it?'

'I've been asking questions,' Joseph replied. 'I won't bother you with the details, unless you want them, but you probably know them as well as I do.' He looked at Corcoran's weary face and felt a pity for him so intense it was a physical ache inside him. 'I think Ben Morven was placed inside the Establishment to be a spy for the Germans, perhaps groomed for it even before the war – one of the idealistic young men who must have peace at any price, and see us as just as much to blame for war as anyone else.'

Corcoran's face tightened, a subtle change in his expression, but one of terrible sadness.

'I think you knew that,' Joseph went on. He was finding it even harder to say than he had expected. The room seemed to be abnormally silent, his own voice thundering, although he was speaking softly. 'And I think that for the sake of England, and the war, you are sheltering him for as long as you need his skill to finish the prototype.'

Corcoran took a long, deep breath and let it out in a sigh. 'And if you are right, Joseph, what difference does that make?'

'You must have him arrested,' Joseph said simply. 'You have no choice.'

Corcoran's eyes widened. 'Must?'

'He murdered Blaine. He'll kill you, Shanley, the moment he thinks he doesn't need you. And possibly Iliffe too, if he gets in his way. Or Lucas, for that matter. But I'm not going to lose you.'

Corcoran's face was soft, his eyes gentle. 'My dear Joseph, it is not about me, or about you. It is about England, and the war.

Morven will not harm anyone until he has the final answers. I am safe until then.'

'And you are sure you will judge that correctly?' Joseph challenged. 'To the hour? To the minute?'

'Are you returning to Ypres, Joseph?'

'Don't evade the subject.'

'I'm not. Are you going?'

'Yes.' He was surprised that he did not even hesitate. 'Yes, I am.'

'And might you be killed?' Corcoran asked.

'Yes,' Joseph said quietly. 'But more probably not. I won't run any unnecessary risks.'

Corcoran smiled for the first time. 'Rubbish! You will go out into no-man's-land just as you have always done. And if you die Hannah will mourn for you, and her children will, and Matthew, and Judith. And so shall I. But I shan't tell you that you cannot go. You must do your duty as you see it, Joseph. And so must I. But it matters to me immensely that you cared enough to come and try to prevent me. The fact that it is utterly wrong, and against all you believe yourself, is a mark of your affection I shall not forget. Now please allow me to wish you good night, before I become too tired to keep my feelings under control, and embarrass us both.'

Joseph was defeated and he knew it. Corcoran's argument was unanswerable. There was nothing for him to do but say good night and go out to find Archie. He did so with a heavy heart, but as much grace as he could manage.

Archie was due to leave on the early train next day. There was no more time left for Hannah to waste. It was late. They were both tired, but if she missed her chance to ask for the truth now, there might be no other time. When he left, she would miss him in every way: his voice, his touch, his laughter, the light in his face, the smell of his skin. But more importantly, this might be her last chance of knowing the man inside the shell, the thing that was unique and eternal.

She sat on the bed and watched him move his small case to

230

where he could pack it in the morning. She must speak now. Tomorrow he could avoid her, the children might interrupt, there would be any number of reasons and excuses.

'Lucy Compton called to see me a few weeks ago,' she began. 'You know Paul was killed in France?'

He looked up. 'If you told me, I'd forgotten. I'm sorry. How was she?' There was pity in his face and a kind of crumpled sadness, as if he were seeing Lucy in her, or perhaps her in Lucy.

'Full of regret,' she answered. She hated doing this! It was not too late to leave it, not try to force him to tell her. Let him have a last evening at home in peace. Leave the war until tomorrow.

He did not understand. 'Regret? You mean grief?'

She steeled herself. 'No, I did mean regret. There was so much she didn't know about him, about his life, what he cared about, what he felt. Now it's too late.'

'You never know all that people care about,' he said, pushing the case away behind the wardrobe, back where he could not see it.

She forced herself to continue.

'A friend of his came by and told her all sorts of things about him,' she said, 'in France – what a good officer he was, what a good friend. That was when she realized that this man knew her husband far better than she did.'

'I'm sorry. But there's nothing you can do to help her. There's no point in thinking about it.'

Was he misunderstanding her on purpose?

'No. But I can help myself!'

There was a closed look in his face, touched with anger. 'What are you talking about? No, don't bother explaining. It doesn't matter.'

'It matters to me,' she insisted. She was sitting still in the bed. He was less than a couple of yards away, and it could have been miles. 'You never tell me what your life is like at sea. I don't know anything about the men you serve with, who you like, who you don't, or why.' She gulped and went on, speaking too quickly now, and aware of it. 'I don't know what you do every day, but far more than that, I don't know what hurts you, or frightens you, or makes you laugh.' She could see the surprise in his eyes, and the defence already. 'Archie, I need to know!' she insisted. 'I want to! Please – it isn't really a kindness to shut me out. I know you're doing it to protect me, and probably because you don't want to talk about it anyway. You want to keep a place where war can't intrude, somewhere clean and separate.'

He was staring at her. 'For God's sake, Hannah! Can't we just have a pleasant evening? I have to go tomorrow.'

'I need to know!' she said with rising desperation. She knew she was angering him, risking pushing him further away. They might even part with a quarrel! That would be unbearable. It could be for the last time. That thought beat in her mind, almost choking the words, her throat was so tight. 'When you're gone it's as if you disappear!' she said hoarsely. 'I know a part of you so well it's as if we'd always been together, but there's a whole world, terribly important, that I'm shut out of as if I couldn't understand and don't belong. But at the moment it's the biggest part of you, it's what you spend your life doing, it's what makes you who you are, what you believe, what makes you real. I need to know it, Archie!'

'I can't tell you,' he said with patience that obviously cost him a tremendous effort, almost more than he possessed. 'It's ugly, Hannah. It would give you nightmares and your imagination would torture you. You can't help! Just—'

'I'm not trying to help you!' Her voice was rising in spite of her effort to keep it under control. 'Can't you see that I'm trying to help myself! And if I have to, help Tom. What if something happens to you, and Tom asks me what you were like? What am I going to say? "I don't know? He never told me"? Do you think that will satisfy him, when his father's gone and he can't ask? Do you think it will satisfy me? We need to know, Archie. Maybe it will hurt, but that's better than a lifetime of hating myself because I didn't have the courage to face it.'

'Tell you what?' he said wearily, sitting on the floor and crossing his legs as if he had given up. 'What it feels like to live in a few square feet that's never still, even when the sea's calm? Do you want me to tell you how cold it is? The wind off the North Atlantic whips the skin from your flesh. How tired you get when you've only had a couple of hours' sleep, and day and night blend into each other till you can't think, can't feel, can't eat and you feel sick? You know what it's like to be exhausted. You've done it with sick children – babies, anyway – up every half-hour, or more.'

'It's not the same,' she said, wondering if it was.

'At sea you stare out at the ocean till you're blind with it,' he went on, almost as if ignoring her. 'You know every wave could hide a torpedo. One moment you are standing on the deck, pitching and sliding, and the next you're deafened by the noise of tearing metal, and you know you could be pounded, broken and suffocated by icy waters, dragged down into the darkness and never come up again. You imagine your lungs bursting, and pain obliterating everything else.'

She sat frozen, her muscles locked and aching.

He went on; his voice was softer, cut across with grief. 'Shall I tell you about fire at sea? Or what it's like to see a gun turret hit, and bodies of men you know cut to pieces, blood everywhere, human arms and legs lying on the deck? Or would it be enough if I just stick to the long days and nights of monotony while you wait and wonder, cold, tired, eating sea rations, trying to work out how you'll deal with the attack when it comes, how you'll keep the men together, keep heart in them – be worthy of their trust in you that somehow you can get them out of it? And how you'll live with it if you fail?'

She blinked. 'It's horrible,' she whispered. 'I don't even know how to imagine it. But if that's your life, then shutting me out of it would be even worse . . . maybe not straight away, not now, but in time it would. It hurts to be shut out. A different kind of hurt, but a real one.'

'You don't need it, Hannah!' He stood up, easily, moving with grace in spite of his inner tiredness. The leave had not been long enough. But he had told her only about life at sea, and little enough of that. He had not told her about himself.

'Yes, I do need it,' she argued. 'Either I belong to you, or I don't. If you shut me out, even if you're right and I don't have the strength or the courage to bear it, then—'

'I didn't say that!' he protested, turning to look at her angrily.

'You meant it,' she retorted. 'And when Tom's confused and hurt, when you're not here, I have to try and explain to him why you won't trust any of us.'

'It's not trust!' He was frustrated by her refusal to understand. 'It's to protect you from the nightmares I have! Can't you see that? What's the matter with you, Hannah?'

'Do you think Judith needs protecting?' she asked, controlling her feelings with an effort. This was the time when she must be strong. She had asked for the truth; there was no place for emotional manipulation.

Archie was startled. 'Judith? That's different. She's—' He stopped.

'What?' she demanded, keeping her voice level with intense difficulty. 'What is she that you think I'm not? Tell me!'

Archie stared at her. His eyes were so tired they were red-rimmed. She knew he was sleeping little.

'What is it?' she insisted. 'You're not protecting me, you're shutting me out. I need to know you! Don't you trust me to love you, even if you're afraid sometimes?' The words were out, irretrievable. She could not take them back now. Her stomach churned with fear.

He looked startled. 'No, of course I'm not shutting you out! Is that what you think?'

'I don't know what to think,' Hannah answered. 'Do you imagine I expect you to be perfect? I don't. I never did. That isn't love, it's . . . for goodness' sake, even Jenny doesn't expect that! It's vanity!'

He winced, as the mention of Jenny's name hurt him unexpectedly.

She was accusing him now. 'And total lack of faith in us!' she went on. 'I never thought you were perfect, any more than I am! Or is that it? You really believe I'm not strong enough to hear about what you have to live through?'

He leaned forward, intensely earnest. 'I don't want you to have to think about it, Hannah. Did you tell me how it felt to give birth? I heard you screaming, but I couldn't share it.'

234

She took a deep breath. 'Then let me hear you scream some-times,' she begged. 'Or at least know what it's for. I know you might get killed. I do know that! Then I'll lose you, and for the children's sake, I'll have to go on by myself, whatever I feel like. And they'll have to go on too. But I want to have the real you now! I want to know what I will have lost.'

He turned away from her. 'You don't understand what you're asking. Joseph doesn't tell you what it's like in Flanders.'

'I'm not married to Joseph.' That made all the difference in the world. 'But I would listen if he did, if it helped him.'

'And if he didn't want to tell you?' Archie asked, still not looking at her. 'What if I would rather have you just as you are, not knowing, not changed by it, not part of that life?'

That hurt. Joseph had refused to tell her. She felt the sting of it like a hand slap. She had difficulty controlling the tears coming to her eyes. 'I'm shut out, as I am from you, and I will have to live with it,' she said quietly. 'I will be alone. Perhaps you have other people you want to share yourself with.'

'Hannah! That's not . . .' He sat down slowly on the bedroom chair, lowering his head so she could not see his face. 'If you had any idea what it's like you wouldn't say that.'

'I don't have any idea because you don't tell me!' she retorted. She couldn't and wouldn't go back now. 'I only have my imagin-ation and my own nightmares. Is it any worse than reality?'

He was speaking quietly now, almost as if in a way she had beaten him. 'Yes it is! You've never been as cold in your life as it is at sea. Your eyelashes freeze, the tears on your face are ice. It hurts to breathe. Your bones hurt with it, like having toothache all over your body. Land could be only a hundred miles away, but it might as well be beyond existence.'

He lifted his head to look at her. 'There's nothing but you and the ocean, and the enemy. He might come over the horizon, a black silhouette against the sky, or he might heave up out of the water right in front of you. More likely you won't know anything at all until the torpedo hits, and the deck under your feet erupts in fire and twisted metal and blood.'

It was not the words – she had heard them before – it was the horror in his face, because he was letting himself live it now. It was in his voice, his hands clenched on his knees, scars showing white against the wind-burned brown of his skin. A part of her wished she had not started this.

'Do you hate it all the time?' She did not want to know the answer, but she had to ask.

He was surprised. 'No, of course I don't. There's laughter, and friendship. Some of the jokes are even funny. There's immense courage.' He looked away from her again to hide the nakedness inside him. 'Heroism you can't bear. Men who keep going in blinding pain, dying . . . Hannah, you don't want to hear this. You've never seen a human being blown to pieces, or worse, torn open and bleeding to death, but still conscious and knowing what's happening to him. That was the way Billy Harwood died. I can still see his face when I close my eyes.' He gasped. 'There was blood everywhere. We did everything we could, but we couldn't stop it. There was just too much. You haven't seen fire in a gun turret when there's nowhere to escape to and they have to stand there and burn to death, and we watch them. A child shouts in the street, and I hear that again – men like torches in the night.'

Very slowly she moved closer to him and kneeled down. She could see there were tears on his face. He was right, she did not want to know this. Her imagination would build enough for her to have nightmares, waking or sleeping, from now on, but she had to.

This was not the man she had first loved, who had gone to sea with pride and enjoyment in it, ambitious to succeed. This man was older, at once stronger and more vulnerable, a stranger in her husband's skin, whom she wanted passionately to know. She needed to start again, assuming nothing. She reached out her hand and slid it over his very gently.

'We sank an enemy ship a couple of weeks ago,' Archie went on; his voice was shaking and she could feel the locked muscles making his legs tremble, even though he was sitting.

'It was at dusk. It was a good manoeuvre; partly luck, but mostly skill. We'd been shadowing each other for days. He fought hard, but we had the first shot and it damaged him badly.' He was looking beyond her, into his own vision. 'The water was grey like lead, pitted dark by wind and rain. We fought for nearly two hours. We took some bad hits ourselves. Lost a dozen men, killed and wounded. The man next to me lost both his legs. Surgeon tried to save him, but it was too much.'

He took a deep breath, searching her face, trying to read her emotions, what she thought of him, how much she was frightened or sickened.

She wished she could think of something wise or generous to say, but her mind was empty of everything but the numb misery of it. He must not see the fear in her, the longing to deny it all.

'We sank him just after sundown,' he went on, saying the words slowly and carefully. 'We hit his magazine, and he went down with all hands. That's the thing I dread more than anything else – being carried down inside, the water rushing in and I'm trapped, going down all the way into the darkness, with the sea above me, for ever.' His breath was ragged.

'They went down,' he said quietly. 'All of them. We didn't save a soul. There was no triumph, no victory, just silence. I lay awake all night seeing it again and again. When it comes to it, they were seamen, as we are. We probably would have liked them, if we'd met a few years ago, before all this.' He was looking at her again, waiting for the confusion at his feelings, the revulsion for what he had done.

She blanked her mind. She must not show it, not even a glimmer, whatever it cost. There must be something to say, and she must think of it quickly.

'You're right, it isn't easy,' she agreed. 'It's horrible. But we don't have a choice. We go forward together, or we go forward alone. I don't want to be ashamed of myself because I refused to look. But don't tell Tom too much, just a little, if he asks. Tell him some of your men were killed. He'll understand that was hard to take. Please don't leave him out altogether. He loves you so much.'

His voice caught and there were tears on his cheek. 'I know.'

She smiled, blinking hard. 'So do I.' Please God she would have the strength to go on meaning that, if it got worse, if she woke up with the horror of her imagination night after night when he was not there beside her. She would remember all the laughter, the hope, the tenderness between them, and picture the dark, icy water suffocating the life out of him as he struggled and beat against it, and was crushed and plunged to the bottom of the sea, to places no human being ever imagined. Her heart would go with him. At least she would not be cut off, separate and unknowing.

'Hannah!' his voice broke through her thoughts.

'Yes!' she said quickly. 'I'm here.'

He pulled her into his arms and held her.

Chapter Twelve

Matthew had just returned from Cambridgeshire and a visit to the Scientific Establishment that had been one of the most wretched of his career.

'No, sir,' he said quietly.

Shearing looked drawn. The usually smooth flesh of his cheeks was hollow and the web of fine lines around his eyes was cut deeper as if the skin had no life in it. 'No hope?' he asked, looking up at Matthew.

'No, sir, not in any time we could put a name to.'

There was a tension in the room already, as if tragedy were only waiting to be acknowledged. Matthew realized how afraid he was. For once he wished he were a fighting man, so he could at least do something physical to make himself feel better. And perhaps knowing less would also be easier now, a single enemy in front of him to fight, rather than the darkness all around, massive and closing in.

Shearing sat very still. Even his hands on the top of his desk were motionless, no pen, no paper in them.

The blow was numbing. Corcoran had been so certain he could complete the prototype, even with Blaine dead. He had worked on it himself, night and day. Ben Morven had helped him, taking over Blaine's calculations. Lucas and Iliffe had continued with their work.

Shearing lifted his eyes and stared at Matthew. There was fury in his face, and fear. It was the first time Matthew had seen it, not fleeting but steady and unconcealed.

'A fatal flaw?' he asked.

'Yes.'

'But Blaine knew the answer?'

'Possibly. Or maybe they hadn't got far enough yet to realize it.' Shearing's hands on top of his desk clenched tight, knuckles gleaming. 'When we find the man who killed Blaine I'll tie the rope around his neck myself, and pull the drop.' There was hatred so deep in his voice it rasped in his throat. 'Who is it, Reavley?' That was a demand, almost an accusation.

'I don't know, sir. Probably Ben Morven, but there's no proof.'

Shearing looked beaten. He had been counting on success.

So had Matthew. He realized now just how much. He had believed Corcoran could make the prototype, even without Blaine. Corcoran was a giant. He had been there all Matthew's life – kind, funny, wise, above all clever.

Matthew could not think of anything more to say. The sense of loss filled him with rage. Whoever had murdered Theo Blaine might have lost Britain the war, the survival of everything that was good and sweet and of infinite value. He could not even imagine the end of his home and his life in the way he knew it. No more afternoon tea on the lawn, irreverent jokes about the government, country churchyards, quiet rituals, freedom to go anywhere you wanted, to be eccentric and make your own mistakes.

'Reavley!' Shearing's voice was suddenly sharp.

It brought Matthew back to the moment with a jolt. 'Yes, sir?'

'We must salvage something from this. Someone in the Establishment murdered Blaine and smashed the prototype.'

'Yes,' Matthew agreed. 'Almost certainly the same person.'

'Probably Morven, but not beyond doubt,' Shearing went on. 'A German sympathizer?'

'Naturally. There's no other reason for doing it.'

'Is he on his own?'

'I doubt that.'

'Has Corcoran told him he's beaten and is giving up?' Shearing leaned forward across the desk. 'Be certain, Reavley! It could all hang on this! Who knows it's a failure, apart from Corcoran himself?'

'No one.'

'Are you absolutely certain? Why? How do you know?'

'Corcoran still wants to keep working on it,' Matthew replied. 'He can't get Morven, Iliffe or Lucas to do that if he admits it's over.'

The irony touched Shearing's mouth for an instant, then vanished. 'Good! Excellent! We'll send the device for sea trials,' he said wryly. 'On Archie MacAllister's ship. He's already prepared.'

For an instant Matthew was stunned – it seemed so pointless – then he realized what Shearing meant to do. Morven must be reporting to someone who could not take the chance that the device did not work. They would have to steal it! 'You'll need someone on the ship!' he said urgently. 'May I go? I've got nothing here that—'

'I have every intention that you should go,' Shearing cut across him. 'Why do you suppose I'm telling you? I'll have papers prepared for you and inform MacAllister. You will be a signals officer, newly drafted from a shore job, which will explain your unfamiliarity with naval discipline and the sea in general. We'll change your name to Matthews. Reavley is too well known; the association would be immediate. We can get you on board the day after tomorrow. We need to be quick, but still give them time to get their man on as well. Be careful. It will not be easy. You will not know who he is, and there may be more than one, although I doubt it. It will be hard enough for them to get even one man there at this short notice.'

'Yes, sir . . .'

Shearing leaned forward over the desk. 'Which means he will be good, Reavley! There are new men every voyage because losses are heavy. That's all you'll know about him. And you must appear like every other new man, no favours. MacAllister will not be able to do anything for you, except cover. He may tell some of his senior officers, but I have told him not to, unless in an extreme emergency. We can't rely on them not betraying you accidentally. They are trained for the sea, not for espionage.'

'I understand.' Matthew felt his pulse beat harder, high in his throat. It was something physical to do at last, a real, immediate chance to catch whoever had murdered Blaine. He half hoped, and half dreaded, that it would be Hannassey himself. It was too late to grieve for Detta. That was a pain inside him he did not dare even examine.

He looked across at Shearing and saw his dark eyes studying him. It was a steady, penetrating stare, no readable emotion in it.

'Be careful, Reavley,' he said again. 'Whoever comes after it, he will not be a fool, and he will be expecting us to guard the prototype with everything we have.' His mouth turned down at the corners, a delicate acknowledgement of defeat. 'After all, it was supposed to be an invention which will turn the war for us. If we don't guard it with our lives, they will know immediately that we failed.'

'And you'll arrest Morven, or whoever it is!' Matthew insisted.

'Is that a question?' Shearing said bitterly, a flicker of savage anger back in his face again.

'No, sir, I apologize,' Matthew said sincerely. He hesitated a moment, trying to think of something further to say, but there was nothing. He glanced around the room with its impersonal furniture, its one painting of the London docks at twilight. He still did not know if Shearing had the painting because it held some meaning for him, or simply because it was beautiful, or perhaps reminded him of somewhere else.

He went out without speaking any further.

That evening the Peacemaker stood at the window of the house in Marchmont Street and looked down at the footpath below. He saw the young man from the Establishment in Cambridgeshire step out of the taxi-cab, pay the driver and walk to the door. That was remiss of him. He should have stopped a block or two away, for the sake of discretion, as Mason always did. The Peacemaker's lips tightened in irritation. He did not like to have to tell someone anything so elementary.

He heard the bell ring, and then a few moments later the light, rapid footsteps on the stairs, and the tap on the door.

'Come in,' he said abruptly.

The young man was flushed, his thick hair a little windblown as if he had been running, and he closed the door behind him with a sharp click, his hands shaking. He did not wait for the Peacemaker to speak, which was highly uncharacteristic.

'They are going to test the prototype!' he said, his voice sharp and high. 'At sea. On the *Cormorant*. Day after tomorrow. We'll have to be very quick.'

The Peacemaker was astounded. In spite of his usual self-mastery his heart was beating faster and the palms of his hands were wet. All thoughts of discipline for the carelessness of stopping outside the door vanished from his mind. 'Sea trials?' He tried to keep his voice level, and failed. 'So you've completed it? You told me there were still problems!'

'There were. Corcoran told us he was abandoning it, or at least we were. I didn't believe him.' His face was a strange mixture of expressions, unreadable. 'I didn't think he would admit defeat, but I had no idea he had the answer, and was just going to cheat us out of having a part in it. I suppose I should have seen it.'

'Are you certain?' The Peacemaker could not suppress the excitement bursting up inside him. This could be a superb victory! The device completed, and stolen for Germany. It could end the war in months. 'Absolutely certain?' This gamble had proved a stroke of genius. His heart was lurching in his chest, making his breath uneven.

'Yes,' the young man answered. 'They are taking it down to Portsmouth tonight and putting it on board the *Cormorant*, ready to sail in the morning.'

'Who are they sending with it? You?'

'No. I don't know who's guarding it. Probably someone from Naval Intelligence, but it's supposed to be used by ordinary gunners.'

'Gunners?' The Peacemaker was surprised. 'Not scientists?'

'No. Unless they have plans they haven't told us. But if it were anyone from the Establishment it would have to be Iliffe or me, and it isn't.'

The Peacemaker steadied his breathing with an effort. 'You have done extremely well,' he said gravely. He must not praise the young man too much. It was the cause that mattered. Arrogance always cost in the end, and there was much ahead for this man yet. He would be rewarded appropriately, no more. He smiled. 'Now I understand why you came so hastily, you over-looked the rudimentary precaution of getting out of your taxi a street away. Don't do that again.'

The eagerness did not dim in the young man's face. 'No time,' he said simply. 'You'll need to move immediately. Whatever you're going to do, it will have to be right now.'

'I'm prepared. I assume that if the police had progressed any further in learning who killed Blaine, you would have told me.'

'Of course. But it doesn't matter now. It's finished without him.'

'On the contrary,' the Peacemaker said with a touch of chill, 'it matters even more. Since it was not us, and would hardly be British Intelligence, it means there is some other interest of which neither of us is aware.'

'Domestic tragedy after all?' the young man said, but there was not quite the same certainty in his voice as before, nor the bright edge of intelligence.

'And smashed the first prototype?' the peacemaker said sarcas-tically.

The young man blushed. 'Sorry,' he apologized. 'It has to be Lucas or Iliffe, but I have no idea which one.'

'Then go back and find out,' the Peacemaker ordered. 'I need to know.'

'Yes, sir.' The young man's face was paler now, the fire within him under control.

'Go,' the Peacemaker said softly. 'I have much to do. You have done brilliantly, Morven. Your action today may have saved a hundred thousand lives.' He held out his hand.

The young man hesitated, suddenly uncomfortable. 'I'm doing

what I believe to be right,' he said quickly. 'I don't want thanks for that. I do it for myself.'

'I know.' The Peacemaker's voice was gentle, a different kind of warmth in it, almost a tenderness. 'I know you do. Go back. You are not finished yet.'

Morven turned and went to the door. Outside he took a long, deep breath and his whole body trembled. Then he controlled himself with a passionate effort, and went down the stairs to where the servant was waiting at the bottom to let him out into the street.

As soon as he was alone the Peacemaker picked up the telephone. He had not expected the guidance device to be completed so soon; in fact he had come to the conclusion that they would not be able to do it at all. Now suddenly they were going to test it at sea. He had to send someone with the skills and the resources to get themselves into the crew of the *Cormorant* at a day's notice, and the strength, the iron nerve and the ingenuity to steal the device. That meant a man of wide experience and the ability to blend into any group of men and seem to be one of them, but also with an organization behind him who could and would do whatever they were asked.

And of course he would also have to inform Germany of it, so they could send a U-boat to intercept the *Cormorant*, which would take skill and some planning. If the device were as brilliant as Morven had said, it was the ultimate weapon!

There was only one answer: Patrick Hannassey. He was perfect. If there was any man in Europe who could get himself on to the *Cormorant* as a member of the crew, and be unremarkable, competent, a man whose face or mannerisms no one would remember, and yet have the intelligence, the imagination and the cold, brutal instincts to kill if necessary, it was he.

He would get the prototype into the hands of the Germans. And in so doing, would have to go with it himself. The Germans would probably have to employ more than one U-boat, and in all likelihood end in sinking the *Cormorant*, which was a loss the Peacemaker regretted. Still, bitter as that sacrifice would be, it was small as a price for ending the war now in May 1916, instead of God knew when!

And it had the added, and now quite urgent, beauty that a word from the Peacemaker to his cousin in Berlin, and the Germans would keep Hannassey, get rid of him if necessary. He must not be allowed to return. A mention of his aims, a free and peaceful Ireland, demanding money, an even larger share of power and total independence, would be sufficient to see that Berlin removed him from the scene.

Yes. It was excellent! A better outcome than he would have dreamed possible, even this morning.

Matthew reported for duty on board the HMS *Cormorant*. He was familiar with the sea from having spent holidays on the coast in small boats, but this would be very different. It was a relief to be able at last to do something personally to strike against the enemy who had, until this point, outwitted and outplayed him at every stroke. Somewhere on this ship, unless both he and Shearing had totally misjudged, there would be another man placed as late and as artificially as he was. He would be here to steal the prototype for Germany, just as Matthew was here to catch him, and through him the murderer of Theo Blaine.

He had never been on a warship before, only seen them from the shore, low and sleek, grey castles of steel on the grey water, decks dominated by bridge and gun turrets. There was very little rigging, just one relatively small mast and two cross-spars, enough for signalling and radio. Funnels proclaimed the power of mighty engines. There was no grace and beauty of sails as at Trafalgar, or sound of the wind in canvas. They were more like wolves than swans in flight.

Once on board the differences were perhaps less great. He was welcomed without ceremony, merely one of eight new men replacing those killed or injured. As an officer, albeit junior, he had a cabin to himself. Perhaps that was Archie's doing. He thought, as he unpacked his few belongings and stowed them in the space under the high, hard bunk and in the chest of drawers, that such cramped quarters shared would have made his task severely more difficult.

The only other furniture was a washstand, and a hinged table, which let down as a desk, and a chair. The whole thing was about five paces by three, with a port over the bunk. But then the entire ship was less than two hundred feet long.

He must familiarize himself with it as soon as possible, learn every passage, stairway, every fitting and its use, every room, and at least something of every one of the other seven new men aboard, and what his job was. One of them was his enemy.

He must go up and report to the signal room, and he could not afford to get lost. All the passages were narrow, so that one could barely pass anyone without touching them. On the floor was a curious substance, rough to the feel, a mixture of cork and Indian rubber known as corticene. Everything else was metal, with the occasional glass light bulbs.

When he came above into the air, he found the deck itself was wood, but there was still the steel of gun turrets, and the mass of the bridge and signal house above, the only place from which almost everything could be seen.

He felt the thrum of engines and the surge of power. They were already under way; the safe, familiar outline of Portsmouth harbour was slipping astern. Soon there would be nothing around them but the grey water, and whoever else was on it, or under its concealing surface.

Matthew thrust the thought from his mind and clambered up to the signal house to report for duty, not to Archie, but to the chief signals officer who was a quiet man of about thirty-five, with a plain, intelligent face and sandy-red hair. But when he spoke there was a sincerity in his voice and an authority of manner that earned almost instant respect. There was no dissembling in him and no bravado. He made it known he required the same of others.

He did not betray by any flicker of expression that he knew Matthew was any different from the ordinary replacement: raw, uncertain of himself, but adequately trained.

'Matthews? Settled in?'

Matthew stood to attention. He had no seniority here, he was a new recruit, given rank only because of his knowledge of signals. 'Yes, sir.'

'Good. My name is Ragland. You'll report to me. I don't know what you did ashore, but here obedience is exact and immediate, or you'll end up at best in the brig, at worst at the bottom of the sea. There is no room for hesitation, individual will or taste, and certainly not for any man who doesn't fit in. We rely on each other, and a man who can't be trusted is worse than useless: he's a danger to the rest of us. Understood, Matthews?'

'Yes, sir.' He thought bitterly of how companionable that sounded, that perfect fellowship, the sort of thing people described in the trenches, and it did not apply to him at all. He could trust no one, except Archie, and Archie was remote from him in the hierarchy. He was more alone than he had ever been in his life. He knew the rudiments of his job, little more. He did not know the sea. To none of the men he would see day by day could he tell anything of the truth, nor dare he trust them. Somewhere on this ship there was a German agent who would think nothing of killing him, if he blocked his path to the prototype. It was Matthew's job to find him, before he found Matthew.

He had to do his job in signals without relying on anyone else. He could confide in no one and at all times must guard his tongue, the way he responded to anything, even the silent betrayal by his ignorance of duties, perhaps most of all the physical fear he had never had to face before.

'Then you had better familiarize yourself with your station, and the ship in general, and get about it,' Ragland told him. 'You can start now.'

Matthew spent the rest of the day doing exactly as he was told, and trying to look as if it were natural to him. By the end of the evening he was becoming more used to the smells of salt, oil and smoke, the sound of ship's bells, and on deck the constant hiss and whine of wind and water. He was glad that at least the movement of the sea was something he was acquainted with.

Below, he had eaten in the officers' mess, listening a great deal more than talking. The food was good enough, but they were newly provisioned and he expected it to get worse. At least there was enough of it, and they were not under fire. He was a lot better off than Joseph had been in the trenches most of the time.

He wondered about Joseph, aware that his conscience had driven him to go to Flanders in the first place, and perhaps it was all that made him consider returning now. His physical injuries were healing, but the wound to his mind and his emotions appeared to be deeper. Something in him had changed, and here in this close, crowded room, with other men who also faced the enemy every day, and the possibility of mutilation or death, Matthew found that the change grieved him. Joseph was not a soldier in fact, but he was in spirit. He was as much part of the regiment and of its battle to survive and win as any other man.

Matthew ate silently, answering only if he was spoken to, and he watched the others. He had no idea if the man here to steal the prototype was an officer or a seaman, but he must not rule out any one of the new crew members until he was certain. He must learn everything he could of each of them, because his life might depend on seeing the tiniest element that did not fit in. He might not be given more than one chance before it was too late.

The crew was complete without him. They had a bond he would never be part of. They were not unkind, but they knew his inexperience and mistrusted it. He would have to earn his place. The jokes passed over his head. He did not understand the teasing, the laughter, the references to one man's boots, another's compulsive tidiness, a third's lapse of memory. They were based on terror and violence shared and endured together, tolerance of moments of weakness easily understood, the loss of friends and, above all, the knowledge of horror yet to come, and that they might not survive it. They knew each other's values, and that tomorrow or the next day their own survival might hang on that courage and willingness to sacrifice even life for the good of the many.

Matthew slept badly, aware all night of the shifting and turning of the ship, the sound of footsteps along the narrow passage on the other side of the door, and, of course, every half-hour the ship's bell ringing the time. About three in the morning he heard running, and a brief burst of gunfire, but there was no alarm. He lay rigid in his bed, gulping air.

Now, for the first time, his mind became aware of physical possibilities of war, shells tearing apart the metal of the ship, men injured. He was not afraid of pain – he never had been – but since the murder of his parents, violent death horrified him in a new way. The reality of it reached inside him and touched his innermost being. Now the knowledge that he was on a warship that might become involved in the slaughter and injury of battle turned him nauseous and a little cold. But at least it would not be personal, face to face, as it was for Joseph. He might see the injured or the dead, but they would be people he barely knew, and above all, he would not have to inflict injury himself. The enemy would be distant, a ship, not men. Except, of course, for the one man on the ship that he had come here in order to find.

It was over an hour before he went to sleep again. His rest was uneasy and full of violent dreams.

The next two days were difficult and exhausting. It took all his concentration simply to learn his job and he was embarrassed at the mistakes he made. Ragland was patient with him, but he made no allowances. He could not afford to. At home in St Giles, Archie was a friend. They had known each other over fifteen years, but mostly at family occasions, bound by a love for Hannah, taken much for granted. Here on the ship his word was law, his decisions governed the life of every man on board – and very possibly the death also.

On the one occasion Matthew passed him in the narrow passage up towards the signals room, he remembered to salute only just in time, and received a brief acknowledgement in reply, an instant meeting of the eyes. Then Archie was past him and on the steps up to the bridge, and the isolation of command.

It was a strange, artificial situation, and yet unbreakable. Here the sea and the enemy were the only realities. Friendship and duty were the core of survival, but neither must ever trespass upon the other. In his own way, Archie was every bit as alone as Matthew could ever be, and with a burden of trust enough to break the mind, if you allowed yourself to think about it. Better not to. Just act, each moment for itself. Do your best.

At the end of the third day Matthew lay on his bunk staring up at the ceiling and realized he ached in every muscle and his head throbbed from the tension of concentrating on getting each decision right, and drawing no attention to himself. He hadn't had any chance at all to try to find the man sent here to steal the prototype. When it happened it might be swift, too late then to learn who it was.

Presumably they would be ambushed by a U-boat. There would be no point in torpedoing them. The last place the Germans wanted the prototype was on the bottom of the Atlantic.

Time was short. What would he do, in their place? Have a U-boat shadowing them, stalking, and keep in touch with them somehow. Radio signals. A sharp burst, too quick for anyone on the *Cormorant* to detect. Just sufficient to keep in touch and mark their position. A destroyer was not an easy target to disable adequately enough to be certain of getting the prototype off before sinking it. They carried four 4.7 inch guns, two pairs of pom-pom guns and four torpedo tubes, and they could move through the water at twenty-five knots. They were the wolves of the sea, swift, manoeuvrable, and often ran in packs. But even alone, they would fight hard for their lives. It would take two U-boats at least to be sure.

Matthew knew he must begin immediately in the morning, even if he had to get Archie's permission to delegate some of his signalling watch duties to somebody else.

But he did not get the chance. He woke in the dark to the urgent sound of alarms. All hands on deck. He scrambled into his jacket and boots and, heart pounding, made his way up to the bridge, feet slipping on the steps.

The ship seemed to be alive with movement, men running, shouting orders, manning the gun turrets. The wind was rising, sharp and startlingly cold for the end of May. The ship bucked and slithered on the long, Atlantic swell. Over in the south-east there was a grey blur across the horizon. It would be dawn in half an hour.

Matthew scanned the surface of the sea for any sign of the black presence of a U-boat, but he saw nothing except the glimmer of waves as the half-light caught their backs, and the occasional paler tips of spume.

'You won't see them,' Ragland said from beside him.

'What do we do?' Matthew asked.

'Wait,' Ragland replied. 'Listen. Be ready to act.'

Minutes dragged by. There seemed to be noise everywhere, the wind on the metal of the ship, whining in cables, wires, against the housing of the bridge, the rhythmic hiss and crash of the water, and now and then footsteps of men. Matthew found his breathing was ragged, his muscles ached and he was so cold his legs were numb below the knee.

Suddenly the order came and they changed course dramatically, swinging to the west, and a few moments later back again. The light was broadening in the sky. Then he saw it, a long silver trail in the water to the left. He knew what it was – a torpedo. It had missed them, but somewhere under that dark, heaving sea was the U-boat that had fired it.

A moment later there was another, closer this time. The U-boat commander had anticipated their turn and moved more rapidly.

The *Cormorant* replied with a torpedo of its own, but no one expected to see wreckage on the paling water.

They zigzagged again, avoiding more torpedoes, and discharged their own back sporadically, not to waste shot. The game of hunter and hunted went on for four more tense hours. The torpedoes shot past in glistening trails, many times far too close. Twice the *Cormorant*'s crew knew the U-boat passed directly under them. The depth charges exploded with deep rumbling violence, churning up gouts of water, but still no wreckage.

If this was the U-boat sent to take the device, why only one? Was another going to appear on the other bow and take them down? Hit them where they would sink slowly enough for one man at least to leave them and board the U-boat with the proto- type, presumably the man on the ship who was signalling them? He was here, wasn't he? One of the seven other new men on this voyage?

Matthew stood in the signal house, cold, hungry, eyes aching, his muscles locked with the tension of waiting. He turned to the east and in the sunlight bright on the water saw for an instant the black conning tower of another submarine. An instant later the *Cormorant*'s guns blazed in a deafening roar.

Matthew was totally unprepared for the sheer noise of it. Then he was thrown off balance as the ship veered again, and he felt a violent jolt as if they had been slammed in the side of the hull. They had been struck! This was it. They would begin to sink. That ice-cold, grey sea would suffocate them after all. At least he must make sure they did not lose the device. The Germans must never know whether or not it worked.

He swung around to Ragland. 'I've got to get below, to the torpedo room!' The man would go for the prototype. At least Matthew would get him before they went down. Then he was filled with white-hot rage. The whole crew would be lost, and this man was responsible for it. God knew how many women would be widowed or lose their sons and brothers. Hannah! Even thinking of that choked him so he gagged for breath. She would lose her husband and her brother in one night. How would she bear it? How did anyone?

And Joseph. He would never see Joseph again. Would he go back to the trenches, or would this imprison him in St Giles . . . ?

Ragland's hand was on his arm, hard enough to hurt. It was the pain of his fingers digging in that stopped him.

'It didn't explode,' Ragland shouted at him. 'They'll deal with it. Get on with your job.'

Matthew felt the sweat break out on his body, in spite of the cold. But it was not over. This would happen again and again, until one time it really was the end. How in God's name did they bear it?

There were shouts, commands. A long raking salvo of gunfire on the starboard side towards the east, and the sea erupted in water, smoke and flying debris, then the *Cormorant* changed course again, and again. Torpedoes streaked past the sides and disappeared.

An hour later Matthew was standing in the captain's cabin and

Archie was leaning back in his chair. He looked pale and haggard from lack of sleep, but calmer than Matthew felt. How many times had he been through this?

'Was that an ambush for the prototype?' Archie asked.

'Yes, sir, I think so,' Matthew replied. The 'sir' had come to him so naturally he only realized it afterwards. Archie was no longer his brother-in-law – he was his captain. They had sunk a U-boat, killing the men on board it suddenly and violently. They had looked back and seen the other U-boat combing the seas, but there were no survivors visible. It was a terrible thing to do. Twenty-nine men were dead.

In one morning Matthew had learned with his heart and his gut what war was. And it was nothing like the imagination, even with the knowledge of the figures from all the battle zones of the world. This was as intimate as one's own churning stomach, the blood and bile in the mouth, the sweat on the skin, the dark water waiting to swallow them all.

'How close are you to finding him?' Archie asked. His voice sounded far away, an intrusion into Matthew's racing mind and its horrors.

He wanted desperately to give him a positive answer, but he knew the cost of lying, even by implication.

'There are seven new men on this voyage, apart from me,' Matthew said. 'Coleman is only seventeen, which excludes him from having the knowledge or the connections. Eversham's just lost a brother in France and I think his grief and his anger are both real. That leaves Harper, Robertson, Philpott, MacLaverty and Briggs.'

'It's not Briggs,' Archie said flatly. 'His parents were killed in a Zeppelin raid on the east coast. I know that's true. Knew his elder brother as well. That leaves you four. You haven't much time.'

'I know. We have to assume that was only the first attempt, and there'll be more.'

Archie nodded, lips thin. 'Apart from that, how are you getting on?'

Matthew smiled. 'I think when this is over I'll go back to

intelligence,' he replied ruefully, 'and work twice as hard.' He said it lightly, but he meant it. Emotions of all sorts were banked high inside him, like a spring tide; a respect for the men who defended the sea that was now a gut-deep passion; and the beginning of a new perception of what Joseph felt, a glimpse of how much there was that he would never know.

'No risks,' Archie warned. 'Whoever it is, he'll kill at the drop of a hat. Remember that. He'd have sent the whole ship down this morning. The only thing stopping him from killing you is that so far he may not know who you are, any more than you know who he is. But he'll be looking for you!'

A flutter of physical terror twisted in Matthew's stomach. His lips were dry. 'I know.'

'Don't forget it – ever,' Archie warned.

'No, sir.'

'Right. Go back to your duty.'

'Yes, sir.' He saluted and left.

They steamed on northward beyond the coast of Ireland, and then east into the North Sea. Matthew moved very carefully, but he knew every hour mattered. Whoever it was would expect the sea trials of the prototype to begin, or they might suspect there was something wrong. How could the Admiralty not wish to deploy such a weapon as soon as possible?

He became so used to the movement of the ship that most of the time he barely noticed it. He still had to count the bells and work out what they meant, and think in watches: five of four hours each, and the two half-length dog watches.

He had studied the plan of the ship, but found no believable excuse to be in the engine room or the magazine. However, he knew the names and service records of every man, though the majority of them he could not recognize by sight.

Gradually he learned enough about both Philpott and MacLaverty to eliminate them, leaving only Robertson, a large gunner with a dark sense of humour and quick, intelligent eyes; and Harper, a skilled engineer in his late forties. He was lean and muscular, moving with a grace that suggested both strength and speed when necessary, but oddly colourless features and fairish brown hair as straight as rain.

The second U-boat attack came not long after midnight, about two hours into the middle watch. Again Matthew was woken by the alarm. He could roll out of bed and into his jacket and boots almost automatically now. Knowing what was coming did not make it better. In an instant he thought of going to where the prototype was stored rather than up to the bridge, but then Archie's warning brought back some sense. To do that would give him away immediately. And it would then be only a matter of time, perhaps minutes, before Harper or Robertson, whichever it was, would kill him and put him over the side. During the battle with the U-boat would be the ideal time.

Instead he went with the other men, hurriedly. Feet were pounding along the narrow, corticene-floored, metal-walled passages and up the steps, boot soles clanging and scraping, all the way up to the bridge.

He got there before Ragland. The duty officer looked tense in the yellow glare of the lights, his eyes searching the rain-swept night, and the endless black waves around them.

'Bastards are bloody invisible in this,' he said bitterly. 'The sooner we try this damn invention we're supposed to have, the sooner we'll have a chance! What the hell are we waiting for – Jerry to sit there in the middle of a calm sea so we can take a shot at him and see if we strike? Damn it, we can do that already.'

'Wish I knew,' Matthew said sympathetically. 'Maybe it needs daylight to see the results? I've no idea.' That was an approximation of the truth. He did not know how they would have tested it so as to be certain of its abilities.

Further conversation was lost in the noise of gunfire, and it was several minutes before Matthew realized the sound was not depth charges going off, nor torpedoes being fired at them. It was a surface vessel opening up with their four-inch guns and the shells were landing only just short, the water shooting up in columns and falling back again. They were being attacked from the surface and beneath.

They changed course and returned fire, orange flame blossoming from their guns. The noise ripped through the night, bruising the senses.

The next hours passed in a haze of chaos, with smoke and flame so thick it choked, then ice-cold air hurting the lungs, then more guns again. Every now and then Matthew saw through the clearing smoke the silver trail of a torpedo or the pale gout of water leaping two hundred feet high as a depth charge exploded in the sea, or a shell fell wide and burst.

Then the shooting got more accurate. Shells tore into the decking, sending splinters of hot metal flying. One gun turret erupted in fire and there was a desperate scramble to get the injured men out. Matthew was sent with a message, stumbling down the gangways, choked with the acrid fumes of cordite and the smell of burning rubber from the corticene.

He saw smoke-grimed faces bent to guns, stokers heaving coal into the boilers, bodies gleaming in the red light of flames, skins almost black, other men injured, blood on their uniforms, eyes hollow with shock.

This time there was no conclusion, no strike of depth charges and wreckage spewed up and floating on the sea, no wait for bodies, just a long, slow winding down of tension and release of fear as time stretched out after the last burst of gunfire.

Two men were dead and thirteen wounded, most of them with flesh injuries or burns. Three were serious, one would be fortunate to survive. He had been in the gun turret that was hit.

Matthew was coming up from carrying a message to the ship's surgeon, and on the way back up to the bridge, when he passed Robertson in the passage. For a few moments they were alone, the thrum of the engines loud, like a mechanical heartbeat, the air close, suffocating with the smell of oil and smoke and rubber, the swing and surge of the sea now so familiar they both adjusted to it without thinking.

Matthew was the senior. Robertson stood aside for him. He was broad-chested and heavy-shouldered. His face was expressionless except from the illusion of lopsidedness created by streaks of oil on his nose and left cheek.

It was a chance that Matthew could not afford to pass by, little as he wanted to take it. He was exhausted as well, and he realized how physically afraid he was. He had just survived a battle and he wanted to escape and be safe, even if only for a few hours. He stopped. He needed to say something, provoke an answer. With every hour there was less time ahead.

'Are you all right, Robertson?' he asked. 'Is that blood on your face?'

Robertson looked alarmed. He brushed off the smear then put his hand to his nose. His relief was palpable. 'No, it's oil, sir.'

'Good. Makes one wonder why I chose the navy and not the army,' Matthew said with a slight smile.

Robertson met his eyes squarely. 'Why did you, sir?' In the narrowness of the corridor he was about two feet away from Matthew.

Matthew drew in his breath to answer just as the ship juddered and pitched, and Robertson lunged forward, throwing his arms out to save himself, and catching Matthew, pinning him to the wall.

Matthew lifted his knee to jab Robertson in the groin just as Harper came around the corner. 'What the hell's going on?' he shouted at Robertson. He charged forward ready to attack him.

Matthew felt a wave of relief so intense he almost burst out laughing; he could feel the laughter well up inside him, hysterical and absurd.

Robertson looked stunned. 'Sorry, sir,' he said with alarm. 'Suppose I haven't got my sea legs as well as I thought.' He turned to Matthew. 'Didn't mean to hurt you, sir. Meant to go against the wall.'

Matthew did not believe him, but there was no point in saying so now.

'No harm done,' he replied, straightening up. 'Thank you,' he said to Harper. There was no need to let him know what he had interrupted. 'All a bit tired, I expect. It must be dawn soon.'

Harper stretched his hand out to look at the watch on his wrist. 'Yes, sir, in about half an hour.'

Matthew stared at it. It was beautiful, wrought of mixed silver and gold, with a green line around the face. He had seen it before, when Detta had showed it to him as the gift she had selected for her father.

Matthew was standing in the bowels of the *Cormorant* facing Patrick Hannassey. That level, hard gaze, the bony features that looked so ordinary at a glance, were those of the Peacemaker who had caused the murder of so many men, and at least one woman – Alys Reavley.

He must get out of here, quickly, before he betrayed himself even if only by his shaking body or the sweat on his skin, the ashen colour in his cheeks.

'Thank you,' he gasped, his voice hoarse. 'We must be well into the North Sea by now.' He nodded briefly and walked away, his legs like jelly, forcing himself not to run.

He went straight to the bridge and asked for permission to see the captain. It was refused.

'The captain gave me a particular duty to perform,' he said urgently, hearing the panic inside himself. 'I have to report a conclusion. Tell him so, and do it now.'

Something in his manner must have caught the man's belief. He returned and conducted Matthew up to where Archie stood alone, staring across the grey water, Cape Wrath to the south, the open North Sea ahead.

'Yes?' he asked.

'It's Harper. I have no doubt at all.'

Archie smiled, his eyes brighter, something inside him easing. 'Good. I'll have him put in the brig. Well done. Now you can go and get some sleep.'

Matthew knew that it would be a long time before Archie himself could sleep. There was no one else to carry any of his burden. He was alone.

Matthew stood to attention. 'Thank you.'

Chapter Thirteen

Matthew slept easily that night.

He woke in the morning to the news that the Grand Fleet had been ordered to sea and the German High Seas Fleet had left harbour. For one idiotic moment, feeling the steel steps under his feet and the rail in his hands, he wondered if this was what it had been like on the morning of Trafalgar a hundred and eleven years ago. There would have been the silence of wind and sail then, but the same tingle in the air, the unbearable sweetness of life bound up in the knowledge that this could be the last day of it for thousands of them. Then the British fleet had been outnumbered and outgunned, and knew Napoleon was massed on the shores of France.

Now they faced the Kaiser, and the might of Germany and Austria. France was driven to the wall and England desperate again.

Matthew tightened his grip and pulled himself up on to the level of the bridge. Ragland was in the signal house, surveying a calm, slightly hazy sea.

'Looks as if you're going to have more than you bargained for, Matthews,' he said. 'I'm afraid it's all hands on deck.'

'Are we going to be in time?' Matthew asked.

Ragland smiled. 'Of course we are. But at least you've got your man. If you want to ask him anything, you'd better do it now.

By midday you may not have the chance. We'll probably catch up with the main fleet about then.'

Matthew considered it, but what could he ask? What was there that he didn't know already? He did not want to face Hannassey, but perhaps he must, even if there was nothing to learn.

He accepted the advice and went back down into the bowels of the ship and along the narrow passages, steel-enclosed. He could feel the entire hull vibrate with the racing of the engines. The stokers must be shovelling coal till their backs ached and their muscles felt as if they were tearing off the bones.

Hannassey was in the brig, guarded by armed men. They knew who Matthew was and let him in, but with a warning to be careful.

Hannassey was sitting on a wooden bench. Stripped of his assumed naval uniform he was a lean man, hard-muscled with a flat stomach and broad, supple hands. But it was his face that held Matthew's attention. He was no longer pretending to be ordinary, and the cold, brilliant intelligence in him was undisguised. His features were powerful, his eyes bright blue-green. He looked at Matthew with amusement. 'Well, I never thought I'd go down in the belly of some damn English ship!' he said wryly.

Matthew searched to see if he could recognize anything of Detta in the man in front of him. His colouring was utterly different, pale, washed out, where she was dark and vivid with life. He was cold where she was warm. He was all angles, she was fire, soft lines, and grace.

Hannassey smiled. 'Looking for a resemblance, are you? You won't see much. Detta's like her mother. But she's mine, all right, heart and soul of her. She had the measure of you, boy.'

Funnily enough, it was his smile that was like hers, the set of his teeth. The memory of her tore inside him. 'Did she?' he responded.

'Oh, yes.' Hannassey's smile widened, colder than the wind over the sea. 'You were desperate to trick her into confirming what you guessed about the sabotage of your munition ships. You hoped that if she believed you knew it all anyway, she'd tell you the rest. She gave you nothing! But she learned from you what she needed.'

'Oh? And what was that?' Matthew heard the shiver in his own voice.

'That you're desperate,' Hannassey replied wolfishly. 'You know nothing. You're guessing and fishing around for proof of anything at all.'

So Detta had told him what Matthew had wanted her to. She had believed the code intact. Then he felt an ice-cold fear for her. Without meaning to, he looked at Hannassey.

Hannassey saw the fear and understood it in a flash of revelation. 'You did break it!' he said, his face bleached white. His voice choked in his throat as if he were gagging blood. He lurched forward, hands stretched out to grasp and crush him, but the chain on his ankles held him. 'Mother of God, do you know what they'll do to her?' he cried. 'They'll break her knees! My beautiful Detta . . .' He stopped, looking up at Matthew, his eyes burning with hate.

Matthew froze. He knew she would be punished for failure, when at last they found out. He had thought it would be later, a long time, when there was so much lost one more person would not matter.

'She'll be alive,' he whispered the words, emotion choking him. 'My parents are dead, and God knows how many others. You too, now, whether this ship goes down or not.' He had nothing more to say. He was sick with the thought of Detta mutilated, never to walk with that easy grace again.

He turned and left without looking back at Hannassey and his pain-twisted face. He heard the guards lock the brig door, but he said nothing to them.

Up in the signal house again he found himself jobs to do, anything to keep his mind busy. He went down to the transmitting station where the fire-control table was continuously recording the data for the range and bearing of whatever enemy ship was targeted. All around the walls were different electrical instruments for sending the information up to the guns – voice pipes and telephones. There were about twenty men there, each with his own job to do.

On the deck again he took the glasses and scanned the horizon, trying to force Detta from his mind.

The weather was calm, the swell slight. There was a haze over the water, the wind from the south too little to dispel it completely.

Everyone was looking for something to do to take their thoughts from the mounting tension. All the watertight doors were thoroughly examined, every piece of apparatus was tested and spare parts broken out to be handy if needed in emergency. Was this going to be it, the big one at last? Perhaps by this time tomorrow it would be over. Trench warfare went on and on, a battle of slow wearing down, death month by month, a matter of who could survive the longest.

Here at sea the war could be lost in a day because without naval supremacy, Britain was finished.

The afternoon passed slowly, minute by minute. Matthew obeyed his occasional orders and waited, watching Ragland's face, his self-controlled calm. What was he thinking? Did his stomach churn with fear too, with the imagination of physical pain, of not being good enough, clever enough, quick enough, above all brave enough?

What about Archie on the bridge? In the final count it all depended on him. A hundred and twenty-seven men. Would he make the right decisions, every time? Did he dare even think of failure? Had Hannah even the remotest idea what it was like for him? Matthew had never ever imagined loneliness like it.

It was just short of four o'clock in the afternoon when they saw the smoke of gunfire on the horizon and after that, sighted the rest of the fleet spread across the sea to the east. Bugles and drums sounded the 'General March' to call all hands to battle stations. Within minutes every station reported to the bridge that it was ready for action.

After that Matthew was occupied with signals, messages flashing back and forth. The whole German High Seas Fleet was engaged.

He saw smoke on the starboard bow, and a few long, dragged-out minutes later he could hear the gunfire. There appeared to be at least two light cruiser squadrons coming across their bows. The roar of gunfire was now almost incessant, and great plumes of water shot into the air, up to two hundred feet high where the shells exploded on hitting the surface.

Matthew found himself shivering uncontrollably, but there was a strange kind of excitement inside him as well, a mixture of fear and a driving hunger to be involved, part of the action striking back.

They were ploughing through the water at tremendous speed. There was gunfire, heavy and continuous, somewhere to the rear but, through the clouds of smoke and the towers of water in all directions, it was hard to have any clear idea of what was happening.

Twice he saw torpedo tracks racing towards them, and the ship swung hard, screws thrashing, hull juddering under the strain as infinitely slowly, they turned in the tightest circle possible. He heard a shout and saw through a break in the chaos the vast shape of a battle cruiser, bow high, stern wallowing. He was unaware of crying out. The thing was sinking, belching smoke, forward guns still blazing. It was struck again and the bow lifted higher, steam roaring, flame yellow as the magazine caught. He was sick with the horror of it, vomit bitter in his mouth.

Shot fell only six hundred yards short of the *Cormorant* and Matthew saw the water drench the deck, bridge and signal house.

'Bloody close!' Ragland said tersely.

The next instant Matthew felt the lurch and jolt as a shell hit the upper deck and exploded. He swung round, instinct driving him to do something, anything. He felt Ragland's hand on his arm hard enough to hurt.

'Not yet!' he shouted in the noise of returning gunfire from their own turrets. 'Sounds like the boys' mess deck, or the after dressing station. Others will attend to it. There'll be enough here for you to do if the signals get hit.'

Matthew made an intense effort to control himself. His brain told him he had his own job to do and people relied on him to be in place and keep the communications open at all times.

They were past where the cruiser was sinking. He swivelled to look, but he couldn't see it. It must be behind the smoke.

Another shot fell five hundred yards short of them and again the bridge and signal house were drenched with black, foul-smelling water.

'It's gone!' Ragland told him.

Matthew was stunned.

'It was German!' Ragland added. 'Pay attention to what you're doing!'

'Yes, sir.'

Again they changed course sharply and this time Matthew could see that they were steering straight into the area where the previous shots had landed. He looked ahead to the bridge but he could not see Archie. He must be there, knowing everything depended on his judgement.

There were ships all around them. One moment he could see the German ships ahead and the British fleet to the port and starboard – dreadnoughts, hard grey outlines knifing through the water, spurting flame – the next he was blinded again.

The noise was almost unbearable, the roar and crash of shot, the churning of the sea and the screaming vibration of the engines. There was oil and water everywhere, towering into the air, crashing on the deck, splinters of shell flying from shots exploded on the sea, and clouds of mist and smoke.

Matthew worked in the signal house, hearing the intermittent bleep of the radio, voices on the telephone, shouts. He had to concentrate to make sense of it, disentangle one message from another.

Then came one that turned his stomach cold. The British battle cruiser *Indefatigable* had been sunk, all hands lost. It was hideously real. In the noise and the violence men were dying, crushed, torn apart, burned and drowned.

Time passed in violence, half-blindness and mind-bruising noise. The ships moved with what seemed like agonizingly slow motion, the sea dragging at everything, pulling against escape, against change, against turning or manoeuvring of every sort. It was a chaos of destruction. Matthew had no idea what was going on, or even if they were winning or losing.

It was growing dusk. The *Cormorant* took several more hits, one shell going straight through the armour plating but failing to explode. There was a bad fire aft, and Matthew was sent to help get control of it. The blast of the shell had momentarily put out the lights, but candles were lit. There seemed to be shards of broken glass everywhere, and the resin out of the corticene covered everything with a black, sticky glue-like stuff that smelled ghastly, filling the throat and churning the stomach. His was too empty to be sick now.

Some men were struggling to put out the flames, others to pad and block the hole in the plating, more to help the injured. Matthew had no experience, no skills. He could see in his mind's eye the Zeppelin, a sheet of flame, descending out of the sky on top of him, feeling the heat of it, Detta beside him.

He wished he knew what to do. He knew nothing about fire, or the force of water trying to crush a steel hull from the outside. He moved, lifted, passed, everything he was told, carried bleeding men, staggering under their weight.

He was up on the deck again before dark, his skin singed, eyes aching and gritty with smoke. As it cleared in the wind he could see a burned-out gun turret, charred wood, broken rigging and a German battle cruiser ahead, just within range. The starboard guns fired from the good turrets one after another and Matthew saw at least half a dozen plumes of water spout up. They were just short of the battle cruiser, but closing.

There was another destroyer to the port side, about two thousand yards away, as near as he could judge, and beyond it, almost obscured by smoke, another. The battle cruiser was firing. A salvo of shells landed almost on them, sending up mountains of water, drenching the entire ship. They veered across rapidly to avoid the range, hull shuddering under the strain, and then swerved again, coming closer.

All the starboard guns fired, the noise a kind of hell in itself. A gun turret on one of the other destroyers was hit and Matthew knew the men in it would all have been killed. He found himself praying it would have been outright, not slow burning to death. He had seen the men's white faces when they saw it happen a hundred yards away, and knew that even if they had been on board, there was nothing they could have done.

Was this how Joseph felt, battered and deafened by sound, watching men being torn apart, struggling to fight, to survive, to do all that was asked of them? Matthew had experienced it for a few hours, not yet even twelve. Joseph saw it every night, and knew it would go on, maybe for years. You knew men, you cared for them, laughed, shared jokes and memories, pictures of your family, food when it was scarce, the long day watch, all the time knowing the chances that sooner or later they would be killed, or mutilated beyond recognition.

How did Joseph bear it and keep sane? Or Archie? Above all, how did Joseph find something to say that was anything but idiotic in the face of such reality? The kind of courage that it demanded amazed Matthew and awoke a staggering admiration. He would never be able to look at Joseph, or even think of him again in the same casual, familiar way as before. As a child he had regarded Joseph as a hero because he was his elder brother, but this was entirely different. The Joseph he had known all his life was only part of the man; the core of him was a stranger that until now he could not have seen.

The noise was incessant, guns in every direction, huge steel monstrosities, ten, twenty feet long, firing shells it took two men to lift and load. When they struck they tore apart plate steel, and if they hit magazines, exploded in sheets of white-hot fire that engulfed whole decks, burning men to death in minutes.

The sky and sea were lit up by muzzle flashes all around them. Matthew knew it must be nearing midnight by now. They were still firing at the German cruiser. Radio signals were stuttering from all directions, some making sense, others too broken to read. The losses were appalling, innumerable ships and thousands of men. The sea was now rough, choppy; the wind swung round to the west.

The *Cormorant*'s guns were silent for minutes. They were closing on the cruiser.

Then they opened fire again, the noise mind-numbing. There seemed to be flame and smoke everywhere, searing the skin and hair, choking the lungs. The bridge and signal house were shrouded by it. Matthew had not the least idea whether anything was hit or not.

He stared to the east, straining until the smoke cleared. Ragland beside him seemed to be holding his breath, his face mask-like in the glare of the lights.

Gradually the wind blew the smoke away, cold salt instead of burning cordite, and they saw the cruiser engulfed in flame. The magazines had taken a direct hit and exploded, breaking the ship's back. It was listing already, in the first terrible throes of its long plunge to its tomb in the depths.

Matthew was speechless. The tactics had been brilliant. The *Cormorant* had sunk an enemy cruiser with more weight, more guns and more men, but there was no sweetness in it at all. The fact that they were German, and would have sunk the *Cormorant* if they could, seemed almost irrelevant. They were close to a thousand living, breathing men, seamen like themselves, going to a fearful and certain death. It was all he could think of as he stood transfixed with pity, watching as the great ship burned lower and lower in the water. Ammunition still exploded, tearing her apart until she slid beneath the black surface, shining in the flames of other gunfire, leaving the sea littered with struggling men and the debris of death.

There was no one there to help, and no one came. They were under the guns of the *Cormorant*. Please God Archie would not have shot at a rescuer, but they could not know that, nor could the *Cormorant* risk going any closer to the array of German destroyers on the further side, well within firing range.

Matthew turned away, sick in his stomach, and saw Ragland's face in the light. The same wrenching pity was in his eyes, the tight line of his mouth, although it was impossible to tell in the red and yellow glare of muzzle flames and the smeared darkness of drifting gun smoke, if he was as ashen as he looked. The noise had started again closer to, others joining those of the injured ships around them. There was no time for shock or mourning. The battle raged on.

Midnight passed. In the signal room they heard that both the *Ardent* and the *Fortune* had been sunk.

At two o'clock news came that the armoured cruiser *Black Prince* had blundered into the German firing line and been lost with all hands. For the first time Matthew began to believe that the British fleet might lose. It was a strange thought, alien and hard to grasp. Britain had not lost a crucial battle at sea since before the Spanish Armada in the reign of Elizabeth I, over three hundred years ago. This would mean the end. Without a navy to guard the shipping lanes, to evacuate the army from France, to prevent the German army landing on the beaches of Britain, the war was lost. In a month, two months, the fields and trees of England could be trampled by German boots, burned, torn up, destroyed by an occupying army.

What then? Retreat to the hills of Wales, Scotland? Fight in the forests and fens until there was no one left? Or submit, sue for peace and some kind of survival? On what terms? Would that be to betray the dead who had already paid so high a price, only to have it thrown away now? Or the living, who had to make the best of what was left? At what point was it no longer worth fighting?

He listened to the signals coming in with a kind of grim despair. He thought of Hannah and the children, the village, the fields under the great, silent elms. Were they better destroyed in the last battle, or conquered, surviving, and changed for ever?

He was still thinking of that, angry and tormented, his ears deadened by the noise, when he heard shouting and saw Archie waving his arms, signalling frantically to the men on the deck below him.

Ragland peered forward. Then Matthew saw it as well – a German cruiser coming straight towards them. He realized what Archie's order had been – 'Clear the foc'sle!'

The next instant they crashed together with an impact that hurled Matthew off his feet and the whole room seemed to pitch over on one side and then right itself and send him back again, staggering against the table. The whole ship rolled over to starboard, and the next moment there was the roar and crack of fire raking the length of the ship.

Matthew clambered to his feet, shaken and hurt. Ragland was doing the same but, with more presence of mind, he made for the door, threw his weight against it and burst it open. Matthew followed him. The front glass was shattered. Only then did he see on the port side the vast, towering bow of the German cruiser almost cleaving them amidships, buckling and ripping off the steel plating.

'God Almighty!' Ragland gasped, standing momentarily rooted to the deck.

Very slowly the German ship eased back into the sea and the *Cormorant* rocked violently and righted itself a little, wallowing hard in the water.

The German guns had cleared the decks. The foremast was toppling, the for'ard searchlight had fallen from the fire-bridge down to the deck, and the funnel was blown back until it rested between the two foremost ventilation cowls. The boats had come down and even the davits were torn out of their sockets. The cruiser's guns must have been elevated too high to rip open the deck, or the *Cormorant* would have been on fire by now, and settling in the water.

Matthew knew it before the order came to man the boats: they were sinking. There was no way to save her. A wild terror assailed him that Archie would go down with her. He swung around, looking for him, but the bridge was invisible through the smoke.

Someone was manning the guns, firing with everything they had at the German ship, spewing shell, flame, smoke in choking clouds. They'd go down locked together!

Except that the German ship was not holed. It was still well afloat.

One of the boy sailors, not much older than Tom, came scrambling up the steps, shouting something. Matthew tried to read his lips and the meaning in his wildly swinging arms.

'The brig's burst open!' the boy yelled, the words piercing a sudden moment's lull.

Hannassey! He'd go for the prototype. He didn't know it was no good. And perhaps it wasn't? The Germans might be able to finish it!

There was no point in trying to explain anything to Ragland. The roar of the guns had started again and he would hear nothing anyway. Matthew pushed past him and plunged down the steps, now twisted and torn loose at the bottom.

Men were running up. Smoke caught in Matthew's nose and throat, half-blinding him, making him cough and his eyes stream, but he was determined to catch Hannassey, at all costs. If they were going down, all of them, Archie, Ragland, all the men and boys he had eaten with, worked beside and whose courage and good humour he had known, then Hannassey was bloody well going down with them. He was not going to escape to the German ship that had rammed them, not even for a few minutes before it too sank. Perhaps it wouldn't? Maybe someone would survive and it was not going to be the Peacemaker!

Where would he go when the brig burst open? To the proto-type, surely. He wouldn't leave the *Cormorant* without at least trying to get it. He was not a man to save his own skin without playing the last card!

Matthew swivelled in his tracks and went instead towards the torpedo room where the prototype was stored, theoretically ready for testing.

It was difficult to keep his balance – the list to starboard was growing worse. He kept sliding, losing his footing and having to catch himself, one hand against the bulkhead, then an elbow, then a shoulder as he ran. He stumbled over bodies and wreckage. The guns were still roaring, as if the crews were determined to take the German ship with them. There was shattered glass on the floor and the air was thick with the stench of gun smoke, burning oil and rubber from the corticene. And it was getting hotter all the time as he got closer to the fires.

There was another explosion, a tearing thunder of sound, and the whole ship juddered and sank lower, throwing Matthew forward on to his hands and knees, then rolling him over, bruised and wounded, hands cut, burned, streaming blood. He clambered to his feet again, gasping and coughing, retching to catch his breath.

Was Hannassey still somewhere ahead of him? What if he was wrong, and he had abandoned the prototype and was even now saving his own life by jumping to the German ship? It would be possible. It was lower in the water now, at least from the raised port side.

He hesitated. Which way?

The ship lurched again. Was it even lower? There seemed to be smoke everywhere, and the heat was intense! Were they on fire? Please God, if they were, they would explode! Better to be consumed in a fireball, blown apart in an instant, than to sink knowingly, wide awake, into the darkness and the crushing weight of the ocean, struggling for breath, or drowned as the water poured in, black and ice cold from the lightless depths.

But he'd get Hannassey first! If he'd already got the prototype, and was struggling to carry it, which way would he go?

Portside, of course. It was higher. If she listed any more there was a risk the starboard side would actually be below water level, and if it were holed either by enemy shot or their own gun turrets or magazines exploding, that would be the end.

It was not his imagination, it was getting hotter. His hands hurt from the broken glass. Somewhere there was burning. It could reach the magazine any minute. He had no idea where the fire was, or how bad. A voice inside him screamed to go up, towards the light and the air! Escape . . . escape . . . escape!

The smoke was thicker. He was having trouble breathing. His eyes were streaming and he could hardly see. He fell over another body, inert and wet with blood.

But he would get the Peacemaker, and die knowing for certain that he had destroyed him. It was worth it. Don't die for nothing. He just wished he could have told Joseph that he'd done it.

And Judith and Hannah – they deserved to know too. Especially Judith. He could not tell Detta, he could never tell her, but she deserved to know, for the way he had used and broken her also, and taken from them both what they could have had.

He went to the port side, sliding on the floor as the tilt became steeper, grabbing at anything he could reach to help himself, and finding it slick with oil. The noise was roaring in his ears, the engines racing, the shrill hiss of steam, the crash and boom of guns.

Then he saw Hannassey about five yards in front of him. He was balanced with the prototype in his arms. It was easy enough to carry, a wide, thick disc like a clock, a little over a foot in diameter. He saw Matthew at the same instant.

'Told you you'd go down,' he shouted above the din. 'Never had time to use your marvellous invention, did you?' It was a sneer. He was almost laughing, his teeth gleaming in what was left of the lights. Then his face changed. All triumph vanished in a snarl of rage and furious, total understanding. 'It doesn't bloody work!' he screamed. He hurled it from him, towards Matthew as if he could hit him with it. 'The goddamn thing's no use! You didn't use it because you can't! Mother of God! All this for – nothing!'

Matthew avoided the hurled prototype easily, the pitch of the ship carrying it hard against the other wall, and Hannassey stumbled with the release of the weight.

'That's right!' Matthew shouted back at him. 'You came for nothing! You'll die for nothing! You'll never see your bloody Empire!'

'I don't . . .' Hannassey started, but the rest of his sentence was drowned in another bellow of gunfire. He turned and clambered over wreckage towards the steps upward.

Matthew went after him, clawing his way along, feet slipping on burning corticene and broken glass, climbing over twisted iron and crumpled bodies he could not help, Hannassey always just a few yards ahead of him.

There was another crash somewhere above and the ship heaved, sending them both flying. There were several more explosions as ammunition caught fire, and a roar as a gun turret burst into searing flames. The heat hurt the skin and tore the breath away even where Matthew and Hannassey were sprawled on the burning floor in what was left of the passageway.

Then Hannassey shot forward and dived for the steps hanging loose-ended from the mangled deck and hauled himself up, swung his body over, and went on.

Matthew ran at it and jumped, catching the third rung, and flailed wildly for a moment or two before his feet found the bottom one and he swarmed up it after Hannassey.

He reached the deck and blessed air just in time to see Hannassey running into a pall of smoke under the blackened gun turret. The bow of the German ship was only yards below them.

It had heaved away but now it was coming back. Deliberately for Hannassey? He could make it. He had only to leap. He turned for an instant, jubilation in his face, that wide smile, showing his teeth.

Matthew hurled himself forward and caught Hannassey at the knees, overbalancing him. Hannassey fought, kicking, gouging, tearing at Matthew's face, his hair, anything he could reach.

This was the Peacemaker, the man who would have sold England in the greatest betrayal of its history! But for Matthew, overpowering it like a drowning wave, was the fact that he was the man who had murdered John and Alys Reavley, simply because John Reavley had stumbled on his plan. Matthew thought only of their bloodied bodies in the car, and his grip was unbreakable unless Hannassey could have crushed the bones of his hands.

They were near the rail. The German ship was only fifteen yards away, less, and closing. Even through the smoke he could see the vast darkness of it.

He pulled away with all his strength, then lunged forward, catching Hannassey on the jaw with his head. Hannassey gasped and let go for an instant. It was enough. Matthew scrambled to his feet. He made the decision without thinking. He bent and grasped Hannassey and heaved him over the side.

He heard him scream as he went down and in the light of the fires saw him flailing in the water for long, desperate, terrible seconds until the steel bow of the German ship crushed him like a fly against the hull of the *Cormorant*.

Matthew clung to the rail, nausea sweeping over him, the deck lurching beneath his feet till he fell to his knees, still clinging on. He had killed Hannassey. With his own hands he had thrown him to a hideous death. He would remember that thin scream above the guns' roar. The falling figure, arms wide, was seared on to his brain, and then the crunch of flesh and bones lost in the din of the sea, the flame, and ear-splitting explosion of the rear gun turret. Then everything vanished in smoke and darkness, his lungs bursting, the deck heaving violently beneath him. He would die with the ship and all the men in it, but the Peacemaker was gone for ever.

Chapter Fourteen

Joseph had been to see Gwen Neave again and was walking back on the road homewards, Henry at his heels. He was no longer even aware of the slight ache in his leg. He had been over seven weeks away from his regiment, and he was actually in better health now than many of the men who were still there. The thing that kept him at home in the warmth of the sun and the quiet peace of the fields was his fear for Shanley Corcoran.

His feet crushed the stems of the grass and he could smell the sweetness of it in the air. The larks were singing above, high up beyond sight, less than a black dot against the blue.

Then why had Corcoran not told Perth yet? Lack of proof? Or did he still need the man, assuming it was Ben Morven? It was a dangerous game to play. No wonder his voice had sounded strained on the telephone. There was so much to win, or lose.

Archie had just gone back to sea, and Matthew had telephoned to say that he too would be away for perhaps a week or more.

Then it struck him like a physical blow. The prototype was finished and on trial at sea. That was why Matthew was gone.

And here was Joseph walking through the grass with the may blossom heavy in the air as if there were nothing to be done but drink in its splendour.

It must be Archie's ship being used for the sea trials. Archie had said Corcoran had talked to him about sea trials on the night

Blaine was killed. They had been at the Cutlers' Arms, over at Madingley.

No, Corcoran had said that was where they were. Archie had said . . . He stopped. It was absolutely clear in his mind, as if it had been only minutes ago: Archie had said they had met at eight, when Blaine had still been alive, and at the Drouthy Duck, here in St Giles.

Could Archie be mistaken? Surely he must be. It did not matter to him where or when it had been. No one could have suspected him of being involved with Theo Blaine either personally or professionally. To Corcoran it was far more important, because he had said it was where he had been at the time his best scientist was murdered. Presumably that was what he had told Perth also, if he had asked. He would have, wouldn't he, as a matter of course, if nothing else, to find out if Corcoran could have seen anything, or heard anything? Not that he would normally be anywhere near Blaine's house. Corcoran lived in Madingley. Except that he was out that evening, which was unusual. He worked far too hard to take time off, except for the most important occasions – such as discussing sea trials.

He must simply have made a mistake, in tiredness and anxiety, even grief for the loss of his best scientist, and a friend, and been uncharacteristically careless. And, of course, it was impossible now to check with Archie so he could correct it.

Why did that make him feel uncomfortable? Why was he even considering the possibility that Shanley Corcoran could be lying about where he had been? What was it he thought? That somehow Corcoran knew the truth, and was lying about it? He already knew that he was protecting whoever had murdered Blaine because he needed him to complete the project. There was little doubt in his mind that it was Ben Morven. Lucas could not have killed Blaine, and Joseph did not believe it was Iliffe, although it was not impossible.

Was it conceivable that Corcoran had guessed beforehand, and gone to Blaine's home to prevent his murder, and been too late? What tragic irony.

But why had he then lied about it? To prevent any possibility of having to betray Morven, before the work was completed.

Had he gone openly, or in secret? Joseph now felt cold in the sun and the larks sounded tinny and far away. Did Morven know? Had he seen Corcoran there? No, surely not, or he would have killed him before now. He could hardly afford not to.

No, worse than that, he was waiting for Corcoran to complete the prototype, just as Corcoran had been waiting for him?

But if Joseph was right, then it was completed and already at sea! Was Morven waiting for news that it worked? Hardly – it would be a wildly unnecessary risk. Far more likely he was simply seeking the right moment to kill Corcoran so that he was safe himself, and the only man left who could recreate the machine.

Joseph started to walk quickly, calling Henry to follow him. He took long strides, ignoring the trampled grass. He reached the gate to the orchard and flung it open, slamming it behind him as soon as Henry was through, and sprinted under the trees to the hedge and the end of the garden. He was out of breath by the time he got to the back door and into the kitchen, oblivious of trailing mud over Mrs Appleton's clean floor.

He went straight to the telephone in the hall and asked the operator to connect him to Lizzie Blaine. Please heaven she was at home. She was the only person he could think of who would take him to the Establishment. He waited impatiently while it rang. Why should she be at home? There were a dozen other places she could be.

He heard her voice with intense relief.

'Mrs Blaine? This is Joseph Reavley. Can you take me to the Establishment please, right away? It's extremely urgent.'

'Yes, of course,' she said immediately. 'Is everything all right? Has something happened?'

'Not so far, but I must go there and warn them so that it doesn't. I'll be waiting in the road. Thank you!'

It was ten minutes before she arrived, during which time he apologized to Mrs Appleton and left a message for Hannah that he had gone on an errand, and would be back in the evening.

Lizzie swept up in the Model T. She looked anxious, her hair falling out of its pins and a smear of dirt on her cheek. Obviously she had taken him at his word as to the gravity of the occasion.

'Thank you,' he said, climbing in and closing the door.

She eased out the clutch and increased the acceleration before replying. 'Are you going to tell me what it is? Do you know who killed Theo?'

'Yes, I think so,' he answered as they turned the corner into the High Street. 'But I've got to make sure he doesn't kill Corcoran as well. I believe they're testing the invention, and if it's a success he won't need Corcoran any more.'

'He wouldn't kill him for that,' she said, increasing speed on the open road and narrowly missing the may branches sloping wide. 'It would be a stupid risk.'

'Not because they don't need him,' Joseph explained. 'This man killed your husband, and Corcoran knows it. I don't know why he hasn't turned him in already.'

'Perhaps he has no proof,' she suggested, her knuckles white on the wheel as she swerved with considerable skill and straightened up again. 'Are you going to tell me?'

'Yes, when I'm absolutely sure. With Corcoran gone he would be the only man left alive who knows exactly how to recreate the invention.'

She concentrated on her driving for several minutes in silence, her face intent on the road.

'I'm sorry,' Joseph said in sudden contrition. He was speaking of the murder of her husband as if it were incidental to the scientific achievement, not the death of the man she had loved, probably more than anyone else in the world.

She flashed him a sudden smile, and it vanished as quickly. 'Thank you. I'm not sure how much I want to know what happened. I thought I did, but now that it could be revealed any minute, it's more real, and a lot uglier. In a way it was better to allow it to drift into the past unsolved. Am I a coward?' There was pain in her voice, as if she cared what he thought and had already decided it was harsh.

'No,' he said quietly. 'Just wise enough to know that answers don't always help.'

'I'll miss you when you go back to France.' She stared ahead, deliberately avoiding his eyes. She put her foot down and increased the speed, now having to concentrate fiercely to keep on the road. The silence settled between them as if by agreement. They both had much to think about.

She screeched to a halt at the gates of the Establishment and Joseph got out, thanking her and leaving her to wait. He spent nearly a quarter of an hour explaining to officials that he had to see Corcoran urgently, and then waited, shifting his weight from one foot to the other, while messages were sent, answers returned, and more messages sent in reply.

It was nearly twenty-five minutes after arriving that Joseph reached the waiting room, and a full quarter-hour after that before he was ushered into Corcoran's office. Corcoran, pale and tired, looked up from a desk littered with papers.

'What is it, Joseph? Surely it could have waited until this evening? You would have been welcome to come over to dinner.'

'I don't think it can wait,' Joseph answered, too tense to sit down in the chair opposite him. 'Not safely. And I couldn't have said it in front of Orla anyway. You've got to have Perth arrest Morven before he kills you as well.' He leaned forward on to the desk, refusing to allow it to separate them. 'I'm not going to let you run this risk any more!' He nearly added that he cared too much, but it sounded melodramatic, and selfish.

'The work—' Corcoran began.

'It's finished!' Joseph said impatiently. 'It's on sea trials, isn't it? With Archie. You said he was going to do them. Isn't that where Matthew's gone?'

Corcoran's dark eyes opened very wide. 'You think I know?' he said slowly, surprise and a flicker of fear in his face.

'Don't affect ignorance!' Anger welled up dangerously inside Joseph, too close to breaking his control. The danger was real, and he could not bear to lose Corcoran as well. It was as if the past and all he loved in it were being taken from him piece by piece. 'You may not know where they've gone, but you know you finished the prototype and they took it! And Morven knows it.'

'To test!' Corcoran shook his head. 'There's so much that you don't understand, and I can't tell you. Morven will not kill me—'

279

'He can't afford not to!' Joseph was raising his voice in spite of himself. 'For God's sake, you were there that night! You saw it, or something! Enough to work it out.'

Corcoran gulped. 'What makes you think that, Joseph?'

Joseph's patience was close to ripping apart. 'Don't treat me like a fool, Shanley! You lied to me about where you were when Blaine was killed. You said you were with Archie at the Cutlers' Arms. You weren't.' He saw Corcoran wince as if he had been hit. 'I'm not checking up on you!' he said angrily. 'Archie told me where he met you, at the Drouthy Duck! I just today realized what you'd said.'

He steadied his voice, dropping it to be gentler, hearing his own anguish in it and unable to moderate it. 'You were protecting Morven because you needed his gifts to finish whatever it is you were making. Well, it's finished now! And the first chance he gets he'll kill you. Give him up!'

Corcoran stared at him, amazement and grief battling in his face. He looked old, almost beaten. There was only a last shred of will left to hang on to.

'Shanley, you can't protect him any more!' Joseph pleaded. God, how he hated this war! Year by year it was stripping him of everything he loved! 'I know you may like him,' he urged, his voice panicky, too high. 'Damn it, I liked him myself, but he killed Theo Blaine. He stabbed him in the neck with a gardening fork and left him to bleed to death in the mud under his own trees – for his wife to find!' He leaned further forward. 'And he'll do the same to you, but I won't let that happen!'

'We . . . we still need him, Joseph,' Corcoran said slowly. 'It's only sea trials. It may need work yet.' He sat forward, elbows on the desk, his face almost bloodless only a yard away from Joseph's. 'This is the greatest invention in naval warfare since the torpedo. Perhaps even greater. It could save England, Joseph!' His eyes burned with passion. 'The whole British Empire rests on our mastery of the sea.' His voice trembled. 'If we master the sea, we master the world, and lay peace on it. I can't turn him in yet!'

'And if he kills you first?' Joseph demanded. He heard what Corcoran said about England, about the Empire, even about victory and peace, words that sounded like the vision of a forgotten heaven of the past, a glory remembered now like the gold of a dream. But he could not bear to let go of the love he still had, the memories of all certainty and goodness bound up in this man. 'Morven is a spy! He killed Blaine, and he'll kill you!'

Corcoran blinked as if his vision were blurred and his eyes so exhausted he had trouble seeing. Then very slowly he sank his head on his hands. 'I know,' he said softly, his voice little more than a whisper.

'Tell Perth!' Joseph reached across and placed a hand on Corcoran's wrist, a touch more than a grip.

'I can't, not yet.' Corcoran lifted his head. 'Leave it, Joseph. There's more to it than you know.'

'I won't let you be killed!' He thought of his father. The pain of his loss ached inside him like a bruise to the bone, as if he had been beaten and it hurt even to breathe. Why couldn't he make Corcoran see his danger? His father would have known what to say. Even Matthew might have done better than this. He wished Matthew were here with his judgement, his sanity. But he wasn't. There was no one else.

Corcoran stared at him, his face gaunt, almost like dead flesh. 'Leave it, Joseph,' he said again. 'I know what Morven is. I've known for months. But it's not time yet!'

'Why not?' Joseph demanded.

'I can't do without him until we're sure the prototype works.' Corcoran tried to smile. He looked like an old man staring death in the face with all the courage he could still grasp. 'Please, Joseph, let it go for now. I know what I'm doing. He caught Blaine by surprise. Poor man had no idea. I do, and I'll be careful. It's not in his interest to kill me yet.'

'Is that why you were there?' Joseph asked, still struggling with the idea of asking Perth to end it all now, while he was sure Corcoran was alive and well.

Corcoran looked inexpressibly weary, as if suddenly his mind had lost the thread. He blinked.

'Were you trying to save Blaine the night he died?' Joseph insisted.

Corcoran sighed and pushed his hand across his hair, as if to take it back off his brow, but it had grown suddenly more sparse, and the gesture was pointless. 'Yes. I was too late.'

'Tell Perth!' Joseph urged. 'Let him put more men here!'

Corcoran smiled. 'My dear Joseph, come back to reality! I know you are afraid for me, and it is just the love and concern I would expect from you. You have always been the most like your father, the most passionate, tender-hearted.' He blinked as if to hide tears, and his voice was softer. 'You have much of his intellect, but not his power to separate the dream from the practical. This is an establishment where we do work which may save thousands of lives, tens of thousands, even end the war with a British victory and save England, and all the literature, the law and the dreams that have built an empire.' His lips tightened. 'Perth is a decent man, adequate in his way, but it is totally impossible to have him or his men in here except for an hour or two at a time, under supervision, as they have to be. And I need to get back to my work. There are other inventions, other plans. Had you been anyone else I would not have taken the time from them to see you.' He rose to his feet stiffly. He looked as if every year of his age weighed painfully on his shoulders. 'But it means much to me that you care so deeply. I shall make time to see you again before you return to Flanders.'

Joseph felt curiously beaten. There was nothing for him to do but say goodbye and leave.

He found Lizzie waiting for him in the car, parked just beyond the gate. He climbed in and sat down, closing the door. He felt drained and inexplicably defeated. Corcoran knew, but still Joseph had not been able to do anything to ensure his safety. And although he realized the murderer was beyond question Ben Morven, it was still an ugly thing to have it confirmed. He had liked Ben. He had thought there was something good in him, something of gentleness and honour.

Perhaps, Joseph thought, he himself was a complete failure as a judge of people? He saw what he wanted to see. To judge kindly is a virtue, sometimes the difference between love and self-right-eousness, but to miss the truth altogether, to fail to see evil, allows it to grow until it poisons everything. It is a kind of moral cowardice that leaves the battle to others, while calling itself charity. In the end it is not courage, honour or love, simply evasion of discomfort to oneself.

'Are you all right?' Lizzie said softly. 'You look pretty awful.'

'I'm sorry,' Joseph apologized. 'I'm not even any use. I'll get out and crank. You start.'

When they were a few yards down the road, around the corner into the lane back towards St Giles, she asked again.

'Yes, I'm all right,' he insisted. How could he say otherwise, to her of all people? Of course he was all right. 'Do you need to know or not? You don't have to.' Liar, he said to himself. Of course she has to. 'Well, not yet,' he added aloud.

She smiled. In spite of the circumstances it was warm, lighting her eyes. 'Stop being kind to me,' she said wryly. 'You're like a dentist hovering over a bad tooth. It has to come out! Who killed Theo?'

'Ben Morven,' he answered. 'He's the German spy here. He needed to take Theo's place on the project, so he could have the information it would give him, and I suppose the opportunity to sabotage the whole project.'

She said nothing for several moments, frowning as she turned a sharp corner, and then another. 'That doesn't make sense,' she said at last. 'Ben Morven is very good, but he's not in the same field. To a layman it might look as if they were, but they weren't. Theo talked to me about his work – not the details, of course, but I know what his skills were.' She looked at Joseph quickly, then at the road again. 'They were both physicists, but Theo's specialist field was wave transmission through water, Ben Morven's is servomechanisms. He couldn't have taken Theo's place. Corcoran himself could have, except that he wasn't as good.'

'Not as good!' Joseph said incredulously.

'Not in that field,' she replied. 'Physics and mathematics of that order, inventive, original, are a young man's skills. Corcoran was the best in his time, but that was twenty-five years ago.'

'But . . .' He struggled after explanations, something to rebut what she was saying. It was heading towards an abyss that appalled him.

'I'm sorry,' she said quietly.

He sat stunned. He did not want to think of it, but the reasoning unrolled in front of him just like the ribbon of road ahead, and he was carried along just as inevitably as if he were in a vehicle of the mind that he could neither stop, nor steer away.

Corcoran had lied about Morven, not in order to protect the work, but about their relative abilities, even the nature of their skills. Morven had not taken Blaine's place, Corcoran had taken it himself, or tried to. Was that why the work had taken so much longer? Corcoran was not as good, he had not the keenness of grasp, the agility of intellect.

Lizzie drove on silently.

Other things came into Joseph's mind, like the branches coming into sight as they turned a corner in the road: Corcoran sitting at the family table making them all laugh, years ago, when Joseph was a boy; Corcoran telling stories, complimenting Alys and making her blush, but laugh at the same time; Corcoran talking about his work, eyes burning with pride and enthusiasm, saying how it would revolutionize the war at sea, how it would save Britain. He had not boasted that his name would go down in history as the man whose brilliance altered the course of life, but it was there between the lines.

Only had he lived it would have been Theo Blaine's name that was written, not Corcoran's.

Was that it? Glory? Had he, not Morven, murdered Blaine, believing he could take his place, and then found he could not? The thought was unbearable! What treachery to the past, to friendship, to his father, that he could even allow such a thing into his head! Joseph despised himself that he could do it, but it was there, immovable.

How could he have been so wrong all his life? And his father be wrong as well? John Reavley had loved Corcoran as a friend since university days. Was he so deluded that he had missed such a fatal hunger for fame, for endless adoration?

At last Lizzie interrupted, her voice strained as if she could keep silent no longer. 'What is it?' she asked. 'I have to know one day. You don't need to protect me.'

'I . . .' he started. Then he realized how rude that would sound, saying that it was himself he was protecting, his dreams and his beliefs, all the safety of the past that comforted and sustained now. He watched her face, strong and humorous and brave, trying to find a way through loss. She deserved the truth, and he realized with surprise that he would like to share it with her. It would be easier, not harder for him.

Finding the words with difficulty, he described to her what he had thought, the slow piecing together until the picture they made was inescapable.

It was several moments before she answered.

Had he made a hideous mistake, turned on the one man who was doing all he could for the best, selflessly? Would Lizzie despise him for it as much as Corcoran himself would, and Matthew, and Hannah?

But a voice inside him said that he was not wrong. War could strip a man down to essentials of strength or weakness that the comforts of peace had layered with deceit. It revealed flaws lesser times left decently covered.

Lizzie pulled the car to a stop at the side of the lane and turned to face Joseph. Her eyes were full of unhappiness and a deep and terrible pity.

'I wish I could think of anything to argue you out of that, but if I did I would be lying, and we can't afford anything less than the truth, can we.' It was a statement, not a question. 'I'm so sorry. It would be so much easier if it were anyone else.'

He was not alone in his knowledge. It left him no choice. The dilemma and the guilt of choice were gone, and the freedom. He was propelled forward now, whatever he wished.

'Are you going to be all right?' she asked softly.

'Yes, of course I am,' he answered, looking at her, then seeing her strong, steady face turning away again. There was no doubt in her. She understood all that it meant. 'Lizzie, you must say nothing, not for Corcoran's safety, for your own. Do you understand me?' he said urgently, even roughly.

She shivered. 'Yes. I know. As long as you are going to do something. I'm not going to cover for anyone at all who killed Theo, whatever the reason.' They were in the main street of St Giles. She turned the corner and pulled the car to a halt outside the house and looked at him, her eyes wide and bright from the lights in the doorway. 'He doesn't deserve that. He behaved like a fool with Penny Lucas, but not enough to die for, or be forgotten as if he didn't matter.' She was quite steady now. 'He did matter. He was brilliant, and stupid, brave and vulnerable and thought-less, like most of us, except he did everything more. I'm not going to let him be forgotten. I'm not looking for vengeance, I suppose not even justice. It seems as if half the young men in Europe are dying. I just refuse to let it pass as if it wasn't worth trying to do the right thing.'

'I'll do the right thing,' he promised. He meant it intensely, for her sake as well as his own. 'I'll go to London tomorrow, and speak to the people who can deal with it, but not here, not Inspector Perth. I don't have the kind of proof he would need. It's just my word, at the moment.'

She reached across quickly and touched his hand, then gave a little smile, and nodded.

'Thank you for taking me.' He acknowledged her help, and got out of the car. He looked back at her for a moment and saw her smiling at him, the tears wet on her cheeks in the lamplight. He turned and went inside.

In the morning he took the bus to Cambridge, and then the train to London. He had told Hannah that it was business, but he had not told her the nature of it. She saw the darkness in his face and she did not ask.

He had no idea how long he would be gone, but he had a key to Matthew's flat and if he had to stay in London, then he would do, as long as it was required until Admiral Hall of Naval Intelligence would see him. He would not trust Calder Shearing, because he knew that Matthew did not. This must go as high as he was able to reach. He still half hoped that there would be someone who could prove to him that he was wrong. He would look like a disloyal fool, but he could deal with his own weakness, blame himself and execute the appropriate penance. It would still be better than facing a truth as bitter as that which he knew his mind already accepted.

He went to Naval Intelligence. He knew where it was from his previous experience the year before, after the business at Gallipoli. Of course it was a different man who met him this time.

'Yes, sir?' the man asked blandly.

Joseph gave him his name, rank and regiment, and said that Matthew was his brother. 'I have information regarding the murder of Theo Blaine at the Scientific Establishment in Cambridgeshire,' he went on. 'I can repeat it only to Admiral Hall.'

'I'm sorry, sir, that is not possible,' the man said immediately. 'If you like to write it down it will be submitted in due course.'

Joseph kept his temper only with the greatest difficulty. It was a kind of absurd nightmare that this dreadful task should be so difficult, as if fate were testing his resolve.

'The matter is in regard to immediate danger threatening a device currently being tested in sea trials on the HMS *Cormorant*,' he told the man.

That provided the result he wanted. A quarter of an hour later he was in the office of Admiral 'Blinker' Hall, a short, robust man with a keen face and a shock of white hair. It was apparent within minutes how his nickname had been earned.

'Right, Captain Reavley, what is it?' Hall asked bluntly. 'And don't waste time explaining, I know perfectly well who you are. Well done on the Military Cross.'

'Thank you, sir. I know who killed Theo Blaine, and I fear that I know why. It appears to have nothing to do with the Germans.'

Hall frowned at him. 'You had better sit down and tell me exactly what you mean.'

'Yes, sir. Do you want to know how I reached—'

'No. Just tell me who did what, and I shall ask you what I cannot deduce for myself.'

As briefly as he could, Joseph recounted what he believed to have happened. Hall stopped him every time he needed proof, or the process of his reasoning was unclear, but that did not happen often. The more Joseph laid out his knowledge the more hideously plain it became.

'And I believe you are testing the device now,' he finished. 'When it works, and Corcoran does not need Ben Morven any more, then I'm afraid he may either kill him, or else try to turn him in for the murder of Blaine.' His chest felt tight, as if he could not draw air into his lungs. Put as baldly as that it was logically inescapable, and yet emotionally he still felt as if he had betrayed the past and somehow broken a thing of infinite value that was not his alone, but belonged to his whole family. Most especially it belonged to Matthew, and he would not be forgiven for destroying it. He had created immeasurable pain, and he should have found some way to avoid it.

'That will not happen,' Hall said quietly.

'Yes, it will,' Joseph contradicted him. 'As soon as the *Cormorant* returns and Corcoran knows the device was successful.'

Hall looked at him steadily, his eyes bright and sad. 'It will not be successful. Corcoran could not complete it. Mrs Blaine is right: he has not the brilliance Blaine had. He thought he could do the last little bit himself, but he misjudged his ability. He killed Blaine too soon.'

Joseph was stunned. 'You mean we . . . we've lost the invention?'

'Yes.'

He refused to grasp it.

'But we're testing it! On the *Cormorant* . . .'

'In the hope that the Germans will try to steal it.' A flash of dry, bleak humour touched Hall's face. 'Then we might at least find the leak from the Establishment. But if it was Corcoran himself who killed Blaine, and I believe you, then there may not be one. It looks as if he also smashed the first prototype in order to hide the fact that he was unable to complete it. It bought him some time, and increased our belief that there was a German spy in St Giles.'

'You're not surprised?' Joseph said with profound misery, still fighting to find some shred of disbelief. It was futile, and in his heart he knew it, but he could not let go yet.

'Yes, I am surprised,' Hall admitted. 'But your logic is perfect. More than anything else I am grieved. I know Corcoran – not well, but I know him. I saw he was ambitious and that he loved admiration. He fed on the love of his fellows, which he more than earned.' His clear blue eyes were sad, and perhaps guilty. 'I did not recognize the hunger for glory that it seems finally destroyed everything else in him.' His voice dropped. 'I've seen it before, in military men, and in politicians, where the original desire to win the battle is overtaken by the lust for fame and to be admired, and then finally to become immortal in memory, as if their existence were measured only by what others think of them. They become so addicted to fame their appetite is insatiable. I didn't see it in Corcoran, but I should have.'

'I can't prove it!' Joseph said with a kind of desperation. It was Shanley that Hall was speaking of as if he were a stranger, somebody one could diagnose with impartiality, not a friend, his godfather and a part of his life woven inextricably with every memory he had. 'You won't prove it with Archie's evidence,' he went on, insistent, as if it could still matter. 'Not beyond reasonable doubt.'

Hall looked at him with pity. 'I know. He will have to be arrested immediately and tried in secret. None of this can be known. It is murder and treason. The evidence will be given in camera because of the prototype, and because such a betrayal would cripple morale, and we might not survive that just now.'

'In secret?' Joseph was startled.

'Yes. We will call you when you are needed.'

'Me? But—'

'You must testify as to what Commander MacAllister told you, and Mrs Blaine.'

'But it's hearsay!' Joseph protested. 'It's not evidence!'

'Is it true?' Hall's eyes opened very wide.

'Yes! But—'

'You will swear to it?'

Joseph hesitated, not because he had any doubt, but because it meant that he was casting the final pieces that would weigh damnation for Shanley Corcoran.

'Are you telling the truth, Captain Reavley?' Hall repeated.
'Yes . . .'

'Then you will swear it before the tribunal if you are called. Thank you for coming forward. I realize what it has cost you.'

Joseph rose to his feet slowly, straightening his leg and his back. 'No, you don't,' he said wearily. 'You have no idea at all.' He turned and walked to the door slowly, as if each step were too long, and too slow. He heard Hall speaking behind him, but he did not listen. There was nothing he could say that would do any good.

Joseph returned to St Giles the next day. He walked into the house in the early afternoon and he was barely in the hall when Hannah came out of the kitchen white-faced, her hair coming loose from its pins.

'Joseph, something terrible has happened,' she said immediately, without waiting for him to speak. 'Orla Corcoran telephoned, but I couldn't reach you at Matthew's flat. You must have left already.' She stepped in front of him, so close he could smell the sweetness of the lavender soap on her skin. Her voice was trembling. 'Joseph, someone came this morning to arrest Shanley and took him away. They didn't say what for, and Orla is almost beside herself. She has no idea what it's about and she doesn't know what to do. They told her to say nothing, so she can't even call a lawyer. How can we help? I told her you would know.'

'We can't help,' he replied, seeing the grief and incomprehension in her face. He opened the sitting-room door and pulled her in, closing it after her. He did not want Mrs Appleton to hear. 'It is to do with Blaine's murder,' he explained. 'And the project they have at the Establishment. It has to be secret.'

'They've found the spy?' She searched his face, her eyes serious, probing for honesty. 'Was Shanley protecting him? Is that what's wrong?'

'No, actually they haven't. I'm not sure if there is one.'

'There has to be! He murdered Theo Blaine.' She stated it as fact.

Should he let it go? It would be easier. The temptation was so powerful it burned through his mind like a fire, hurting and destroying.

She saw something of the turmoil inside him and reached up her hand a little uncertainly to touch his cheek. 'Joseph, please don't shut me out. I'm not running away any more. I am sure that whatever it is, it's terrible. I haven't seen such pain in your eyes since Eleanor died. What is it?'

He looked at her. She was so like her mother, and yet stronger. Her innocence was gone; not destroyed but transformed into something else, something prepared to love whatever the cost. She needed him to trust her, and now overwhelmingly he needed her to share the burden with him. He had not intended to, but he told her.

'Shanley killed Blaine himself because Blaine was going to create something brilliant, and take the credit,' he said. 'It was his, rightly. Shanley killed him out of envy, thinking he could finish the work, but he was wrong. He wasn't clever enough.'

He saw the incredulity in her face, then it turned to hurt, then finally grief. 'Oh, Joe, I'm so sorry!' She put her arms around him and held him as if he had been younger than she, the wounded one, the sleepless one whose nights were too long, too dark and too cold to be endured alone.

He was glad of it. It was all he could do not to let the hot tears of disillusion and betrayal burn his face.

Chapter Fifteen

It was a long time before Joseph could compose himself sufficiently to telephone Orla Corcoran and say to her that for the
moment there was nothing he could do to help, and in Shanley's
best interest she would be wisest to say as little as possible. If
anyone should ask her she should tell them he was not well and
could not be reached.

She was unhappy with that advice, knowing that there was
something desperately wrong, but he refused to tell her more. He
left the study, where he had been with the door closed, to find
Hannah in the hall saying that Hallam Kerr was here again, in a
degree of anxiety because Mrs Hopgood was expecting her son
home from France, and he had lost both his legs. The boy was
nineteen.

'Do you want me to tell him to go away?' she asked with a
slightly twisted smile.

'Thank you, but I'll tell him myself,' he replied, walking past her.

'Joseph . . .'

He stopped and half turned.

She gave him a tight smile, wry, soft-eyed. 'Isn't it also time
that you told him you are going back to your regiment, and he's
going to have to deal with her on his own?' she asked.

How did she know? He had not even faced telling her yet,
knowing how much she wanted him to stay.

She looked at his dismay. 'I'm learning,' she said with a touch of self-mockery. She turned and went towards the kitchen, her head high, her back stiff, deliberately not glancing back at him. Their understanding was better than to need it.

Joseph went into the sitting room where he found Kerr standing in front of the fireplace, although, of course, the fire was not lit, and the room was full of sunlight. He looked anxious and there was something close to panic in his eyes. He cleared his throat and his voice was husky.

'I came to tell you about William Hopgood,' he said a little awkwardly. 'I thought you would like at least to know about it. He wasn't in your regiment, but you probably know him.'

'Yes . . . slightly.'

Kerr hesitated, his eyes searching Joseph's. 'I'm . . . I'm going to see him,' he said. 'I've no idea what I can say – God help me! But I swear I'll stay as long as he wants me to. If . . .' he swallowed as though there were a lump in his throat, 'if he tells me to get out, should I go?'

Joseph smiled in spite of himself. 'I don't know any better than you do. Maybe wait until he's told you three times. That should mean he's sincere.'

'I'll be there all night, if that's what he needs,' Kerr promised. 'Two in the morning can be a terrible hour to spend alone. I . . . I know. I've done it. I still have my arms and legs, but I felt as if God had abandoned the world.' He gulped again. 'He . . . He hasn't, has He?' He looked at Joseph with pleading eyes.

Joseph looked back at him, racking his mind for what he should say. Was Kerr strong enough for honesty? Perhaps he was too weak to survive anything else, and forgive? 'I don't know,' Joseph answered. 'There are times when I look at what's happening – young men crushed and dying, the land poisoned and turned to filth, corruption of what I used to trust utterly – and I'm not sure.' He met Kerr's haggard eyes. 'But the things that Christ taught are still true, of that I'm absolutely certain. Meet me at the end of the world when we stand at the abyss, I'll tell Satan to his face just as certainly: honour is still worth living or dying for; no matter how tired or hurt or frightened you are, face forward and seek the light, and even if it's gone out and you can't remember where it was, keep going. It's always right to care. It's going to hurt like hell at times, but if you let go of that then you have lost the purpose of existing at all.'

Kerr stared at him, a slow, almost beautiful dawn of understanding in his eyes, as if he had seen something at last that made sense, one firm step on which to build.

'Yes,' he said simply. 'I'll go now. Thank you, Captain Reavley.' He held out his hand. 'Thank you for everything.'

Joseph took it and gripped it hard, and felt an answering firmness. 'Good luck,' he offered, meaning it profoundly.

Kerr nodded. 'You too, sir.'

The next day Orla telephoned again, and this time it was not possible to put her off with evasion. Her voice was harsh with fear and exhaustion, and unquestionably with anger as well.

'Joseph? Shanley has asked me to speak with you. He sounds terribly ill, and he won't tell me what is wrong. He says that he has some information about an enemy in the Establishment. I suppose he must be referring to whoever murdered poor Theo Blaine.' Now the anger in her was very forceful. 'I think that Shanley has realized who it is that is betraying us to the Germans. He dare not trust anyone except you. He says he cannot even speak to Matthew, and you will know why, but it is extremely urgent. You have to go to him, Joseph. He sounds dreadful. I've never heard him like this before.' Her voice dropped. 'I think it must be someone he is very fond of, someone he really trusted. Disillusion is one of the most painful of all human experiences, especially for a man like Shanley, who cares for people so much. Please go immediately, Joseph. Promise me?'

She spoke of disillusion! What searing irony. It was the very last thing he wanted to do. There was nothing to say, nothing to add except recriminations, and excuses neither of them would believe.

Was it conceivable that Corcoran knew anything about information going from the Establishment to the Germans? From whom? Ben Morven? There was nothing new in that. Surely Naval Intelligence would get everything from him that there was?

Or could it be that Corcoran knew something that Morven would never betray?

He did not believe it. But he would go, not for Corcoran to tell him anything from Naval Intelligence, but because he wanted to look at Corcoran again and see if he could understand how he had been so blind all these years to the truth of him. Had the weakness always been there? How had he missed it? What did he really understand of human good or evil if he misread a man so close to him, so badly?

And had his father been so blind as well? Had he chosen not to see, or not to believe it? Had he thought that to hope, against reality, was a kind of charity, a faith in the best? Should the deepest friendship close its eyes deliberately? Was that what loyalty was, or ought to be?

He was standing at the telephone in the hall. Everyone else was in the kitchen. He could smell bread baking.

'Yes,' he said, clearing his throat. 'Yes. Of course I'll go. I imagine they will let me in. Where is he?'

There was a moment's silence. 'Don't you know? Shanley said you did!'

'No, I don't. But I imagine I can find out. It may not be today, but I'll go.'

'Thank you.' She did not press him or ask him to swear or promise. She believed his word. It made him feel worse.

It took Joseph several telephone calls and a lot of waiting before finally someone in Admiral Hall's office told him where Corcoran was, and gave him permission to visit because he was an ordained chaplain in the army. Corcoran would not be permitted a civilian lawyer, but he would be allowed a military one, and the military priest of his choice. Apparently that was Joseph. A car would pick him up the following afternoon, and return him afterwards. He was to speak of the visit to no one, most particularly not to Orla Corcoran. Joseph gave his word; it was a condition of the visit. And he was to wear uniform so there could be no misunderstanding of his status.

The countryside was glorious, dappled sunshine over the fields, hedges still white with blossom, trees billowing in the wind, their skirts flying. There were shire horses leaning into the harrow, necks bent. Clouds piled up, scudding away in long mare's tails, like spindrift off the sea. For once he did not see it.

It was a long journey and he lost sense of direction, except that it was generally towards London. It took over two hours. When he finally arrived at the building, he found it was an old prison made of stone and smelling as if it were always wet. It seemed to carry with it the darkness of old griefs, bitterness and lost dreams.

Joseph identified himself again, and was taken inside.

'I have been told to allow you an hour, Chaplain, but it will only be this once,' the officer in charge told him. 'I don't know what he's here for, but it's very serious. You must give him nothing, and take nothing from him. Do you understand?'

'Yes. I've seen military prisoners before,' Joseph replied miserably.

'Maybe, but this one's different. Sorry, Chaplain, but we've got to search you.'

'Of course.' Joseph submitted obediently, then finally he was conducted along a narrow corridor. His footsteps, instead of echoing as he had expected, were eaten by the silence, as if he had not really passed that way at all.

Corcoran was in an ordinary room, indistinguishable as a cell except for the fact that the window was above head height, and the glass was so thick that nothing was visible through it. The single door was made of steel with no features at all on the inside – no hinge, no handle.

Corcoran himself was sitting on a bunk bed with a bare mattress.

He looked up as the door closed and Joseph was left alone with him. He was an old man, his face withered, his skin without life. His eyes seemed smaller, more deeply sunken into his head.

Joseph felt a wrenching pity inside him like a cramp in the stomach, and even a kind of revulsion. It would have been unimaginable a week ago. This was Shanley Corcoran! A man he had loved all his life, whose face and voice, and whose laughter were woven into the best of all his memories. And he had killed Theo Blaine, not in anger or passion, not in defence of anything good, but because Blaine was going to achieve the glory of saving Britain,

296

leaving Corcoran to be no more than a footnote on the pages of history.

That glory in other men's minds had mattered to him more than the project itself, more than Blaine's life and, God forgive him, more than the lives of the sailors who would have used the thing, whatever it was. Had he thought of them?

Joseph stopped just inside the door, standing because there was nothing on which to sit. He had to say something, keep up the pretence.

'What is it you know, Shanley?' he asked. He could not bring himself to say, 'How are you?' That would be absurd now, and dishonest. His state was painfully obvious, and Joseph could do nothing to help, even if he wished to, and he was not sure that he did, or what it was he felt now, except misery.

Corcoran gave a bitter little laugh. 'Is that all you care about, Joseph? After all these years, the sum of it is, "What do you know?".'

Joseph felt a stab of pity and disgust that almost made him sick. It was like a physical twisting of the stomach. 'That's why you sent for me,' he replied. 'And incidentally, why they let me in.'

'And the only reason you came?' There was accusation in Corcoran's face.

It was even worse than Joseph had feared. The room was not hot, but it was airless, and he could feel the sweat running down his body. He could not ask Corcoran when the corruption had started, or if it had always been there. He played the farce. 'Is there another spy in the Establishment, Shanley?' he asked.

Corcoran looked up at him. 'You know, I have not the faintest idea. There might be. It could even be one of the technicians or guards, for all I could say.' Now there was anger in him, as if he had been let down. 'But I knew you wouldn't come unless you thought there was some glory in it for you, some prize to take back to Admiral Hall.' His mouth twisted in a sour grimace. 'You're nothing like your father, Joseph. He knew the value of friendship, through fair weather or foul. He would never turn his back on a lifetime of loyalty, all the human passion and treasure of the past. But for all your pretence of religion, your self-right-eousness going out to the trenches where you can pose the hero, you're shallow as a puddle in the street.'

It was ridiculous that it should hurt! It was grossly unfair, distorted by fear and, please God, by guilt as well, but still it left Joseph gasping with the pain of it. 'Don't use my father's name in this,' he said between his teeth. 'Most of the time I miss him with a constant emptiness. I keep thinking of things I want to ask him, things to tell him, or just to share. But I'm glad he doesn't have to see you now. He would have found it unbearable because you've betrayed not only the future, but the past as well. Nothing looks the same as it used to. All my life I've thought that you, above all men, were honest. You're not, you're a liar to the soul. I just wondered if you had always been, and somehow we missed it!'

Corcoran stood up, easily, the aches and stiffness forgotten. 'You're ignorant, Joseph, and with the arrogance of all people who think they speak for God and morality, you judge without understanding. I had no choice.' He stared at Joseph, his eyes burning with anger. 'When I said I had no idea who the spy in the Establishment was, that was only half true. I don't know who's left now, who smashed the prototype and who could still be in touch with the Germans.' His voice rose a pitch. 'Theo Blaine wasn't nearly as clever as everyone thought he was, not anywhere near! Oh, he was bright!' He said it bitterly, as though it were somehow a condemnation. 'Very advanced in his field, but there's all the difference in the world between bright, and genius. Like Icarus, he flew too close to the sun. Thought he could design a machine that would guide torpedoes and depth charges so they would hit their target every time. He said so!'

Joseph's mind swam. The idea was vast! It really would have changed the war for ever. Whichever side had such a thing would destroy the other out of the sea. That was what Archie was testing now, and Matthew with him. Did they know the truth – that it was useless? Why in God's name had Corcoran killed Blaine, if Blaine had not had the genius to do it?

'It makes no sense,' he said aloud. 'If he couldn't finish it, why kill him?'

'Now you doubt I did it?' Corcoran was raging. 'Suddenly you're sorry, and on my side again?'

Joseph was staggered. Could he have been so immensely wrong? It was a moment's wild, beautiful hope. But Blaine had certainly not torn his own throat out with a garden fork!

'Because he couldn't finish it he was going to sell it to the Germans, you fool!' Corcoran spat. 'Anything rather than admit he wasn't up to it. That way we would never have known. It was his chance to cover himself. But maybe the Germans could have finished it, built on what we had! They have brilliant men.' He leaned further forward. 'Don't you see, Joseph? I had to do it! I had no choice. Who could I tell? No one else in the country knew enough to understand whether I was right or not. The fate of the war depended on it . . .'

Joseph was stunned. Was it possible? It made a hideous sense – a scientist who boasted of what he could achieve, who overrated his own ability, brilliant as it was, but not genius of that splendour. Then when he was at his wits' end, staring failure in the face, and his own humiliation, he sold it to the enemy rather than admit the truth. What fatal arrogance!

'I tried to stop the spy as well,' Corcoran went on, his voice strengthening. 'But I missed him. Blaine wouldn't tell me, but I have no doubt now that it's Morven.' He moved until he was almost close enough to Joseph to touch him. 'You have to take it from here. I don't know who to trust. Matthew's at sea on Archie's ship. He doesn't trust Calder Shearing, he told me that himself. Hall won't listen to me. You have to do it – for England – for the war. For everything we love and believe . . .'

Joseph looked at him. It hung in the balance, all the past love, the memories, sweet and close, the desperate hunger to believe, like clinging to a dream as the shreds of it slip into waking.

But honesty forced itself on him. Corcoran was lying. It was there in the details, the pattern that shifted with each retelling of the story, always to lay the fault on someone else. He remembered Lizzie's words about Blaine's skills, and that Morven's were not the same, but Corcoran's were. And now he could see it in Corcoran's eyes, the sheen on his skin, in his imagination he could even smell it. It was the same terror of dying that he saw in the trenches, but out there, for all the horror and pity, it was in a way clean.

He turned away, sick to his heart. 'You're lying, Shanley,' he said quietly. 'Blaine might have finished it. It was you who stopped him so you could do it yourself and take the fame in history, the glory of saving your country. But you were willing to let the country lose rather than have Blaine crowned in your place.'

'You don't know that!' Corcoran shouted at him. 'There's nothing to prove it, except your word! You could be wrong . . .'

Joseph turned back. He hated meeting Corcoran's eyes and seeing the terror and the self-pity in them, but to look away now could be a cowardice he would never be able to mend. 'No, I'm not wrong. You didn't kill Blaine to save the project; you killed him to prevent him from eclipsing you. You have to be the centre, all eyes on you.'

'Don't testify!' Corcoran's voice cracked. 'You don't have to! You are my priest, you can't be compelled to!' His face was slick with sweat now and he was trembling. 'Your father wouldn't have done. He understood friendship, the supreme loyalty.'

Joseph thought of all the arguments in his mind. He thought of Archie at sea, and of Gwen Neave's sons, and the loss and the grief still to come. Whatever betrayal he felt for himself, he owed them better than to run away now. He turned and walked to the door. He reached it and banged with both fists.

The guard came and let him out. Only when he was outside in the sun and the wind of the courtyard did he realize that his face was wet with tears, and his throat ached so violently that he could not speak.

It was the first day of June, warm and still. A few clouds drifted like bright ships across the sky, sails wide to catch the sun. In the orchard the blossom was over, the fruit setting. The garden was dizzy with colour and perfume.

Joseph was in his shirtsleeves, working with pleasure. It was good to feel his fingers in the earth, pulling the thick, lush weeds, and to move with only a slight awareness of an ache, no pain, no fear of pulling on a muscle or tearing open the healing flesh. He could not stay much longer, only until he had testified for Admiral Hall, and then all this would be forfeited again and become just a treasure in the mind.

Hannah came out of the back door towards him, her face pale, her voice breathless.

'Joseph, there's been an enormous battle in the North Sea, off Jutland. Our whole Grand Fleet against the German High Seas Fleet. They don't know what's happened yet. They don't even know if we've won or lost, but lots of ships have been sunk on both sides.' She stared at him, eyes wide.

What should he say? Hope? Cling on to the belief in good until the last possible moment? And if it was smashed, if Archie and Matthew were among the thousands lost, what then? Did trying to prepare yourself ever do any good? Was the blow any less?

No. It always hurt impossibly, unbelievably. Would it have been easier to bear, quicker to recover from if he had imagined his parents' deaths, or anyone's? Would he have missed Sam's friendship any less, been able not to lie awake in his dugout in the mud of Ypres and not wonder if Sam was still alive, imagine hearing his laughter, or what he could have said to this, or that?

He touched Hannah gently, both hands on her shoulders, but softly; the slightest pulling away would have released her. 'Far more will come home than have been lost,' he said. 'Think of them and don't face anything else unless we have to.'

She controlled her fear with an effort so intense he could not only see it in her face but feel the power of it through her body. She blinked several times. 'Thank you for not telling me to have faith in God.' She smiled a little twistedly. 'I want a brother, not a priest.'

'Have faith in God too,' he answered. 'But don't blame Him for anything that goes wrong, or imagine that He ever said it wouldn't. If He promised you that Archie and Matthew would come back, then they will. But I don't think He did. I think He said we would have all that we need, not all that we want.'

'All we need for what?' she asked, her voice trembling.

'To realize the best in ourselves,' he answered. 'To practise pity

301

and honour until they become part of us, and the courage to care to the last strength we have, to give everything.'

She frowned. 'Do I want all that? Wouldn't "pretty good" do? Does it have to be "perfect"?'

He smiled, widely, a warm, genuine laughter inside him. 'Well, decide what you don't want, and tell God you'll do without it. Maybe He'll listen. I have no idea.'

'You still think He's there?' she said perfectly seriously. 'Will you think that if they're gone?' She wanted an answer, the gravity was there in her eyes.

'It's still the best option I know,' he answered her. 'Can you think of anywhere else, any other star to follow?'

She thought for a moment. 'No. I suppose the alternative is just to stop trying. Sit down. There are times when that seems a lot less trouble.'

'You have to be pretty certain you like it where you are to do that!' He let go of her and touched her face, brushing a stray hair off her cheek. 'Personally I think this is a sod of a place, and I have to believe there's a better one, fairer to those who hadn't much of a chance here.'

She swallowed and nodded. 'I'll make lunch. There's nothing to do but wait. Please don't go out, Joe.'

'Out? Don't you think I care as much as you do?'

'Yes, of course. I'm sorry.'

It seemed an endless afternoon, every minute creeping by. Time after time Joseph drew in breath to say something, and then found he did not mean it, or it was pointless anyway, only making more obvious the fears that crowded his mind. He looked at Hannah and she smiled, making a little grimace. Then she returned to her ironing, going over and over the same sheet until she was in danger of scorching it.

The news came in the early evening. The *Cormorant* was among those ships lost. Joseph and Hannah stood together in the sitting room, holding each other, numb, minds whirling over an abyss of grief, struggling uselessly not to be sucked into it.

Not just Archie gone, but Matthew as well. They would never know how; blown apart, burned to death, thrown into the sea to struggle in the water until their strength was gone, or worst of all, imprisoned in the ship itself as it plunged downward into the darkness of the bottom of the ocean until it was crushed and the sides caved in and the water suffocated them.

The loss was overwhelming, unbearable. Time stopped. The sun lowered in the sky and darkness came. The children went to bed and neither Joseph nor Hannah found any words even to begin telling them what had happened.

'There's been a big battle at sea,' Hannah said, her voice oddly flat and steady. 'We don't know how everybody is yet.' It was a lie. She needed the time. Perhaps she needed to grieve alone and do her first, terrible weeping before she gathered strength to share it with them.

Joseph too needed time. He hurt for Hannah, and he hurt bitterly for himself. He had always loved Matthew, but it stunned him how intensely Matthew was inextricably woven into the fabric of his life. It was as if John Reavley had died again, a large piece of him gone in a new and heart-numbing way. He had not expected that Matthew could be in any danger, even going to sea to test the prototype. The loss was too vast to take into his mind. Matthew could not be gone!

Was it like this for everyone? The world falling apart, reason and joy disintegrating into an all-engulfing darkness?

And that created the need for another decision. Could he go back to the trenches now and leave Hannah and the children alone?

He found her in front of the looking-glass in her bedroom. She had an old dressing wrap on and her hair down around her shoulders. Her face was bleached of all colour, every shred of blood drained away, but she looked quite composed. She just moved slowly, as if afraid her co-ordination would not keep her from knocking things, or perhaps even falling over.

She looked exactly as he felt. He understood totally.

'I won't be going back to Ypres,' he said quietly. 'I expect you know that anyway, but I thought I'd tell you, just in case.'

She nodded. 'We'll tell Judith . . . but not yet. I'm . . . I'm not ready.' She looked at him curiously, her face crumpled. 'Joseph, how does everybody do it, how do they keep on, how do they live? Everything I've said to other women who've lost husbands or sons is idiotic!' She frowned in amazement. 'How did I dare? Were they kind to me, or just too beaten and numb to care about anything else?'

'I'm not sure that anything we say touches people in those times —' he corrected himself — 'these times. It's worse when the shock wears off and feeling comes back. But I'll be here. I won't leave . . . or let you leave me.'

She turned away from him quickly. 'Go to bed,' she said, her voice cracking. 'I'm not ready to weep yet. If I do I won't be able to stop, and I have to think how to tell the children, especially Tom. Please!'

He obeyed silently, closing the door behind him.

He slept fitfully. He heard Hannah up and down the stairs, he lost count how many times. At five o'clock he got up as well and went down to the kitchen, knowing he would find her there.

She was dressed, scrubbing out the pantry. The whole large cupboard-like room was empty, nothing left on the shelves. It was all piled on the kitchen table and on the bench above the flour and vegetable bins and the cutlery drawers. There were boxes, bags, tins and barrels everywhere. She had her sleeves up to her elbows and an apron on over an old dress. She had not bothered to put her hair up, but it was in a loose braid, like a schoolgirl's.

'Can I help?' he offered.

'Not really,' she replied, pushing her hair out of her eyes. 'I don't know why I'm doing it, it's just better than lying in bed.'

'Do you want a cup of tea?'

'If you can find the kettle and the tea, yes.'

Half an hour later all the shelves were scrubbed but still wet, and Joseph had made some sort of order out of the piles of groceries. They were both sitting at the kitchen table and it was broad daylight, the sun shining in through the window as if it were any other day.

The telephone rang.

Hannah gripped her cup so tightly she slopped tea over on to her dress and arm. The sight of the mess upset her, tears gleaming in her eyes, simply because it was a hair crack in the façade and it cost all her strength to keep from letting go.

Joseph went into the hall and picked up the receiver. 'Joseph Reavley,' he said quietly.

'Good morning, Captain Reavley,' a voice said, on the other end, sounding tinny and far away. 'This is Calder Shearing.'

Joseph did not want to speak to this man. He could not cope with talking of Matthew's death, not yet.

'Mr Shearing . . .' he began.

'I have news you will want to hear,' Shearing cut across him. 'There were quite a number of survivors from the *Cormorant*. Captain Reavley and Commander MacAllister are among them. Their injuries are trivial. They spent some time in the water, but they will be perfectly all right.'

Joseph found his voice was gone, stuck in his throat, his mouth dry.

'Captain Reavley?'

He coughed. 'Yes . . . are you sure?'

'Of course I am sure,' Shearing said testily, as if some emotion had drained him as well. 'Do you imagine I would have called you if I were not? The battle was appalling. We estimate casualties of over six thousand men, and at least fourteen ships. Your brother and brother-in-law will be home within two or three days.'

'Thank you . . . yes . . .' Joseph gulped. 'Thank you.' He replaced the receiver and walked back to the kitchen, bumping into the jamb of the door and numbing his elbow. It should have been painful, but he was unaware of it.

Hannah stared at him. There was no fear in her face, there was nothing else left to hurt her; the worst had already happened.

'It was Shearing . . .' he began.

She frowned. 'Who is Shearing?'

'Intelligence Service. Hannah, they're alive! They saved a lot of the crew, and Archie and Matthew are among them! He's sure! It's no mistake, he's absolutely certain.'

She looked at him, eyes wide. Now she was afraid again, afraid to believe, to grasp the pain of hoping, going through all the torture of love and fear and waiting and dreading. 'Is he?'

'Yes! Yes, he is! Absolutely!' He strode around the table and pulled her to her feet and put his arms around her, clinging on to her and feeling her cry, great gasping sobs of all the emotion, the agony she had held in, and now at last letting it go.

He was smiling, tears on his face as well. Archie was alive – above all, Matthew was alive! Matthew was alive – he was all right – he would be coming back.

And that meant, of course, that Joseph would have to return to Ypres. But not yet, not today.

There was twenty-four hours' respite, then Joseph went to London to testify at the trial of Shanley Corcoran. He was charged with high treason. The trial was held in a closed room; the only thing to make it different from a place where any kind of business might be conducted was the situation of the chairs, the height of the windows above the ground, and the armed and uniformed men at the doors.

As with any other trial, Joseph did not hear the testimony previous to his own. He waited in an anteroom alone, pacing the floor, sitting for a short time on the hard-backed chair, then pacing again. He turned over and over in his mind what he would say, if he would simply answer what was asked of him, in a sense leave his contribution to truth or justice in someone else's hands. That would take from him the final responsibility, the blame for Corcoran's fall, and whatever happened to him because of it. It should not be Joseph's decision to weigh his guilt.

The door opened and a small, quiet man in a dark suit told him it was time.

Joseph went with him.

The room was silent as he entered. He saw Corcoran immediately. There were only a dozen or so people there, no jury. This was not a trial at which any member of the public could be present. Both its evidence and its findings would remain secret. It reminded Joseph of a court martial.

He had not intended to meet Corcoran's eyes, but his gaze was drawn in spite of himself. Corcoran sat at a small table with his defender beside him. He looked ashen pale, stiff-bodied but somehow smaller than Joseph remembered him. But then at heart he had been different from the way Joseph remembered him for a long time, perhaps always.

Now he was angry, his dark eyes brilliant, still a question, a demand in his expression – would Joseph finally measure up to the loyalty his father would have given, the loyalty to all past love and laughter, passions shared, and which he was convinced he deserved?

The prosecutor began. 'Please state your name, your present occupation and where you live,' he directed. His voice was soft, very polite; he was a rather elegant man.

'Joseph Reavley. I am a chaplain in the army. I live in Selbourne St Giles, in Cambridgeshire.'

'And why are you not with your regiment now, Captain Reavley?'

'I was injured, but I am due to return as soon as you permit me,' Joseph replied.

'When your duty here is completed, you mean?'

'Yes.'

'Just so. How long ago were you wounded, and when did you go from hospital to St Giles?'

Joseph gave the answers, and detail by detail the prosecutor drew from him his involvement with solving the murder of Theo Blaine, his acquaintance with Blaine's widow, his conversations with Hallam Kerr and with Inspector Perth. It was a meticulous, almost dry, account, but then there was no jury to impress, no emotion to manipulate. The three judges would deal only with facts.

Throughout it all it was a battle between Joseph and Corcoran, who sat staring as if Joseph were the betrayer and he the victim, a man in an impossible situation who had been beaten by circumstance, and in the end turned on by the one person he trusted like a son. Such was the agony in his face that Joseph became more and more certain that he had actually convinced himself it was so.

Worse was to come. The defence lawyer, a lean man with fair, receding hair, stood up and walked towards Joseph, stopping a couple of yards in front of him.

'Would you like to sit down, Captain Reavley?' he asked cour-
teously. 'I know you received serious wounds, which must be
barely healed. We do not wish to cause you unnecessary pain.'

Joseph straightened his shoulders and stood even more crisply
to attention. 'No, thank you, sir, I am perfectly recovered.'

'I understand you have been awarded the Military Cross for
your heroic efforts in bringing back dead and injured soldiers from
no-man's-land in Flanders?'

Joseph felt himself colour. 'Yes, sir.'

'Is that part of an army chaplain's duty?' The defence seemed
surprised.

'Not technically, sir, but I believe it is morally.'

'So you are willing to define your moral duty outside the army's
terms of reference?' He smiled very slightly, his voice still soft.
'The army tells you one thing, but you have added to it others
far more dangerous, risking your own life and very nearly losing
it, because of the way you perceive your own duty?'

Joseph could see the pitfall ahead, he had dug it himself and
there was no honest way to avoid it. 'Yes, sir. But I am far from
the only chaplain to do that.'

'Ah, I see. Soldiers must obey orders, but chaplains have a
higher master, a different morality, and can do as they themselves
think fit?'

Joseph could feel the heat in his face and knew it must be plain
to others. 'Most soldiers will risk their lives to save their friends,
sir,' he replied stiffly. God, he sounded self-righteous. He loathed
it. 'If you had someone you were responsible for,' he went on,
'some young man of nineteen or twenty who had gone out to
fight for his country, was lying injured, bleeding in the mud of
no-man's-land, and you had it in your power to go and look for
him, perhaps bring him back alive, wouldn't you?'

There was a faint rustle of movement in the room, a kind of
sigh.

'What I would do is immaterial, Captain Reavley,' the defence
replied, shifting his weight and then taking a step or two to face
Joseph from a different angle. 'We are establishing what you will
do. It is quite clear from what you have said that you make your

own rules, answering to what you believe is a higher authority than human law.'

The prosecutor rose to his feet.

'Yes, yes,' the central judge agreed. He turned to the defence. 'Mr Paxton, you are drawing too high a conclusion. We take your point that Captain Reavley is a man who follows his belief in morality without being ordered to. Please proceed.'

'Thank you, my lord.' Paxton turned to Joseph again. 'I shall not ask you to repeat your testimony regarding the death of Mr Blaine, or your growing acquaintance with Mrs Blaine after her widowhood. It all seems to be perfectly clear. But I will ask you to repeat what she said about her husband's ability. And then, if you would be so good, tell us what you did to ascertain for yourself that it was indeed true. What is Mrs Blaine's knowledge of the situation at the Establishment, other than what her husband told her? And it is regrettably beyond doubt that he was more than willing to deceive her in matters surely more important to her than his professional standing, relative to that of Mr Corcoran.'

Joseph had no choice. Reluctantly he admitted that he had accepted Lizzie's word, without corroboration.

'You seem somewhat gullible, Captain Reavley,' Paxton observed. 'Well meaning, but easily led where your affections, or your own perceptions of your duty, are concerned.'

'Is that a question, my lord?' the prosecutor demanded, his voice edgy, his face pale.

'Perhaps it should be,' Paxton rejoined immediately. He looked at Joseph. 'You seem to wish to be all things to all men, Chaplain. No doubt a noble and Christian desire, but you may well end in betraying one in order to be loyal to another. And I fear in this instance it is your lifelong friend Shanley Corcoran who is going to suffer for your very mixed emotions, and what you feel to be a higher duty than that which you have been given. My advice to you would be to do what you have been commanded to, and do it well. Leave the rest to others, before you meddle where you do not understand, and end in doing irretrievable harm, not only to individual men, but to your country.'

Joseph stood rigid. Was it true as he had feared? He tried to be all things to all men, and was in truth nothing inside, empty? He looked at Corcoran. There was sweat on his face, but his eyes were gleaming. He had seen hope, and he would allow Joseph to be destroyed if he had to, to save himself. In that ugly, final moment Joseph was certain of it: Corcoran would survive at all costs.

Joseph turned away, sick at heart. He faced Paxton. 'That is very good advice,' he said distinctly. 'And it is what I did. Mr Corcoran had said to me that he had killed Theo Blaine because Blaine was incapable of finishing the project they were working on, but to protect his own scientific reputation he was going to sell it to the Germans.'

Paxton's eyebrows shot up. 'Even though it did not work?'

'I didn't believe it either,' Joseph replied, and saw Paxton's face flame. 'I went to Admiral Hall of Naval Intelligence and told him all I knew. He would be able to check on Theo Blaine's abilities, and those of all the other men working at the Establishment.'

Paxton shifted his position again. 'And if Blaine could not complete the work, Captain Reavley, but intended to betray what there was of it to our enemies, what would you have done in Mr Corcoran's place? You, who exceed your own orders and go "over the top" into no-man's-land to bring back the dead? Is this not actually what you received your Military Cross for? Was not the journalist Eldon Prentice actually dead? It was a corpse you risked your life to bring back, was it not?'

'Victoria Crosses are given for a specific act of extraordinary valour,' Joseph corrected him. 'Military Crosses are for a number of lesser acts. Lots of men go out to bring back the injured. You can't always tell if they're dead or not until you reach your own trenches. It's wet and cold and dark out there, and you're being shot at. Sometimes men die before you get them back.'

There was a moment's silence.

'Very moving,' Paxton said. 'But irrelevant. There are many kinds of courage, moral as well as physical. I repeat, if you knew for a certainty that the most brilliant scientist in your Establishment was also a traitor, but you could not prove it to others, what would you do, Captain Reavley?'

Joseph closed his eyes. This was the moment. Corcoran was sitting rigid, staring at him. He could feel his eyes as if they burned a scalding heat on to his skin. 'I would do what I have done,' Joseph replied. 'I would take the evidence to Naval Intelligence and let them deduce from it what they would. I could be mistaken.'

'And was Mr Corcoran mistaken, in your opinion? Did he act in error?'

Joseph's mouth was dry, his heart pounding. 'No. I do not believe so. He described a scientist whose ambition and hunger for glory was so consuming that he would betray everything and everyone else, rather than yield the ultimate achievement to another. He would sooner have Britain lose than win with someone else's invention. But it was not Theo Blaine he was describing, it was himself.'

Paxton flung out his arms. 'You have known the man all your life!' His voice cracked with incredulity. 'He was your dead father's best and dearest friend, and this is what you think of him?' Now there was derision in him, and stinging contempt. 'What changed your mind, Reverend? A loss of faith in everything, perhaps even in God? What happened to you in the trenches, in the no-man's-land you describe so well, the cold, the wet, the agony, being shot at?' He waved his arms. 'And you were hit, weren't you? Are you lashing out at a God the Father who did not protect you from all this?' He gestured again towards Corcoran. 'Or at the father who died and left you to face this horror and deal with it alone? What changed you, Chaplain? What turned you into a betrayer?'

What had been the moment, exactly? Joseph searched in his mind and he knew.

'You are right when you said I tried to be all things to all people,' he replied with a strange, aching calm. 'It was when I was talking with the minister in St Giles, about what to say to a young soldier who has lost both his legs. Sometimes there is nothing you can do, except be there. He asked me if I were sure that there is a God, quite sure. Sometimes I'm not!'

There was a movement in the room. Corcoran's stare did not alter.

'But there are things I am sure of,' Joseph went on, leaning forward a little. 'The things Christ taught of honour, of courage and of love are always true, in any imaginable world. And whether you choose to follow them with all the strength you have or not, has nothing to do with anyone else. And if you stand alone, then you do. You don't do it to give to this person or that, as a command, or out of obedience, and certainly not for reward. You do it because that is who you choose to be.'

Paxton started to interrupt him.

'You will never know how it hurts me to look at Shanley Corcoran and see him as he is,' Joseph overrode him. 'But my alternative is to betray the good I believe, and I can't do that out of loyalty to anyone. If I were to, then I would have nothing left inside me to offer to the men in the trenches, to those I love, or to myself. Judgement is the court's, not mine, but I have told you the truth.'

Paxton knew he had lost, and he gave in with grace.

The verdict was immediate. Shanley Corcoran was found guilty of treason and sentenced to be hanged. He faced it with terror and self-pity, the sweat running down his ash-grey face. He seemed to shrivel inside his clothes, leaving them hanging on his body. For all the laughter, the warmth and the intelligence he had had, there was a core of emptiness inside him, and Joseph could not bear to look at his nakedness.

Three Sundays must pass before the execution, but something had died here today; an illusion of warmth and beauty had finally evaporated, leaving only a void.

But as Joseph walked out on to the steps in the sun, he knew also that he had acknowledged betrayal, and survived. He had been forced to look within himself, and seen not a weak man trying to find his purpose in becoming whatever others needed of him, but a knowledge of good that did not depend upon anyone or anything else. He would love, and he would need people for many reasons, but not to heal his own doubts or to fill an emptiness within himself.

He walked into the street smiling, to return to his friends, and his purpose.